Out of the Blue offers a tender glimpse at how yesterday's wounds affect today's purpose. Charming banter, endearing characters, and a heartwarming love story grace the pages of this enchanting contemporary romance. Add the beautiful backdrop of lakeside Michigan, and you have an unforgettable novel that is certain to captivate readers. Highly recommended!

~ **Rachel Scott McDaniel**
award-winning author of *The Mobster's Daughter*

Out of the Blue is summertime perfection, harkening back to long-lost memories of warm summer camp nights and dreams of a romance under starry July skies. In addition to her unique setting, Tuttle's knack for creating beautifully complex characters shines with guarded Gwen and fun-loving and sweet (not to mention loyal, protective, and charming) Nate. Their quick-witted, flirtatious banter will make you smile, and their kisses, laced with the depth of healing and new mercies one can only hope to experience after tragedy, will bring tears to your eyes. Fans of Becky Wade, Melissa Tagg, and T. I. Lowe are sure to add Susan L. Tuttle to their list of favorite authors after this gem of a story.

~ **Janine Rosche**
author of the Madison River Romance series

From Michigan campgrounds to a romance that will have you swooning, there is so much to love about *Out of the Blue*. Susan L. Tuttle has crafted a powerful story of forgiveness and redemption that will stay with you long after you turn the last page.

~ **Tari Faris**
author of the Restoring Heritage series

Other Books by Susan L. Tuttle

Love You, Truly

Along Came Love Series
At First Glance
Then Again, Maybe
Never Too Late

Resort to Romance Series
Met her Match

Out of the Blue

SUSAN L. TUTTLE

IRON
STREAM
FICTION

Birmingham, Alabama

Out of the Blue

Iron Stream Fiction
An imprint of Iron Stream Media
100 Missionary Ridge
Birmingham, AL 35242
IronStreamMedia.com

Library of Congress Control Number: 2022930777

All scripture quotations, unless otherwise indicated, are taken from the Holy Bible, New International Version®, NIV®. Copyright © 1973, 1978, 1984, 2011 by Biblica, Inc.™ Used by permission of Zondervan. All rights reserved worldwide. www.zondervan.com The "NIV" and "New International Version" are trademarks registered in the United States Patent and Trademark Office by Biblica, Inc.™

ISBN: 978-1-64526-376-0 (paperback)
ISBN: 978-1-64526-377-7 (ebook)

1 2 3 4 5—26 25 24 23 22

To my father-in-love who walked out his life verse,
Romans 14:8, with grace and a deep love for Jesus that
still resonates through this family today. And to my
mother-in-love who misses him dearly and whose love
and faith in Jesus through life's good and bad moments
has touched all our hearts.

Acknowledgments

With any book I write, my first thanks goes to Jesus Christ, the author and finisher of my own personal story. I have loved this journey of writing with him. Pursue whatever gift he's given you because doing so only draws you closer to him. To Jesus be all the glory.

I also want to thank my hubby and my kids. They enrich my life every day. I am far from a perfect wife or parent, and yet they love me with endless grace. By far, this family is the best thing I've ever had a hand in making.

Another person who always lands on this page is Jessica R. Patch. Honestly, God threw us together in this writing world as only he could, and my writing and my life in general has only been better for it.

To my agent, Linda S. Glaz, you are a warrior woman. Thank you so much for your honesty and your encouragement within this tough industry. And thank you for always pointing to Jesus first.

To Jessica Nelson and Linda Yezak. It has been a journey, and one that made me better as a writer. I have been blessed by you both as my editors. You've pushed me, kindly challenged me, encouraged me, and also made me laugh along the way. You are two amazing women, and I have been blessed by your help in shaping my books. Love you, ladies!

Chapter One

Someone really should develop a warning signal for mornings when life was about to take a two-hundred mile per hour hairpin turn. At least then maybe a person could be prepared. Strap in. Hold on tight.

Or avoid it all together.

Gwen Doornbos stared across the table at the weathered-faced man who'd practically raised her—only right now, she wasn't so sure aliens hadn't overtaken his body. "What do you mean we're not selling this place, Granddad?" Camp Hideaway had been in their family for two generations, but she wasn't making it three. "I thought we agreed."

Granddad pushed his thick black glasses up on his nose, his smile faltering. "Well, see, that's the thing. You talked. I listened. But I never actually agreed."

So what was all that nodding he'd done then? In her world a nod meant yes.

She dialed back the snark. Granddad deserved her respect. Dad and grandparent rolled into one, he loved her selflessly—opening his home to her not once, but twice since her childhood. There was no one she trusted more.

Which made his sudden change of direction even harder to swallow.

She stood and paced his tiny cabin, ready to finalize a deal that had been in motion for nearly a year. "What's going on? Crossroads Church is on their way here."

Over one hundred and twenty acres, Camp Hideaway nestled within a nature preserve at the tip of Michigan's thumb, its western border creating the eastern edge of Hidden Lake. Concealed among the trees, the balloon-shaped lake narrowed to join Lake Huron. Their acreage contained the only stretch that allowed lodging. People could hike, kayak, even picnic along Hidden Lake's borders, but this was the only place they could build, making Camp Hideaway prime land.

And the only prime buyer for her was Crossroads Church.

Granddad folded his hands over a middle that had become more padded than firm in the past years. "I want to keep this camp open." He said it matter-of-fact, as if it were that easy.

It wasn't.

She slumped into a seat. "There's a list of reasons that won't work, Granddad." Ones they'd already hashed out. "The biggest is you can't run this place another season. The last season nearly did you in." The years were catching up to him. His pace slowed on their evening walks, his muscles protested lifting what they used to, and on more than one occasion, she'd found him wheezing. They'd only stayed so he could reach his fiftieth anniversary running the camp. A decision that had nearly split her in half, but she understood the drive to meet a goal.

Granddad nodded. "I know."

"Then why are you reneging?"

He hesitated.

"Granddad?"

His chair scuffed against the rough wooden floor as he pushed away from the table to grab something off the cabinet behind him. He slid a worn notebook with poppies on the cover across the table.

"Grandma's journal?"

He flipped it open to an entry dated five years ago this summer, months before Grandma passed. Gwen looked up from the perfect cursive handwriting. Like ripping off a Band-Aid, she wanted the information quickly. "Just tell me what it says, please."

His fingertip ran over Grandma's words. "Next to your mama and you, this place meant the world to her."

"I remember."

"And I promised her it would continue." His watery eyes nearly undid her.

Covering his hand with hers, she stilled his trace of the ink. "And you did for as long as possible. Grandma would understand." She watched his struggle, her guilt niggling. She was capable of running this place. Had the know-how and the ability. She simply didn't have the want any longer. Oh, she possessed a whole host of other emotions . . . fear, anger, even bitterness, but absolutely no desire to work with teens. She'd barely survived living in the background here these past four years. "If things were different, Granddad, you know I'd do it." After Grandma died, she and Danny had planned on coming back. But then, he was gone. "I can't . . ." Her throat tightened.

"I understand, sweetheart. I do." This time he squeezed her hand. "But Camp Hideaway has life left in her. I'm not closing our camp or selling off her land. I hope you'll eventually understand."

See. Hairpin turn. No warning. She attempted a roadblock. "But if you don't sell, we won't have money to build our new house or the yoga studio." Which would provide for them when he retired. She'd already started working on her logo, website, and certification. All that remained was her building, but money was tight—had been since she'd returned. Granddad refused to increase prices, and the camp had needed several improvements. To help complete a few, she'd invested Danny's life insurance. The income from the sale would reimburse that money and take care of them until Gwen's studio found its footing. "We're on schedule to break ground next week."

He'd already detoured the block. "Lew can still break ground." His saggy cheeks pulled into his old familiar smile. "Not on the house, but I made sure you can have your studio."

Did he hold a hidden bank account? "How, if we're not selling?"

"I found a renter for this summer. And with what he's paying, there'll be enough to cover payments on the construction loan for your studio and support us until it's running."

Nerves humming, she barely dared to ask, "You're renting? To whom?"

Their plan included building on the few small acres they weren't selling, land along Hidden Lake and adjacent to this camp. Whoever moved in would be their neighbor, and she already had the perfect one picked out—quiet and predictable Crossroads Church. They'd use the space for retreats and a few family camps. No teens with sharp edges and rougher attitudes. Kids she'd once thought she could help but now painfully knew different.

A knock at his door snagged both their attention. White and green checkered curtains, the same green that matched the large pines outside, obscured the view through the half window. Granddad lumbered over, running a hand over his downy gray hair in what remained a losing battle to settle his cowlick in place.

Something told her she was about to embark on her own battle with whomever stood behind that door.

Granddad spared her a quick glance. "Be nice," he said as he opened it.

She pasted on a smile. Sunlight streamed in behind the stranger standing there, and all Gwen could make out was his tall form—well over six feet.

Granddad offered his hand. "Good to see you again, Nate."

"You too, Arthur." He ducked inside.

His sheer size should distract her. Muscles strained against the short sleeves on his gray T-shirt, and his broad shoulders tapered to a thin waist. Warm blue eyes settled on her like he was already an old friend, and his full smile could be contagious. Something flickered in her . . . awareness? It wasn't the time or place for her heart to stage its comeback. She shut it down and focused on Granddad's use of the word "again." This must be who he'd rented to.

She stood and looked to Granddad who nodded toward the man. "Gwen, this is Nate Reynolds." A pause. "And Nate, meet my granddaughter, Gwen Doornbos."

"I've heard a lot about you, Gwen." Nate held out his hand.

She stiffly shook it. "Wish I could say the same."

He cut a glance to Granddad. "You haven't told her about me?"

"I was getting there."

Nate's teeth tapping together punctuated the awkward silence. "Should I come back later?"

"Now's fine." Granddad waved him off.

He studied them. "You sure?"

"Not entirely." She'd rather replace him with someone from Crossroads Church. "But I believe I have no choice."

"You always have a choice." Nate held her stare, unblinking. "Especially when it comes to attitude."

"I know. Which is why I'm controlling mine."

"Lucky me." He tugged his hand through his thick brown hair, pulling its soft waves straight before releasing them into a mess on his head.

Granddad motioned toward the table. "How about we sit down?"

Uh, no. She'd already given up enough ground today. This time she refused to be the first to move.

With a tiny one-side-edged-up smirk that blew his friendly grin out of the water, Nate took two long steps to the table and held out a chair. "Ladies first."

Granddad's throat clearing halted her hesitation. She begrudgingly slid into her seat.

Nate bent close as he pushed her in, his breath tickling the nape of her neck. "Pleasure to finally meet you, Gwen."

Straightening, Nate didn't miss the soft scent of roses coming from Gwen's tanned skin. He'd worked his rear end off at a greenhouse one summer to put food on the table for him and his little sister Calloway. His fingers still stung from those thorny beasts. So why did the fragrance suddenly evoke pleasure, especially when coming from this prickly woman?

Arthur shuffled to the counter. "Coffee, anyone?"

"Already had my cup, Granddad."

"Is there a one-cup limit around here?" Judging by how tightly wound Gwen appeared, maybe there needed to be. Everything about her was rigid, and it had nothing to do with the toned muscles clearly visible in her shorts and tank.

Arthur plunked a mug in front of him. "Nope. Drink up."

Nate added cream and sugar to his, well aware how Gwen's eyes remained on him. Blue as sapphires, hard as diamonds. Yep. Buckets of fun coming his way.

Arthur settled into his seat. "I'm sorry I didn't tell you about Nate sooner, Gwen."

While her grandfather spoke, she didn't release Nate from her harsh stare. Did she blame him for Arthur keeping her in the dark? Yeah, well, color him surprised too. He'd push for an explanation later, but right now it appeared Gwen needed one more.

She turned to Arthur. "I don't understand why you didn't tell me, but I'll get over it." Next, she faced him. "And I'm sorry I was rude. This caught me completely off guard, and I don't do well in situations like that."

The tension continued ebbing. Only one deep line remained between her brows now.

"It's all right." He maintained a soft, smooth voice.

"Thank you." She rubbed a long scratch in the table. "So would you two catch me up, please? Because until five minutes ago, I thought we were closing our camp, Granddad was retiring, and we were selling a majority of our land."

She thought they were closing this place? Yeah, she had been caught off guard.

Nate pulled a banana Laffy Taffy from his pocket and unwrapped it. "Want one?" He held another out.

Her lips wrinkled. "No thanks."

Arthur waved his hand in decline too. "Nate visited camp last month when you were at Bay and Colin's wedding. I'd already been on the fence about selling, but wasn't sure what to do. After he shared his heart and vision, I knew. So I offered to rent the place to him."

"And his vision is . . .?" Gwen prodded.

Arthur rubbed his hand against the salt-and-pepper whiskers on his chin. His mouth opened, then shut. He'd been onboard, enthusiastic even, every other time they spoke. What worried him now?

After a second, the old man spoke. "Nate, why don't you tell her about it?"

Why was Arthur tossing the ball into his court?

Something was off, and Nate had no clue how to dig for an answer when the question wasn't clear. But his gut screamed there was a specific reason Arthur held off informing Gwen about his arrival, and it wasn't something small.

Gwen's hand stilled on the table, and her big eyes fixed on him with expectation. "Nate?"

"Right." He cleared his throat. The moment reminded him of an old jack-in-a-box toy. His words were the twirling lever, and a thrumming apprehension in him said things were about to pop. Though he didn't know when. "For several years now I've wanted to open a nonprofit camp but haven't had the capital to sustain it. I recently had a potential investor express interest in backing me, but he'd like to see a working model first—and he'd like to see it this year. I'm renting your space for the summer as a trial run to prove to him my idea has merit."

"And if you succeed?" she asked.

"*When* I succeed, I'll purchase your land with his help and use Camp Hideaway as the first of many future camps."

She clasped both hands in her lap. "What's your camp model?"

Nate scooted closer to the table. "Like I already mentioned, it's a nonprofit, and it's for underserved kids. The ones who can't afford camp but would love to come." He was gaining her interest, but not the good kind. She straightened in her chair as he continued speaking. "So many need a safe place to go. A place to be reminded they're still kids, help them laugh, show them they're loved." He paused, searching for a way to connect. "Show them how much God loves them. Isn't that what Camp Hideaway is here for?"

But instead of a connection, the pink in her cheeks drained. "Yes. Sort of. We were a church camp helping teens deepen their faith. Where . . . where would your kids come from?"

Right here he'd stop turning the lever on the jack-in-the-box, but unlike that old toy, there was no way he could stop playing this tune.

"A little southwest of here. It'll be small. Only forty kids—twenty boys, twenty girls—with a possible ten more coming who'll need to work off community service hours. We're partnering with the Juvenile Correction Services. That's what I'm most excited for, and the program I hope to expand eventually. So far, all the key players are on board as long as this place is ready to go on time. Which is why I'm so thankful for your help. I couldn't do this alone."

With that large swallow, she was definitely close to bursting. "JCS?" The three letters squeaked out like she'd sucked in helium.

Nate nodded at her pasty complexion.

"What city, exactly?" She directed the question at him, but her stare landed on her grandfather.

"Macon."

And that was the last twist.

Like the clown erupting from the toy, Gwen launched to her feet.

"Did you know?" Her hands splayed across the tabletop, and she leaned on them. "Before you rented this place, Granddad, did you know these children were coming from Macon?"

Wisdom and deep love, not remorse, swam in Arthur's eyes. He nodded.

Tension strummed off her. "You're keeping the camp open, bringing in kids from the Macon JCS system, and you told him we'd help?"

Another nod. "I did."

She ran her hands along her smoothed-back hair and glanced from Arthur to Nate. "I need out."

Nate met her at the door. "Don't you think we should talk? Clear the air?" Especially because he was clueless as to what polluted it.

Gwen trembled. A head shorter than he and all muscle, she had a wildness in her eyes that promised she could do some serious damage if she lost her current battle with restraint.

"Move." Her tone caught somewhere between a command and a plea.

"I'd rather talk this out." Deal with the issue head-on before it grew into a monster. "It's obvious you don't want me or the kids here, but I'm not leaving. So let's figure out how we can work together."

Breath puffed from her nose in sad laughter. "We can't." She sidestepped him, her shoulder brushing his as she stormed away.

He remained in the doorway. What world had he walked into? He rejoined Arthur at the table. "It's starting to make sense why you didn't tell her about me." His fingers wrapped around his mug. "She's not even close to being on board." Outside a woodpecker drilled into a tree. "Are you sure this is what you want? Because she seems furious." But something more bubbled under that anger. "And . . . haunted."

Arthur said nothing at first. He fiddled with the tattered edges of a journal and stared out the door. "Gwen's had a tough few years"—he blinked—"but yes, I'm sure. So let's talk about your camp."

The swell of excitement typically arriving with that thought shrank to a ripple. "It's not heaping onto her problems?" Whatever they were.

Arthur tapped the table. "No, it's part of the solution."

Didn't feel like it. Which might spell trouble. Nate had accumulated all the research he could unearth on running camps, but book learning wasn't his strength. He learned best by diving in, and he'd discovered it was smart to have a swim instructor nearby. That's why he wanted someone who lived and breathed camp life—something his investor also strongly suggested. A sounding board for all the ideas in his head, and guard rails to keep him on track. With opening day around the corner, he couldn't run off course. Arthur and his granddaughter's experience proved priceless.

Good thing too, since he'd dropped all his pennies into the rent and renovation of these grounds.

"Will she help?" Felt callous to ask, but he had to know.

"Give her time."

Time wasn't something he had to give. He needed this camp to be up and successfully running by summer, or he'd fail before he even crossed the starting line. Not that God couldn't work miracles. Nate was a walking one. But he'd counted on Arthur and his granddaughter's help to achieve this one. Because, ready or not, forty kids—fifty, God-willing—in need of their own miracles would arrive in five weeks.

Chapter Two

S team had to still be coming out of her ears.

And a knife handle out of her back.

What had Granddad been thinking?

Gwen swallowed the lump in her throat. Granddad loved her. If she repeated that truth a thousand more times, maybe it wouldn't feel like a lie anymore. Because if it were true, why would he do this? He'd nearly drowned in all the tears she'd cried into his arms after Danny died. How could he bring those kids to their doorstep?

Gwen swerved into a parking spot shared by both Lew's Lumber and NovelTeas. Right now, she should be reviewing her window choices with Lew, not calling an emergency meeting with her girlfriends. But between the elevated pollen count and her high anxiety level, her lungs were constricting, and she didn't have the time or patience for an asthma attack. The morning was already crazy.

Gwen slammed the door on her old Ford truck and stomped to the sidewalk. Sunshine warmed her, and she took a moment to stare at the cloudless sky. Suck in a deep breath. Order her thoughts. Calm.

Something tugged on her pocket, pulling her off balance. She looked down and couldn't stop smiling if she tried. Had to be her own personal cherub peering up at her.

"Hello, cutie." Gwen greeted the little girl.

"Penny?" The tiny toddler with big brown eyes set in a round face and pigtails in a matching dark color held out her palm.

"Lexie!" The girl's mother rushed toward her. "I'm so sorry. She knows you stock the horses with pennies. The cup was empty, and I was digging for my own, but she must have seen you while I wasn't—"

"It's okay." Gwen offered a smile to the mom before producing two shiny copper coins for the sweetheart in front of her. "That pony is magical. If you close your eyes when you're riding her, she'll take you to a field filled with pretty flowers."

Those huge walnut eyes widened in wonder. Her plump hands grasped the pennies, and she raced for the pony.

"I'm really sorry." The mom was halfway between her daughter and Gwen.

"Don't be." Gwen jingled the remaining change in her pocket. "She's adorable."

With a relieved smile, the mom hurried off. Gwen turned toward NovelTeas. For as long as she could remember, horses painted as intricately as ones found on the world's best carousels lined the shops on Waterway, Hidden Lake Township's main road. Gwen ensured the tiny coin cups beside these penny-per-ride ponies stayed full so that magic could always be found by little ones with boundless imaginations.

She could use a little of that magic today too. The kind that would make Nate Reynolds disappear. But she'd seen that look on Granddad's face before and didn't believe a disappearing act was in Reynold's near future, so she'd unload on her friends and regroup. Figure out how to put up with this temporary setback. Because it *was* temporary.

Inhaling, Gwen clomped up the stairs of NovelTeas. Bay Willow—no, Dugal now—owned the shop and lived upstairs with her new husband, Colin. Bay had transformed this old cottage that once housed the town's library into a tea shop where she now loaned books from her own expansive collection. Gwen never stopped in when there wasn't at least one patron reading, snacking, or relaxing.

Didn't hurt that Bay was an amazing baker as well.

Inside, the dark wooden floors creaked as Gwen crossed them to join her friends at their table in the corner.

"Hey, you." Bay slid a tall plastic glass over to Gwen, a wide blue straw sticking out of it. A floral apron covered Bay's loose blouse and skirt, and she'd pulled her sandy blonde hair into an equally loose braid. "I know it's no substitute for Rock N' Rye, but I hope it'll do."

As hard as Gwen had lobbied for her favorite soda to be stocked in this place—it was a Michigan treat after all—Bay refused to give in. No soda in her tea shop. Behind her sweet smile lay a steel will. Bay had provided, however, a close second in drinks Gwen now loved.

Gwen grabbed the Boba Tea and sipped, savoring the spicy chai taste. "Guess it'll do." She smiled at her friend, then chewed the tapioca bead that had glided up the straw.

"So what's up?" Lucy Burnett tucked a long strand of her caramel hair behind her ear, her sage green eyes steeped in curiosity. Typical journalist.

Beside her, Elise Wilder slipped a bookmark into her latest read and nudged Lucy. "Give the woman a second to unwind. She's tighter than a square knot."

"I would, but I'm booked on a three o'clock flight to Ireland. I don't have time for her to unwind." Lucy scrunched up her face. "Sorry, Gwen."

"It's okay." She didn't need to prolong this story. "Granddad rented our camp for the summer."

"Rented?" Bay asked.

"I thought you were selling," Elise said. "To Crossroads."

"Obviously not. Hence this meeting." Lucy leaned in. "Who's renting the place?"

Gwen's lips puckered. "Nate Reynolds."

"And he is . . .?" Bay prodded.

Gwen leaned forward, elbows on the table, and held her head in her hands. "Trouble." In spite of his huge smile. Actually, that trait strengthened her assessment.

"How's he trouble?" Lucy's pen drumming against the table matched the pounding in Gwen's head. "Is he planning on running a brothel or making moonshine on your land?"

Elise broke off a piece of her muffin. "Who uses those words anymore?"

"Me." Lucy snagged a fluffy chunk off Elise's plate and popped it in her mouth.

Chuckling, Bay stood as a customer entered. "Sorry. I'll be back."

Gwen's friends were trying to lighten her mood, but there was nothing remotely funny about this situation. "He's running a camp, and he's bringing in kids from Macon."

That stopped them. Bay stumbled and recovered, then hurried to the counter.

Gwen pressed her fingers against her eyes. "Not only from Macon, but the same kids Danny and I worked with."

"From the JCS?" Elise's alto voice softly prodded.

"Yes. Forty underserved kids with ten JCS delinquents thrown in."

"Your grandfather approved this?" Lucy collected unbelievable facts, but her tone said she found this one completely implausible.

And why not? These were the kids responsible for Danny's death. Oh, not the same exact one who pulled the trigger, but from the same place. Maybe the same families, friends, groups.

Gwen nodded, the pain from almost four years ago more fresh than she'd had to withstand in months. This was to be the year she finally walked out of her past and reclaimed her new future. She'd endured the living nightmare of Danny's death. Survived burying him. Clawed her way through the trial and somehow pieced together enough of her broken dreams to create a new picture.

And today it had all shattered.

That Granddad played a part in this debacle cut deep. He loved her. He must have convinced himself he was helping her right along with the kids.

He wasn't.

"Gwen?" Elise grabbed her hand. "You okay?"

"No." She gulped. Her lungs squeezed. Not now. She didn't need this now. "You guys talk. Anything. Animals, books, trips—I don't care. I need a moment."

Lucy nodded. "So, Bay," she called across the room, "you got Shane McCoy's newest release?"

Elise nearly spit out her coffee.

Bay's eyes widened. "Not hardly." She leveled a stern look that would have silenced a motorcycle gang. It nearly made Gwen chuckle. Nearly.

"You'd have to scrub your eyes out with sanitizer if you read it." Elise made a gagging noise.

"What do you have against romance anyway?" Lucy picked at her.

"McCoy's books are *not* romance." Bay slid into her seat.

"Boy pursues girl. Boy gets girl." Lucy tipped her head. "Romance."

Lucy and Bay kept the debate moving, while Elise remained quiet. She lived in a Carhartt coat and Timberline boots, her deep red hair always in a low ponytail, and her emerald eyes creating a bright contrast to her pale skin. Romance was as foreign to her as high heels, and it didn't seem to bother her. At least Gwen never thought it had. But with the way she wrapped that lock of red hair around her finger like a tourniquet, maybe Gwen had been wrong.

She straightened. "How's the farm coming, Elise? Did you get your sheep?"

Her pensiveness cleared into a small grin. "Wild Animal Park and it was a llama." Elise's steel-toed boot nudged her. "So you ready to talk about this Nate Reynolds?"

Burying her head in the sand sounded like a better option, even if it wasn't viable. "I'm still trying to process how this happened. Everything was coming together and now it's . . ." She tossed her hands in the air. "There's no way I can work around those kids. I barely survived hanging behind the scenes these past four years, and our campers weren't troubled teens."

"The purchase plan may have changed, but that doesn't mean you still have to live there. Does it?" Ever logical, Lucy focused on details, not feelings.

"We do unless we buy a house elsewhere." She shook her head. "Which I refuse to do when I know this camp won't last. I just have to wait Reynolds out." Wasn't how she'd envisioned spending her summer, but she long ago realized life didn't go according to plans. "I called Crossroads on the way here, and they said they'd still be interested if he backs out."

An alarm on Lucy's phone dinged and she stood, winding an aqua scarf around her neck. "I hate to leave before we have your problem solved, but I gotta scoot." She bent and side-hugged her. "I'll be thinking of you."

"Thanks, Luce." Gwen squeezed her back.

"Be safe." Elise waved.

"And call when you get there," Bay added.

Beside her, Bay and Elise picked up the conversation, doing their best to distract Gwen from her troubled morning. But her mind kept wandering to finding a faster way to get rid of Nate Reynolds and her life back on track.

Second time around the camp's perimeter, and Nate still wasn't sure what to do. While he understood the motivation behind Arthur's decision, he didn't agree with it. Especially when it added to his already uphill battle. Elliot Payton had several places vying for his money. If things didn't run smoothly, he'd never choose Nate—even if they had known each other for years.

Without Elliot's investment, Nate's first year would also be their last. Effectively shutting down this camp and all the ones he wanted to follow it.

These camps needed to happen, as much for himself as the kids. They'd give meaning to his messed-up past and value to everything he'd gone through growing up. That whole "God uses all things for good" verse? Maybe he'd finally see it occurring in his own life.

Nate stood at the lower half of the land. Towering pines, rounded oaks, and maples flanked the carved path worn through the grounds. The camp's right half had been sectioned off for the boys, the opposite side for the girls. Straight down the middle. The Commons held indoor games and a full-size basketball court with bleachers. All this against the backdrop of a gently rising hill with soaring firs that separated two open fields. But the truly breathtaking portion lay hidden in the northwest corner.

The lake. A glittering blue jewel.

And he had a vision for every single portion. Except after this morning . . . He trusted God, but had he gotten ahead of Him? Wanted this so badly he'd forced open doors meant to stay shut?

Nate pulled his phone from his back pocket and hit a name. Two rings was all it took before Ryker Zane's voice boomed across the line. "Nathanial, you standing in the middle of your dream?"

"Standing in the middle of a camp." Jury remained out on the dream sequence.

Loud music softened in the background as a door shut. "The guys and I were going through the show. Making a few changes since you left."

First event he'd missed in nearly a decade. Ten years of buses and hotels, crisscrossing the nation to speak with youth groups and teen conventions. He missed the camaraderie, but—he sucked in the wide open air—it felt good to stretch his legs. "You encouraged me to leave, remember?"

"Wouldn't have things any other way." A chair squeaked, most likely protesting Ryker's size. That's what happened when a wall of muscle landed on it. "So what's got you bothered?"

Always to the point. Ryker's habit was where Nate had picked up the trait. "Got in this morning. The place is more amazing than I remember." He and Ryker had hiked the camp back when winter struggled to hold on. They'd been booked for a show at a local youth event, during which Elliot phoned with his proposal. He was interested in several nonprofits and wanted to invest in one before this year ended. He'd make his decision by October after seeing each in real time this summer.

Nate had shared his dream and the problem facing it with one of the pastors at the event; though Elliot was looking for a place to invest, Nate owned no land for his camp. That pastor suggested checking out Camp Hideaway. Nate drove out with Ryker, and even through the gray skies, mounds of black slush, and a carpet of wet leaves, this place hooked him. Amazing how a few weeks made a difference. Now, with fresh buds on the trees and spring's crisp scent spilling through the air, Camp Hideaway's beauty reawakened.

Nate sighed. "I finally met Arthur's granddaughter this morning. Name's Gwen, and she's furious I'm here."

"Okay." One word tossed in a tone full of meaning. With Ryker, there was no such thing as a stumbling block to God's plans. Only hurdles meant to be leapt and keep a person's faith strong.

But Ryker hadn't seen Gwen's face. "Not okay. She freaked out when she heard where the kids were coming from. I don't need to be stepping on any toes, and those kids don't need someone around who is already against them." It wasn't right that she seemed to have judged them by their rough edges. Her hackles had risen before she'd even met them. "I need people here who can love on these kids."

"So God got it wrong, bringing you there?"

"I didn't say that."

"Then what's this phone call about? Because if you believe he got it right, you wouldn't be calling and asking me to confirm it for you."

Blue sky peeked out above; the kind of blue that made him think it was a lake and everything was upside down. He scrubbed his forehead. Perfect picture for today. "I don't think God got it wrong. I wonder if I heard him wrong. About this place. Maybe the camp was meant to be somewhere else."

"So the prayers, the confirmations, those all were wrong too?"

The man never let him off a hook.

Ryker clicked his tongue against the roof of his mouth. "Nate, you've had this dream for years, and God's lined it up. Pretty fast, I'll give you that, but He's prepared you, given you what you need even when you didn't know you'd need it, and now it's time. Did you honestly think there wouldn't be opposition? That you wouldn't have some more work to do?"

No. Nate had figured on work. More physical, less emotional—at least until the kids arrived. "You're right. I know you are. This morning took me by surprise is all."

"And that's fine." A nod probably accompanied those words. "But don't let that be a force to knock you off track."

"I won't." Though he nearly had. "Momentary setback."

"Let's get you moving forward again, then." Ryker never wasted time. "You hear back from JCS?"

"Not yet. Jude will call once he does."

Jude Walker, Nate's closest friend, ran a kids' shelter in the heart of Macon. Open 24/7, the shelter mainly helped kids during the after-school program hours, but Jude had open beds for the ones who needed a safe place at night. The number of homeless teens was growing, and Jude felt called to combat it. He'd developed a thick relationship with the police and JCS in that area.

If everything lined up, Nate would too.

"What's first on your agenda now that you're there?" Ryker continued to refocus him.

He tugged on the tips of his hair. "Too many in that slot to count. I made notes on what I thought we'd need, but I have no clue where to start." He scanned the area. Arthur hadn't been lying when he'd warned they hadn't prepared for campers this year. "If I had more time, I'd dig in and learn as I go. I know I'm capable." Trial and error were his best teachers. "But I don't have it. I need Gwen and Arthur's experience."

"Can't give you that, but the guys and I will be over that way in a few weeks. Anything we can do—"

"I'll call."

Ryker's muffled voice spoke to someone else, then he was back. "Pastor from the host church just arrived. I should get moving."

"All right." Nate started moving too. "Stop by when you get close."

"We will." Ryker offered his good-bye and hung up.

Nate held his phone, staring at the woods encasing the camp. Making a list went against every grain in his body, but he'd created one when Elliot requested it. A paper proposal before Elliot would entertain investing in the camp. Once in Elliot's hands, he'd liked what he'd seen and bumped Nate to this level. He needed to complete a trial run of the proposal. Elliot also offered the strong suggestion that he find seasoned help to guide him.

Good advice.

Nate spun in a circle.

No, great advice, because he didn't know what needed to top this new list. He'd counted on Gwen and Arthur to tell him. They had connections in their town that could benefit him.

They knew what to look for in interviews. What equipment should be replaced first. Which camp activities on his agenda went over best; which were flops.

And so many more things that would push this place toward success and secure Elliot's investment to take Nate one step closer in bringing this model national. He could reach more kids, change more lives, finally make sense of his rocky past.

His stomach growled. No time to eat though. Arthur had walked him to his cabin soon after Gwen had stormed from his, cautioning that he'd not had time to finish cleaning it. He hadn't been lying.

Good thing messes never bothered Nate.

Because it seemed he'd landed smack-dab in the middle of one bigger than the cobwebs swinging from the corners of his new home-sweet-home.

Chapter Three

——◦≋◦——

Gwen kicked a stone out of the way as daylight slowly extinguished the darkness along the rocky shoreline where Hidden Lake met Lake Huron. Unable to sleep, she'd donned her soft cargo shorts and a light sweatshirt, then made the short hike through the forest to Little Blue, a tapered lighthouse on this small strip of secluded land separating the two lakes. Though accessible by both foot and car, most people only saw Little Blue by boat. But with its steady presence and beach of smooth stones in brilliant colors, this was one of her most favorite places to come. To think.

And she had more than enough to contemplate.

She settled on the small wooden bench handcrafted from fallen logs. Soft blue shadowy hues clung to the earth in that place between nighttime and morning. Peering up, she tried to sort her chaotic thoughts and soothe her bubbling anxiety. This land encapsulated her hiding place. Here, life had slipped back into focus after losing Danny. She'd crafted a plan. Knew what to expect. Taken back control.

Until yesterday.

"Morning."

She startled and swiveled sideways.

Nate stood a few feet from her.

"Morning." Did he have to invade all her special places? "How'd you find this spot?"

"Your grandfather brought me here yesterday." Before or after he'd found Gwen and apologized, again? "It's a beautiful place." He pointed to the bench. "Mind if I sit?"

Politeness won over honesty. "Sure." She scooted as far to the other end as she could, not wanting to share one more thing with this man. Over the lake, sunlight continued to break open the blackened sky.

Nate relaxed against the bench, his eyes on the show straight ahead. "I'm sorry your grandfather didn't tell you about me. If I'd known, I'd have asked him to do it differently."

By her foot, a trio of ants did their best to shoulder a dried berry twenty times their size. She could relate. "Not your fault." Or his problem.

"I know. But I'm sorry all the same." He propped his elbows on his knees and rubbed his hands together.

They sat in silence until all the blackness in the sky lightened to varying shades of blue. Finally, the question bubbling since yesterday broke across her lips. "Why this camp?" She turned. "You could start anywhere, so why here?"

He straightened and angled his body toward her, bending one leg onto the bench. "Because this is where God brought it together."

It was that simple?

Maybe not, because Nate continued.

"I have a good friend, Bryce Payton, whose father recently turned sixty-five and decided to retire. Name's Elliot, and he'd like to diversify his investments and make sure they're spelled out clearly in his will." He brushed away a mosquito buzzing between them. "I'm one of several nonprofits Elliot's interested in seeing more from, and we all have until October to snag his partnership." He smacked the annoying bug. "Proposing a summer camp didn't leave me much wiggle room with the calendar, but I know we can make this happen. And when we do, he'll add his funding, allowing me to expand to numerous other sites."

"What are the other proposals he's looking into?"

"Not sure. He hasn't provided that information." Nate straightened. "Which is fine by me. I don't want to waste time worrying about competitors. I barely have enough to make this camp a reality."

And he had no clue what he was asking for with his desire to birth his crazy concept. Right here in her safe spot. She rubbed her earlobe. "You still haven't answered why you're here. On my land."

A motor's buzz drifted on the air as a boat raced toward the open water. Nate watched it for a moment before answering. "I was in town visiting and shared my hopes for the camp. Someone told me to check out your space and when I did, I ran into your grandfather. He offered to rent. I accepted."

That condensed version gave her every detail but . . . "And he never mentioned we already had a buyer lined up?"

"No." Strong word balanced by his soft look. Maybe this wasn't so easy on him either.

"Thank you." She offered a smile. This entire situation still completely bothered her, but she could acknowledge he wasn't at fault. "For indulging my curiosity."

He leaned in. "Any time you have questions, Gwen. I'm an open book."

The moment stretched, and he didn't move. This close she caught a dimple hiding under the dark scruff on his cheek.

Down the beach a colony of seagulls took flight. Instead of the noise grabbing his attention, Nate kept it on her, his dimple deepening before he finally looked away, stood, and walked toward the colorful rocks. "This beach is unique."

Gwen stood too. "It's one of my favorite places."

Now how had that escaped? No need to share personal tidbits with the man. But his long look had unsettled something inside, leaving her slightly off balance and grasping at a figment of emotion.

He glanced over his shoulder. "I can see why. There's every shade imaginable in these stones." Bending, he picked one up and tried to skip it across the water.

Gwen poured over the rocks until landing on the perfect one. Snagging it, she flicked the thin oval across the lake. One, two, three bounces.

Nate's eyebrows raised. "Show-off."

She shrugged.

He stepped across the colorful ground. "Your grandfather showed me some photo albums yesterday. This place has touched thousands of kids' lives." Another failed attempt at skipping a stone. "I'm excited to join that legacy."

Except they were talking apples and oranges. "There's a world of difference between the church kids who've come here for years and the teens you're bringing." Didn't he see that?

With the way his face tightened, the only thing he saw was disapproval over her words. "You're right." He softened his grimace into a near smile. "They need us even more."

She used to agree. "This isn't a good idea." With a flick of her wrist she skipped another rock.

He watched it bounce, then, "I get you believe that, but why?"

Personal tidbits were one thing. Her scars, another. No way she'd let those slip past her lips. "I won't stay once the kids come, but I will help you ready this place. Granddad can't do all the work alone."

He didn't press his unanswered question. "You're worried about him."

"I am. He's all I have left."

"He seems stubborn as a mule. I don't think he's going anywhere."

She'd thought that once about Danny. They'd only had five years of marriage. No growing old together. If she could add to Granddad's years by removing extra stress and work, she'd do almost anything—including helping Nate Reynolds.

"The last few years have been rough on him, and he can't handle this place like he used to." She dredged the next words up. "Come to me before you do him."

Simple assurance lingered in his nod and words. "I can do that."

With no clouds in the sky, it promised to be a beautiful spring day. Sunlight bathed Nate, highlighting the dips and curves of the muscles in his arms and legs. Obvious strength without the bulk. Warmth curled through her that wasn't from the rising sun.

Her eyes flicked back to his. Darn things had strayed all on their own, and he'd caught them. That dimple on his right cheek deepened.

She backed away. "I need a shower and breakfast. Let's meet at the office,"—she glanced at her watch—"say nine? You know where it is, right?"

"I do." The lines around his mouth crinkled in amusement. Probably at her fast retreat.

But nothing about this was a laughing matter. Nothing at all.

"Don't be late." She hustled away.

Digging the bristles of a broom into the far corner on his tiny porch, Nate pushed last fall's leaves and grime toward the open edge. He hadn't expected to run into Gwen this morning but was glad he had. They'd started toward some unspoken truce, at least it seemed so until she nearly bolted away. He chuckled, remembering the look on her face. Like a kid caught with her hand in the cookie jar, and he was the cookie. Only she couldn't drop it fast enough once captured.

His stomach rumbled. Maybe food analogies weren't the best idea right now. He'd eaten his last beef stick for breakfast. Should have hit the grocery store last night. An empty stomach delivered a flood of memories he preferred to keep stacked away and broke a promise he'd long since made to himself to never go hungry again.

His phone rang, and he dug it out, noticing Jude's number and the time. Oops. Nearly nine.

He leaned the broom against the siding and answered. "Hey, there."

"You settled in?" Question for a greeting. Typical Jude.

"As settled as I get." Nate stepped inside to grab his ball cap. "How are things there?"

"Great. The kids are ready to leave today."

Forty junior highers from the school districts surrounding Jude's youth center had signed on for the opportunity to attend this camp before it had become a reality. Nate hadn't decided how to feel over the fact that most parents hadn't checked into this place. Spoke volumes to their homelife. Some parents believed anywhere was better than the streets they lived on, but most wanted the kids out of their hair—didn't matter where they went. It was the latter Nate related to.

Spotting his cap, he grabbed it from the messy pile on his floor. "Maybe remind them they need to finish the school year first."

"I have. Repeatedly." Like a broken record, he'd guess. "Spoke with the JCS today."

Jude's upbeat voice fueled Nate's hope. "Where are we with them?" An additional ten beds would be filled by kids needing to fulfill community service hours, if he could get approval from the JCS that the tasks he'd have them doing would meet the requirements.

"They emailed some forms. I forwarded them to you."

"Thanks." Bright sunlight flowed through his cabin's windows. "How soon do they need them back?"

"Yesterday."

"No problem. I'm about to head to the office." He'd clean up the clothes spilling from his bag later. "Anything else?"

"Just a few things. I sent you a checklist."

Great. Checklists. His favorite.

"I'll get right on it." Nate upended his bag of Laffy Taffy and snagged one to eat on his way out the door. "On another note, has Elliot contacted you with a date for his visit?"

"Bryce said they'd be here sometime in August."

"Perfect." Someone knocked. "That gives us time to get kinks worked out." Gwen stood at his door, rosy cheeked. With that tight jaw, the blush wasn't lingering embarrassment from the beach. He checked his watch and nearly bit his tongue. Nine-oh-four. "I've got to go."

"Sure. I'll text you when I find out anything."

"Sounds good." He started to hang up, but Jude's voice caught him.

"You hear from Calloway again? Know where she is?"

His fingers clenched around his phone. He did. But his little sister asked him not reveal her location. Where she was concerned, though, Jude wasn't just anyone.

Jude sighed. "Your hesitation is answer enough. Tell her my phone is always on."

"She knows. Keep being patient."

"I'm trying."

More than he could say for the woman pounding on his door. His hand rested on the knob. "Really got to go."

They hung up, and Nate swung the door open as Gwen's fist rose again. He grinned as she stopped mid-air.

Her brows jolted up, then relaxed as she assessed him with that cool blue gaze. "You're late."

"Sorry. I started cleaning this place and lost track of time."

She peered around him, taking in the clothes on his floor, his mound of candy and lone wrapper on the counter, and finally landing on all the dust riding the sunbeams streaming through the window. "If that's your definition of clean, we're in trouble."

He stepped on the porch, closing his door. "I started on the outside."

Now she scanned his porch. "Just don't be late again."

"It was only a few minutes." By the look on her face, one was more than enough. "You could have waited for me."

"I did."

He looked at his phone—nine-oh-six—then raised a brow at her. "It's a five minute walk."

"Or two minutes by golf cart." She hustled down the steps. "Come on."

He followed, catching the mumbled *this is never going to work* that floated behind her.

"Look," he began, taking the seat on the bench beside her, "I get you're flabbertated, and my being late didn't help anything, but if we're going to work together, we need to find common ground." And stay on it. Otherwise this summer would be torturous.

Her hand stilled on the reverse lever. "I'm what?"

He rewound over what he'd said. Ah. He'd been making up words for so many years he barely registered when he did it anymore. "Flabbertated," he supplied.

"Flabbertated." The word came out as slow as the nod that accompanied it.

"Flabbergasted over the surprise of me being here and agitated about the change." He shrugged. "Flabbertated."

He didn't know a sigh could be so deep and long. "If we're going to talk, can we keep it to real words?" The cart jarred backwards.

Wouldn't promise what he couldn't deliver.

They rode in silence until they reached the office. "What's your grandfather up to this morning?" Hadn't seen him around.

"Helping his little sister." She hopped off and managed the four steps to the office in two. "She lives west of here two hours and needed some help buying a new car. Hates shopping of any kind, but she calls and he drops everything."

He followed her to the door. "I have a little sister. I understand."

A small smile tickled her lips. "I hear they're the Achilles' heel to any man."

Was this a glimpse of her teasing? If so, he liked it.

"You heard correctly."

With a breathy laugh, she unlocked the entrance, pushed it open, and flicked on the lights. She followed a short hallway to an office. Everything inside was wood, including the paneling on the walls. She crossed to a desk, opened its drawer, and pulled out . . . a clipboard with a list attached. No. Pages of lists judging by the stack of paper.

She grabbed a red pen and looked at him. "Before I go over this, I'd like to hear your agenda."

So much for the flash of fun Gwen. "My agenda was to enlist you and your grandfather's help. I have ideas and a schedule, but need your knowledge to tell me if they'll work or if I'm way off base."

She rolled the pen between her slender fingers. "Have you ever been to camp?"

"I've visited several and interviewed a few directors." All in his preplanning stages. "Like I mentioned earlier, this came together faster than I'd anticipated, and I'm doing my best to roll with it."

"Roll with it." Straight tone and slow, like she was trying to interpret another language.

"Yeah." He pointed to the computer. "Mind if I print off some documents before we tackle your stack-o-paper?"

With a twitch, she straightened. "Be my guest."

Nate circled the desk and switched on the computer. It asked for a password. "You mind?" He nodded to the screen.

She nudged in close and leaned over the keyboard. Again the soft scent of roses floated to him, and she was close enough for the few strands that had escaped her bun to tickle his chin.

"You set?" Her gaze caught his over her shoulder.

He attempted focus. Without trying, she'd thrown his head for a loop, and it had been a while since any woman had done that. "Huh?"

Based on her wide eyes and large step away, she seemed to catch she was the distraction—and not like it. Which only made his attraction more confusing.

"You good?" She pointed to the screen.

"Yeah." Dragging his attention from her, he fired up his email and printed the documents. "Mind if we head outside? It's too gorgeous to be stuck indoors." Closed quarters weren't his thing, and right now, it seemed they both could use some extra space.

"Sounds good." Gwen provided a wide berth for him to pass, then followed, shutting off the lights and locking the door as she did. On the porch, she added another foot of space between the two old white rocking chairs and slid into one, laying her clipboard on her lap. "Let's start with counselors."

They spent nearly the next hour covering more details than he'd realized were involved with running this place. As they finished, he took the plunge and offered an idea he'd had. "What do you think about cabin rewards?"

"Cabin rewards?"

She sounded skeptical, but at least she hadn't shut him down. "You know, make accomplishing their assigned tasks into something enjoyable."

"And these rewards would be . . ."

"Extra tickets to spend in the canteen. Double dessert. Another hour of swim time." He shrugged. "We could make a rewards wheel for them to spin."

She tapped her pen against the clipboard and stared off in the distance. Slowly, a smile filled her face. A tiny victory and he'd take it. "That's actually not a bad idea."

"Wow. You're still breathing."

The look she leveled classified him as certifiable.

He shrugged. "Figured giving me that compliment would kill you. But see? It didn't."

Her lips inched up before she caught them. Huh. Seemed she had to fight to dislike him. Meant there was a part of her he could wear down until they became friends, a status he wanted with her. He'd played the bad guy in enough circumstances. This was his chance to finally reverse that role permanently.

"So you think we can have this place ready in time?" he asked.

Her tongue clacked against the roof of her mouth. "It'll be close, but if we stay on task, it should work."

He nodded to her clipboard. "So, what else is on there?"

"Inviting a different set of kids, for starters."

If that was her attempt at continuing their humor, it fell flat. They needed to clear this topic off the table once and for all.

He softened his voice. "While I understand that's how you feel, it's not going to change." How many times had Ryker said the same words to him about things he wanted to fight about? "There's a lot we can compromise on, but not this."

She drew herself straight. "Another will be our belief in your camp's potential for success, because this place isn't going to work."

"Is that your honest assessment or hope?"

Her eyes flashed. "That's harsh experience."

Broken. It was written all over her. And her sharp edges kept scraping against him. If he could dull them a little, maybe he could sneak past. "I'm sorry for whatever happened to you."

Her chair creaked as she pressed against it. "Then don't open your camp here. Let Crossroads buy this place. Please."

Her trembling plea nearly undid him. She was desperately reaching for control in a situation she had none in, but he couldn't supply the answer she wanted. Couldn't even wrap her in a comforting hug. So he did all he could. "It's going to be okay." It wasn't an empty assurance. He'd had enough of those in his life. This one he firmly believed.

Apparently he was the only one.

Her eyes closed in a long blink before focusing on him again. "No, it's not." She stood and gathered her things. "I hope no one gets hurt before you realize how wrong you are."

Her words rang more like a warning than concern, but she bolted down the steps before he could reassure them both.

Chapter Four

$\cdot$ ❧ $\cdot$

No breakfast tasted more heavenly than peanut butter smeared over a toasted English muffin, then topped with sweet apricot preserves. Gwen popped the last bite of deliciousness into her mouth and chased it with a sip of coffee. The combination was almost enough to make her forget life wasn't so perfect outside these doors.

Her phone dinged a text, and she snatched it up. Ireland's rolling green hills stared back at her along with a message from Lucy: I'M HERE. I'M ALIVE.

All right, so perfection still existed in some corners of the world, just not currently in hers. Not that it was a permanent situation.

Her thumbs flew across the tiny keyboard. GLAD TO HEAR. BE SAFE. HAVE FUN.

Two more texts chimed in, one from Bay and another from Elise, as they answered too. Gwen set her phone down and padded to the bathroom. Across the room the conversation continued to ding, but she ignored it. A hot shower came before further interaction with the world.

Half hour later she slipped a thin sweater over her tank, pushed up the sleeves, and jammed her freshly painted toes— one good outcome of a sleepless night—into her sandals. The forecast had predicted a week of early morning spring sunshine that sprouted into humidity and heat. Michigan was going for extremes this year with its record cold winter that spiked straight to summer temps.

Wrapping her hair into a high bun, she scuffed into the kitchen and grabbed her things before stepping onto her small porch. The humidity in the air already erred on the far side of thick. Worse than she'd expected. Coughs immediately erupted as her lungs tightened. Didn't help that the pollen count was growing daily.

Anxiety and frustration joined forces inside her. Even the weather fought against her bid for life to be calm again.

Stepping back inside, Gwen hurried to her bathroom medicine cabinet, concentrating on slow, measured breaths. She pushed the inhaler past her lips and took two quick puffs, inhaling immediate relief. Bracing one hand against her sink, she confronted herself in the mirror.

Slow. Easy. Stay in control.

Thirty seconds passed as her breathing returned to normal, or normal enough to know she'd be okay. Still, she pocketed her inhaler. Should have had it with her anyway.

This time she made it to the golf cart and then drove to the parking lot where the camp's ancient cactus-green Ford F100 pickup sat. Switching vehicles, she fired it up, cranked the AC, and pointed the nose toward Hidden Lake's main street.

The shops on Waterway created a small town with a Norman Rockwell feel and a Monet color palette. She rolled to a stop in front of Lew's. He had a final question about the plans before breaking ground next week. As bad as the past two days had been, this was her bright spot. Sure, Nate's presence threatened to blow clouds over it, but she continued to brush them away. By fall her yoga studio would almost be finished, with Nate a mere memory.

Opening her truck window, she let the humid air outside mingle with the chilled inside to avoid the jarring shock between the two. After a minute she hustled toward NovelTeas, first dropping pennies by the small pony she passed. Inside, Bay and Colin greeted her with smiles.

"Morning." Colin stood from the small table they shared and wrapped Gwen in a hug. "Heard you had a hard day yesterday."

"You could say that." The air swirled with yeast, spicy teas, and sweet fruits. Her stomach caught the scents and growled. She slipped from his embrace. "I thought you'd be working."

"Traded shifts with another doc whose wife recently had a baby." His smile rested on Bay. "Hoping he'll be able to return the favor soon."

Bay blushed and turned to Gwen. "Tea?"

"Not this morning. Just a cherry turnover for Lew. I'm on my way to see him."

Bay scurried behind the counter. "I thought building was on hold."

Gwen had been so worked up the other day, she'd forgotten to tell them. "For our house, yes, but we're still starting on the yoga studio."

Colin joined them by the register. "You're not going to wait until you see what happens with the camp?"

Uneasiness pricked at her as she pulled a few bills from her wallet. "I don't need to wait. Nate's idea can't work." Grabbing her words for confidence and her turnover for Lew, she said her good-byes.

"Call us if you need anything." Colin's offer followed her outside.

The only thing she needed was for life to return to normal.

She descended NovelTea's staircase, then walked next door to Lew's. Pulling open the door, she caught with full force the scent of shaved wood and ink. Piles of plans covered the front desk, and Lew Thompson hunched over a set a few feet away. He looked up and smiled. "Gwen." He started for her, hand out. With his red and black flannel shirt rolled to his elbows, a grey knit cap, thick black beard, and barrel chest, Lew could be Paul Bunyan's twin.

Rather than the handshake he was aiming for, Gwen offered the brown paper sack holding his treat. "Brought you a cherry turnover."

The grin on his lumberjack face was priceless. "Needed something to go with my coffee this morning." He placed it on his desk. "You here to look over some plans?"

"Yes. I'm excited to see them."

He grabbed a thick roll of papers, the rubber band snapping as he slid it off. "While you're here you want to peek at the ones Nate had me draw up?"

Nate was working with him?

"What plans?" Concern pressed her brows together.

He pointed to a nearby paper. "The ones for your camp."

Nate requested work for the camp? Making permanent changes only gave an illusion of ownership—which wasn't going to happen. Nate Reynolds might be thinking long-term, but he was a short-term problem in her book. She peered up at Lew. "Show them to me."

Nate finished his morning stroll around the campground, half hoping to bump into Gwen. The picture of her standing there yesterday, pleading with him to go somewhere else, had branded itself on his brain. This wasn't only about upsetting whatever plans she'd made. It was so much more, and he'd tossed ideas in his mind all night long. Most people he could read, but Gwen was like a set of hieroglyphics, and he didn't have the key. A few pieces were obvious, like her hurt and need for control, but he had no clue how they fit together.

He also didn't have the time to figure her out. Right now, every second belonged to this camp.

Munching on his protein bar, Nate stood dead center in a sprawling field at the camp's peak. Tall pines, trunks bare for the first twenty feet, bordered three sides of a wide, grassy area waiting to be filled with a fun new attraction. Yep. This was going to be one of their draws.

Swallowing the last bite on his bar, he crinkled the wrapper and shoved it in his pocket. Luckily he'd found the grocery store last night and then scouted out Lew Thompson's office ahead of today's appointment.

Ten minutes later, Nate drove around the curve that wound into downtown Hidden Lake, the town's namesake on his left as he circled around it. He'd always pictured Michigan as a flat state. He'd been wrong, at least as far as this area went. Hills rose, dotted with trees, and Hidden Lake shimmered inside the bowl they created.

Sunlight reflected off the navy water and a few boats puttered along the edges as he turned onto Waterway, the main street bordering the water's north side. He pulled in front of the first building, its large glass window decorated with gold letters: Lew's Lumber.

Nate jogged up the steps and opened the heavy, wooden door. Stepping through, he jolted to a stop. Gwen, talking to Lew, turned at the sound of his arrival. Perhaps one day she'd smile when he entered a room. Today was not that day. "Gwen? I didn't know you'd be here."

"Surprise." She lifted her hands. "I'd come to finalize my plans, but I'm learning more about yours."

The door clicked shut behind him. "You have plans too?"

"For the yoga studio I'm building."

He'd forgotten. "Right. Arthur mentioned that." Her rigid body mirrored the last time he'd seen her. "I meant to tell you about mine yesterday, but. . ." But she'd run off. Her slightly narrowed eyes challenged him. He opted to continue neutrally. "We ran out of time." He pointed to the table. "Have you seen the drawings, or would you like to look at them with us?"

"Lew was just showing them to me." She strolled his way. "What I want to know is who's paying for the changes?"

"I am."

She stopped. "You are?"

He nodded and her lips slightly parted. Yeah. She'd grasped the cost he'd incur and connected what that meant as far as his bank account. It wasn't something he wanted to talk about, though. "I'm footing the bill for getting this place up and running with all the necessary changes, but by summer's end, my pockets will run nearly dry. That's why I need outside help."

This was where he kicked himself. He should've had more than enough money to open this place indefinitely. But he'd had no clue how his life would change or that it even needed to. The thought of how much cash he'd wasted on old compulsions could, at moments like this, make him almost physically ill. If he hadn't run into Ryker when he had, there wouldn't be anything left in his accounts.

Be thankful for the small things. Ryker had drilled that into his head, and he was living by it.

Gwen tipped her head. "By outside help, you mean Bryce and Elliot Payton?"

"Just Elliot. Though Bryce is interested in what we're doing too." He nodded toward Lew, who stood shuffling through the plans. "Do you want to stay? Add any ideas you may have?"

Bringing her into the process might make her more open to the changes. To him, each one was necessary. The teens would flip out over the activities, and each item would help secure the camp's success. Elliot needed to see Nate didn't do things halfway. These kids deserved the best, and he intended to give it to them.

Slipping a soft blond tendril behind her ear, she straightened. Her shoulders were as tight as her lips, but her response remained civil. "Thanks for the invite, but I should go." Her brittle smile turned to Lew. "You'll break ground next week?"

His gray eyes flicked from Nate to Gwen. "I was told to do Nate's job first. His timetable is shorter."

Gwen sucked in a deep breath. "You'll still have my place ready by fall though, right?"

"That's my goal."

With a clipped nod, she exited into the afternoon sun.

Lew chuckled. "Sorry. Not a laughing matter, but boy, you're in for a world of difficult."

Nate pulled his gaze from Gwen's retreating form. "I'm figuring that out." He held in his groan and tugged on the ends of his hair instead.

"How about I show you those plans?"

"Sounds good."

Lew spread out the papers. "Tell me what you think."

Nate scanned them, his excitement building and removing the hesitation Gwen left in her wake. By the water, a zip line provided a fast drop to the lake. In the field where he'd stood this morning, an expansive ropes course for the kids to get lost in and a soaring rock wall beside it ate up the now empty grass. Both those courses would help build confidence and trust, two very important traits these kids needed.

"This looks great. How long will it take?"

"Least three weeks."

Then they needed to get moving. "Can you start tomorrow?"

"Seven too early?"

"Not for us."

Nate nodded and shook Lew's hand. "Pleasure to finally put a face with a name."

"You too."

With a wave, Nate stepped out into the warm spring day and paused. Gwen knelt beside the camp's ancient Ford pickup, twin furrows chiseled between her brows as she stared at her flat tire.

He strolled over. "Need some help?"

She startled and fell on her rear. "You shouldn't sneak up on people."

It's not like he'd tiptoed over.

"Sorry. I figured you heard me." He offered his hand.

She ignored his help, stood, and brushed off her shorts. "I was slightly distracted."

He flicked his gaze from her long, tanned legs to the tire. "I can see that." Kneeling beside her truck, he picked up the wrench she'd dropped.

She stretched out her palm. They held a stalemate until she wiggled her fingers. "I appreciate your offer, but I've got this." Went against everything in him to sit back and watch her change the tire, but at least in this area he could give her what she wanted.

He set the tool in her palm, and she shoved it onto a bolt, pushing counterclockwise. It was as easy to see she knew what she was doing as it was to note the bolts were rusted in place. Knowledge didn't equal muscle, no matter how hard she'd like to think it did.

He stood and leaned against his Bronco, giving her another minute to try. "Sure I can't help you?"

Gwen didn't look up. "Nope. I've got it."

All right. He'd let her work her energy until she tired, and maybe then she'd allow him to apply his own to the bolts.

Pocketing his hands, he started up the street whistling. Ice cream sounded good. Ten minutes later, he returned. His chocolate cone nearly gone, a peanut butter one for Gwen dripping down his fingers, and her still working on the same bolt.

He lowered the cone. She didn't look up. "No thanks."

He wiggled it slightly.

She pushed it away. "Again. No thanks."

Her loss. Nate tipped the peanut butter cone upside down and smushed it onto his.

Now she turned. "You're eating them both? Like that?"

With her wide blue eyes and slightly opened mouth in what he guessed was disbelief—or disgust?—he almost laughed.

"Why waste it? Besides, chocolate and peanut butter are a classic combination."

Her eyes grew wider. "It was peanut butter? I thought it was vanilla."

"Looks can be deceiving. You should have asked."

With an eye roll, she turned back to her tire.

Nate finished his cone, then walked his napkins to the nearby trash. She shot him a frustrated look as he returned. "Could you stop that please?"

He raised his brows. "Stop what?"

"Whistling."

"Okay." Hadn't realized he'd started again.

After a few more minutes, he crouched beside Gwen, who'd yet to make progress. The tattoo on her left wrist caught his attention. He tilted his head, studying it. "What's your tattoo say?"

The wrench slipped from the bolt. She tipped forward, catching herself with both palms against the pebbled asphalt. A hiss escaped her lips.

Nate grabbed her by the shoulders, helping her back to a crouched position. He squatted to gently inspect her hands. "You okay?" Angry red marks scratched the surfaces of her palms, and he wiped the tiny stones still clinging to her soft flesh away.

She shuddered and pulled away. "I'm fine. Thanks." Dusting her hands against her shorts once again, she reached for the wrench.

He grasped it first. "How about you let me take a swing now?"

Hesitation flickered across her face, but then she nodded and stood. "Be my guest."

With firm pressure he loosened the first bolt. Moving on to the second, he questioned her again. "So your tattoo?" He glanced over his shoulder.

She rubbed the single word on her wrist, her entire attention focused on the black ink as if she was trying to decipher it. "It's 'live' in Greek."

Nate loosened two more bolts. "Cool. Where'd you come up with that?"

She didn't answer right away. Then, "From my husband's favorite verse, Romans 14:8."

His turn for the wrench to slip. It clanked to the ground as his focus swung to her. "You're married?"

Her pause spoke more loudly than her words when they finally choked out. "Not anymore." She spun and disappeared into NovelTeas.

Chapter Five

It had been three days since her flat tire and just as long since Gwen had seen the man who fixed it. In this case, space proved a good thing. Life had been off-kilter since she met Nate. Then, standing beside her truck, he'd completely knocked her off her emotional axis. Frustration built as she fought that tire. To need a man and not have hers there . . . it still stung. But what pierced even more? A part of her wanted to slide over and accept Nate's sweet offer to help. The entire situation made her angry, which only made her press harder, but that stinking bolt refused to move.

Then he had to ask about her tattoo.

Her eyes closed for a moment, her skin still tingling at the memory of his careful touch as he helped her up from the pavement. His brushing away the pebbles from her hands set her off balance enough to finally step back and let him fix her flat.

It had been so long since a man had taken care of her. Accepting his help, his attention, rekindled something inside that should have felt natural but only wound up putting her on defense.

Those roles belonged to Danny. Moving forward was one thing. Casting someone new in his place was something else completely—even if it had been for one small moment. Especially when that someone intended to bring to her doorstep those accountable for snatching Danny away from her.

So she ran straight back to camp with her thoughts tumbling like someone had upturned the basket they resided in.

She was so tired of things being a mess.

Which explained why she'd spent the last three days cleaning. She'd already completed the registration building, staff quarters, and portions of the main hall. Today's undertaking consisted of the kitchen and mess hall while Granddad continued working on the cabins.

As for Nate? Each morning she left a checklist that kept him busy on tasks far away from hers. Filling the open employee slots remained daily at the top. More people provided more opportunities for keeping Nate occupied and away from her.

At the top of the hill, the sound of power drills, hammers, and electric saws sliced through the morning. Lew Thompson and his crew had been putting in full days. Their noisy echoes should be coming from the opposite corner. Those tools should be building her new dream instead of a playground for the kids who'd stolen her original dream from her.

She pulled up to the dining hall. Cleaning kept her calm. She couldn't bring order to her life currently, but she could to this building. A tangible victory to erase her intangible losses.

But she'd save the bathrooms for Nate.

Grinning, she balanced a bucket of cleaners in one hand and opened the back door with the other, then stepped inside. She lined everything up on the kitchen counter and took out her clipboard. Flipping through the pages, she located the one labeled Mess Hall to place on top.

Kitchen area came first. Specifically, the dishes. Twisting open a bottle of Rock N' Rye, Gwen took a large sip, the sweet and creamy taste one of her favorite pleasures. Placing it on the counter, she set to work hauling out all the pots and pans. An hour later she inhaled the lemony scent of a job well done, finished off her drink, and crossed off the first box on her list. Her muscles began to relax.

Next came the cupboards. She donned a mask to avoid the dust as she eyeballed the one over the massive refrigerator. Only way to reach it involved climbing on the counter. She hauled herself up, then precariously stretched across the top of the fridge.

Nearby, the back door creaked, and Nate's deep voice startled her. "What on earth are you doing?"

She wobbled and clutched the cabinet door which swung open. Nate grabbed her waist, steadying her. Heat shot up her skin at his touch, surprising her, and she glared at him. "Stop sneaking up on me."

His hands remained curled around her waist. "The squeaky screen door wasn't heads up enough?"

Not when it was his voice that threw her off balance. His strong hands weren't helping either.

She attempted to wiggle free. "I'm fine. You can let go now."

Was that a slight hesitation before he released his grip?

And why did his touch bring a measure of security?

Because he stopped you from falling and breaking your neck. Anyone's grip would feel secure.

Nate stepped away but kept his eyes on her. "What are you doing up there anyway? And what's with the mask?"

"Cleaning out this cupboard." She pulled it down. "And allergies."

He tipped his head, but left it alone. "Do we actually store stuff up there?"

"No." She wiped it out. "But it needs cleaning anyway."

He remained quiet and waited for her to finish. Gwen hopped to the ground and peered up at him. "Did you need something?"

"I found a trail I'd like to explore, but I'm not exactly known for my directional abilities." He leaned against the counter and crossed his arms. Pretty sure she could bounce a quarter off those biceps. "You said if I needed anything to come to you first. Well, I need a guide."

"Huh?" She pulled her focus from his arms, cheeks warming, and tapped her list. "I'm busy."

He twisted the clipboard around so he could read it. "This all looks like cleaning. And here I thought you were busy creating ways to keep me out of your hair."

She fought the lip twitch and reclaimed her clipboard. "And I thought you were busy arranging interviews. Isn't that what I put on your list for the day?"

"Yes, but then I checked the forecast. I can call on those tonight or tomorrow when it's raining."

His procrastination made her skin itch.

"Why'd you ask me to make a schedule if you aren't going to keep it?"

"I will keep it." He pulled a Laffy Taffy from his pocket, ripped it open, then bit into it. "Except maybe not in the order you wrote it."

"Do you have a secret stash of those someplace?"

He finished chewing and swallowed. "I do. It wasn't on the handy clipboard you left me, but I ordered candy for the camp store. It arrived this morning, and I thought I should test it out."

"It wasn't on your list because we don't do that. We sell T-shirts, water bottles, small toys. We don't sell candy."

His laughter had to originate at his toes, it was so deep. "A camp for kids and you didn't sell candy?"

Not that she needed to justify her decision, but . . . "Kids have enough energy, they don't need sugar to amp it up."

His lips scrunched to the side, and he pinned her with those blue eyes. "Yeah. Think I'll still go with the candy and take my chances."

Why wasn't she surprised? "Well, good luck with that, Willy Wonka."

"Willy Wonka. Hmm . . ." He nodded, then picked up the broom leaning against the wall. "Pretty sure I'll need more luck with this thing."

Gwen reached to take it from him. "It's okay. I've got this."

He didn't release his hold. "But if I help, you'll be done faster, and we can hit the trail."

She pulled. "I never said I was going."

"And let me get lost in the woods?" His tug proved stronger. Gentle but unyielding, and he tucked the broom behind his back. "You wouldn't let that happen."

Seriously. What did he lift to get those biceps?

Ugh. What was up with her and his arms?

"Don't bet on it." She stepped away. "But if you insist on helping, we don't start with sweeping."

His hand scrubbed across his mouth. If she didn't know better, she'd believe he was holding in a laugh. "You really like order, don't you?"

Why did he constantly make her feel like she was going to implode?

"Yes." She tried to keep her response sweet, but it came out more like an awful tasting artificial sweetener than the real thing.

"Because order matters." He said it like he was trying to fit puzzle pieces into her broken places.

"It does." She pointed to her checklist, fracturing their held stare. He had a way of seeing inside her that flared old memories. "If you want to help, this is how we do it."

"Fine." His voice soft, he leaned the broom against the wall. "Where should I start?"

Gwen peered at her paper. Order was important, but so was moving him to a room she wasn't in. The man unsettled her. And no one had done that since Danny. It was a trip she wasn't going to take again.

Not that she would with Nate. They were too opposite. But she wasn't blind or numb. As much as he infuriated her, something inside stirred when he was near. Could as easily be annoyance as attraction, but each was enough to keep her distance.

"Here." She pointed to the second section on her checklist. "Start with the chairs out there."

With a salute, he grabbed supplies, then strolled into the dining hall. A minute later his off-key whistling rolled into the kitchen. Gwen leaned back and looked through the open serving window. Nate pulled chairs into one long line, then began wiping them. About every other note he whistled tickled her brain, but he never stayed in tune long enough for her to place it.

Half hour of whistling later, she stepped into the doorway. "Okay. I give. What song is that?"

He looked up from the row of chairs. " 'Stand by Me' "

The man was tone deaf and didn't realize it.

"That's not 'Stand by Me.' "

"Sure it is."

Gwen shook her head. "No. This is." She whistled the first several bars.

"Exactly." He joined in a few, then stopped. "That's what I've been whistling."

She laughed. "It's so not."

Nate straightened. "Yes. It is."

No use trying to convince him. She lifted her shoulders. "All right. It is." Smirking, she returned to the other room.

"It is." His emphatic response pulled more laughter from her.

She bit her tongue.

Because there was no way Nate Reynolds was getting on her good side.

Nate brushed the last cobweb from the corner of the room. He was covered in dirt, sweat, and grime. Gwen joined him, looking about the same. A smudge of brown streaked down her temple, the mark stopping where her mask had been.

"Looks good." She nodded at his progress. "Gotta say, I'm impressed."

"Didn't think I could actually clean?"

"After seeing your cabin?" She tilted her body to the wall. "No."

She didn't hold anything back.

"Deserved." He gathered his supplies. "How's your portion?"

"Would pass a white-glove test."

Of course it would. He raised a brow. "Maybe I should administer one." She was fun to needle.

Her tiny shrug showed she wasn't the least concerned.

"Unfortunately, I left my butler gloves in my cabin." He joined her in the doorway between the dining room and the kitchen.

"Never to be seen again, I'm sure."

In her teasing he caught a glimpse of the woman under the layers of hurt. But it wasn't that woman who intrigued him. It was this one right in front of him. The one with all the cracks and crevices still running through her. Those unsealed edges of pain allowed the light seeping past to burst forth, warm and golden, against the darkness, almost like the solar eclipse he'd once watched as a child hiding out in his backyard. He hadn't been able to stop staring then, even though he knew he was supposed to.

He was having the same problem now.

Her brows drew together under his scrutiny. He reached for the first words he could grab. "So, lunch first, then we hit the trail?"

She blinked. "Nope." And pushed off the wall. "Lunch and then more cleaning. My checklist isn't finished yet."

Susan L. Tuttle

Because veering from it might make the world stop rotating.

He captured those words before they escaped. They could eradicate their tentative teasing line. "But here's the thing. You wanted me to put together a camp calendar." Number five on those blasted lists she'd left on his desk this week to try and keep him out of her hair.

"Yes." She drew the word out.

"That means I need to check out a few activities I have in mind to see if they'll make the cut. These trails are one of them." That slightly lifted brow kept him talking. "Today's the only nice day all week." He pointed to her list. "And that's all stuff you can do when it's raining. We can't hike the trails then."

"So we abandon our schedule based on the weather forecast?"

"No. We rearrange our schedule based on the weather forecast."

Her gaze caught on the sunshine outside before settling on him. "Which trail?"

He shrugged. "I don't know the name. I saw a section on the map and wanted to check it out."

"Show me."

He dug out a map from his back pocket and unfolded it, then pointed. Gwen leaned in, and he caught a whiff of roses. She squinted at the dark brown line beneath his finger. "Looks like the Potawatomi Trail."

Pot-ah-what? "Thought you told me to stick to real words." He turned, close enough to see the dark green lines filtering through her sky blue eyes. Like a tiny piece of the camp had been embedded into her very being.

She grinned. "Potawatomi. It's an Indian name." She traced the line. "Goes for several miles. People use it year round. I'm sure you'll enjoy the trek."

"*We'll* enjoy the trek." Nate refolded the map. "I can't do this without you."

• 51 •

"And I can't leave Granddad with all this work." She continued gathering cleaning supplies from around the room. "Easing his load is the only reason I agreed to stay."

"Which is why I came to you first—like you asked. He can take the afternoon off while we check out this trail." Nate picked up a sponge. "I'm the one with the ticking time clock. I understand what needs to be done, and I promise you, we'll finish the cleaning later this week." He tossed the sponge into her laundry basket. It landed with a thud, and he pumped his hand into the air. "Three points!"

Exasperation weighted her features and words. "Those were my clean rags." Pinching the sponge's frayed edge, she transferred it to a plastic bag. Then she scooped up her basket.

He hustled to open the door for her. "Look. It's hard to admit, but I really am directionallenged."

"Thought we agreed to use real words."

He grinned—"Directionally challenged"—and followed her down the steps. "That better?"

"Much."

But she still hadn't agreed. He jogged past her to stop in her path. "If I tackle the trail alone, I might never come back."

"You say that like it's a bad thing."

If her lips weren't struggling to stay in a straight line, he might get offended. "Please?"

She tipped her head. "You really need a tour guide?"

He hated to admit it, but, "Yes." The map fit back into his pocket. "I have many talents. Navigation is not one of them."

She dodged him and dropped her basket on the golf cart's rear seat. "A man asking for help with directions. I'm impressed."

"Yeah, well, I learned the hard way my ego takes a much smaller dent asking for help than having a search party launched for me."

"That bad?" Pure surprise and—he bet—a hint of curiosity lifted her lids as she stared at him.

"Come with me, and I'll tell you about it."

Tugging her earlobe, she consulted her checklist.

Nate pried the thing from her. "Come on. Take advantage of the spring sun."

Her hesitation lingered.

"I'll help with all the cleaning this week. Promise."

Both her eyebrows arched in challenge. "Even the bathrooms?"

"Even the bathrooms."

She shook her head and looked down. "All right, but I'll need to change."

"I can wait."

Her pause gave way to a decisive nod. Maybe even a little excitement. "Fine. I'll come, but let me run by Granddad's first to tell him that he can take the afternoon off."

Nate walked backward up the trail. "Meet you at the truck in twenty?"

"Sounds like a plan."

One of the best he'd had all week.

Chapter Six

What was wrong with her? She had a list of things to accomplish at a camp she hoped never opened, for a man she didn't even like, yet she was ditching her plans to run off and spend the day with him.

Had to be curiosity. She wanted to know more about Nate and his story. What had him so convinced he could change these kids' lives? His hope seemed so fresh.

Hers was tattered.

She filled her water bottle and set it on the counter so she could pull on her hiking boots. Granddad had been easy to convince to lay low for the day. Said he'd head into town for lunch at Bay's and not to worry about him.

As if that would ever happen.

Boots on, she stuffed her bottle into a small backpack and glanced at her inhaler. Today's perfect spring temps with low humidity said she shouldn't need it . . . but she tossed it in anyway. She had no clue how fast Nate would push the hike.

Stepping out the front door, she caught him smiling from his perch on a golf cart. "Ready?" he asked, his eyes hidden behind dark sunglasses. He'd changed into frayed cargos and hiking boots, but his grey T-shirt remained along with a flannel that covered his broad shoulders. Might as well have plucked him straight from an outdoor magazine. "You going to be warm enough?"

"Huh?" Gwen looked down at her cut-offs and tank. There was a light breeze, but she could stand to cool off a little. "I'm good." She slid onto the bench. "I thought we were meeting at the truck."

"Figured I'd give you a lift." He cranked the lever to reverse.

The more time she spent with him, the more his caretaking gene became evident. "Thanks."

"Welcome." He executed a Y-turn and headed for the parking lot. Dust swirled as he swung into a spot beside his black Bronco and hopped out. "I packed us lunch too." He reached for the cooler behind him.

"That thing is ginormous." She slipped to the passenger side as he walked around the vehicle. "How much do you think I eat?"

"Obviously a lot."

Gwen stopped. Looked at him. He slipped the cooler into the rear, whistling off-key, then pulled open his door and met her gaze across the seats. "What?"

"I can't believe you said that."

"I can't believe you asked it."

Slowly shaking her head in amusement, she climbed in beside him.

He fired up his Bronco and turned down the long driveway. "Nice neology, by the way."

"Can you go one afternoon without making up words?"

"Neology is in the dictionary. Look it up."

"Or you could tell me."

Dust swirled outside their windows as they bounced along the dirt drive. "It means the use of a new word."

She rolled back over what she'd said. "Ginormous?"

He nodded.

"Ginormous is in the Oxford Dictionary."

"But it wasn't always." He grinned.

She issued an eye roll along with directions. "Take a left."

"Aye-aye, Captain."

Ten minutes later they pulled into a small parking lot at the head of the Potawatomi Trail. Both jumped out, and Nate offered her a granola bar. "Want one?"

"Sure." Her fingertips slid over his as she grabbed it. Like before, the touch jarred something in her. It wasn't as if she hadn't had contact with men since Danny died, but this was the first time a touch or look from another man stole her attention. And she wasn't sure what to do about it.

Gwen examined the bar wrapped in parchment paper and sealed with a navy blue oval sticker. The outline of a white tea cup with a book resting inside was stamped in the middle. "You went to see Bay?"

"I went to see Lew, but NovelTeas is right beside him." He closed the cooler. "Does she pump the smell straight from her oven out her front door? Because I swear it lured me right in."

Gwen chuckled. "You're not the first man who's been sucked in by her baking. Too bad for you, she's taken."

"It's a good thing, actually." A breeze ruffled the edges of his hair across his forehead, and he shoved the waves back. "I'd be the size of a walrus if I married someone like her."

"You're the farthest thing from a walrus." Her cheeks went solar-hot the second the words left her mouth.

Nate grinned. "Good to know."

She bit her lip to keep anything else from escaping.

"So. Shall we hit the trail?"

"Yep." Gwen slid on her backpack and eyed the path, which lay wide open for about twenty feet before the forest swallowed it. "How far do you want to go?"

"I was hoping to hike to the picnic area. Looked like there's one about three miles up."

"Sounds good."

They stepped onto the trail, branches tightening around them in a way that felt more cozy than confining. The baby leaves were nearly full grown, squeezing out all but a few sunbeams with dancing dust. They walked in silence for a few minutes. Her shoulders slowly relaxed. These woods had always been her haven. It's why she'd run to them when Danny died. She stepped over a downed tree. Brown needles carpeted the forest floor, muffling their footfalls except for the occasional snap of a broken branch cracking under their boots, and she breathed in the loamy scent of dirt.

"The farther we go, the more beautiful it becomes." Nate spoke from behind her.

She glanced over her shoulder. "For once we agree on something."

"We haven't disagreed on everything."

"Only most things."

"See." He grinned. "We agree again."

They kept going, the silence creating a comfort level they'd yet to achieve. She'd witnessed snippets, but it seemed like whenever they spoke for a length of time, any marginalized edge of friendship they'd gained was lost. Maybe if they stayed this quiet the rest of the summer, they'd both survive.

"Awfully quiet." With two giant paces, he walked beside her.

So much for staying silent.

She looked his way. "Enjoying the scenery."

His boyish grin came out to play. "Thanks."

"You're incorrigible."

"Or confident." His arm brushed against hers.

"I think you're making my point for me."

Squirrels dodged across the branches above, their chattering broken by the occasional robin's tweet. Beside her, Nate took in everything as if seeing a forest for the first time. His blue eyes as wide as a child's—except he was no child. Scruff covered the sharp angles of his chin and rode along his cheeks, the rough look softened by the waves that rolled through his thick hair. More than once she'd thought of stretching to finger a strand off his forehead. He was at least six inches taller than her. And while those things drew her attention, it was his strength that pulled her to him. Not only physical, but emotional. To know him as briefly as she had and already see that aspect promised he was a force unlike any she'd known.

He looked down, caught her staring, and cocked half a grin.

That wasn't good.

"You owe me a story." She pushed to step ahead of him. "About your amazing directional abilities, I believe."

"Right." His voice rumbled close. He wasn't letting her far out of reach. "You would remember."

She tapped her head. "Steel trap."

His deep chuckle curled up her spine. "And humble."

"You're not distracting the conversation."

"Wouldn't dream of it."

She nailed him with a contradictory look rather than words.

"Fine." Nate relented. "I was in Yellowstone with friends. We were hiking, and I had to um . . . use the facilities. So I took off by myself."

"Isn't the number one rule of hiking to never go off alone?"

"Isn't the number one rule of an audience to hold their questions until the end?"

She couldn't help it, laughter escaped. "Okay. Keep going."

"In full disclosure, my friends may have mentioned the same rule as I've never been known for my directional abilities, but I opted for privacy." His long legs made half-strides to remain in sync with hers. "I left my backpack with them—"

"You didn't."

He gave her a look.

"Sorry."

"And took off. When I tried to head back, it was like I'd entered another dimension." He held a low branch for her. "I thought I was hiking south to the trail. In reality, I was going west. Didn't know it until search and rescue found me—ten hours later."

"You're kidding."

He lifted one brow.

So he wasn't kidding.

"I hold the record for the longest bathroom break in Yellowstone history."

"Do you have the T-shirt?"

"Nope."

She grinned. "Then it never really happened."

The trickling of water drifted through the trees. Nate broke course.

Gwen tossed her hands in the air. "And that's how you get lost," she called.

"I won't get lost." He glanced back, his dimple showing. "That's why I brought you." Then he dodged through the trees.

Gwen sighed and followed. So much for their conversation. Her eyes darted heavenward to mark the trees she passed and the sun's location as she pushed aside the bushes he'd disappeared through. Coming out on the other side, a pebbled shore gave way to wide flowing water, sunlight glinting like diamonds off its rippled surface.

The Potawatomi River.

"Did you know this was here?" Nate stood on a small boulder along the water's edge.

"When we get back, I'm putting *Find My Friends* on your phone." She nodded to the river. "And yes. It's what the trail is named after. Didn't you see it on the map?"

"The blue line?"

"Blue typically refers to bodies of water on a map. Were you absent that day in school?" She lobbed the verbal jab with a friendly toss.

It landed with a thud at his feet. His lips thinned. But it wasn't anger in his eyes. Embarrassment? Insecurity? Whatever it was, it was aimed at himself. "Guess I must have missed that class."

Gwen swallowed. Stepped forward. He might not be her favorite person, but he wasn't a bad guy. "I was only teasing. I pretty much slept through anything math related. I mean, I was great at math until they decided to bring the alphabet in."

He chuckled and combed his hand through his hair. "Yeah. Numbers and letters don't pair well, do they?"

"No, they do not."

He held her gaze. Blew out a breath and smiled. "So what's *Find My Friends?*"

"An app you desperately need." More than any person she'd ever known after that story. "I'll show you how to use it and link it to my phone. If you're ever lost, I'll be able to find you."

"So we're friends?"

The word *what* almost escaped her lips until the app's name answered the question. "I guess so."

"Good." He pointed to the river. "Where does this lead to?"

Things that had been hard for years seemed easier with him.

She planted her foot on the boulder where he stood. "Lake Huron." Most people loved the bigger lakes. She appreciated them, but the small beauty of Hidden Lake captured her heart. "This river collects run-off from several smaller lakes— Hidden Lake included—and runs to Lake Huron."

"So, in theory, we could tube from Hidden Lake to the Lakeshore?"

"You could." In theory. "But I haven't done it since I was a girl. I'm not sure what the river looks like all the way through."

Nate jumped down. "Then we'll have to try it."

"No way." She shook her head. "That water is freezing."

Nate bent and ran his fingertips through the water. "It's not bad."

She dipped her own in and shivered. His idea of cold and hers were two vastly different things. "We're back to not agreeing on things."

"I'm not suggesting jumping in right now—"

"Good, because I wasn't planning on it."

"We don't even have tubes. But maybe in another few weeks, if the days stay as warm as they've been." He looked up at her, the navy rim around his blue pupils a near match for the river's water. "Could be fun."

He stood. She backed up. Not fast enough to escape the light scent of pine he wore. Or maybe it was the woods around them.

Yep. She was going with that.

Gwen wiped her hands together. "Or it could turn us into popsicles."

"Might be a little uncomfortable at first, but if you go in slow, you'll eventually warm up." He had a way of studying her that pricked at her heart. Like a tiny needle seeing if that area had healed enough to feel again. "And you might find something amazing."

Numbness wasn't her problem right now. The little zings of reawakening hurt. Especially when there was no understanding the *why*. She hadn't been looking. And definitely not at this man.

Nate broke their stare and swiveled around. His brows drew together. "I can't see the trail."

She turned. "That's what happens when you leave it." Well, if you left it without paying attention, which he had. But she'd studied the trees as she stepped from them. Now she pointed to them. "Those are the trees we want."

The river behind them gurgled along. "I knew I brought you for a reason."

"And here I thought it was for my good company."

He leaned in close, his eyes flickering over hers. "That was the bonus." Then he brushed past. "Come on. Haven't made it a mile, and I'm already hungry. Let's find that picnic site."

She shook off the lingering heat from his stare and trudged after him. Had it been so long since a man paid attention to her that she was misreading signals? And why did a part of her wish she wasn't?

Because, in spite of his faults, Nate was safe. She'd already determined that answer. So what if clouds kept rolling over it.

Her cell phone's chime startled her as much as it did the birds.

"You get service out here?" Nate asked.

"Apparently." She pulled it out but didn't recognize the number. "Hello?"

"Gwen Doornbos?"

"Yes?" She raised her shoulders at Nate's questioning glance.

"Ms. Doornbos, this is Nurse Sutton from County General. We have your grandfather here."

Chapter Seven

Nate handed Gwen a Styrofoam cup filled with coffee. The smile she granted him did nothing to alleviate the worry in her eyes. She shivered as he took the seat beside her, the vinyl chair crinkling as his weight settled into it. He set his cup on a worn oak table marred with watermarks from the other coffee cups it had held during the years of loved ones waiting in this same spot. Next he shed his flannel shirt. She'd refused it in the truck and again when they arrived, but one more time and he'd force her goose-pebbled arms in the sleeves himself.

"Please put this on." He held the offering out.

"I'm okay."

"You're not." The shirt hung from his finger. "Stop being stubborn and take it. The last thing Arthur needs is for you to get sick." He'd really rather not strong arm her into it, at least not physically.

Her blue-green eyes wavered back and forth across his stare, as if holding it was too intense for her. "Really, I'm—"

"See, now you're being exaspertinating."

She straightened. "What?"

"Exasperating and obstinate."

Silence. Then, "That was your worst one yet."

"I made it up under extreme duress." He shook the shirt. "And if you want me to keep trying more words, I suggest you deny the shirt again."

She snatched it from him and slipped it on. "Happy now?" The sleeves extended past her fingertips, and she began rolling them up.

"I am." He grabbed his coffee, and then reclined in his chair, closing his eyes.

"I was worried you might start whistling next."

"The people in this waiting room should be so lucky."

A tiny bubble of laughter skipped past her lips. "Thank you."

He peeked open one eye. "You're welcome."

Now that she was warm, he'd let her have quiet. They'd arrived to Bay's husband, Colin—an ER doctor—waiting for them. Colin's shift was ending when the paramedics brought Arthur in. He informed them Arthur had fallen off a ladder, shattering his hip, and they'd taken him into surgery. After passing on the info, he disappeared into the O.R., coming out periodically to provide updates.

Murmurs mixed with the voice of Judge Judy blaring from the TV in the corner. Not his choice of programs, but at least it wasn't a soap opera. The judge was chewing into a young man who'd found himself on the wrong side of the law. Nate sympathized with the defensive stance the kid took. About the way he used to look when authority of any kind laid into him. Didn't mean he hadn't deserved it, only that if someone had delivered the message with kindness instead of judgment and disgust, maybe he would have listened sooner.

Too many lost years.

Soft clicking to his left returned him to the here-and-now. Gwen's unzipped backpack sat by her feet, and on her lap lay her iPad, the small keyboard cover open as she typed. "You brought your iPad on our hike?"

"You were scouting the trail for possible use. I might have needed to take notes."

He peered over her shoulder. A medical website filled the screen. "What's that for?"

"Researching Granddad's injury. Trying to figure out what he'll need."

He covered her hand with his. "They'll assign a case manager who'll work with your insurance. You don't need to worry about any of this."

She looked at their joined hands, then up to him. Her mouth opened but words didn't immediately pour out. It took a few long seconds. "I know, but it's a good distraction. I don't do hospitals very well."

Why? The word hovered on his tongue. He swallowed it. Earlier her teasing had spoken to him, now her unexpected vulnerability did. It allowed him to see another sliver of her and stoked something protective inside. The urge to pull her from the shadows still covering her life rose within him, but he'd need to earn her trust first.

He squeezed, then let go, leaning in toward her iPad. "So what have you found?"

Air puffed from her lips, and she cleared her throat. "He'll need a few things for his bathroom, a wedge for his chair, possibly a hospital bed—though it's not necessary . . ." Her voice slipped away, then her eyes lifted to his. "I should have stuck to the list today."

And there it was. The guilt she'd been nursing since she'd gotten the call. He'd worried its heat would forge anger, and she'd aim it at him. Instead, she unloaded her burden. He'd help shoulder it as long as allowed. "This isn't your fault."

"But if I'd followed my plans, I'd have been at camp when he needed me."

"And the ladder still could have tipped."

"I wouldn't have let him on it."

"Then you'd be the one in surgery."

Gwen rubbed her thumb against her fingernails. "My hip could have handled that fall."

"But what about your head? Your arm?" The door swished open and a doctor came through—not Colin. "Look, Gwen."

She gave him her attention. "We can play the what-if game all afternoon. You can hit one to me, and I'll lob it back. But in the end the facts won't change—and honestly, it's not a very fun game. So how about instead we give thanks that Arthur wasn't hurt worse?"

Her lips thinned. "Thanks for the sympathy."

"You have my sympathy. I'm truly sorry your grandfather got hurt." He shrugged. "What you won't receive is me agreeing you could have controlled the situation. Stuff happens, Gwen."

"Stuff happens?" Her voice raised a notch.

He nodded, lowering his voice. "Yes. Stuff happens. Big stuff. Sucky stuff. Uncontrollable stuff." He paused. "But also amazing stuff. Beautiful stuff. Miraculous stuff—like your granddad not getting hurt worse. Like his cell phone being in his pocket and not broken so he could call for help. Like an ambulance being only five minutes away." Emotions turned circles behind her eyes. "Focusing only on the bad creates an unbalanced picture."

She blinked and looked away. "Sometimes the bad is so big you can't see past it."

The shift in her voice . . . They'd moved beyond Arthur. Whatever pain had touched her, it hovered over the surface like a fog she couldn't see clearly through. Life had a way of doing that. Giving a person such huge hurts or insurmountable obstacles that they coated their view of every future experience. He should know. Pretty much described his entire youth.

But those clouds eventually lifted. He'd love to help hers do the same. "Then you have to look harder."

God could heal her hurts and fill her holes. Nate was walking proof. And if he succeeded this summer, every kid who attended his camp would be another testament to that truth. He prayed Gwen collected those pieces of evidence and arrived at his same conclusion: God could change hearts, and this was the place for him to do it.

Because if this camp didn't succeed, then what was his own past for?

Beside him, Gwen shifted. She'd been staring at her hands, he'd been staring at the wall. Both needed a distraction. "Show me more of what we'll need once Arthur comes home."

"We?" Confusion dragged her brows together.

"Yes. I plan—"

"Gwen!" The door to the waiting room shoved open, and Bay, along with a red head—Elise, based on an earlier phone conversation he'd overheard—rushed through. Gwen dropped her iPad to the chair and hugged them both. "I told you guys not to come."

"And you thought we'd listen?" Bay released her.

Elise did the same, brushing dirt from her jeans. "I had to track down Mac, and Bay had to wait for one of her employees to cover the store, or we'd have been here sooner."

"You left your brother alone at the farm?" Gwen grabbed Elise's arm.

Guess that wasn't a good thing.

Elise waved a hand through the air. "I told him to feed the snakes. He loves that."

Snakes? Weren't farms more like cows and sheep?

Gwen pulled on her earlobe. "Sorry to mess up your day. I could have kept you updated over the phone."

"You didn't mess up a thing," Bay reassured. "And we can't hug you over the phone."

Nate stood and held out his hand to whom he guessed was Elise. "Hi. I'm Nate Reynolds."

She smiled, her emerald eyes lighting. "Elise Wilder." Her hands were calloused and strong, a stark contrast to the smooth, soft skin of her face and her tender smile. "Thanks for staying." Then she turned back to Gwen and offered the iced coffee she held with some weird gummy-looking beads floating in the bottom.

"What is that?" he asked.

"Boba Tea." Gwen showed him the cup. "These are tapioca pearls floating in the bottom. It's really good."

"I'll take your word for it." He wasn't a tea guy to begin with. And he definitely wasn't into chewing his drinks.

Bay produced a bag that had to be responsible for the savory aromas rumbling his stomach. "Don't worry. I brought you real food." The gauzy wide sleeves of her blouse slid up her slim arms, and her skirt swished around sandaled feet as she wiggled the bag. She bore a beautiful bohemian vibe, but in the short time he'd known Bay, her spirit proved most attractive. Colin was a lucky man.

Nate snagged the food from her and lifted it to his nose. Yep. Colin was a very lucky man. "Thank you."

"Anytime." She guided Gwen to a seat.

Elise took the one on the opposite side and all three leaned their heads together. Gwen rested in good hands. Nate settled into a corner and quickly polished off his roast beef sandwich. His stomach full and Gwen cared for, he leaned his head against the wall.

An agitated voice awoke him. He blinked the haze from his eyes. Gwen stood, her legs touching the edge of her chair, while an older couple whispered harshly with her. Her bottom lip caught between her teeth. She cast a furtive glance his way, her eyes widening when she caught him watching. Her focus slammed to the couple, but they'd already seen her reaction. The woman turned and red filled her cheeks.

Nate stood. He looked to Bay and Elise, who offered no further help other than sympathetic smiles which—judging by the looks aimed his way right now from whoever stood beside Gwen—were about as good as tossing arm floaties to a full-grown man drowning in the middle of the Pacific.

He reached the threesome and held out his hand. "Hi. I'm—"

"Nate Reynolds. We know." The older gentleman addressed him. "We're David and Marlene Doornbos."

Gwen's parents. He held out his hand. "Pleasure meeting you."

They didn't shake it. The red in Marlene's cheeks turned molten. Tears filled her eyes, and she shook her head. Her husband wrapped his arm around her. Nate slipped his hand into his pocket and arched an eyebrow at Gwen.

She resembled a deer in the headlights.

What was going on?

"Gwen?" he nudged.

"I, um . . ." Her palms brushed against her sides.

"How could you?" Soft but strong, Marlene's voice rang out.

Nate shifted to her. "I'm a little lost as to what's going on here."

"Not you." Marlene's body shook, but her stare held strong on Gwen. "You." Gwen recoiled, but Marlene didn't stop. "Allowing him into your life? With those kids?"

"Marlene," her husband's voice warned.

But she plowed straight ahead. "I thought people heard wrong. That there was no way this could be the truth. But here you are"—she jabbed a finger toward Nate—"with him."

Gwen's mouth opened, but no sound came out.

Fine. He'd speak. "She's not *with* me."

"Then why are you here?" Marlene pulled her hand away, clenching it at her side. "How can you do this?"

David wrapped his arm around her. His face compromised somewhere between a glare and grief, he nodded to Gwen. "We wanted to make sure Arthur was all right." He swallowed. "And you too." A brief glance at Nate before returning to Gwen. "But we see that you are."

Then, his wife in his arms, they walked away. Bay and Elise rallied around Gwen who still hadn't spoken. Bay squeezed her arm. "You okay?"

Nothing.

Nate cast a concerned glance toward Bay, who simply shook her head.

Yet Gwen's silence spoke volumes. Puzzle pieces began joining together. Her intense pain laced with anger. The tattoo on her wrist. Hating hospitals. The parents he'd just met; neither referred to Arthur as dad or treated Gwen like their daughter, and yet they shared the same last name.

The picture coming together presented one he didn't want the final piece too, but at the same time desperately needed it.

"Gwen?"

Chin still dipped toward the floor, her eyes slowly peered up at him. Exhausted didn't begin to describe the emotional state breathing off of her. She blinked.

"Who were those people?"

"My husband's parents," she offered so quietly he almost missed it.

"And your husband . . ." he prodded.

Bay and Elise moved in closer to Gwen.

"Is dead."

It was the puzzle piece he'd held but didn't want to slide into place.

Gwen's chin lifted, her eyes strong and clear now. "Killed by the same kids you've invited to my camp." Then she spun away from her friends, pushed through the waiting room doors, and disappeared.

Shock glued him to the ground. The kids he'd . . .

It was like expecting a firecracker and experiencing the atom bomb.

What had God dropped him in the middle of?

Chapter Eight

Something soft draped over her chest. With both hands, Gwen pulled it up and snuggled her chin deep into the smooth fabric, refusing to open her eyes. Except her back ached, so did her arms, her legs, her neck. Whatever rested on top of her might be soft, but whatever lay underneath her might as well be rock.

She blinked her eyes open.

"Sorry. I didn't mean to wake you, but you looked cold." An entirely too fresh and clean Nate stood beside her chair. "Your blanket was on the floor when I came in."

She straightened in the chair where she'd fallen asleep and blinked a few more times. Under the blanket she clutched, she was a rumpled mess. The squeal of cart wheels along with muffled voices drifted through the closed door to her left. She looked to her right. Granddad slept soundly, soft puffs of air escaping through his lips.

Pushing the blanket off, she stood. "It's okay. I wasn't really asleep."

There went his dimple.

"Okay," she confessed, "but it wasn't a deep sleep."

"That I'll believe." He held up a duffle bag. "I brought you some fresh clothes and a toothbrush."

She sucked in her bottom lip. That was sweet. But he'd gone through her stuff?

He must have picked up on her discomfort, because he offered a reassuring grin. "I called Bay. She stopped by before opening NovelTeas and put the bag together. I'm only delivering it."

Much less weird, much more sweet. Gwen accepted the bag. "You didn't have to come back."

"I wanted to see how Arthur was doing."

"I have a phone."

He stared at her for a long moment. "I wanted to see how you were too."

They hadn't spoken this many words since she'd rushed from the waiting room after her bombshell confession. He hadn't chased her, and he hadn't asked the questions she'd seen burning in his eyes when she returned nearly an hour later.

No. He'd sat in the corner of the waiting room until Colin slipped out to say Granddad made it through surgery. They could see him, but he wouldn't be coherent. And still Nate waited until Gwen had kissed Granddad's cheek in recovery, forced down half a bagel for dinner, and eventually found the room they'd settled him in for the night. All that time, the most he said to her was "keep it" when she tried to hand him back his flannel shirt before he left.

His shirt. Gwen looked down at the red plaid. She started to shed it. His hand raised. "It's pretty cold in the hallway. Wait until you've changed."

"You'll still be here?"

He nodded. "Thought I'd sit with Arthur until after you get a shower."

Granddad's fall changed things. Surely Nate knew that. It had consumed a large part of her own thoughts last night as she planned what the next few weeks would look like now. And still, he was here. Helping her when she could no longer help him.

"Thank you." She started for the door. "I won't be long."

"He's not even stirring with us talking. I think you're safe to grab breakfast too." He settled into the chair she'd vacated.

Smiling, she stepped into the hall and toward the bathroom, which contained the shower lacking in Granddad's room. Locking the door behind her, she dropped her bag to the floor. The past week arched through her mind like a boomerang's path. Her plans to sell had been flung from her, but then Granddad's broken hip soared them straight back. He couldn't help with this camp now. His injury not only killed their timetable for readying the place—she needed to be by his side, not Nate's—but he'd need calm and quiet to recuperate. The destruction of Nate's plans meant her original ones with Crossroads Church could move forward.

A bubble of conflicting emotions burst inside. Okay. So she didn't want those kids on her land. But even she could see Nate was a good guy. People's true colors illuminated under pressure. Last night, when Marlene arrived, guns blazing, Gwen was reminded of her passive-aggressive ways. Marlene wasn't there because of Granddad; she showed up because she'd heard about the camp. While Nate stayed for Granddad first. Her second. And when things went crazy, he hadn't pushed for his own answers.

Undressing, she ducked beneath the warm spray from the shower. Her muscles relaxed, even if her brain couldn't. She didn't want to feel badly for Nate, but she understood him. He had a plan, and it was about to change due to circumstances beyond his control. They were like two perpendicular lines, intersecting on this point but going in two completely different directions.

Shower finished, she quickly dried off and twisted her hair into a bun. A small toiletry bag rested at the bottom of the duffel. She owed Bay a huge thank you too.

Smacking her minty lips, Gwen hurried to the cafeteria. She snagged two cups of coffee, two muffins, and two bananas. Juggling it all with her duffel over her shoulder, she rushed back upstairs. She'd only been gone twenty-five minutes. A deep chuckle poured out the cracked-open door of Granddad's room. Only twenty-five minutes, but of course he'd wake up while she was gone.

Pushing inside, she was greeted by Granddad's grey-blue eyes and a smile. "Hey, princess."

His gravelly voice nearly brought her to tears. He was going to be okay. How many times had she repeated that sentence in the past eighteen hours? It was only a broken hip. Colin said surgery went amazingly well and that Granddad was strong. But until she heard his voice . . .

Gwen beelined to his side, dropping her pseudo-breakfast on the swivel table by his bed. "Don't ever do that again."

He lifted his cheek to meet her kiss. "Well, that's a fine good-morning."

Her palms fit against his wrinkled cheeks, her nose inches from his as she stared into his eyes. "Good morning." She kissed his forehead. "Now don't ever do that again."

She released him, and he chuckled, sliding a glance to Nate. "She's even bossier when she's tired and hungry. Better keep that in mind."

Her hand stopped over the banana she reached for. "Why does he need to keep that in mind?" Because after today, Nate would be packing up and heading home. There was no way they'd try to keep the camp moving forward now.

"With me out of commission, you two will need to work more closely. Thought I better give him some pointers." His light words aimed to tease, but they sunk into Gwen like heavy weights.

"Except we won't be working together anymore." Her gaze flicked between the two. Both looked genuinely surprised by her words.

"Why not? I broke my hip, not burned the camp down."

Was he being serious?

She looked at Nate. "You understand, don't you? There's no way we can help you get ready for the season now. And even if we tried to meet your deadline, Granddad can't recuperate with those kids running all over the place."

Nate opened his mouth, but Granddad beat him to it. "I broke my hip, Gwen, but my brain works fine." He waited for her to meet his eyes. "I can still help."

"You'll be down for three to four months."

"My legs, not my mouth." Steel fortified his jaw, she was sure of it. "My broken hip doesn't mean the end of this camp."

They were cut from the same cloth—and a thick swath of stubbornness edged it.

Nate's voice joined the discussion. "His first question when he woke up was about you. The second was to ensure everything still moved forward."

Seriously? With what she told Nate last night? With Granddad sitting in a hospital bed? Nate lobbied for his camp to continue?

She was taking back that good-guy thought.

"We're not continuing with this plan." Her fingers clenched around her hips.

"We are." Granddad's voice rang surprisingly strong for how tired he must be.

And she recognized the tone. He wasn't budging. She'd waste her breath trying. So instead she turned tactics. "Fine. Let them still come, but you're moving into Elise's with me." Her friend already offered the extra rooms in her home once the kids arrived. Gwen had immediately taken her up on it. Granddad obstinately refused, but now would have to agree. "I'll call her and make sure it's okay if we come a few weeks earlier than planned." She spared Nate a look. "If you have questions, you can find us there."

He nodded.

Granddad shook his head. "I already told you, I'm not moving into Elise's."

"That was before you fell off a ladder and broke your hip. You've got a long road ahead. You can't stay alone. You'll have therapy—"

"Then hire me a nurse, because I'm not leaving my home."

After all the years he'd cared for her? Walked her though her darkest moments? No way. "Granddad, I'm taking care of you." She wouldn't let anyone else do it.

"Then it looks like you're staying at camp for the summer, because I'm not leaving it."

"You can't be serious." He wouldn't force this impossible decision on her. Not when he knew the hell she'd been to and wasn't back from yet. But he looked calm. Much too calm.

She paced. Two steps to the wall. Two steps to his bed. "You're not serious." The last whispered out as a question begging for a *no*.

Granddad's eyes held compassion as deep as his voice. "I am."

She needed air. Her lungs tightened.

"Gwen." He wrapped her name in his calm, steady voice. "It's going to be okay."

People really needed to stop saying that, because it wasn't. Not with Nate taking over her hiding place and filling it with darkness, and Granddad thrusting her into the center of it all. "I can't stay there." And she couldn't leave him. Each pulled with equal force, tearing her apart. "Granddad, please."

Nate drew a hand across his whiskered jaw. "Elise's house is the best place for you both."

The full strength of his stare weighed on her. Not probing, simply sacrificing his wants for her needs. She might not agree with one tiny speck of his plan, but in this moment she glimpsed the drive behind it. He had a huge heart. And right now its boundaries engulfed her.

Granddad cleared his throat. "I'm not going anywhere but my cabin." The firmness in his words functioned as a brick wall.

"Art."

"Granddad."

Their voices melded, but Granddad lifted his hand. "My home." He tried to push up in his bed, but his lips pulled into a straight line, and his face grew ashen.

Gwen hustled to his side, and Nate took the other. "Let me help." They gently grasped his arms to help him into a comfortable position with pillows behind his head and shoulders. A faint sheen of sweat beaded on his upper lip.

Might as well split her down the middle; it would be less painful.

"Better?" Nate asked.

Granddad nodded.

She sank into the chair beside his bed and leaned forward, head in her hands. "I can't be there with those kids, and I can't leave you."

Why was Granddad forcing this?

Granddad sighed, then reached for her. She let his rough, worn hands hold hers in complete security. "I know Danny's death still hurts, but you can't let it steal any more than it already has."

"It stole everything." A tear seeped past her closed lids.

Nate paced in the corner.

"No. It stole Danny. It stole the future you planned with him." He softened his voice but tightened his grip until she looked at him. "But it's never stolen the future God had planned for you all along."

Now the tears came in buckets. She thought she'd shed every tear her lifetime held. Apparently not. "I can't be around those kids."

"They aren't the boy who killed Danny."

"But they're exactly like him." She dried her damp cheeks against her shoulder, vaguely aware Nate had stopped moving while his focus remained on her. "I thought we could make a difference in their lives, but we didn't." Bitterness swelled.

"They did. In mine. And I'm not naïve enough to think this time around will be any different."

"Then you're limiting God." Granddad squeezed her fingers. "I'm going back to my cabin. What you do is your own decision."

Pure exhaustion seeped from every pore. Their matched stubbornness had always produced good results. Until today. Now it felt like the spring on one large trap holding her down. Wiggle all she wanted, she was stuck.

Chapter Nine

N ate watched Gwen tug her hand from Arthur's grasp.
He'd nearly lost it when her tears started, but it wasn't
anywhere near his place to offer her comfort. Instead, he tried
to provide a way out. When that didn't work, he paced and
prayed, attempting to focus on his silent words rather than her
broken ones.

Now his attention returned to her red, puffy face as she
pulled away from her grandfather. "I need time. You need
rest." Hand shaking, she brushed his hair from his forehead
and pressed a good-bye kiss there. Even in her hurt and pain,
she was still caring for him. She loved deeply. It was beautiful
to see.

It also kept her trapped in a place that rubbed against open
wounds.

Nate didn't utter a word as she slipped away. What could he
say? He didn't know enough about her past to offer wisdom,
and this wasn't the time or place to seek more details. There
were plenty at his feet to process for now.

A throat cleared. Nate shook his head and looked at Arthur.

"I'm guessing you have some questions?" The old man
correctly assumed.

Stuffing his hands in his pocket, Nate crossed to the foot
of Arthur's bed. "They can wait."

"Not wondering who Danny is?" Bushy gray brows rose
over his matching eyes.

"No. I figured that out after last night." The shock still reverberated. "Didn't know his name until today." Though hearing it brought a whole new level of reality.

"She told you about him?"

Nate shook his head. "His parents came to the ER."

Arthur's eyes closed. "That had to be tough for her." He blinked them open. "And you. They weren't due back from Florida until the end of the month. I wanted to tell them about the camp in person."

"Apparently someone called them."

"It's a small town. I should have figured word would get out." Arthur sighed, then looked directly at Nate. "So how much do you know?"

"Enough to wonder why you accepted my offer."

Arthur motioned to the chair beside his bed. He waited for Nate to sit. "I accepted because I believe God wants you and those kids here."

"Even if Gwen's paying a pretty steep price?"

"She already paid a hefty price." He rubbed his jaw. "It's time for her to stop living in the debt of it."

Felt like his presence only cost her more. Questions and doubts started to form somewhere deep inside.

Wetness lined the old man's eyes. "Gwen had a heart for anything lost or hurting long before Danny came along. She'd mother any stray that crossed her path from the time she toddled around the camp." Gruff laughter coated his memories. "Her heart was so big, we worried it'd swallow her whole. Then she met Danny."

"Her husband." The label sharpened Gwen's pain.

Arthur nodded. "He wanted to be a missionary, and they would have gone overseas if my wife hadn't gotten sick." His voice trembled on that last word, and he cleared his throat. "They stayed and started working with inner city kids in Macon. And Gwen, she blossomed."

Surprised, Nate nodded. He could understand that work, the way it reached inside your very core, carving impressions that lasted a lifetime. But he hadn't pegged Gwen as someone who shared the desire.

"She wanted to make a difference. Believed in her whole heart she could."

"Then Danny was killed." He didn't need Arthur filling in that detail. It was the only place this story could lead.

Arthur nodded. "Shot by one of the boys they'd been mentoring. He was a part of their program for a year, seemed to be getting his life together, then out of nowhere . . ." His pain and sorrow reflected in his eyes. "She's not been the same since."

"How long has it been?"

"Almost four years." He picked at the medical tape securing his IV. "She's hidden long enough."

Nate stood and paced, rubbing the back of his neck. He wouldn't force her to stay. "I know you and I had an agreement, and I appreciate that you want to hold up your end, but you need to do what's best for Gwen now. And yourself."

Arthur didn't speak for a long moment. "I won't pretend this is easy, that I know what God is doing or what will happen to this camp. But I prayed that, if this is where Gwen needs to be, God would do whatever it takes to keep her here." He tapped his blanketed legs. "And here I lie."

Was this all part of God's design to get through to Gwen?

Nate had no clue. But this wasn't how he'd have chosen to do things. He'd planned to reach kids, not a broken widow. And yet Gwen's pain-filled eyes mirrored theirs in so many ways, even if she couldn't see the similarities.

If only he didn't have to be the cause of her most recent pain.

Arthur's eyelids drooped closed, and he batted them open. Then, like someone had attached weights to them, they lowered again.

"I should let you rest."

Barely a nod escaped the old man. Chin to his chest, he released a soft snore. No surprise. These conversations would take it out of a healthy person—they had for Nate. He pressed the button to recline Art's bed, hoping he'd grab enough sleep before they woke him to walk. He snagged his flannel shirt from the chair before slipping into the hall.

Anxiety twisted around him the closer he drove to camp. In the past twenty-four hours, his entire picture of this summer shifted. It had been hard enough to deal with Gwen not wanting him here, but understanding why only validated her arguments. He wouldn't want him here, either.

Did he stay or go?

As if he had a real choice. These kids needed him. Their expectations already swelled, and he couldn't smash them. Not to mention the huge chunk-of-change he'd sunk into this place. He simply couldn't afford to pick up and move. Time and money wouldn't allow it.

Dust swirled behind his Bronco as he parked in the gravel lot. He slammed his door and surveyed the two fields that Lew was working in. Morning rain had kept them away, but right now the drops remained inside thick clouds. Manual labor sounded good. Conversation didn't. After grabbing tools, he sought out the overgrown footpath separating camp from Hidden Lake.

Why had God sent him here? His dreams were someone else's nightmares. Made no sense.

Using his muscles, breaking a sweat, had saved him many times over. His mind cleared with each swing. God's plan wasn't always his, but he'd learned years ago to follow it. Wasn't easy. He couldn't even say he'd always liked it. But God remained faithful. He supplied all his needs. And the destination was always a thing of beauty.

A tiny smile broke out as he struck another tree in his way.

Okay, God, I'm seeing the parallel.

This path was the right one to take. Didn't mean there wasn't hard work involved to carve it.

Half-hour in, progress became visible. No way he'd clear the entire trail on his own, but the work proved necessary. The pain in Gwen's eyes continued to flash through his mind. How could he help someone find healing when he was the one keeping the wound raw?

No clue.

Like he'd had no clue that Gwen's heart once shared the same passion as his.

Did a part of her still contain that desire?

He swung at another tree.

Gwen closed her cabin door and jogged down the steps, bypassing the golf cart. Energy zinged through her as she headed for her beach and yoga. She needed a physical outlet to numb these bouncing thoughts after the emotional whiplash of this week.

As she crested the hill, *thwacks* echoed from the trail she aimed for. Nearing it, she saw Nate's broad shoulders. Sweat dampened his grey T-shirt and curled the edges of his hair. He lifted an ax, his muscles carving ridges in his forearms and across the span of his back with the motion.

He must have sensed her, because he stopped and turned. "Hey." That same sweet look he'd leveled on her several times at the hospital shone in his eyes with an all-encompassing focus.

"Hey." *Please, oh please, oh please, do not ask about earlier today.*

Neither moved.

Nate cleared his throat. His gaze traveled over her form-fitting yoga gear. "Headed for yoga?"

She fought a blush. His look might be completely innocent, more in answer to his own question, but the full force of his stare effected as much pressure as a hurricane. Gwen pointed around him. "Yeah. Mind if I squeeze by?"

"Sure thing." He stepped into the brush.

"Thanks." She pushed her pace till the tree branches filled in adequate space between them. Her toes touched the beach when footsteps sounded behind her.

"Gwen," Nate called. "Wait up a sec. I wanted to let you know—"

But it wasn't his voice that stopped her. The cluttered sight of her once wide-open lake halted her movement.

"About what was delivered this morning." Hesitation wrapped his words.

She slid an exaggerated peek over her shoulder. "This was you?" Rhetorical, of course. And he was smart enough to realize it, because he kept quiet.

Gwen slowly scuffed to the water's edge. Her beautiful view had been obliterated by the largest inflatable known to man. It had to be twenty feet wide by at least fourteen feet high and held so much of her focus she nearly missed the unfinished dock feet away. Beyond that, piles of lumber lay stacked high and wide.

What was he doing to her beach?

She turned. Nate stood in the tree line, ax in hand, waiting her out.

Well, she needed a sec. Trying to sift through her words, she stared at the hard packed granules beneath her feet. After a moment, she trudged to him. "What's with the blob?"

"It's called The Iceberg, and it's the start of our swimming area."

"Start?" As in more was coming?

Nate nodded.

She didn't let his open mouth supply more words. Not when to his left stood the transparent silhouettes of her yoga studio and new home—plans he'd already forced her to wait on. Not when her choice to escape had been taken. And definitely not now that this would steal the one piece of sanity she had left. "No."

He tilted back. "No?"

"No." She straightened. "Either you take that thing out of the lake, or I'm sticking a pin in it."

"The size it is, a pinhole won't hurt it."

"Fine. I'll find something larger."

He sighed. Turned. And started walking. After a few steps he called over his shoulder. "If you want to keep this conversation going, I suggest you follow."

What? Did he seriously . . . After about thirty seconds, anger and curiosity propelled her forward.

Nate sunk his ax into a tree, yanked it out, then delivered another whack before she reached him, steam fairly pouring out her ears. "I don't really know—"

He held his ax out, handle first.

She stopped. "What are you doing?"

"I'd rather you take your frustrations out on the tree than me." His words sounded matter-of-fact, but a tense current ran under them. One that promised he wasn't someone to back down.

Neither was she. Gwen crossed her arms and stared him down.

He wiggled the handle. "Trust me. It'll make you feel better."

"No. You removing that blob from my lake will make me feel better."

"Not happening." The tree behind him swayed, its trunk cut nearly through. "But you're not mad about that, you're mad about everything else. And I may understand, but I'm not willing to be your punching bag."

Seriously? "Look. I might not have done a happy dance when you showed up, but that doesn't make you my punching bag. I'm adjusting. But now you're messing with my lake view—"

"I meant your plans changing. The kids coming." Barely a breath of a pause. "I meant Danny."

Her entire body tensed. "You did *not* just bring him up to me."

"I did." His voice softened but never lost its strength.

Heat curled like a vine, twisting from her toes to her eye sockets. She trembled from its squeeze. "Who are you to come to my home and throw Danny's name at me?"

"I didn't throw it." Nate lowered the ax. "And I'd like to be a friend."

Gwen snorted. "Not going about it very well."

Silence slipped in as he resolutely held his stare. "You're angry Danny died."

"You think?" The thick words acted like a large cotton ball rolling from her throat to her mouth and sucking all the moisture from her. She couldn't even form a tear.

"And everything is still so out of control."

It wasn't supposed to be. "Why did you have to pick my camp?" The question ran on repeat in her mind.

Nate looked to the sky and gave a tiny shake of his head. "I wonder the same thing too, Gwen. But I'm here and this is happening." His eyes met hers, and he held out the ax. "So how about a little manual labor?"

He was as confused as she; it lined the crinkles around his eyes. And yet . . . She held his gaze a moment longer. Peace. The absence of her own made his stand out even stronger. She took the ax. His manual labor must be like her yoga, and he was right, she could really use this right now.

Her fingers touched his as her hand closed around the handle. Something connected between them. A common ground that shouldn't be.

He stepped away from the tree he'd nearly leveled. "Go ahead."

Gwen swung, the tool heavier than she expected. It slammed to a stop in the trunk, ripples of energy flowing up her arm. Didn't hardly add to what he'd already accomplished. Wiggling it free, she aimed again, this time ramming almost through.

Nate wrapped his hands around the rough bark and shoved hard. "Now push."

She added her weight, and the tree toppled over. A small bead of sweat trickled between her shoulders, and she kept going. Tree after tree she attacked. Blisters ached on her palms, and her muscles screamed. But she continued.

Nate was right. This was good. This was pain she could meet head on and barrel through, and it would heal. She could control this pain.

He silently worked beside her, tearing out brush and bushes. About an hour in, he grunted. She turned. He tugged on the base of a massive plant. Every muscle in his arms tightened, but his strength wouldn't budge the plant. It refused to give up its space.

Nate caught her watching. "The thing is stubborn." He rubbed his forearm across his cheek.

"It was here before you." She shrugged. "Maybe let it stay and you work around it." Holding her hands in front of her, she gently massaged her palm.

His lips twisted to the side. "Maybe I will." He walked over and grasped her hand, stopping her motion to assess her raw, pink skin. "I think it's time for a snack."

His words barely registered. Her attention remained on their joined hands. She'd bumped into men or received hugs from them in the last few years. But Nate was the first to hold her hand since Danny died. Like each interaction that sparked between them, it wasn't a move. Not a romantic gesture. But while it didn't feel right, it also didn't scream wrong, and that fact had her pulling away. "We're not done."

"We are if you still want use of your hands. They're barely healed from when you fell in the parking lot."

She waffled. "But these trees aren't going to clear themselves."

"Which is why I hired someone to do it." He headed for camp. "Come on, I hear ice cream calling."

Gwen followed him. "You mean we wasted an hour on those trees when there's a list of work we could have been tackling?"

"You really are all about the checklist, aren't you?" He waited for her to catch up. "Don't worry. We'll get it done."

"Before those kids arrive?"

They stepped from the woods onto the camp's asphalt paths. "Honestly? If this place isn't britossy the day they arrive, these kids won't care. Even in its worst shape, things here are far better than where most of them come from."

"Britossy?"

"Bright and glossy."

"Really?" She amped up the sarcasm.

Nate smiled down. "Really." He led her to his cabin's door and held it open for her. Inside, he pointed to a metal stool pulled up to his chipped Formica countertop. "Sit."

She eyed the candy wrappers littered across his counter.

He had the good grace to grow pink cheeks before sweeping them into the trash container. "Sorry."

Gwen half grunted, half laughed. "It's okay."

His hand rested on the freezer door. "Float or sundae?"

"Float."

She rose to wash her hands, and his glance caught on them. "I should have found you gloves."

"I'm a big girl. I know where we keep them." She gingerly dried off before retaking her seat.

"So do I, and I should have gotten them." He plopped ice cream into the two glasses he'd grabbed, then put the container away and rinsed the scoop.

A question pressed on her tongue as she watched him. Their new comfort coaxed her to voice it. "Do you really think you can change these kids?"

"I do. Even if it's only one."

No hesitation. Only conviction. He sounded so much like Danny, it carved into her. "But you can't." The words scratched past her throat as she stood. "And it's dangerous to try."

The edges of his blue eyes crinkled slightly, hurt carving the crevices. Only it wasn't his pain driving those lines; it was hers. A thread of emotion connected them. Not pity. She'd seen that sentiment in enough faces to recognize it. But this, this complete reflection of herself in his eyes stirred something inside her.

Then he pulled a burgundy can out from his tiny pantry. The hiss of a pop can opening broke the silence.

"Rock N' Rye?" She couldn't stop the grin.

"I'd grabbed a few cans for our hike." He poured it over both their ice cream, dropped in spoons and straws, then plopped a foaming glass in front of her. "Never heard of the stuff before I came here."

"It's a Michigan thing."

"One you think I'll like?"

"Only if you have good taste."

He stopped, his straw inches from his mouth. "I have impeccable taste."

She watched his first sip, telling herself he wasn't flirting. "So?"

Nate's focus remained trained on her. "Amazing."

Okay. Maybe he was a little.

Sweet, creamy, goodness fizzed in her mouth as she took her own drink. "I agree." She smiled at him. "Thank you."

"You're welcome." He tapped his cup against hers. "Sometimes it's the little things that make the biggest difference."

He was making his case.

But he hadn't stood where she was living.

Still, she couldn't go back any more than she could tug him forward. They were in two separate places.

"I really appreciate this." Rain began pattering on the roof above. "But ice cream floats—even with my favorite pop— won't change the world."

"But the people drinking them might."

If only it were that easy. She took another sip. Better soaking in this sweetness than letting out the bitterness.

"Are you going to be okay?" His hip pressed into the counter. "Being here all summer?"

There was no easy answer to that question. "I'm going to have to be, aren't I?"

"No." He straightened. "I'm not talking about how you'll act." He moved so close, she couldn't see beyond his broad shoulders. "I want to know how you're doing. Really."

The warmth embedded in his voice would have been enough. But that look? As if the strength of his concern for her pressed in on him. The man didn't need words because his eyes spoke all on their own. The intensity of them pinged right in the middle of her stomach.

It wasn't fair, wanting to let him in and push him away all at once. Even if she could blur Danny, just enough to move forward with this part of her heart, Nate wasn't the man to do that with. It wasn't fair to any of them.

She rubbed the pads of her fingers over her brows before sliding them through her hair. "I'll have a list on your desk in the morning. We've got a lot to do, so get some good sleep tonight."

Turning, she darted out his door into the raindrops. Avoidance and escape had never really been her things, but they seemed a fantastic idea right now. If she stayed, if she risked one more shared look, the connection building between them would become one strand stronger. They needed to be co-workers. Possibly even friends.

But they could never be anything more.

Chapter Ten

After a week stuck inside, Nate might very well lose his ever-loving mind. The sooner he could hire an office administrator, the better. But the last three people he'd interviewed for the position didn't fit the bill. Unless he wanted to bring in a good, old-fashioned typewriter and ditch the computer. Ditch all signs of technology created after 1980, really. Or, better yet, make up a fake fiancée. He shook his head. That last interviewee seemed more interested in his qualifications as future husband material than her qualifications for the job. Didn't matter if his age surpassed hers by a solid ten years.

He tugged on his hair. He needed out of these four walls.

With the rain paused and over an hour until his next interview, he sensed his chance for temporary freedom and claimed it.

Outside, fresh air mingled with the sunlight struggling to puncture the clouds. He was made to be outdoors, not stuck inside staring at a screen. Creating spreadsheets, keeping track of data, ordering supplies . . . He could do those things, but they weren't his strengths. They actually scraped against every natural grain in his body. But this wide open space? The only thing missing were the kids, and he couldn't wait until they arrived. His mission was to reach at least one. His hope was to reach them all.

Gwen's cabin slipped into view. He hadn't come outside with any plans other than breathing freedom, yet here he stood. The woman excelled at avoidance techniques. Other than notes left on his desk or clipboard lists hung on the nail inside his office, he hadn't seen any evidence she remained on the grounds. She'd spent time with Arthur, at least one note disclosed. If things went well, he'd be home within the week.

He should ask if she'd need help getting his cabin ready or transporting him back here. Jogging up her steps, Nate rapped his knuckles against the door. After a moment he tapped again. No response. Honestly, it would have been a bigger surprise if she answered. By this time of the day, she'd be working through her own checklist and happily avoiding him.

Resuming his walk, he followed the path to the heart of the camp. The double doors to the chapel stood open, the strands of "Chopsticks" echoing from the piano inside. Nate followed the music to Gwen, who had her back to him as she lightly pounded out the childhood song.

"This is me, not sneaking up on you," he called.

She still startled, whipping around to face him.

"Don't stop on my account." He slid beside her on the bench and picked out the accompaniment.

By his second time around, she relented and added her melody to his. They played one full round, then Gwen lifted her hands from the keys but Nate continued. As her fingers rejoined, he began to embellish his part. She jerked a glance his way but didn't miss a beat.

As the last note echoed, Gwen took her hands from the keys. "How on earth can you play like that yet not hit one correct note when whistling?"

He chuckled, swiveling to look at her. "What can I say. I'm full of many surprising and hidden talents."

"Maybe try and keep the whistling one a little more hidden."

"And deprive the world of such amazingness?"

A snort of laughter lifted her shoulders. "Any others you care to reveal?" Her growling stomach nearly ate her words.

"I make a mean BLT."

"Maybe when I'm not swamped with work I could try it."

He snagged her clipboard and wrote one word on it, then returned it to her.

Her brow lifted as she read. "Lunch?"

"Now it's on your list." He stood and offered her his hand.

She ignored him but stood too. "Too busy." A cough barked from her.

That didn't sound good. "You okay?"

"Yeah. Dust and my lungs don't always get along, but that's nothing new." She nodded to the top of the piano. "I have my inhaler, should I need it."

"Sounds like you do."

Instead, she grabbed a rag from the bucket on the floor.

Nate snagged it from her. "A half hour. Come on. Fresh air. Lunch. This mess will still be here."

"I know."

The defeat in her voice struck him. His grip slipped from the rag to her wrist, forcing her full attention. "Putting this room back in order is not going to put your life back in order, Gwen."

"Maybe not," she whispered, "but it certainly feels that way."

After a gentle squeeze, he released her. "Coming from someone whose messed-up life threw him into his own habits, can I share something?"

"You used to be a neat freak?" Her lips attempted a smile.

"I wish mine were as constructive." He shook his head. "But habits are habits, and their cycle will continue until you're ready to give up control to the only one deserving of holding it."

She might not have voiced her question, but he read it on her face all the same.

"Gambling, for one," he answered. "The others I'll share with you over lunch."

Would she take the bait?

She rubbed her ear, and he seized the moment. "You know, running yourself ragged isn't going to help your granddad. He's coming home in a few days, and he'll need you strong."

"Pulling out all the stops, huh?"

He grinned. "I find he's your weakness." Apparently those were fighting words because her spine immediately straightened. "Please don't spin that into an argument. You know what I meant."

"That you use my grandfather to get your way?"

"I won't fight with you when you're ravenausted."

She groaned.

"In case you missed it that was ravenous and—"

"Exhausted. I caught it, even if I tried to duck." She started for the door. "You could have said hangry."

"Nah." He joined her and opened it before she changed her mind. "Too overused."

Down the steps and to her golf cart, Gwen plopped into the driver's seat. As she drove, he looked her way. "By the way, if your plan is to communicate via Post-It notes all summer, I should let you know that doesn't work for me."

"Was my handwriting illegible?"

"Not at all, but I prefer face-to-face interaction."

She spared him a short glance. "Too bad we don't always get what we want."

The woman tested his peace-loving resolve.

But just as quickly as her snide remark shot out, her apology followed. "Sorry. I guess I am more tired and hungry than I realized."

They stopped in front of his cabin. "So how about you let me help rather than holding me at arm's length?"

A glimmer of lightness sparked in her blue eyes. "I'm letting you make me lunch."

"True. I guess that's a start." He hopped out and they walked to his door. "Ready for the best BLT you ever had?"

"You sure don't lack confidence, do you?" She ducked past him and went inside.

While he pasted on a smile and offered her a fast comeback, he mentally couldn't shake the fact that where she was concerned, he sorely lacked confidence. Not in who he was, but in what they could be.

Good thing he had hope.

Nate must have put something into the BLT sandwich he made earlier in the week, because by the time Gwen finished it, he'd convinced her they would accomplish more by working together—and she'd agreed. They spent the next several days hiring the rest of the staff, prepping Granddad's cabin for his return, and completing the bulk of the remaining cleanup. Though the yard still needed help, the buildings sparkled and stood ready for campers to arrive. Staff quarters shined, the kitchen cupboards were stocked, and The Commons waited to receive all the new games Nate had ordered.

Another accomplishment happened over the weekend when the JCS approved Nate's plans. They'd stopped by yesterday to check on the camp and give their official stamp of approval for certain campers to complete community service hours while here. Gwen could still see the smile on Nate's face. Feel it actually—the beaming grin radiated off of him.

As much as his palpable joy beckoned her, she couldn't join in his excitement. She didn't wish him ill, but no positive outcome existed when it came to these kids. If only he'd listen, because he inched toward becoming a friend, and she didn't want to see him hurt.

But something bigger played into her reluctance. Agreeing with Nate's optimism required letting go of too much. Logic said she needed to forgive. Grace demanded it. She simply didn't possess the ability. Why should everyone else be released from paying a price she remained in debt for? Danny's death shouldn't be forgotten. It should make a difference.

And it would. She might be helping prep this place, but she refused to stop touting her misgivings. Maybe she'd eventually change Nate's mind. Enough time remained to reverse this crazy idea. A small upheaval for him now would prevent the depth of pain she'd endured later. She'd spare her worst enemy from that suffering, and though not full-fledged friends, Nate no longer fell into the enemy camp either.

Gwen stretched her legs down her cabin steps and leaned back, her elbows propped against the top stairs. Memorial Day had dawned with a crystal blue sky and temperatures reinforcing that this year, Michigan skipped spring in favor of summer.

Her phone rang, and she picked it up, checking the number first. Surprise licked through her at Marlene's number on the screen. She hadn't spoken with her mother-in-law since the hospital.

Gwen answered. "Marlene, how are you?"

"Summer is always hard. July will be here before we know it." A long pause before she hit the heart of the matter. "Are you and Arthur really staying on?"

"We are." Gwen clenched her phone. "It's not ideal, but this is Granddad's home, and he's not ready to leave it."

"Not ideal?" Marlene's voice raised a notch. "Are you in agreement with what they're doing there?"

"No, but the decision wasn't mine to make." She debated leaving things there, but a small part of her still desired to soothe Marlene's hurting heart. "I don't see this being successful. Nate hasn't secured his investor, and he can't continue past this season without him. I have no doubt once the investor realizes what he's opening himself to, he'll back away. I only hope no one gets hurt in the process."

"Like Danny."

Her eyes closed. "Like Danny."

The line buzzed with silence. Finally, Marlene broke it. "I should let you go. Do you have someplace to be today? If not, our door is open."

"I'm actually getting ready for Granddad. They're releasing him tomorrow. I'll probably grab some groceries. Maybe watch a movie tonight."

"If you get lonely—"

"I'll come over." But if she gave in to that, she'd be there most nights.

Except that familiar pang of loneliness had lessened recently.

Turning the thought over in her mind, Gwen said her good-byes and pocketed her phone. The whir of a golf cart caught her attention. Nate sped down the path, and his grin grew with his proximity. "Sleep well?" he called out.

Was he really the reason her empty nights felt a bit fuller lately? She smiled. "I did."

He stopped and held the steering wheel. "Got plans?"

"Plenty. I'm going to paint my toenails, get some groceries, maybe watch *Notting Hill*."

With each word, more wrinkles carved across his brow. "Got any fun plans?"

Danny had always made her laugh with tickling. Nate's words and expressions pulled laughter from her. She shook her head against the unsought comparison.

"No? Then are you ever lucky I made some for you."

What? Wait. He'd misinterpreted her headshake. "That's okay, I'll stick with mine." An afternoon with him might invite more comparisons she didn't need to be making. Or worse, deepen new impressions she hadn't been searching for.

"But mine are more fun." His dimple came out to play. "And made with you in mind."

The fact he'd planned anything was amazing. That he'd done it with her in mind, endearing. Made her want to run all the more. Question was, in which direction?

Nate leaned back and crossed his arms. "We've got as much done around here as we can. It's the holiday. And after today, I don't know when our next break will be." His tongue pressed against his cheek as he waited her out. After a minute, he shrugged. "Okay. But you'll be disasorry." He flicked the cart into reverse.

"Wait."

He stopped but said nothing.

"Disappointed and sorry?"

"Yep."

Yep she would be, or *yep* she got it right? Probably both. "What are these plans?"

He patted the seat. "You'll have to come along to see." A challenge deepened the blue in his eyes. "Think you can do that? Take a leap without it being planned out?"

No one had ever pressed her to. Everyone knew she did best with lists and order. They never challenged that fact.

But Nate did.

She tipped her head. Last time she went with him, Granddad broke his hip.

"Things don't always work out perfectly, Gwen. Planned or not. But that doesn't mean you stop living."

How'd he always read her so easily?

She looked at the tattoo on her wrist. Pulled in a breath. And stepped forward.

Chapter Eleven

Gwen stood on the banks of the Potawatomi River, black rubber innertube in hand. Cold water lapped over her toes, and she tilted her face to the sun, combating the water's chilliness. It was like fire and ice.

She preferred the fire.

Nate's face shifted into her thoughts. He'd driven them to the parking lot only to find her friends waiting there. Seemed last night he'd called Bay and Colin, who helped him put this together, inviting the rest of the group to float along the river today. After piling coolers and tubes into the van, they piled themselves in too and headed for the small trail she and Nate hiked last week. He'd decided Memorial Day created the perfect excuse to combine work and play. Had to admit, she liked the idea of achieving another checkmark on their list. Didn't like so much that they'd turn into human popsicles to do so.

"I should have asked what we were doing before I blindly agreed to come." Rhett James, Elise's cousin and Gwen's oldest friend—more like a brother—snuck up behind her. Now living in Chicago, he owned a small plane and flew in as regularly as he could, which wasn't as often since he'd taken the promotion as Editor-in-Chief at "The Best Of" food magazine.

Gwen half-turned, slipping into his hug. "You'd have shown up anyway."

He sighed. His sandy blond hair spiked on top, the cut a little longer than he normally wore. And he'd grown more of a beard than scruff. "Probably." He held out her pinky finger. "I need to cut this sucker off."

She swatted him. "You are not wrapped around it."

"Tell me that again when I'm floating down the local Arctic Ocean."

"It's a river." Lucy joined them. "You're an editor, get your words straight."

He tweaked a strand of Lucy's hair. "Creative license."

"Is what all writers want. Yeah, yeah. I hear ya." She smiled at him, then turned to Gwen. "You look like you're getting along decently with Nate."

Rhett nudged her. "Yeah. By the way Luce described it, I thought I was flying in to help grab you from his evil clutches, not join his river-rafting party." Again he glanced at Lucy. "Though the woman is prone to exaggeration."

He sidestepped her swat, stepping on Colin's toe as he, Bay, and Elise joined them.

"Everyone sure about this?" Colin asked.

Gwen's cough barking over all their yeses yanked their attention her way. "What?" she croaked. "A girl's not allowed to cough?"

Colin narrowed his eyes. "Pollen count is high today."

"And I have my inhaler." She patted her pocket as she cleared her throat. "Secured in a plastic bag and all."

Across from them, Nate tossed additional tubes into the water, tying a few together. Then he loaded coolers on top with one foot in the water and one on the sand, the muscles in his arms tightening as he lifted. "Everybody ready?" His blue T-shirt a perfect match for his eyes and that dark scruff covering his jaw, he wasn't doing anything to help with her breathing.

Her friends started for the water, but Gwen lingered, stuffing her rebellious thoughts away.

Rhett remained by her side. "I'm keeping my eyes on you today." He lowered his voice for her alone. "Seems like yours are occupied too."

She stiffened.

"Don't freak out." He picked up his tube. "So you noticed a man. Danny wouldn't expect you to become a nun, Gwen."

"Rhett." A subtle warning edged her words. She wasn't ready to acknowledge these new emotions slicing through her numbness. Stand-in-brother or not, Rhett couldn't either.

He lifted one hand. "That's all I'm going to say."

"Good."

With a soft squeeze to her upper arm, he brushed a kiss on her forehead and walked toward the water. Nate watched them, a vertical crease pulling his brows together. He strolled the few feet to her, eyeing Rhett as they passed. Rhett slowed and quietly spoke words she missed but Nate caught because he nodded.

What had he said?

Whatever it was erased the crease from Nate's face and softened his blue eyes. By the time he arrived nearly toe-to-toe with her, his focus solely on her and the heady scent of woods and pine rolling off of him, unruly thoughts rose against her control.

Warmth swirled through her middle. She clenched her stomach muscles as if she held a vertical plank, but her defense fought a losing battle. Too much about Nate proved enticing in ways she hadn't prepared for.

Thankfully, if he'd noticed his advantage, he didn't capitalize on it. Instead, he nodded at the saying on her Michigan T-shirt. "Not for sissies, huh?"

"Not our winters." Laughter echoed from the water as her friends jumped in. She crept toward the river, Nate beside her. What about him set her on edge and relaxed her all at once? She never knew those two feelings could exist in one breath.

"Not that you'll be here to see it." She snorted. "Huh. I just proved my own point."

Head cocked, he tugged the towel from around his shoulders and held it out. "Here."

She took it. Next he peeled off his shirt. The man had to work out every day. Every single stinking day. Muscles sculpted his chest into . . . She wasn't a writer, she didn't have the words.

"Gwen?" He now offered his shirt and sunglasses to her, a full-on smirk lining his lips. She reached for them. His lips moved from that smirk to a satisfied smile before he dove into the river.

When he stood, water droplets trailed down his bare chest. "Think I blew your point out of the water. Literally."

She rolled her eyes, the motion landing her focus on her audience of friends. Great. Curiosity blazed across their faces.

"You coming?" Nate's deep voice snagged her attention back to him.

"I'm not sure I'm ready." In so many ways. She worked her bottom lip.

"The water's not bad once you get in," Rhett called from his tube.

Nate held her gaze, sizing her up in his way that originally unnerved her but lately needled her in unexpectedly pleasant ways. Breaking their stare, he looked over his shoulder to motion her friends on. "You guys go ahead. We'll catch up."

No one moved until Gwen nodded. "We'll meet you at Eagle's Landing if we don't catch up before."

"Hold up a sec first." Nate snagged his things from Gwen and dumped his T-shirt and towel in one of the coolers secured to Colin's tube before the group floated off. Arms up, body tense, Gwen tiptoed farther into the water as he did.

"Come on." Nate sloshed back her way as he coaxed. "It's not that bad."

"Tell that to your face ten seconds ago."

His laughter peppered her. "You're not much of a jumper, are you?"

She was once. But one leap had cost her everything. Her very heart.

"Nope." She waded a little deeper, waited another moment, then nudged out another few inches.

Once her rear end became level with the tube, she sank onto it, sucking in a squeal as icy water raced up her back. Beside her, Nate hopped on his without even a flinch. They floated in silence for a few minutes, trailing behind the rest of the group. Birds danced in the branches above, their dips and caws creating a delightful visual and audio backdrop. Her muscles slowly relaxed. She peered over at Nate. With his Aviators and slight scruff, he looked at home in his tube.

He caught her watching and grinned.

She smiled back. "So . . . gambling."

His eyebrows rose over his sunglasses.

Hers did too. She slapped a hand over her mouth. Where on earth had that come from? Sure, they'd gotten distracted and never circled back to the topic the other day, but this wasn't the time or place. "I'm so sorry. Must be too much sun."

He chuckled. "Melted the filter right off your tongue, huh?"

"Seriously." She typically maintained better control over herself. "Forget I said it. Please."

He twirled around until he was floating backwards and facing her. "No. I'm the one who brought it up originally, then never followed through. It's on the table." He held her tube. "So what do you want to know?"

This time she sorted her thoughts before letting words out. "As much as you're willing to share with me."

He didn't miss a beat. "Everything then."

Nate had been waiting for the questions since he'd shared with her. When she didn't bring the subject up, he wondered if she simply wasn't interested in learning more about him.

The current carried them slowly downriver. He maintained his hand on her tube, the warm black surface steadying him. His past didn't shame him so much anymore, but it still wasn't an easy topic. Not with someone like Gwen. She didn't come from the same messed-up background as he had. Would she see him differently with every layer he allowed her to peel back?

Did she even want to peel them?

Her soft voice lifted above the trickle of water, "If you don't want to—"

"No. Sorry. I do." He squeezed her tube. In. Out. In. Out. It provided a release for his nerves. Gambling constituted the easiest part of his past. He could share this. "I grew up pretty poor." The simplest place to begin his story. "It's one of the ways I relate to the kids who are coming here."

She nodded. He wished he could hear her thoughts.

"Not too big a leap from there to see I wanted a way to change my life. No one told me about God, so I was busy finding my own ways to change things." Each one led to some form of pain and a past he hoped he could one day make sense of. This camp would help do that. "Gambling came easy. I had a knack for numbers that translated into cards. At first I played online games, the ones that don't actually take money." It was where his addiction began. "When I realized how good I was, I decided to play a site that lets you start small."

"You were poor yet you had a computer?"

"No. But the library did." It was safe and quiet there. And eventually a place to make money. "Wore headphones over one ear, listened with the other. Entered a fake age with my real address, used the reloadable Visa I'd purchased at Walgreens." With money he'd stolen out of Mom's wallet. "Eventually, I used a fake ID."

"Where there's a will—"

"There's most definitely a way." Bright sunshine warmed their tubes. He cupped his hand into the water, capturing its coolness and trickled it against the rubber where their tubes met. "I kept winning. So I kept playing. Anything I could get my hands on. My bank account went from negatives to slowly building into the small thousands." They floated around a curve.

"To a kid with nothing, that had to feel like a million."

She had no idea. "Yeah. But gambling wasn't all I was—"

"You're alive." Rhett's voice intruded.

Nate turned. The group bobbed in the river where they'd latched themselves to a fallen log. So nice of them to wait.

Gwen offered a commiserative smile. "Guess I'll have to wait for the rest of the story."

He nodded, though she had no clue what she was really asking. His tale would either open her heart toward the kids arriving soon or close her off to him for good. The latter he wasn't ready for, because he couldn't deny his attraction to her. He wanted a chance to discover if there could be more between them then this tentative friendship. Guess there still remained a part of him willing to play the odds.

Gwen pushed off his tube to join her friends, laughing at something Rhett said. When he first met the man and seen them interact, a pit formed in his stomach. It deepened after Rhett's hand on her arm and that kiss back at the beach. But then Rhett offered his low warning; he considered himself Gwen's protector—and if Nate messed with her, he'd answer to him.

His respect for the man rose.

"I tried to hold them off, but Rhett insisted we wait." Elise paddled over. "Thought we should travel as a group."

Yep. Stand-in big brother. "No problem."

"Right." Lucy grinned.

"Now that the gang's all here,"—Colin tossed a ball in the air—"how about girls against guys. Keep-away." He tossed the ball to Nate, and Gwen landed on him in a second, her arms pressed into his tube, tipping him off balance. Her hand grasped the ball, her face set in victory.

More than that. It was fierce competition.

He held his breath as the water closed over his head. This was going to be fun.

Nate hauled himself to shore, never so glad to feel solid ground beneath his feet. In front of him, Lake Huron created the perfect landing pad for the sunlight dropping from a cloudless sky. As they'd neared where the river dumped into the lake, the trees on their left had given way to sandy dunes, while on this side they hung tight, creating a canopy to picnic under. About twenty feet from the tree-lined bank, a berth of soft creamy sand spread to meet the lake. Later, after warming up and eating, he'd pull out a few of the games he'd brought.

A cough erupted behind him. Nate slowed, waiting for Gwen. He grabbed her tube along with his as another cough escaped her. "You okay?"

She smiled and held up the ball. "Girls won. I'm great." The lightest of blue tinged her lips. If he hadn't been staring at them, he'd have missed it.

With the way he'd grown nearly numb in the water, he'd bet his own lips sported the same color. Everyone else climbed from the river and dropped their tubes on the sand while he jogged to the van they'd parked here earlier. Unlocking the door, he pulled out a pile of towels. He placed the thickest around Gwen's shoulders before handing the rest out. "How about you go sit in the sun while we get the campfire going?"

"I can help."

"And deny me the pleasure of starting the fire?" Rhett stood beside her.

Gwen clenched the towel around her shoulders. "Fine. The girls and I will set up the picnic table."

Within fifteen minutes, the fire pit blazed with wood they'd brought from camp. Nate had found plenty of dried leaves to start it up, and the smell reminded him of the dreams he'd had as a boy. Dreams he'd finally gotten to experience as an adult. The same ones he hoped to make reality for the teens coming next week.

"Hot dogs anyone?" Bay lifted the package from the spread the girls had laid out nearby. She only touched the corner, but her face resembled a toddler presented with Brussel sprouts.

Swooping in, Colin rescued her from it. "Looks like you're about to break into hives."

"Because I am." She wiped her now empty hands against the cover up she'd donned. "Do you know what they put in those things?"

"Nope." Elise jammed one on a roasting fork. "And I don't want to."

There was an easiness about this group. He'd invited them out for Gwen, but found they'd opened their ranks to include him without a second thought. Okay, so Rhett had a moment's hesitation, but he couldn't fault the guy for it. Nate had only known Gwen a few weeks, and already a strong protective instinct stirred in him too.

Adjusting one of the logs, he looked a few feet to where Gwen played musical chairs with the smoke from the campfire. He strolled over. "The smoke bad for your allergies?"

She startled, like he'd caught her completely off guard. But he was sure she'd seen him coming. "How'd you guess?"

"Every time the wind shifts, you find a new seat."

"That obvious?"

When he couldn't seem to keep his eyes off her? "Yes."

She shrugged.

"Is that why you were coughing earlier?" The rough, deep coughs had started to worry him. "Because of your allergies?"

"Kind of. Coughing is actually because of my asthma, but that's provoked by my allergies. Today's high pollen count didn't help." She nodded to the fire. "And smoke is always bad."

"Why didn't you say something? We could have driven back to camp and grilled."

She tipped her head and smiled at him. "Because life isn't always perfect, but that doesn't mean you stop living."

His own words didn't sound nearly as great coming from her mouth. Not when she used them to justify putting herself in a difficult situation. "Not what I meant, and I think you know it."

"I do." She popped a blueberry into her mouth. "But you need to understand asthma is something I *live* with, Nate. I'm not going to let it stop me from having fun with my friends." She patted her pocket. "I have my inhaler with me if I need it."

"You do?"

Such a soft smile. "I do." She studied him for a long moment. "Thanks for caring." She uttered her gratitude so quietly, he nearly missed it.

But he hadn't. "Any time."

"Gwen." Lucy's voice broke through. She patted the chair beside her, smack dab in the middle of all the girls and down by the water. Away from the smoke. "Get your food and come down here."

He brushed away her polite hesitation, wanting her to sit where she could breathe most easily. "Don't worry about me. I'll grab a plate and sit with the guys."

They moved through the food options at the picnic table together, then Gwen wandered to the water's edge. The soft breeze blew the loose strands of her hair against her neck. She was completely at ease here. Laughter poured from her lips at something her friends said. This side of her pulled him in. It offered a glimpse of the Gwen he'd be lucky enough to know if he could make it past all the layers she'd built up. And without question, he wanted to know her.

She headed to nab seconds of something at the picnic table. Already there, Rhett lifted his arm, and she slid under it, laying her head on his shoulder. Her entire body relaxed and a soft smile curved her mouth. In Nate's life he'd wanted to be other men many, many times, but never as badly as he did right now.

Until she looked up at Rhett.

No. He didn't want to be him.

Because if he *was* ever lucky enough to hold Gwen in his arms, he wanted her eyes, her smile, even her touch to say he was so much more than a brother.

Chapter Twelve

Under the right conditions, Gwen could disguise herself as a morning person. Eight full hours of sleep. Waking naturally to silence that lasted until she reached the bottom of her first mug of coffee. And a yoga session, preferably on the beach for as long as Michigan allowed it, before facing a fresh day with its new checklist.

That was not how the past couple weeks were trending.

Gwen pushed off Granddad's couch and shuffled into the kitchen. The time on the clock stabbed at her like the enemy it was. Though she'd cut back on sleep, the day still didn't contain enough hours to accomplish everything in front of her.

Granddad had been home a week and needed help with his recovery. The staff reported a few days ago and needed training. The campers would arrive in a little over a week and needed this place ready. Between playing full-time nurse and camp director, she'd exceeded her threshold of exhaustion. And she'd yet to check in on Lew, who'd finally broken ground on her yoga studio and needed answers to a few design questions.

Fresh coffee in hand, she peeked in on Granddad. His soft snores said he'd be asleep for at least another hour. She checked the journal beside his bed that held info on his medicines and appointments. His physical therapist would arrive at nine. Just enough time for Gwen to head to her cabin and freshen up.

Hitting the trail, she sipped from her travel mug as she walked. At least all this busyness severely limited her alone time with Nate. Other than moments around other staff or her handing out a task which placed him on the opposite end of camp, they rarely saw one another.

The river had been fun.

It had also scared her. And she wasn't ready to dive deeper into those waters. Still, with each interaction, her toes inched closer and closer to the edge.

A golf cart whirred near, cutting out the morning chirps of the cardinals around her. She didn't turn. Nate drove by each morning offering a simple smile and wave. He'd slow to inquire if she needed a ride, then continue on when she answered no.

The cart pulled into her periphery, and Nate maintained pace with her strides. She readied for the routine, but instead he held out a muffin. "Thought you could use more than coffee for breakfast."

She spared him a quick glance. The muffin looked heavenly, and his taking care of her rivaled its sweetness. Avoiding them both would be the healthiest choice. "I'm good. Thanks."

The muffin disappeared. Nate didn't. "You're wasting away."

"Ha. Hardly."

He continued to putter along beside her.

Such a quietly stubborn man.

"Fine." She took the blasted muffin.

His grin boasted his victory. "Want a ride?"

She had to draw a line someplace—and stick behind it no matter how much that dimple beckoned her. "No thanks."

The cart creaked over a bump. "Thought you were in a hurry."

"I am, but I need the exercise." She sipped her coffee.

He pointed to her and then to the muffin. "So you're consumercising."

Offering a breathy snort, she pushed through the brush. His cart couldn't follow her shortcut. "Good-bye, Nate."

The sweet smell of blueberries and streusel wafted up to her, and her stomach rumbled. She bit into the muffin and polished it off by the time she closed her front door. Fifteen minutes later she returned outside, wet hair tucked into a bun, old clothes ready to be destroyed, and inhaler in her pocket.

With the humidity growing every day, it made more sense to complete her outdoor list during the morning hours, then spend the afternoon going over office work. Today's two items included power washing the deck off the back of the dining hall and mowing grass in the smaller clearing. She'd added the lawn yesterday. Whatever landscape company Nate had hired never showed, and he either didn't realize it or didn't care. But Granddad tried escaping his wheelchair after catching sight of the wild mess yesterday. If she didn't mow it today, she'd find him trying to hijack a lawnmower by nightfall.

In fact, she'd start there first. She detoured to their equipment barn. Rolling open the doors, she spied the mower in the corner. Granddad upgraded from his ancient contraption to this new beast last year. Luckily, he'd given her a lesson on it, even if he rarely allowed her to tackle this chore. He enjoyed keeping the grounds perfectly manicured far too much.

Gwen hopped on and fired up the engine. The entire thing vibrated beneath her, and she tapped the gas, lurching forward. Dust kicked up behind as she followed the gravel path to the fields only to push to a jarring stop. Wonderful. She'd completely forgotten about the hay targets Nate had brought in for archery. Five massive squares plunked smack-dab in the middle of the first area she needed to mow. She hopped off the mower and trudged to the first one.

Bending low, she wrapped her hands around the hay bale and lifted, her nose twitching. She should grab a mask, but that would take longer than moving these targets. Above her, small, puffy clouds obscured the morning sun, keeping the heat off her back. She scooped up the target, her bare arms itching from the poking straw. The edge of the clearing stood steps away. She dropped the first target, scratched her arms, and then plodded off for the next target.

It was going to be a long morning.

Ten minutes later, her T-shirt clung to her sticky skin, and her lungs pulled tight. Between the moldy hay and the physical labor, this job pushed her limits. She sat on the last target and took a drag on her inhaler, wiping her damp bangs off her forehead with her free hand. One more.

A golf cart bumped across the grass aimed straight at her. Even from this distance, Nate caused her nerves to jolt. The more she tried to ignore the feeling, the more her brain latched on to it. She refocused on her task until he stood a foot away, blocking her path. She set down the bale and brushed her hands together. "Yes?"

He took off his sunglasses and eyed her warily. "What are you doing?"

She pointed to the field. "Getting ready to mow this section, then moving on to the larger one before the day gets too hot."

"Think that's a smart idea?" He towered over her, but he wasn't a threat . . . at least not physically.

"Very smart." She straightened. "By this afternoon I'd like to be power-washing the back deck. It's shaded and the mist will keep me cool." Sweat trickled between her shoulder blades. "They said it's supposed to be a scorcher today, but I think we're already there."

"Not what I meant."

She reached for the target, but he sat on it.

"Hey."

He didn't budge. "Would you let someone help you?"

"Well, 'someone,'"—she air quoted that last word—"said he'd hire a grounds crew, and yet the lawn still needs mowing."

He drug a hand through his hair, pulling on the tips. Judging by his set jaw and thin lips, he was biting back some choice words. Finally, he looked at her. "I did hire someone."

"So you said, and yet the grass remains knee high."

Another long pause while he glanced heavenward. His mouth moved slightly. Was he counting?

Again, he slowly returned his gaze to hers. "Look, Gwen, just because you don't see someone working doesn't mean they aren't. My timetable might be slightly different than yours. My methods not the ones you'd choose. But I keep my word."

She'd upset him. Those intense blue eyes contained a storm in them, turning gray and foggy. But an upset Nate didn't pose near the threat that helpful Nate did.

He stood, hands on his hips. "I hired a crew, but they screwed up their schedule. I've been on them all week, and they're coming out Saturday, free of charge." The clouds moved and a direct beam of sunshine swallowed them, turning up the heat. He leaned in. "Word given. Word kept."

Because helpful Nate was also reliable, kind, and caring. She inhaled. And he smelled amazing too, a hint of pine and that sweet scent that always followed him. The scruff on his cheeks and jaw only made him look more like he belonged here in the woods.

But she couldn't let him belong here. It felt like a betrayal to Danny and the future they'd planned.

"Thank you, and I apologize for misunderstanding." She darted in the opposite direction. "If you still want to help, can you move that last one? Because until your crew shows up, yard maintenance remains on my checklist, and it needs to be done."

And she needed away from him.

This woman simultaneously drove him crazy and sucked him in. "Gwen, wait."

She turned around. "That target too heavy for you?"

Again he yanked the ends of his hair. By the end of summer, he'd be bald. "No, I'll move it and I'll mow. Go and tackle the next thing on your list."

Deep lines creased her forehead. "You're going to mow?"

"If it's that important to you"—he shrugged—"then, yeah."

The woman could teach a master's class in facial expressions, with a special emphasis in disbelief. "You're going to mow this entire area, the hill, and the other clearing."

"Yep."

"Around all the posts for the rope course?"

Did she have to sound so skeptical?

"Yes."

Her skepticism turned into laughter. "Sure you are." She turned and kept on toward the mower. "Move the target."

Instead, he sat and waited, not bothering to hide the smirk from his face. In fact, he was about to deepen it in three . . . two . . . one.

Gwen reached the mower, looked at the empty ignition, then spun and headed straight for him.

"Need something?" he asked.

"The keys."

He tipped his head. "What keys?"

One eye narrowed. "Nate."

"Gwen."

Neither budged.

She needed to learn she couldn't control everything and everyone.

"Do you even know how to use that lawn mower?" she challenged.

"I can figure it out." He nodded to the wide-open space around them. "I have plenty of room to practice."

She nudged her chin at the hill. "Fine, but that could kill you."

"And breathing fresh grass clippings will be a cake walk for you." He tilted his head. "Plus the pollen count is high today. I checked it when I got up." He'd been checking it daily since their tube ride.

"I'll be fine."

Did she think he was blind or just stupid? He pointed to her front pocket where the shape of her inhaler pressed against it. "That's why you were using that when I pulled up."

"It's why I carry it."

"Good. Then carry it right on to whatever is next on your checklist for the day."

She sighed.

He stood and picked up the target. "I'm not changing my mind on this, Gwen."

A moment's hesitation ended with her skeptical, "All right, then." Hands in her back pockets, she retreated.

By the time he'd dropped the target at the edge of the clearing, she'd disappeared with the golf cart. Gwen may have acquiesced, but he had a sneaky suspicion he hadn't heard the last from her on this. He strode to the lawn mower and climbed on. No steering wheel. Who the heck made a motorized vehicle with no steering wheel?

No problem. He took out his cell phone and googled lawn mowers.

Sure enough, a few minutes later Gwen returned with the cart and a brown bag. She kicked her legs up on the seat and pulled out a sandwich.

"Need something?" he asked.

"Nope. Got my lunch and my entertainment." She bit into the bread. "I'm all set."

"I thought you had a list to take care of."

"Everyone has time to eat. Remember?" Her smile was equal parts sass and sweet. One kiss would tell him which those lips held more of.

And probably get him smacked in the process.

Better to focus on this stupid mower.

He studied the short video, then tried to orient himself, but this vehicle wasn't exactly the same.

With a sigh, Gwen pushed off the cart and strolled to him. Her hands covered his. "Press this down for left, this for right." She demonstrated. "Up for reverse." Then her fingers slid across his skin. "This is for raising and lowering the blade. We like it cut to a three."

Maybe he should pretend he still didn't get it.

His cell phone rang before he had the chance. He checked the screen, then answered. "Jude. Things all set on your end?"

"They are."

A twinge shook his stomach at the hesitation in Jude's voice. "What's up?"

"Do you know a David and Marlene Doornbos?"

He looked at Gwen. "What about them?"

"Sounds like David called Elliot and tried to get him to back off investing with you. Said you don't have the town's support and wanted to make sure Elliot knew he wasn't investing in a simple nonprofit but rather a camp for criminals."

"You're kidding me." He straightened. "What'd Elliot say?"

"Told him he knew what he was doing, and thanked him for his concern," Jude answered. "But Bryce said it did shake him a little."

"I've been open with him from the start."

"But he doesn't like the idea of negative publicity."

They were working with troubled teens. As great as their motives were, not all publicity would be positive. Nate squeezed his forehead between his thumb and forefinger. "How'd they find out about Elliot?"

Gwen's gaze stayed on him, curious.

"Don't know. I hoped maybe you would."

Only people he'd told were Arthur and a certain blonde. "Can I call you back, Jude?"

His friend hesitated. "I guess. Sure."

Nate hit the off button and slid his phone into his shirt pocket. "David and Marlene called my investor to warn him off."

Her brow jarred up. "What?"

Was she surprised or bothered?

"How do they know about Elliot?"

She nibbled her lip before offering a befuddled, "I honestly don't know." Then held up her hand as he opened his mouth. "I told Marlene you had an investor, but never mentioned who."

Anyone could find out anything with a few clicks these days. "Why did you mention it to her?" The thought that she'd had a part in this twisted something inside. She made no secret about not liking why he was here, but he didn't see her as someone who'd sabotage his plans. Then again, people could hide their true intentions behind all sorts of fronts. "Were you hoping they'd be able to stop the camp?"

She took a step back. "I haven't been silent about my feelings on this, Nate, but it's the decision my grandfather made, and I think I've proven to you that I'm working to respect it."

With his silence, twin lines appeared between her brows. "Besides, if I wanted to mess with Elliot investing, don't you think I'd have called him myself?"

True. He shook the frustration from his head, needing to see past his confusion. "Can you call them? Tell them to back off?"

Those lines pulled tight.

He gentled his voice. "This is about the kids."

"Which you keep forgetting are the ones who killed my husband."

"I haven't forgotten yours or the Doornbos' loss." He wished they didn't have to suffer it. "But these kids are not the same one who brought that loss. And even if they were, they still deserve grace."

The words slipped out, and Gwen sharply inhaled, but he didn't wish them back. How could she not see that everything,

everything, could be covered by God's grace. Didn't she still believe God could make someone new?

He restrained himself from reaching for her. "I'm not saying you have to have a relationship with these kids, Gwen. But you can't exempt them from God's grace or your forgiveness. And you can't penalize others for having a similar background."

"I don't."

"You do. You are."

His heart hurt from both that thought and from the pain on her face. But if they had hopes of friendship, she had to believe change could occur and everyone—regardless of their past or where they came from—deserved the chance to start new.

Yet she refused to agree. "You don't understand."

"I do." He tapped his chest. "I know what it's like to live with people's prejudices, and I also know what it's like to have someone believe in me." He held her stare, willing her to see the ability she held in her hand to make things better—or worse—for these kids depending on her words and actions. "Give them a chance. Please."

Her eyes searched his, flickering back and forth as if her emotions did the same.

"Gwen, I turned out okay. These kids can too."

With a slow shake of her head, she closed her eyes. After a long moment they reopened. "You did, Nate, but being poor and gambling is a far cry from how most of these kids live. Please don't get hurt in the process of discovering that." She turned and walked away.

He didn't call her back. He needed to. He needed to reveal his full past. But if the lens of her own painful history blurred how she saw these kids, how would she ever see him clearly once he revealed all he'd once done?

Chapter Thirteen

Thunderstorms would be a better pairing for this day. Gwen pushed her hands into the pockets of the denim shorts she wore and narrowed her eyes at the perfect blue sky.

Today marked the day.

The kids' arrival had loomed on the horizon for weeks. She'd buried her head in her checklist, ignoring today's approach, yet it still arrived. Not one part of her wanted to go on this ride, but she remained buckled in. Nate and Granddad had fired this excursion up, and she couldn't locate the brakes. It was as if only she spotted the "Bridge Out" sign ahead, and though she tried to warn them, they barreled ahead.

Now she waited for the crash.

With David and Marlene racing toward them, this undertaking inevitably would.

All she could do was hand off the baton to Nate and hide in Granddad's cabin. There'd be more than enough time to work on the website and logo for her studio. And she could still enjoy the beach during nonswim hours. Maybe not the view any longer, but at least the calm of the lake. Honestly, that would be wonderful. Her muscles missed the daily burn from yoga. Now that she'd completed her task of helping Nate ready this place in time, she could refocus on her own plans for fall.

In between helping Granddad recoup.

His stubbornness was making a strong show, and she neared her wit's end with him. With the few pain meds he remained on, nothing sounded pleasant to his stomach. She struggled to get him walking, and he only tolerated the wheelchair she forced him into for nightly strolls. Before his fall, he'd definitely looked his age, even if he didn't act it. Now it seemed he'd added years to both.

"Granddad?" Gwen entered his cabin.

"Back here," his quiet voice called. "Not that I'd be anywhere else."

She stepped to his bedroom door. His cheeks were sunken, his color more sallow than peachy, and his eyes glassy. Alarm coursed through her. "You need to eat."

"Nate said the same thing." Granddad waved his hand. "I told him I wasn't hungry, and he stalked out."

Nate had been here already this morning?

Gwen looked at the journal. Chicken scratches showed when Granddad had taken his meds. She eyed him. "He was mad you weren't hungry?"

Now a hint of pink graced his cheeks. "I might have refused to eat in a not-so-nice way."

The pain meds had made him a little loopy, but this weaning made him cranky. "Might have, hmmm?" She shut the journal. "Have you been out of bed yet today?"

"Why would I do a fool thing like that?"

"Because your physical therapist told you to." She held up his release papers and instructions. "And I agreed to it so you wouldn't have to go to a rehab center. I could make different arrangements though."

He grumbled. "How's that for respecting your elders?"

"It's called taking care of you." She set down the papers and reached for his quilt. "Like you've done for me my whole life. How many times have you pulled back my covers and made me get up?"

"A few." His eyes misted as he grabbed her hand. "You know everything I've done is to help you, because I love you."

She squeezed back. "I know."

"I hate to see you hurting, but sometimes you gotta push through the pain so you can heal."

With her free hand, she patted their joined ones. A little touch could say more than a whole hour of talking. "Couldn't have said it better myself." She released him to wheel over his walker.

A slight smile pulled up his wrinkled cheeks. "I was going to ask if we were okay, but I can see you still want to torture me."

Gwen kissed his forehead. "We're okay." She wiggled the walker. "And I still want to torture you."

His gruff laughter soothed her heart. "Get me my slippers then."

"Nope." She pointed to the floor. "You're going to put them on."

He grunted.

"I'm not kidding." She planted her hands on her hips. "I'm offering you my arm so you can sit up, swing your legs over the edge, and slide on your slippers. Then we're going for a walk."

Another grunt, but he at least listened. She raised his bed to keep him at the correct angle. By the time he stood, sweat coated his upper lip. "We're not going far, are we?"

"To the bathroom, then to the kitchen."

His eyes narrowed. "I can use the toilet myself."

"I should hope so. I'm not ready to start changing your diapers yet."

"You'll never change my diapers." The walker rolled across the floor.

She followed behind in case he wobbled. "Then you better keep working on regaining your strength."

"I meant because I'll never wear them."

She laughed. "You take care of the bathroom, I'm going to get some soup going."

"I'm still not hungry." He shut the door.

"You're still eating." He wasn't getting a choice in the matter any longer.

Gwen opened his small, one-cupboard pantry and pulled out a can of chicken soup. Grabbing a pan, she dug in a drawer for a spoon. A knock at the front door preceded its opening by seconds.

Nate stepped inside, then jarred to a stop. "Oh. Hey. I didn't know you were here."

She held up the soup can. "I was checking in on Granddad. He said you were by earlier." She placed the pan on the burner. "Thank you."

"No problem." He set a stainless steel thermos on the counter. "I brought this. Thought it might help."

"What is it?"

"A protein drink. He could use the protein and calories to get his strength back, but he keeps complaining he's not hungry. Thought if I could convince him to drink this, it would help."

Gwen rubbed her earlobe. With the way his fingers tapped against the counter, he seemed nervous. Didn't know he possessed that trait.

She tipped her head. "I was going to make him soup, but he's fighting me on that." She picked up the bottle and opened it, sniffed. Yum. "What flavor?"

"Chocolate and peanut butter."

Gwen smiled over the container. "His favorite. How'd you know?"

Nate shrugged. "Saw him eating a peanut butter cup my first day here, so I knew he at least liked the combo."

The bathroom door creaked open, snagging their attention. Shuffling into the room, Granddad nodded at Nate. "You back?"

Gwen pulled out the kitchen chair. "And he brought you something I think you'll like better than the chicken noodle I was making you."

Granddad slowly settled onto the wedged pad on his chair, his mouth thinning into a long line. "Told you two I wasn't hungry."

Nate held out the cup. "Just try this."

After a moment's hesitation, Granddad put it to his lips. With one sip, he actually smiled. "Not bad." He looked to Nate. "What's in it?"

"All the stuff your body needs to heal." He stood over Granddad. "So I'll make you a deal. You do your assigned exercises and keep getting up for a walk every few hours, and I'll bring you as many of those as you want."

Granddad hesitated.

Nate leaned down, his voice going to a stage whisper. "I'd really like your granddaughter to catch up on her sleep, but she won't if she keeps worrying about you.

"She's a bit grumpy when she's tired, isn't she?"

Nate nodded and held out his thumb and forefinger. "A tad."

"I can hear you both."

They simultaneously looked her way. "We know."

Granddad offered his hand to Nate. "You have yourself a deal."

Nate waited around until Arthur was settled in his bed and napping. He followed Gwen from her grandfather's cabin, pausing while she shut the door. She hopped down the few steps to the path beside him.

"Thanks for that."

"What? Making him a shake?"

"Making sure he ate. Watching out for him." She tucked her hands in her back pockets. "Making sure he was okay."

Nate smiled. "He's become a friend."

"He does grow on you, doesn't he?" Her entire face lit. To be the man who made her that happy. The man she bestowed her love on. Danny had been beyond lucky. He'd been blessed.

"He does." Nate hated having to break the peace flowing between them, but he couldn't ignore what was coming in the next hours. "Will you be here all day?"

From peace to a storm. "I will." Her teeth scraped against her bottom lip. A rogue thought of how to help her release the nervous gesture surprised him, but her tentative voice stopped him from chasing the intriguing idea any farther. "I'll help you get ready for arrival. After that, I'll be out of sight but still available for questions. I don't want you bothering Granddad. He needs his rest."

Nate nodded. "Will you be in his cabin?"

"I'll be a little bit of everywhere, but I have my phone on me." She walked backwards. "I've got to set up your beach games."

"Isn't that why we hired the lifeguards?"

"We hired the lifeguards so no one would drown."

"You need help then?"

She stopped, cocked her head, and gave him a look. "Have you even looked at the schedule I made?"

"I skimmed it."

One brow lifted.

"More like glanced its way."

"Maybe you should take a better look." She spun, speaking over her shoulder as she started walking again. "If you can find it on that mess you call a desk."

"Organized mess." He corrected.

Her snort was so loud, the birds jumped.

His phone rang, and he answered it, still watching Gwen. "Hello."

"We're officially on our way," Jude yelled into the phone.

Nate held it from his ear. "You've got a rowdy bunch there."

"Excited," Jude bellowed.

"We're ready for them." At least he was. Okay. So Gwen was too, but it was more like she'd readied for battle.

Now laughter. "You think so, huh?"

"Bring it." Nate shut his phone off, then headed for the office. Anticipation thrummed through him, but he had too much to do to give in to the excitement. Over the next hour he touched base with each counselor, checked each cabin, looked in on what they'd be serving for lunch, and made sure the candy store was stocked. Back in his office, the woman Gwen had helped him hire ensured the check-in table was staffed and ready for the buses which should be arriving right about—

Engines revved, sending the welcome noise into camp before bright yellow buses reached Nate's view. "Let's go." He shouted to the counselors who stood waiting to welcome the kids.

Jude hopped off the bus first. He slapped Nate on the back. "You really ready for this?"

"As ready as can be."

Kids of all shapes, sizes, and colors piled from the buses, their voices drowning out the crickets he'd heard earlier. Nate scanned each face, trying to familiarize himself with them before even learning their names. "How was the ride?"

"Huh?" Jude grinned. "I think my hearing took a huge ding on that bus."

Nate chuckled. "I don't see a reprieve in your future."

The boys formed one line, the girls another. Pretty equal.

Jude's eyes never left the group.

Nate tracked his stare to four boys already causing trouble. Though after being cooped up in the bus, they might have extra energy. He could hope. "What's the story with those four?" He squinted, taking in their size. "I thought we were only taking junior high age."

"We are. But a few kids were held back a year." Jude nodded to the lanky kid with black curly hair, the strands a stark contrast to his pasty skin. His hard eyes shone as dark as his hair. "Like Axel Nellis. He's the tallest in the group and the ring leader. He's also a part of the JCS crew. Pretty sure he has big dreams of forming his own gang."

"Then it's a good thing he's here." Gwen's words about kids who'd been in trouble with the Juvenile Corrections Services threatened to form in the back of his mind, but he shoved them away. Axel represented exactly the kind of kid he hoped to reach.

"I agree." Jude nodded. "The other three are followers. You get to Axel, you'll get to them."

Axel wasn't the only one though. Nate's long gaze strolled over every face, each one showing glimpses of a different story. Stories he hoped to add to this summer. With any luck, he'd change their endings.

Chapter Fourteen

The first week hadn't produced any major mishaps, at least as far as she knew. Gwen managed to avoid everyone, though the evasion proved tiring. Laughter rolled through the trees at all hours of the day. Late night worship songs floated from the open gymnasium doors. Not a moment existed where youthful voices couldn't be heard, and they called to mind memories she thought she'd released. Which was why she spent a good part of her days hanging nearby the jobsite with Lew. His hammers, drills, and saws drowned out all other noise.

Ducking under branches, she slipped from the camp path onto her beach. Early morning sunshine reflected off the still water. Nate had added a few other small inflatables, and the sight wouldn't become normal—ever. But she could deal for a few months.

At the water's edge, with her feet in the firm, wet sand, she moved into Warrior pose. Slowing her breathing, she slid into Reverse Warrior. Focused on the calm stretches, the sunshine on her face. The silence of the moment. This made sense. She opened her eyes to switch to plank, and movement caught in her peripheral vision. Tingles zipped up her spine. She spun.

A girl stood feet away. "I didn't mean to scare you." She held up her hand, palm nearly white against her warm, tawny skin. "I seen you down here most mornings, and I always wanted to learn yoga."

Campers weren't allowed out here at this hour. The reprimand nearly escaped, but those slumped shoulders and downcast eyes halted it. The girl couldn't have been much more than twelve. Short, with more curves than muscles, and wiry blonde hair captured in a sloppy ponytail, she wore navy stretch pants and a baggy white T-shirt starring Olaf. And while her height and apparel said she was still a child, her eyes told a different story.

As if rediscovering a forgotten path, Gwen's heart beckoned to unearth the girl's story, but her mind reined it in. "I'm sorry, but this isn't a yoga class."

Those espresso eyes dimmed. "You don't got to teach me. I'll watch and stay out of your way."

The words ran together like keys that hoped to fit into a lock.

But it wasn't only that. It was her entire demeanor. Like she was lost and wanting to be found.

The shared hope won her over. Gwen sighed with a tiny smile. "Come on."

Head down, the girl stayed where she was. "I'll just copy. I ain't no trouble."

Gwen waited another moment, but the girl refused to move. Not surprised, she readjusted her stance, then continued her morning routine, keeping an eye on the child. Each move proved a struggle for her, but even when she toppled to the sand, she pulled herself up. Gwen's hands ached to help with proper placement, but she hadn't earned the right to be that close. She slowly emphasized each movement, holding it until the young girl conquered what at least resembled each pose. After about thirty minutes, the shrill morning bell rang through the trees.

The girl straightened, shoved on her flip-flops, and raced away, but the intensity of her cocoa eyes remained. It pulled out emotions Gwen had buried with Danny. This wasn't supposed to be happening.

She grabbed her towel and returned to her cabin. After a quick shower and breakfast, she stood with her coffee to peer out her open window. She closed her eyes and listened. All children sounded the same, and the noise stirred memories of summers past, cloaking her with the comfortable sense that Camp Hideaway had been created for this very reason—to effect change in kids' lives.

If only it were that easy.

Needing a break from her warring thoughts, she headed to Granddad's cabin. He was still napping, so she wrote a note and left for the parking lot. Pointing her car toward town, she dialed Nate's number.

"Morning." For such a deep voice, it always contained lightness.

"Morning," she responded. "I'm heading into town for a few hours. Granddad was still sleeping, and he should be okay, but I wanted to let you know."

"I'll check on him around ten."

"Thank you."

Youthful voices filtered from wherever he was. "Not a problem." He cleared his throat. "Haven't seen much of you this week."

Yeah. About that. Instead of the distance creating a buffer between them, it only charged her curiosity. How was he doing? Was he tired already, or did the days energize him? Had he managed to connect with any of the kids like he'd hoped?

So much for keeping him out of her thoughts.

"Gwen?"

"Sorry." She turned onto the main road. "I told you I'd be scarce."

"Scarce around camp, not around me." He paused. "Don't be a stranger."

An unexpected smile lifted her cheeks. "Thanks for checking on Granddad. I'll text you when I get back." Her fingers hit *end call* before her mouth went rogue. At least he hadn't seen the smile his words elicited.

Under the blue sky, the channel bordering Waterway boasted the same busyness as the streets. Gwen parked in front of NovelTeas where Bay served a patio full of customers. She strolled toward the closest painted pony and dropped pennies in the cup before circling back to Bay's shop. Grabbing a treat and a table outside in the shade, she waited for Lucy.

Ten minutes late, Lucy's car screeched into a spot, and she hurried over. "Sorry, I was finishing a story." She dropped into a chair and hauled out her laptop. "Wait until you see what my guy did for your logo. It's phenom."

Gwen slid her plate aside. "I really appreciate this." She'd given up trying to create one for herself. It had become apparent she didn't have enough time or talent for it.

"No problem. You've got enough going on." As if she finally downshifted into the moment, Lucy stilled and looked at Gwen. "How are things going anyway?"

There was no use tiptoeing around the bush. Not with Lucy. She read people too well and expertly asked follow-up questions until she received the info she wanted. Might as well give it to her upfront. "My plan to ignore the campers all summer took a turn this morning."

"Oh? Good or bad?"

Gwen fiddled with her straw. "I don't know." The little girl's face returned full force. "There was this girl, maybe twelve, who showed up and wanted me to teach her yoga. She looked lost, and without really thinking about it, I reached out to her."

"Hmmm . . ." Lucy fiddled with a loose strand of hair. "Can't change who you are, Gwen. You might have put it on pause for the past few years, but it's still there."

"What are you talking about?"

"I really need to spell this out?" She arched a brow. "You love kids. Helping them, building relationships, showing them how to turn their lives around. It's a part of you, and trying to shut it off has put you in a deep-freeze these past few years."

"Grief is what put me in a deep-freeze."

Lucy offered a soft smile. "The only way out of grief is living through it. If you stay frozen in that moment forever, you'll miss the beauty God can still make from life." She covered Gwen's hand with her own. "Pain is greedy. It'll take more than its share if you let it."

Having lost her little sister to cancer, Lucy was the only friend able to truly speak to this spot.

Gwen slid her hand from under Lucy's, placed it on top, then squeezed. "Thanks."

"Always." She waited a beat, then swiveled her laptop around. "Now let's look at those logos."

Nate stood in front of packed bleachers. Fifty kids stared back at him. In place of their last morning activity for the day, the entire group assembled for the inaugural camp rewards. The colorful sea of smiling faces swelled his heart.

"Wondered if you guys liked your first week here?"

Cheers exploded, and his excitement did the same.

The only thing missing from the week was the woman who'd helped him prepare this place. He missed Gwen. His eyes scanned the room for her, a habit that had crept into place over the last several days. She'd been open and honest about making herself scarce when the kids arrived, but he didn't think she'd actually pull a Houdini and disappear.

Forcing himself to refocus, he pointed to the counselors beside him. "It's been an awesome week for us too, all because of you guys. You've pitched in, followed the rules, kept cabins… relatively clean,"—he coughed with a grin—"and been better campers than we could have asked for." He nodded toward the crowd. "We set the bar high, and you're surpassing it."

If possible, their collective smiles grew. These kids didn't hear often enough what a great bunch they were.

"That being said," Nate spoke as he walked to the giant wheel behind him, "there are some rewards we need to hand out."

The campers stomped on the bleachers, filling the room with a thunderous roar much louder than he'd anticipated fifty kids could achieve. He waved his hands in the air, and they quieted. "You need to hear me if you want to know who won."

The noise dimmed, and Nate spun the wheel. After handing out the awards, he turned to a box beside him. Another fun idea he'd instituted. "Since there were no incident reports filed this week, looks like I get to take on one of the challenges you submitted."

The place went wild again.

Investing in ear plugs seemed a good idea.

Nate reached into the box and flicked through a pile of papers. Each cabin had run ideas past their counselors who stuck them in here. They'd been creative, that's about all anyone would tell him.

Fingers closing around one wadded up piece, Nate pulled it out and slowly uncurled it. "Sink three bullseyes or take a pie in the face." He looked up. "Do I get to pick the flavor?"

"Nope." Jude disappeared through a side door before returning.

Pie pans that large were unnatural.

"The kids already decided on mud pie with extra cream on top." Jude's hands gripped a pie that had to be two feet in diameter and a foot high from the swirls of whipped cream.

At least Nate hoped it was whipped cream. "The mud's chocolate, right?"

Based on the laughter from the stands, he didn't need Jude's head shake.

A couple counselors arrived with a target and his bow. "We had things ready just in case."

Sounded suspiciously like a set-up. "You're all very efficient."

A buzz encapsulated the campers.

"You can do it!" A small voice called. Nate scanned the crowd and locked eyes with Tyler Bronsink. The boy had latched on to him the first day and, in a way, reminded Nate of himself at that age. Wiry and short but bursting with energy. He was also in the archery class Nate taught. All week he worked toward his first bullseye. While everyone else hit at least the border, Tyler had yet to nail even the haystack.

Nate grinned at him, then focused on his target. "Here goes nothing." Taking his stance, he pulled back on his bow and let the first arrow fly. It landed in the far side of the solid red circle.

"That's one." He sank the second on the opposite side but still within the border. "Two." The campers started stomping again, all except Tyler, who held still, bottom lip sucked in as he focused on Nate.

Nate set the last arrow in his string and covertly eyed Tyler.

Pulling back, Nate released.

He was going to need a shower.

The last arrow thwacked wide, sticking inches outside the bullseye. The kids went crazy. Nate put on his best grimace and faced the approaching Jude.

"Sorry," Jude offered.

If it wasn't coated in laughter, maybe he'd believe him.

Nate sucked in a breath, holding it, just before nasty smelling sludge they must have dredged from the bottom of the swampy section of the lake slicked across his face followed by more whipped—no, wait. Shaving cream.

He swiped at his eyes as a camera flash went off.

The kids roared with laughter-coated screams.

"All right." Nate took the towel Jude held out. "That was awful. Not so sure I want to see what you come up with for next week, but I'll take it if you earn it." He wiped off his face. "Now go eat."

A few kids high-fived him as they trailed from the room. Tyler slowly approached. "You missed." Pride and worry lined his words.

Nate shrugged. "Everyone misses, Ty. Don't forget it."

It took a second before he made the connection, his shoulders hitching higher and his green eyes brighter as he did. "I won't." He scrunched his nose. "You better take a shower. You kinda stink."

Nate chuckled. "I do, don't I?"

With a nod, Tyler raced toward the door. "See you at archery!"

The counselors followed the kids out, and Jude waited. "You could have made that shot in your sleep."

"Maybe."

"No maybe about it." Jude crossed his arms, smirking.

Nate started mopping up the mess left from his encounter with the mud pie. "Don't know what you're talking about."

"No?" Jude picked up an arrow. "You nail that bullseye three times, and I'll personally clean up this mess."

They'd issued challenges to each other for as long as Nate had known him. He straightened and took his bow. In quick succession, he dropped three in the target. Dead center. "Happy now?"

"Immensely." Jude swerved his glance to the side door.

Nate turned. Gwen leaned against the concrete wall. Hair in a ponytail, shorts letting her long, tanned legs run free, and a loose tank that matched her eyes. She sucked his attention away simply by standing there. Then she broke into a shy smile.

He was toast.

Beside him, Jude cleared his throat. "I wouldn't get too close. You really do stink."

"Thanks." For the compliment and for setting him up.

"Any time."

Wiping his face again with the clean side of the towel around his neck, Nate strolled to Gwen. "Might want to breathe through your mouth."

"Or you could stop there."

He did with a laugh. It was good to see her. Even better to see the softness on her face.

She pushed off the wall but maintained distance between them. He told himself it was because of the mess coating him. When she inched closer, he accepted that excuse and did his best to stay where he was. If he matched her movement, it might scare her into retreat. Better to let her set the pace.

"Wanted to let you know I'm back, and I'm heading to have lunch with Granddad." Hesitation tripped up her next words from flowing easily. "Bay put an extra sandwich in for you, if you'd like to join us. But you probably need to be in the dining hall—"

"I'd love to."

"I'll handle lunch," Jude's answer rolled over his.

"Oh." The word puffed out. As if she hadn't thought through his acceptance and had no clue what to do next.

Nate tossed the towel to Jude. "I'll shower and meet you up there in fifteen." He kept talking as her mouth opened. No way he'd allow her to create an excuse now. "Arthur could use the company, and I'd like to see him. Fill him in on the week. It's been so busy I haven't really had the chance."

Plus, he'd been giving her space. But now that she'd cracked open the door, he was squeezing through.

And he'd make every effort to stay.

She had fifteen minutes to collect her thoughts. To downshift her racing pulse before Nate revved it up again. Watching him easily hit those bullseyes slipped a new awareness inside her. The way his arms tightened and his complete focus rested on one target. What would that be like? To be the center of his attention?

The thought rushed heat through her and nearly stopped the lunch offer from escaping her lips. Apparently, her mouth didn't possess the same reservations as her head because out it popped.

Moving forward wasn't easy. Not in this arena and definitely not with a man who came out of nowhere and provoked her in ways that gave the word positive connotations.

Impossible, yet he managed it with ease.

She climbed the steps to Granddad's cabin. Another picture stubbornly clung to her thoughts: the smiles on those kids faces as they'd raced from the gym. They beckoned her to believe this place was making a difference in their lives. One that would stick. The part of her fighting to resurrect pulsed with the truth of it. They could do this. She could do this.

But the visual of what these teens could grow into pressed against that beat, slowing it until it began to disappear. Both beliefs couldn't live together. Which one to feed?

Gwen knocked gently at Granddad's door then entered. "Granddad. Nate and I brought you a treat."

Silence.

She tiptoed down the hall and peeked through his opened bedroom door. Soft snores drifted from his sleeping form. She retreated to the front porch where off-tune whistling reached her ears.

Nate strolled her way. Dark hair wet from his shower, his T-shirt the right kind of snug across his chest, and the perfect fit on his cargo shorts, his appearance kicked her rebellious pulse into overdrive. The crazy desire to shake Granddad awake assailed her before what remained of her rational side stopped it.

This was all new territory, getting to know a man other than Danny and being fair to them both. Honoring old memories while making new ones seemed impossible because Danny had already claimed her heart. He was the automatic recall on her emotions. Anything that touched them, any way she tried to examine them, his memory filled the moment. It felt like trying to retrain muscle memory.

But this morning, when Nate asked her not to be a stranger, for a moment she'd missed him in place of Danny. No. Not in place of. Just . . . in a different way.

She could do this. Lunch alone but on Granddad's front porch created a solid compromise. A way to explore a new world with the safety of one foot still in the old.

Gwen leaned over the railing. "Granddad's asleep. Mind sitting on the porch?"

He jogged up the steps. "Not at all."

Pine and that sweet scent of his wafted to her. "You smell much better."

"It was pretty bad, wasn't it?" He leaned against the post and crossed his arms. "I worried the smell would never come off. I think they dredged up the stinkiest slime they could find."

"If that was their intent, they succeeded." She picked up the small square table at the far end of the porch. Nate lifted one of the Adirondack chairs. Comfortable silence wrapped them as they situated the furniture. One thing she was learning, Nate wasn't a pusher. He allowed her space and her thoughts. Danny had always liked to talk.

The return of Nate's off-tune whistling pierced the quiet.

She covered her ears with her hands. "Didn't we decide you'd keep that talent hidden?"

"You suggested. I ignored."

"Huh?" She peered up at him. "I can't hear you. Not that it's a bad thing."

He pried her hands from her ears. "People love my whistling." Like other times before, his simple touch zipped through her. Unlike before, she didn't feel the need to run. He gently squeezed her wrists, his eyes flickering over hers before releasing. "Maybe it's your ears that need checking."

"Trust me. It's not." She handed him his roast beef sandwich. "How long do you have for lunch?"

He spooned coleslaw onto his plate. "I'm clear until two. Then I have a call with Elliot."

"How's that going?" She cracked open her Rock N' Rye.

"Okay, I think." He smiled as she handed him a can. He'd like weekly updates."

"Because of Marlene's meddling?"

He shrugged. "I'm sure it didn't help."

"At least you can share that your first week went well." She bit into her sandwich and nearly groaned. Savoring the taste provided the needed moment to contemplate voicing her question. Finally, she swallowed. "How are the JCS kids doing?"

His eyes widened, but he quickly smoothed away his surprise. "Really good. Most of their day is spent working, but in the evenings they have lake time before dinner, and then they come to The Commons afterward."

"What jobs are they doing?"

"Camp store for one." He set his sandwich on his lap. "Then they're covering bathrooms, camp trash, and kitchen duty. Basically everything but the cabins themselves."

"And they haven't caused you any problems?"

"No." Firm but quiet. "Like I said, they're doing well."

But for how long?

They munched on their food for a few minutes. Nate polished his off first.

When he turned to bag his trash, she laughed. "You missed a splotch of mud behind your ear."

As if it was second nature, she reached out and cupped his left cheek, holding it as she swiped at the dried mud where his jaw and right ear met. His stubble prickled against her palm. She flicked her gaze from his cheek to his clear blue eyes. They'd darkened slightly. Her thumb trailed his cheek, the scratch of whiskers familiar yet new. She traced them again. He softly inhaled, and she snapped back.

What was she thinking? She'd seen enough Hallmark movies to not fall for those stereotypical moments, yet she'd stepped right into one.

She tossed his napkin at him. Next time he could wipe his own mess. "You're all clear."

"Gwen—"

Her phone rang, God bless it. She snapped it up without looking. "Hello?"

"Gwen, it's Marlene."

Of course it was. "Oh. Uh, hey, Marlene." Could she sound any guiltier? Did she have a reason to be? Nate's eyebrows drew together. Gwen turned her back to him. "What, um, what do you need?"

"Are you all right?"

"Just a little distracted." Big understatement, and one Nate overheard. She needed duct tape for her mouth.

"With everything going on over there, I understand."

Nate's chair scuffed across the floor behind her. He gently grasped her shoulder, his voice a breath in her other ear. "This distraction is leaving so you can concentrate."

She whipped around, Marlene's voice still buzzing in her ear, but the rumblings of Nate's in her other one had her clenching the phone. She needed to pull it together, and fast.

Refocusing, Gwen caught the tail end of Marlene's words. ". . . my door remains open. We want to take care of you."

"I appreciate that so much." It's what they'd done for nearly four years. The problem was, they didn't want to move forward, and Gwen couldn't keep living in the past. Nothing existed there but memories. Amazing memories, and she'd always treasure them, but the time had come to make new ones. "But honestly, being here makes sense, Marlene. Lew's started on my yoga studio, and I'm close by to keep an eye on it or answer any questions."

"All right." Marlene paused. "You're still planning on next month, right?"

Gwen bit her lip. The anniversary of Danny's death. They'd spend the day reminiscing about his life from birth to death. Have another memorial by his grave. She'd needed those things the first year. But each successive year became more of a must than a want. It would never be a day she'd forget, but she needed to remember it in her own way. "Let me see how Granddad feels. I may have to be here with him."

"Of course. Keep us posted." Marlene said her good-bye. "And remember, if you need anything, we're here."

Gwen would never forget that. Never forget them. They were a part of Danny, so they'd always be a part of her. What couldn't remain in her life, though, was the all-consuming grief.

Chapter Fifteen

⚬━⚬

Mornings were sliding into a new routine, and it made Gwen's breath come easy. Or at least it did when the air wasn't as thick as Granddad's corn chowder. She pulled her inhaler to the top of her bag and rolled out her yoga mat, not bothering to peek at the tree line. Nyla would emerge any second.

Sure enough, Gwen stretched her arms into the air as twigs snapped behind her. She peered over her shoulder with a small grin. Hard to hold the bigger one in, but any large movements seemed to scare the young girl off. While she'd coaxed out Nyla's name the second day, it took three more to convince her to come close. Still, she remained at least ten feet away.

This morning, however, Gwen forged a new plan.

"Ready for some yoga?"

"Yep." The word escaped, but Nyla's eyes averted. Until she spotted the extra mat unrolled beside Gwen's. Her tipped-down head inched up, and she met Gwen's gaze. "That for me?"

Gwen released her stretch. "I thought it might be easier for you to learn if your feet weren't fighting the sand so much."

Nyla stood inches from the mat. "I never used something so pretty."

One of many purchased for her yoga studio. Gwen had retrieved it from storage yesterday. It was a simple yoga mat. A cute one—teal with deeper teal scrolls through it—but still, just a mat. To Nyla, however, it resembled a treasure. Something ached inside of Gwen. "Then I'm glad I brought it."

This time Nyla returned her smile. She stepped onto the mat. Gwen went through the morning routine with her, the air growing heavier as the sun inched higher. Worst day they'd had all summer. Could be a problem. Still early and already the thick air acted like a vice grip on her lungs. If this kept up, she'd need to spend the day inside.

Slipping from plank, Gwen coughed. Enough coughs had already escaped this morning that Nyla finally questioned, "You okay?"

Gwen nodded. "I am. Humid air is hard for me."

"We don't got to do no more."

"We're almost done." Gwen moved into the end of the routine. Yoga brought a sense of stability into her life. Each movement required strength and focus. Mastering them helped her feel in control even when her life wasn't—which was ultimately the skill she hoped to pass on to Nyla.

Nyla's face pinched, but she nodded. They finished their last stretch and dropped to their mats. Another cough barked past Gwen's lips. Nyla turned worried eyes on her. "Don't you got an inhaler?"

Surprised, Gwen faced her. Most people thought she had a tickle in her throat. Some assumed allergies. Nyla recognized the cough.

The young girl pointed to Gwen's bag. "You need ta use it."

Gwen grabbed it and took a puff. "How'd you know I needed this?"

"I got one too." She brushed a tight curl from her sweaty forehead. "Stays with the nurse."

Seriously? She and Granddad had allowed the kids to keep their inhalers. There wasn't always time to wait for them. "Is that what they said when you signed in?"

"Yeah, but it's fine."

Except it wasn't. "I'll talk to them. You should always have it on you."

Nyla shrugged. "Summer ain't hard for me. It's winter."

Didn't mean something couldn't trigger an attack. And when it did, having to wait for the nurse to bring your inhaler could make things far worse. "I'll talk to them, Nyla. I want you to be safe."

Those dark brown eyes latched on to hers. "I'm safe jus' bein' here."

Again, Gwen's heart twitched. Nyla said more in those few words than she had all week. Habits Gwen had packed away years ago resurfaced. They were what kept her from wrapping Nyla in a hug and making promises bigger than she could keep. Stopped her from digging deep into the crevice that statement opened. If she tried either, this tenuous bridge would crumble before she could cross it.

"I'm glad you're here. And thanks for watching out for me." She dropped her inhaler into her bag. "Now it's my turn to look out for you. I'll talk to Mr. Reynolds today."

"Thanks."

"You're welcome." The first morning bell rang. "I'll see you tomorrow?"

With a grin, Nyla spun and ran for camp.

Gwen cleaned up their things before ducking through the trees. She'd shower, check on Granddad, then hunt down Nate. Keeping the inhalers locked up wasn't safe. People who'd never experienced asthma wouldn't think twice about it. But when you fought against a fist closing off the very air you needed, every second counted.

Forty minutes after leaving the beach, she traipsed up the stairs to Granddad's cabin, knocked, and entered.

"Morning." Granddad stood by his kitchen counter, hair wet, and smelling like lemon soap.

"You're up? And showered?"

"And already drank one of Nate's shakes." He pointed to the door. "Promised my PT I'd take a walk this morning. You up for it?"

"Always." His progress meant everything to her. She held open the door as he navigated himself and his walker through. "Where to?"

"I hear the camp store had a little upgrade, and I'd like to see it."

"Not sure stocking it with junk food constitutes an upgrade."

His throaty laugh peppered the air as startled birds flapped away. "Your grandma would have thought so. She loved spoiling the kids." He slowly worked his way down the ramp Lew had built him.

"How about we take the golf cart there? You can walk up and down the candy aisles." She fully supported him pushing himself, just not overdoing it.

"I like that idea."

She settled him on his wedged cushion they'd added to the cart and carefully drove toward the camp store. They pulled up, and she unfolded his walker from the back.

Nate stood in the open doorway as they approached. "Good to see you up and about, Art."

"Curiosity was getting to be too much." He stepped inside. "I wanted to see with my own eyes what you put in here."

Every junk food known to man filled the center of the room, sweetened drinks stocked the coolers, while camp paraphernalia lined the walls. Each day, campers could earn tickets to be used for purchasing anything here.

"I hear something calling my name." Arthur hobbled straight for the peanut butter cups.

Gwen peered up at Nate. "There's something I need to talk to you about."

"Anything to do with my being a distraction?"

"What?" Her cheeks heated. "No."

"Huh. I thought maybe that's why you've been avoiding me these past few days."

"I haven't—"

His chuckle cut her off. "Relax. I'm teasing you." He pushed his hands into his pockets. "What's up?"

The door jingled behind them and loud voices cut off her answer. At first it was laughter, but then a curse word ripped through the air. Gwen straightened, fisted her hands, and spun toward the group of boys. They looked her up and down.

"Who's the new lady?" the tallest in the group asked. "And the old guy? Ain't seen them before."

Nate stepped between her and the boys. "Morning, guys. Care to try those questions again? With manners?"

The other three shifted looks between themselves, but the fourth kept his shoulders back. A boy in a man's body.

Gwen immediately latched on to the coldness in his eyes. She'd once thought young teens posed no threat. They were children, she the adult. Now she knew better. "We need to get going." She tugged Granddad's arm. These boys had to be part of the JCS crew, and she wasn't about to stick around.

"We scare you?" The boy's cool look slid over as if he hoped her answer was yes.

"Axel." Nate's firm voice held control of the room. "You know the rules."

The kid didn't blink. Behind him, one of the others held out his hand. "I'm Josh." Nearly as tall as Axel, his head was shaved bald and his front tooth chipped.

Granddad shook his hand without hesitating. "Arthur. This is my camp."

They all looked at Nate, who nodded. "Arthur's been running this camp since before I was born."

"What's wrong with you?" Another teen pointed to the walker. The shortest of the group, with wiry hair that sprang from his head in all directions, he eyed Granddad with curiosity.

"Took a spill a few weeks back." Granddad smiled. "I'm not as young as you kids anymore. Broke my hip."

"I had my leg broken once." Josh admitted. Nate zeroed in on him. No doubt he'd caught what wasn't being said. Gwen had. It wasn't unusual for these kids to face abuse of all kinds. "Still have a limp."

"Long as I can walk without this again,"—Granddad jiggled his walker—"I'll take a limp."

Josh nodded.

The other two boys introduced themselves.

"Neville." The blond boy nodded.

The one who'd yet to speak added his own clipped nod. "Devon." He stood nearly as tall as Josh with close cropped hair and a gold stud in his right lobe.

Granddad greeted each boy. "Pleasure to meet you boys." He then looked at Axel. "And you are?"

"He done told you my name." Axel jutted his chin at Nate.

"I'd like to hear it from you, son," Granddad pressed.

Nate crossed his arms and stared Axel down.

Another big production of a sigh. "Axel."

"Pleased to meet you, Axel." Granddad offered his hand.

After a moment's hesitation, Axel shook it. His eyes cut to Nate. "Happy?"

"Good manners always make me happy." Nate nodded to the room. "Go ahead and get what you need. Kylie is in the back, and she'll ring you up. I'm going to walk them out."

Gwen's tongue stuck to the roof of her mouth. These boys emanated everything she'd worried about this camp. She shuffled to the door with Granddad, opened it, and practically pushed him out.

The fresh air loosened her tongue. "Those boys are trouble."

Nate closed the door behind her. "I'm watching them, but so far they've earned my trust."

She faced him. "You give it too easily, then."

His look turned tender. "I'm sorry you've been hurt."

"And I don't want *you* to be hurt."

He reached for her, but she backed away.

How had she let that slip out? One sentence, but it said too much. And Nate caught every last drop—a part of her was starting to care for him.

Nerves pulsing, she raced to Granddad. "Let me help you to the golf cart."

Granddad's stare called her out on using him as a distraction, but at least he didn't verbalize it.

She helped him onto his seat, then climbed on too. Nate grasped the roof and leaned in. Would he press? A debate waged in his eyes, but then, "Earlier you mentioned needing to speak with me about something?"

Nyla's inhaler. Her eyes flicked to the store, then to Nate. All she wanted was to flee, but she'd promised to ask. "I ran into a young girl who uses an inhaler. She said the nurse had to keep it, but I was wondering if you'd allow the kids who need them to hold on to them."

His mouth twisted to the side like he gave it a moment's consideration before his head started to shake. "Sorry, Gwen, but all medications need to remain locked up."

"But if she needs it, she might not have the time to wait for it." Gwen prodded. "It isn't safe."

He hesitated. "I get that, which is why we have a plan in place, but too many of these kids face substance abuse issues, and leaving medicine of any kind out in the open poses too big a temptation."

"It's an inhaler, Nate, not ADHD meds or morphine."

"Gwen." With that look, he might as well have added the *c'mon* in front of her name.

She smoothed her hair with both palms pressed against her temples. Then she looked to Granddad, but he'd leaned his head back, pretending to sleep. Big help he was. "In this instance I think the risk to this girl far outweighs the potential risk of abuse. She needs her inhaler. It's not like she'd sell it off to the highest bidder."

"She wouldn't have to sell it for an addict to get their hands on it." He raised a brow. "My decision's been made."

That was it? No further discussion? "I strongly disagree."

"Duly noted."

Frustration built a molten path through her brain. She slammed the cart into gear and tore down the path. *Duly noted.* She'd duly note his poor decision. Didn't mean she had to listen to it.

He hadn't seen Gwen this angry since the day he showed up. Curiosity piqued. Which girl had snuck under her skin far enough she'd be this invested in helping her? He'd been too surprised by her request to ask, but now he wanted to know.

Turning on his heel, he jogged up the steps and returned inside. All four boys stood at the counter, their goods piled high. "Been saving tickets?"

"What else they good for?" Axel made no secret how he felt about the program.

"You could have stayed in Macon, Axel." Nate bagged while Kylie rang them up. "I like having you here, but if you'd rather go home, I can have Jude take you. There's other kids on a waiting list for your place."

It was a risky question, but the game he needed to play. These kids needed to feel wanted, but they also needed to know they weren't prisoners. They had options, something all too few believed. But if they could see choices before them, they could start to understand that making them carried consequences—good or bad.

Nate held out the bag. "So what'll it be?"

"I'm staying," Axel answered.

"Good to hear."

Tossing their tickets on the counter, the boys snagged their stuff and left. When the door closed, Nate returned to restocking shelves. Nearing two weeks into camp and, while he'd made connections with most of the kids, there'd been no real heart-changing moment. Not sure what exactly he'd expected, but whatever his expectations had been, he felt let down.

An hour later the lunch bell rang, and Nate locked up before heading for the dining hall. Jude was in charge of the JCS crew, working in tandem with the counselors Nate had hired specifically for their cabins. He and Jude planned to catch up over lunch, because Elliot was calling later for his weekly update.

Nate chuckled as he walked in the hall. A group of boys swarmed Jude. Probably because he held the tongs to the french fry bin.

"You might want to hand those over before you're overrun," Nate suggested.

Jude grinned over the tops of their heads. "Probably a good idea." Handing them to Tyler, he stepped away. "How's your morning going?"

"Interesting." They retreated to a corner, far enough away to not be overheard, close enough to still keep an eye on things.

"How so?"

"Gwen stopped by the camp store and bumped into Axel and his group." Nate nodded to where Axel stood by Nyla's table. While they looked as different as night and day, Nate had discovered this week that she was Axel's half-sister. Nate recognized a big brother's protectiveness; something he related to. It might be the way to reach him. "In under two seconds Gwen morphed from smiling to bolting from the store, all because Axel and his friends arrived."

Crossing his arms, Jude leaned against the wall. "Can't say it surprises me."

"Me, either. Though I hoped differently." The memory of her request sparked his curiosity. "Strange thing is, she asked about one of the girls needing an inhaler. Wanted us to make sure she could carry it on her."

Jude's lips tipped down as he nodded his head. "Which means she's gotten to know at least one of the kids."

"Right." Across the room, Tyler continued serving fries, ensuring everyone received some. "I'll talk to Paula. See which of the girls uses one." Nate looked at him. "Unless you already know."

"I helped bag the meds at the center before we loaded up, but I didn't look too closely. She's the nurse, so I let her handle things."

The smell of burgers floated to their corner. "All right then, let's grab our food and get started."

They moved through the line, then took the farthest round table. Nate bit into his burger and nearly scarfed the juicy thing down in one huge gulp. He'd ensured amazing food would be served here. Most of the year these kids were lucky to get one meal a day—a lackluster school lunch. Here they'd eat the things they watched others consume year round. He remembered all too well checking out every morsel kids brought from home. Hearing every favorite meal they talked about their moms making. Wondering what it would be like to actually have a favorite other than a sloppy joe slapped on a stale bun next to soggy french fries and canned fruit. Feeling too grateful to grumble about the lack of flavor in those lunches.

Who'd complain when it was free?

There'd be no complaining over these free meals.

Burger nearly gone, he turned to work. "So. Fill me in."

Jude dipped a fry in ketchup. "Been a good week. They've completed every task, including the mandatory reading and discussion times without much complaints." He bit into the fry and swallowed before continuing. "And I laid out their volunteer options for approved projects in town that'll fulfill their remaining community service hours. They're going to vote on their top three later today."

"You'll let me know when you have them nailed down?"

Jude nodded.

Nate pushed his near-empty tray away. "Bryce says Elliot's liked what he's seen so far." Which was more than he got from Elliot, who played things close to his chest. "I hope we can keep him happy."

"Not your job, Nate."

"Kind of is, Jude." Nate attempted to keep the condescending tone from his voice, but by Jude's raised brow, he'd failed.

"You take too much on your shoulders, and you'll buckle under the weight."

"Can't help it. I need this to succeed."

Jude sat back but said nothing.

Didn't need to. True success of this venture didn't rest with him. Nate understood. He truly did. But he didn't need this camp to succeed to prove him a success. He needed it to succeed to prove his past was worth something. That the messes he'd made contained some value. He longed for redemption, and he'd find it through helping these kids.

Chapter Sixteen

⟨ornament⟩

Summer had waged an all-out war, and by the looks of things, Nate battled back with a water balloon fight. Gwen stood by the office window where she'd taken refuge in the air conditioning for the past several days, but shouts of laughter had drawn her to this vantage point.

She scanned the field. Squatting behind the archery targets, Nyla and a few other girls filled water balloons with some contraption Gwen didn't recognize. An entire bucket overflowed beside them, but they didn't see the boys approaching from the woods mere feet away. Nate gave a signal, and they leapt into the open.

It was a massacre. One group pelted the girls while another charged to grab the bucket of balloons, making off with all the girls' ammunition before they could use it. Racing back to their side, they handed out high-fives and slaps on their incredibly dry backs.

Judging by his pointed hand and flapping lips, Nate exchanged smack talk with the girls as they tossed their few remaining balloons. When they missed, Nyla picked up the jug they'd used to fill them with, unscrewed the top, and raced after him. Nate sidestepped her lunge as she tossed the water towards him. It missed, and he did a little dance. Sweat created the only dampness on his shirt. Someone needed to rectify that.

Gwen tipped her head. Looked at the barn. And grinned.

Jude had taken the JCS crew into town to clean up the local park. Left her free to implement her plan. She could take on the humidity for a few minutes, but she couldn't handle running into Axel and his friends.

Sneaking out the back door, she hustled to the panel inside the barn. Opening it, she set a timer, then escaped the room. Next, she stole alongside the building, turning on faucets with hoses. Collecting all five, she hauled them to the corner of the building as she ensured their nozzles were set to *stream*.

Then she found the girls.

"I have a plan."

Kylie Tipton, one of the girls' counselors, looked up from filling more balloons. "What is it?"

Gwen laid it out, and they coordinated their watches while five girls made their way to the barn. "On my signal." Humid air pressed around her, and she gave in to a cough.

Nyla appeared at her side. "You gonna be all right?"

"I am." Gwen reassured them both. "I won't be out here long." Didn't help that the field had been mowed this morning. "You ready?"

Nyla nodded. "Let's get 'em."

Gwen stood from behind the overturned picnic table and sauntered onto the field. Sure enough, Nate saw her coming.

"Look who's decided to join the game." He advanced with a cocky swagger that pulled both laughter and butterflies from her stomach.

"Looked like the girls were outnumbered." She stopped. Kept her focus on his face. "Thought I'd join."

"Better be careful. You make a pretty nice target."

Crossing her arms, she tipped her head and matched his arched brow. Yeah. She caught the double meaning. "Think you can take me?"

His grin grew. "Know I can."

Okay. They were drawing a crowd. Part of her strategy, but not quite how she'd planned it. Kids nudged each other and nodded at them. This age group took any zing of electricity out of the air and fed on it.

"You're a little cocky."

"Like I keep telling you, it's confidence." He stepped forward. She stepped back, leading him as he yammered on. "You don't have any ammo. We took it all."

"Oh." Another step back. Furrowed brow. Sell it.

Now a few boys crept onto the field. Arms filled with balloons, they followed their fearless leader. "Oh." Nate grinned. One of the boys ran up and handed him some ammunition. He tossed it between his hands.

Gwen held up hers. "Nate." She pushed a note of plea into her voice.

"Sorry." He didn't even try to look it. "There's no mercy in water balloon fights."

Her watch beeped. She looked up and grinned. "Exactly." She spun on her heel and ran as the sprinkler system came alive. The five girls jumped out from behind the barn. Hoses in hand, they opened them up, nailing all the boys attempting to run away. Mass chaos ensued—a chaos she could enjoy for once—and she stood on the sidelines, laughing.

Until Nate zoned in on her.

Uh-oh.

She clamped her mouth shut. Tried to stop the giggles. But the water dripping from his face didn't help any. "No mercy, remember?" she called out.

His eyes captured hers. "Oh. I remember." One slow step.

Gwen looked at her watch. "Wow. I need to get back to work."

Nate continued his advance. "I think you have an appointment with the sprinklers. Or hoses." His dimple deepened. "Maybe both."

No way was she turning her back on him to run. She sidestepped, but he lunged. With a squeal, Gwen raced for the office door, her lungs squeezing. He made it there first, a tease in his eyes. "Going somewhere?"

She held up her hands, losing more air to laughter. "I only wanted to make it a fair fight."

"That was your idea of fair?"

"Everyone's wet now, aren't they?" Crud. Wrong words.

He tipped his head. "Not everyone." He lunged again.

She narrowly missed his grasp. Spinning, she raced for the barn. Her chest burned. Too much activity. Too humid air. But just a little farther, and she'd be safe and dry with bragging rights. Nate's feet pounded behind her, his fingers brushing against her back as he grasped for her.

She switched to a zigzag pattern. Nearly there.

Iron clamped around her lungs, asthma demanding its control. One second she was zigging, the next she was on the ground, coughs racking through her. It happened so quickly, she could barely process.

"Gwen?"

She looked at him, eyes wide. Gasps turned to more coughs. He tried to scoop her up, but she shoved him off. Too much pressed in on her. She needed space. Wide open space. Someone to pry her lungs open.

Her inhaler.

It was in the office. She tried to stand, but black spots pressed in on her.

"She needs her inhaler!" Nyla's voice made it through the pressure.

Nate grasped her shoulder. "Where's your inhaler, Gwen?"

Talking required air she didn't have. She pointed to the office. Nate sprinted across the field. Nyla raced in the opposite direction. Gwen tried to call out to her, let her know she'd be okay, but at this moment she honestly had no clue.

She closed her eyes. Focused on control.

Pounding footsteps grew close. The cool metal of her inhaler slipped into her palm. She brought it to her lips. Sucking in puffs, she pictured her lungs opening wide. Pushed past the terror of air not filling them no matter how hard she tried to inhale. Her body was betraying her, and if she didn't do something quick, it would win.

Nate's fingers trailed against her skin. "You're okay. Just relax."

The deep timbre of his voice rolled over her frazzled nerves like honey. She leaned into his touch, focused on his voice, tried for calm.

"Breathe, Gwen."

If only it was as easy as obeying that command. But the medicine wasn't working. Only a breathing treatment would help now.

"Gwen?" Fear edged into his voice.

She wished she could assure him. Hair slicked to her face, she looked up. "Go . . . get . . . nurse."

Her vision started to blacken, and then a thick, round plastic handle touched her hand. A nebulizer. She clasped the lifeline. Medicine already streamed from it. Like the starving person she was, Gwen lifted it to her lips. Tears wet her eyes. Thankfulness? Fear? Helplessness? Probably all of them.

Her airway pressed open a fraction.

Nate settled to the ground beside her, his hand still on her shoulder. He slid it across her back, the tips of his fingers a feather light brush against her skin, and he used his arm to support her. As if natural instinct, she pressed into his strength, his arms as solid as she'd imagined since the first moment she'd met him. They cocooned her. Her lungs inched open. Her body relaxed. She looked up. His concern aimed straight at her. She reached for it and ducked all at once.

His finger trailed along her upper arm. "What can I do?"

Exactly what he was doing right now. Holding her.

Except his hold blurred the memories of Danny.

She forced herself to straighten. "Nothing." Leaning into his strength had been nice. Not going to lie. But she couldn't stay there. "I've got this." Because she didn't know how to lean into him and still hold on to Danny. They both deserved more.

His heart rate contemplated slowing to a near-normal speed again. Each muscle Gwen relaxed coaxed his to follow suit. As her lungs reopened, so did his, the fear that had mimicked her symptoms ebbing.

Then she pushed him away.

He didn't have enough emotional strength to sit beside her and keep his distance. Not after watching her nearly die—least that's what it felt like. Part of why he sat so close was to feel her breathing.

But if she needed space, he'd give it to her.

Nate stood and gripped the back of his neck, squeezing hard. He didn't have a claim on her, even if his heart and mind were starting to formulate one. "I'll go let them know you're okay." He nodded to the group watching from the tree line. Counselors held a few of the girls who were crying. It wasn't that they knew Gwen well. It was because their fun had turned frightening in one moment—something they kept their guard against at home, but had let down here. Hopefully there wouldn't be any lasting effects.

Not with the kids at least.

The picture of Gwen gasping for breath wouldn't leave his mind anytime soon.

Nate hurried over to them. "She's fine." He added a huge grin. "Ms. Johnson is taking care of her right now." Paula knelt beside Gwen to take her pulse. Nate clapped his hands together. "Since our water fight was cut short, how about the counselors take you all back to The Commons and dig into our ice cream supply?"

The counselors caught his distraction tactic. The kids caught the excitement. Within minutes all but one disappeared down the hill. Nate called after Kylie. "You want to wait for Nyla?"

The blonde nodded.

Nate held up his hand. "Give me a sec." Eyes completely focused on Gwen, he retraced his steps, landing right beside her. The near-silent whir of the tiny machine in no way covered her continued wheezing. It had diminished some, but not disappeared. Wasn't this medicine working either? "You're not sounding much better."

Paula's calm voice took control. "She will be. Give her a few more minutes."

Nate's concern still centered on Gwen. She released the end of the tube now streaming medicine in a line of fog. "I'm going to be fine." Her words came around rasps.

He wiped her bangs from her sticky forehead and pushed the medicine toward her. "Keep breathing that stuff."

She smiled around the plastic in her mouth and took a few more slow, deep breaths. "I can talk, Nate."

"Well, don't." He turned to Nyla. "You ran for the nurse. That was smart."

"She needed a breathing treatment." Nyla shrugged. "I got asthma too."

Nate looked between them. So this was the young girl Gwen had asked to change the rules for. He knelt in front of Gwen. "Would the attack have been as severe if your inhaler had been near?" he asked. "Just nod or shake your head."

Gwen's brows drew together. "Can't say for sure, but probably not." She held up her hand. "And please don't lecture me. It wasn't a yes or no question."

Stubborn woman. He pushed the tube toward her mouth. "Finish that up, will you?"

Every word cost her a breath, and she was already in debt.

Nyla sat beside her, watching her. He had a sneaky suspicion if Gwen tried to talk again, Nyla would duct tape the tube to her mouth. He shared a conspiratorial grin with the young girl.

Gwen blinked a glance between them and shook her head.

Nate pointed behind him. "Kylie's waiting for you, Nyla. They're moving the party down to The Commons for ice cream."

She licked her lips but shook her head. "I ain't hungry."

More like she'd learned to be a protector, and Gwen had somehow worked her way onto Nyla's list of people she watched out for.

Gwen recognized it too. She pointed at Kylie, smiled, and nodded.

Nyla's gaze bounced between desire and duty. "You sure?"

Another nod from Gwen.

With a few backwards glances, Nyla slowly retreated. Nate returned to the ground, arms hugging his bent knees before he lost all control and wrapped them around Gwen instead. After a few more minutes, her breathing treatment sputtered, the fog slowing down.

"How do you feel?" Paula asked before he could.

"A little shaky, but all right." She handed the pieces to her.

Paula turned the machine off and packed them up. "Typical after an episode." She stood. "Weather-related asthma?"

"Allergy and activity induced too." She shrugged. "Though activity doesn't seem to bug me as much unless the others are there."

"So summer's your worst season?"

"Spring and fall actually, especially if someone's burning leaves." She picked at grass clinging to her palms. "But humid days like the streak we've been having are another bad trigger."

"I suggest air conditioning until Thursday then. It's supposed to be better by the weekend." Paula tucked some papers inside the bag draped over her shoulder. "If you need anything else—"

Gwen nodded. "I'll let you know."

Nate focused on Paula. "You'll fill out an incident report form?"

"It'll be on your desk by day's end."

"Do any other kids besides Nyla need inhalers?"

"Four others."

"I'd like them carrying them by day's end as well." He yanked on his hair as Gwen's gasps replayed in his mind. "Keep back-ups for them. Talk to them about proper storage and keeping them close, but make sure they have them."

Paula nodded. "They'll know all that stuff, but I'll reiterate it for them." She turned and disappeared down the hill.

Beside him, Gwen's triumphant smile engulfed her face. At one time in his life that look would have erupted rage in him. He'd hated losing fights. Hated losing, period. But he'd come a long ways from that man, and even if he hadn't, this was one fight he'd gladly lose if it meant never seeing Gwen struggling for breath again.

"Thank you." She started to stand.

He pinned her down with his hands on her shoulders. "For my peace of mind—since you're the one who stole it from me—would you please sit still for a few minutes?"

"I just did for nearly ten."

"Then take ten more." He swallowed past a lump. "Please."

She hesitated before reclining on her palms. "I really scared you, huh?"

"You couldn't breathe, so yeah. You did."

"That what made you change your mind on the kids carrying their inhalers?"

"I had no idea how quickly things could go wrong." Deadly even.

She didn't answer right away. Then she touched his arm. "I'm sorry I scared you, but I'm glad it helped you see how important this is."

It made him see how important a lot of things were.

Chapter Seventeen

Mornings like this were what beckoned her through gray, cold winters. Like Michigan's way of rewarding everyone who stayed year-round. Gwen balanced on her forearms, her fingers digging into the sand, back slightly arched, and her legs in a vertical stretch to the sky. She closed her eyes and absorbed the water lapping against the dock, soft breeze tickling her cheeks, even the seagulls, their caws a summer morning's background music.

Behind her a twig snapped.

Nyla had arrived.

Gwen brought one leg then the other to the sand, righting herself. Their routine was nearly comical. Searching the tree line, she caught a pinch of hot pink peeking from behind one of the pines. Even after several weeks, Nyla needed to know she was wanted.

"If you plan to sneak up on people, you should wear a color that blends in," Gwen called amusingly. "Been waiting for you."

Slowly, a face only a shade darker than the brown trunk peered out at her. Gwen patted the sand beside her and focused on the lake. Two seagulls dive-bombed for breakfast before footsteps padded nearby. Nyla tentatively joined Gwen. "I slept in 'cause my cabin used their reward last night. We got our campfire."

Ahh. She'd wondered. Nyla typically rose with the sun.

"Eat a few s'mores?"

Nyla grinned.

A soft breeze accompanied the morning light. For several minutes they stared at the lake. "Sure is beautiful this morning, isn't it?" Mornings on Hidden Lake were unlike anything else.

"Mmm hmm." Nyla dribbled sand through her fist. "You done your yoga?"

And break their new normal? "Not without you."

Nyla jumped up. "Think I could learn that handstand you was doing?"

She loved her ambition. "When you get strong enough." That pose, physically balancing when everything inside tilted off kilter, had soothed Gwen through many moments. Nyla could use the same confidence. "Let's nail a few other things first, like Warrior Pose."

Gwen walked Nyla through the different versions, always impressed with her desire to try, even when her ability sorely lacked. With that drive, Nyla would push past her body's desire to be inflexible and force it to do what she wanted, finding the stability, strength, and control Gwen so wanted her to discover.

Sunlight had shifted to a higher angle by the time Gwen handed Nyla a towel. They wiped their foreheads. "Good job."

"I been practicing."

"I can tell." Gwen accepted the towel back. "Meet me here again tomorrow?"

Nyla's head bobbed fast, but her face froze at something over Gwen's shoulder.

Gwen turned. Nate stood at the end of the path. Nyla hunkered down behind her.

"Ladies." Nate wandered over.

"Nate." Gwen peered over her shoulder and then back at him, delivering a no-clue expression as to the girl hiding behind her.

He smiled and peered around Gwen. "Nyla, you missed breakfast."

Had the bell rung?

"Sorry, Mr. Reynolds." Her voice trembled.

"You're forgiven." Simply stated. "And I'm going to guess you're hungry?"

"I'm used to no breakfast."

He maintained his space but held his authority. "I understand, but one of our rules is that you eat it every day." His glance flickered over Gwen before returning to Nyla. "They also say you're not allowed at the beach until the lifeguards are out here. Do you remember what time that is?"

"After ten." Her voice shrunk even while she straightened. "But Ms. Doornbos ain't doing her yoga then."

Only a marginal lift to his brow revealed his surprise. "Ms. Doornbos is teaching you yoga?"

She nodded. "She's good. You should see her."

Nate's dimple deepened, and he looked at Gwen. "I'm already aware she's rather impressive in most things."

Warmth curled through her.

He refocused on Nyla. "And while I understand this is important to you, so is following the rules. When Kylie didn't see you at breakfast, she was worried." He held up his hand as Nyla tried to apologize again. "You don't have to say you're sorry again. You're already forgiven, but from now on, I don't want to catch you out here before ten. And I expect to see you each morning at breakfast. Got it?"

A slow nod as her heart-shaped face crumpled. Shoulders slumped, she shuffled toward the path.

Gwen nudged Nate. He nudged her back.

"Is it so bad that she was out here?"

"This from the rule-stickler?"

She was, but this was a crazy rule. "It's not like we're doing yoga in the lake." She pressed. "And she hasn't missed breakfast before today."

"But the second she did, it wasn't only Kylie who noticed. All the other kids did too, and they wanted to know where she was. Once they find out, they'll want the same treatment." He held out his hands. "Are you prepared to teach them all?"

Was she? She rubbed her ear.

Nate stared her down.

Ooooh . . .

"Nyla!" Gwen called.

The young girl turned.

"If you follow the rules, I'll add a yoga class to the schedule."

"You will?"

In her peripheral vision, Nate smiled.

"I will."

As if Gwen had showered water on a dying plant, Nyla straightened. "When?"

"We'll add it today." Nate nodded to Nyla. "Get on to the mess hall. Mr. Jude is expecting you."

She dodged through the branches, and Nate turned to Gwen. "That was awful nice, coming from a woman who doesn't want to work with these kids."

"She's different." Gwen shrugged. "Besides, I highly doubt too many will show up for a yoga class, and those who do won't exactly be your roughest crowd."

He stuffed his hands in his pockets. "True." A soft breeze rustled the leaves. "Did you have breakfast?"

"Nope." She smiled. "But I'm not one of your campers."

"You're about as big as one of them."

She laughed. "Thanks. I think."

Nate's gaze roamed the lake. "This place is perfect, you know."

"Minus the giant floating blob, you mean?"

He chuckled. "I kinda like the blob."

"You would."

"So would you. If you tried it."

"Right."

They strolled to the water's edge.

"Arthur looked better today." Nate shed his flip-flops and stepped into the lake.

"You saw him?"

"Brought him some coffee and a donut."

"So you're the one who keeps sneaking him the sweets." She tsked. "I might have known."

"Might have." That boyish grin spread as he waded in farther. "Word is Huron Our Lake has kayaks on sale, and I happen to be in the market for some." His eyes met hers. "Care to ride into town with me this afternoon and make sure I pick the right ones out?"

Eating on Granddad's porch had been one thing. Was she ready to spend an afternoon alone with him?

"I'm not sure you should put those kids on the water," she hedged.

"So. Paintball, then?"

Guns of any kind in their hands?

Smart counter.

"What time are we leaving?"

Nate held the door to Huron Our Lake as Gwen exited, then followed her down the sidewalk. "Thanks. Took me half the time. And you snagged me a great deal."

Sunlight lit her blonde hair. She'd left it down today. He liked it. Liked this easy-going side even more. "I've known Cal most of my life. He's a born salesman. All you have to do is speak his language."

"Too bad I'm not fluent in salesguistics."

"Nobody is." She nudged him. "Because it's not a real word."

"You really should be writing these down."

"I'll get right on it." Gwen nodded toward the small shop ahead. "Froyo?"

He dipped his head toward her. "And you give me a hard time for making up words?"

"Yep. I do." She kept walking. "Now. Do you want frozen yogurt or not?"

"How can I pass up that invitation?" He picked up his pace until they reached the door. Pausing, he waited while Gwen dug in her pocket and deposited change into a small cup by the colorful pony stationed outside the shop. "Making donations?"

"Yep." She nodded to the dark brown horse with stirrups. "A cowboy will chase down a steer on that one." Then she pointed to a pink unicorn across the street. "While a princess rides rainbows over there." She strolled inside. "Pennies don't only buy thoughts, they buy little kids' dreams."

Nate lingered, his eyes on her. Her heart for children still beat under all that hurt. He had every intention of reenergizing its once-strong pulse.

Stepping inside, he sniffed the sweet smell of flavors like salted caramel, birthday cake, and coconut swirling up to meet him. A lady on a mission, Gwen crossed to the paper cups, picked one up, and headed straight for the chocolate explosion. She pulled down the lever and smiled over her shoulder. "Pick a flavor. This time the treat's on me."

"We'll see." He headed for the vanilla.

Her eyes widened, then laughter popped out from her lips. "Could we be more opposite?"

Nate filled the vanilla in his cup not even a quarter of the way. Gwen's chocolate flavor nearly rolled over the sides. "I highly doubt it." He stepped to the toppings. By the time he finished, Gwen nibbled her top layer. He peered at the concoction. "You only added sauce?"

"Peanut butter on chocolate, which we already established as the best combo in the world." She licked her spoon and leaned over his as he placed it on the scale. "Is there even yogurt in that cup?"

Nate pulled out his wallet. "A little. But I didn't want it to overshadow the candy."

"Obviously."

Gwen pushed a twenty in front of his ten. "Told you I was paying."

"I never would have bought them out of candy then."

"Just say thanks and let's eat." Her eyes sparkled.

Nate pocketed his cash. "Thank you."

"Good job." She waited for her change, then slid it into her purse. "There's a table outside."

They snagged one in full sunshine, the metal chairs almost too hot to sit on. The comfortable silence they'd created slid over them as they enjoyed their yogurt. Gwen slipped her sunglasses onto her face.

"I'd like to take the first trip on the kayaks as soon as they're delivered," Nate said, "but how far do you realistically think the kids could make it?"

She shrugged. "We could paddle to the back bay and bank them. Have a picnic. Then paddle back. Easy."

"How long should I plan for that?"

"Since it's their first trip, I'd say a half hour there. However long you want for lunch, then a half hour return."

"Is there a spot to swim where we'll bank them?"

She laughed. "It's a lake, Nate. The entire thing is a spot to swim."

"But am I going to need shears to hack away the seaweed?"

"No. It's clear. Nice sandy bottom." She swiped at a strand of hair the wind blew across her cheek. "And there's two fallen logs the kids can sit on to eat."

"So we'll want at least an hour for lunch? Then maybe another for swimming?"

She nodded. "Give them much more than that, and you run the risk of boredom. Doubt you want that to happen."

"True." He spooned another bite. "And later in the summer, once they're used to the slower pace and their arms are stronger? Where do you suggest then?"

"Then I'd say we kayak all the way out to Lake Huron. It's a full morning trip, or . . ."

"Or what?"

She nibbled her lip.

One of these times he was going to kiss that lip loose.

Refocus.

"Sharing your idea doesn't mean we'll have to do it."

Her yogurt cup empty, she placed it on the table. "We could do the trip late afternoon. Head out to Lake Huron and follow the shoreline to Turnip Rock."

"Turnip Rock?"

She lifted her shoulders. "A big rock that looks like a turnip. Sounds crazy, but it's pretty cool to see." Her fingers drummed across the tabletop. "Granddad knows some of the owners along the shoreline. In the past they've allowed us to camp by their houses and watch the Northern Lights." She shook her head. "But it's crazy to think you could do that with this group."

"How about you let me worry about that?"

"Worry being the operative word here."

Would she ever think these kids worth the risk?

He savored his last spoonful of candy drenched in frozen yogurt. "So maybe we see how they do on the short trips and let them know they're working toward a bigger one." He set his container beside hers. "The rewards wheel has gone over great. Maybe we make this another reward. I don't know." He shrugged. "I'll think it over."

"Sounds good." Gwen stood. "Ready to head back?"

"Yep." He stood too and stretched. "I'm on campfire duty tonight."

"Lucky you."

"You going to come?"

She shrugged. "I'll probably hang out with Granddad. We've been working our way through *NCIS* episodes."

The look on her face showed her pain. "Sounds like you're a huge fan."

"I got nothing against Mark Harmon, but it's not my favorite show." She peered up at him. "I know I'm one of the few to think that."

"Nope. Yet another thing we agree on." Over the weeks they'd uncovered enough common ground to stand on. "So what do you like to watch?"

"Honestly? I'm not a huge fan of TV in general."

"You read then?"

"Nope. Not big on books either."

They stepped around a couple exiting The Art Box. "So what do you like to do?"

"Be outdoors."

"And in winter?"

She looked up at him. "Spoken like a true Southerner."

"I'm from Nevada." Though it'd been a lifetime ago since he lived there.

"Still south of here." His Bronco came into view, and Gwen strolled to the passenger side. "You really plan on staying through one of our winters?"

"You really think I couldn't last?"

"Nope." She stepped back as he opened her door. "I know you couldn't."

Hand on the doorframe, he leaned into her grinning face. "Remember what I said about challenges."

"That's not a challenge, it's a fact." Her eyes flicked over his face.

Nate didn't retreat.

Neither did she.

What would it be like, to be so familiar he could drop a kiss onto those lips? Seal this lighthearted moment with his hand on her waist and his mouth nuzzling her neck, pulling more laughter from her.

She swallowed. Shifted, but not out of his reach.

From teasing to charged in one point two seconds flat. It became harder and harder to be around her without addressing the elephant in the room. It might have been years, but he'd been around women enough to know when attraction flared—even if Gwen hadn't admitted it to herself yet.

Which he sincerely doubted.

"Gwen." He reached for a lock of her hair, letting his thumb brush against her throat softly. Her pupils flamed large. Yeah. She was as aware of him as he was of her. "I've been wondering—"

"Gwen?" An elderly voice pulled her gaze from him to around his shoulder. A stiff smile replaced the easy one they'd shared.

"Mrs. Brown. How are you?"

"I thought that was you." The little old woman looked from her to Nate and back again. "What brings you into town today? I thought you were staying by Arthur's side. That's what Marlene said."

That explained Gwen's brittle smile.

"I needed to help Nate find some kayaks for the camp. Cal would've eaten him alive." Her laugh fell flat.

"Old Cal's a pussycat."

"More like a tiger if you don't know what you're doing." Her bottom lip slipped between her teeth. Then, "I need to get back to Granddad now though."

Gwen tugged her ear when she was deep in thought, but she only nibbled that lip when she was nervous.

"You tell him I've been praying for him." Mrs. Brown issued another all-encompassing glance as if she was writing a short book on what she'd thought she'd seen.

"Will do." Gwen climbed in the door Nate still held open for her.

He nodded at Mrs. Brown before hopping in himself. As he started the car and pulled away, Gwen refused to look at him. She dropped her forehead to her hand.

"You okay?"

"Peachy."

"What's got you so worried?" He had a fairly good idea but wanted her to say it.

"She's going to run straight to Marlene."

"And tell her what? That we were standing by my car?"

"That's not what it looked like."

"Oh?" He stopped at the four-way and leveled a direct look at her. "What did it look like, Gwen?"

Her cheeks reddened. Anger? Embarrassment? Neither were acceptable. Worse was the way her mouth clenched, denying one single syllable a chance to slip out. If she refused to talk, they'd stall before they could even move forward. Not that he had anything more than his gut to go on that she was interested.

Nate shifted into first and took off. "Fine. I'll lead." Air whipped through his cracked-open window "My guess is it looked like two adults about to kiss. You agree?"

She crossed her arms.

He sighed. "It's not wrong, Gwen. You're not married anymore. You're allowed to be attracted to another man." He softened his voice. "Because this man is attracted to you."

Her shoulders stiffened.

So did his. He was willing to be open, share how he felt, take things slow. But she had to at least meet him at the starting point. "Am I way off base here? You say the word, and I'll back off."

Nothing. Not a movement. Barely a breath.

After a mile, he reached out to turn on the radio. Even the country station she'd tuned it to on the way here sounded better than this silence.

Her hand stopped him. She kept the touch until he looked at her. "You're not off base."

He forced himself to return his eyes to the road. "No?"

"No." She waited. "But my heart's not free, Nate, and I'm not sure it ever will be."

Chapter Eighteen

$\mathcal{C}$hurch bells pealed across the quiet morning as Gwen snuck out her front door and headed in the opposite direction of the chapel, checklist in hand. The recording played only on Sunday mornings—Nate's compromise until the real bells in the steeple were fixed.

The humid weather had dissipated after last week, returning the mornings to a comfortable warmth she easily slipped into. Hadn't needed her inhaler over the past two days. With the dining hall emptying, now was the perfect time to retrieve the grocery list their cook should have generated. After that, she'd tackle the other items on her list before she drove into town for her weekly Sunday brunch with the girls. Maybe they could help her finalize the remaining decisions for her studio. Between running this place and taking care of Granddad, she'd shoved those plans to the back burner, but Lew needed answers.

Gwen swung the door to the hall open just as someone pushed out. She stumbled back and strong hands caught her.

Nate grinned down. "You're going in the wrong direction."

They hadn't spoken since their shared confession the other day. Now his touch rippled a churning mix of emotions across her stomach. "Says the directionally challenged man." She shrugged away.

Or tried to.

Nate didn't force the hold, but he also didn't remove his hands. No, he slid his fingertips feather-light over her arms all the way to her wrists where he applied gentle pressure. "Missed you at fireworks last night."

Then he let go.

Her brain spun. Fireworks. The Fourth. Last night.

She swallowed. "I spent the evening with Granddad." Hiding out.

The flick of his brows said he knew it too. "Bet he appreciated the company."

"He did."

"Then I'm glad you were there." The bells rang again, fracturing the moment. Nate cleared his throat. "I should get moving." He started to turn, then paused. "What are you up to right now?"

She wiggled her clipboard. "Finishing this. What's on for today gets done today."

Before she realized what he was doing, Nate plucked the board from her hand. He scribbled across the paper before returning it.

She glanced at his messy handwriting. *Chapel.* In red ink. Right across the top.

"Now it's on your list." He grinned.

A noise escaped her.

His brow lifted. "What was that? Not a laugh. Not a groan." He snapped his fingers. "Groanaughter."

"You truly amuse yourself, don't you?"

"Joy is an important part of life."

"So is completing my checklist." She held it up. "Which you need to stop adding things to whenever you feel like."

"I've only done it twice, and both were items you needed." He tipped his head. "Not that church should be on a checklist."

Yeah. That thought had sliced through her when she saw the word he'd added. But attending church hadn't produced any guarantees for her life. She'd wound up with the same hurts anyone else could experience and a whole bunch of chaos. At least with a completed checklist, she could pretend to remedy one of those things.

"Then you shouldn't have added it." She brushed past him.

He followed. "Would you have listened to my simple invitation?"

"Guess you'll never know."

He stayed on her heels. "Or maybe I will." His deep voice never pushed but always beckoned. "Come to chapel with me, and I'll help you with your list."

"You can't." She ducked into the kitchen and away from his question. "You have one of your very own."

"I do?"

"Yes. It's called making sure the kids don't get into trouble."

Nate propped himself against the door casing. "They're good kids, Gwen."

"Then completing yours should be a slam-dunk."

He did silent too well. So different than Danny that she still didn't know how to react to it. So she kept working. After a moment, he pushed off the door. "I'll save you a seat in case you change your mind."

She wouldn't.

Sitting in chapel hadn't soothed her for years, not like bringing order to things. Yoga, checklists, cleaning—those things momentarily calmed the twisting emotions inside.

Gwen managed to check off everything by the time the lunch bell rang. She'd promised Granddad this hour, and she hustled to his cabin, stumbling as she caught sight of her mother-in-law waltzing out his door.

"Marlene?"

"Gwen." She stepped off the porch and wrapped her in a hug.

"What are you doing here?"

"After our talk I thought I'd come check on Arthur. I wanted him to know we had room for you both at our home."

"What did he say?"

Sadness nipped the edges of her eyes. "That he's staying right where he is."

"I'm not surprised."

"I am." Marlene shook her head. "I don't know how you can both be here."

"I agree it's not ideal, but I won't leave Granddad." She sucked in a deep breath. "I'm surprised you came out."

"I had to." She looked around. "For Danny. We promised him we'd look after you." Her eyes flicked over Gwen's shoulder, and she straightened.

Axel and his friends, their shorts hung low and bandanas snug against their forehead headed up the path to the ropes course. They were supposed to be at lunch, not to mention their attire broke the dress code.

"I have a meeting to attend." Marlene patted Gwen's shoulder. "I'll see you Tuesday."

Gwen nodded, her eyes on the boys. Years ago she'd have followed. Attempted to talk sense into them and usher a reminder of the rules—sure they'd listen.

Now she knew better.

They wouldn't listen, and they definitely wouldn't change.

It was time for Nate to see.

She started down the steps.

"Gwen?" Marlene's voice swam through her fog.

Her eyes remained on the boys. "Hmmm?"

"Tuesday. You're coming, right?"

The request snagged her full focus. She turned, but the *yes* Marlene waited for wouldn't form on her lips. Neither would the *no* she desperately wanted to say. She wasn't strong enough for either answer. "I'm . . . I'm not sure." She spun. "I have to go."

And she took off for the dining hall.

Nate slapped two cheddar brats on Tyler's plate. "You want muscle, you need protein." He'd watched the boy dump his first serving onto a friend's plate.

Tyler's big brown eyes looked up. "I'm okay. Give it to someone else."

Nate ran his hand over the tight curls on the boy's head. As Tyler traveled through the lunch line earlier, he'd snagged the final two brats from a pan. Already one of the counselors headed to refill it. Tyler wouldn't know that though. "Finish those. There's more if you're still hungry."

The look of amazement still punched Nate in the gut. These kids hadn't grown used to the abundance of food he ensured the camp supplied.

"There is?"

"More than enough." He squatted to Tyler's level. "You ever see us running low on something, you come let me know. I'll make sure we don't run out."

Tasked with a job so important, Tyler's grin ran ear-to-ear. "You got it." He bit into one of his brats.

Nate rubbed moisture from his eyes. God was so good to put him here. Dragged him out of the mire and gave his life new meaning. Now if he could assign some to his past.

Across the room Jude chatted with a table full of teenage boys. They'd arrived rowdy, but already Jude held their respect and their ears. Didn't matter what their background was, these kids were as lost as Nate had once been. They only needed someone to show them the way. One person to care. It would make all the difference. Turn their lives around and possibly the lives of their families.

"Nate!" Gwen's charged voice jumped his heart rate.

He spun in her direction and in three seconds stood beside her. "What's wrong?" Her breath burst out in tiny gasps. Was she having another asthma attack? He gripped her shoulder. "Do you need your inhaler?"

Her eyes widened. "What? No." She thrust her thumb over her shoulder. "Axel and his group are headed in the opposite direction of lunch." She lowered her voice. "They're out for trouble."

What were they thinking? The counselors took a headcount at each meal—it's how he discovered Nyla missing the other morning. Their absence would be noticed too.

"I'll check it out."

"I'm coming." She stayed on his heels.

Nate strolled through the door. "Suit yourself, but I'm sure it's nothing."

Her dry snort said she didn't agree.

He climbed on a golf cart and waited for her to sit.

"They were walking toward the ropes course," she directed.

Nate took off. Sure enough, as the cart crested the hill, he could make out four boys leaning against the poles, vaping.

"Guess it's not nothing," Gwen muttered.

Nate shook his head and ignored her. One altercation at a time.

He slid off the cart and approached the boys. They didn't drop their vapes, just eyed him. "Guys." He maintained a steady voice.

"What you want?" Axel stepped forward, his eyes full of attitude. Along with a flatness Nate knew all too well.

He held out his hand, palm up. "Let's start with your vape pen."

"Nah, man, that ain't happening."

Nate didn't budge. "I can wait here all day, Axel."

The boy inched closer and exhaled a line of smoke right into Nate's face. "Don't think it'd be good for your health."

Not even laughter from the others. Just silent watching.

"You keep it, you leave." Nate held his stance. "Give it to me, and you can stay."

"Funny. I thought the rules were they got caught vaping and they had to leave." Gwen's voice sliced the air from behind.

Why hadn't she stayed in the cart? He didn't need her frustrations added into this mix.

Nate remained focused on the boys. "I got this, Gwen."

"Doesn't seem like it."

Devon jerked his chin at Gwen. "She all amped up."

"Aw. Bet he got ways to bring her down." Axel dragged his gaze over her. "Right to his—"

Nate snapped his arm out, thrusting his forearm over Axel's chest and shoving him into the wooden pillar. "Care to finish that statement?"

Fire licked through Axel's eyes, but he shook his head. Nate pressed in. "Now. Your pen."

He didn't release the pressure. He didn't want to hurt the kid, but ground rules needed to be reinforced. Axel needed to understand Nate was in charge.

The other boys' gazes flicked from one to the other.

"Your choice, boys." Nate addressed them without taking his attention from Axel. "You're welcome to stay. It's a great program to work off your community service hours. Three meals a day and plenty of activities after your work hours. But to do that, you need to follow the few rules we have."

Another thirty seconds ticked by before Axel produced a clipped nod. Josh slapped the vape pen into Nate's empty hand along with an additional cartridge. Nate released some of the pressure on Axel. "So we clear?"

"We straight." Right words, but a war still raged in his eyes.

Nate stepped back. Axel tugged his shirt in place and glared. The other three stared at the ground.

Nate pocketed the pen and cartridge after checking to be sure it wasn't one with weed in it. That'd change the boys' entire outcome. "Next, the bandanas. You know they're not allowed."

Through grumbling, they handed them over.

Last thing. "Now, apologize to Ms. Doornbos."

Axel's attention snapped to him, his mouth a thin line.

Nate inched closer. "I'm giving you a second chance with the vaping. I won't with this. Respecting the women here is not negotiable, Axel." He looked at the other three. "You want to be real men, you'll get that straight."

Four mumbled "I'm sorrys" met his admonition. Axel's clenched jaw said more than the words.

Gwen nodded, but stayed silent.

"Okay." Nate nudged his chin toward the path. "Now get back to the mess hall. Lunch is nearly over."

The boys dispersed. "You ain't following us?" Devon asked.

"Do I have to?" Nate looked at him. "Or can I trust you?"

Devon nodded, and they took off.

Nate watched till they disappeared, then turned to Gwen. She still stood with her arms crossed, jaw so tight he was surprised it didn't shatter.

"Go ahead." He planted his feet shoulder-width apart and crossed his own arms loosely.

"I'm not sure where to start." Anger rolled from her.

"I'm sure you can pick a place."

She did. "They broke the rules. You need to kick them out."

"They weren't hurting anyone but themselves."

"So vaping is healthy now? And what about the law?" She lifted her hands. "They're under eighteen. And you and I both know they most likely swiped that stuff when Jude had the kids in town this week."

Nate dragged a hand over his face and down to his chin.

Wisdom. He needed wisdom, because she bore as many wounds as those boys.

"It's called grace, Gwen." Her eyes widened, but he kept talking before she could interrupt. "I only have this summer to get through to them. I'm not letting one smoke break stop me from that."

"Did you see his eyes?" She stepped closer. "That boy is lost. You could have a lifetime, and you still couldn't save him."

"I disagree."

She threw her hands into the air. "Oh, pull your head out of your—"

"Gwen." His gentle voice stilled her wild one. "What happened to you?" He dug his gaze in. Danny's death had stolen enough from her. Pieces it never should have touched. Could she remember the heart she used to possess? The passion for these kids. The faith that, with God, they could reach them—even if it was only one.

"I stepped into reality." Her dry laugh hurt more than the wetness in her eyes. "No. I was thrust into it. And I won't sit here with you in your dream world." She shook her head. "I can't believe you let them walk, Nate."

Wisdom. Focus. Patience. Yep. All three were welcome about now. He slid his fingers through his hair. "Yet you were fine when I didn't punish Nyla for breaking beach rules to do yoga with you."

She went completely still. "It's not the same."

He shook his head. "It is, Gwen. Rules are meant to bring order. They need to be followed. But sometimes you make an exception to a rule because it's what's best for that person."

"Nyla on the beach is nowhere near those boys stealing a vape and smoking it. Not to mention their attitudes."

"They all broke camp rules. They all deserved punishment, but I gave them grace. Hopefully in doing so, I gained a small measure of their trust, and they begin to see the picture of God's grace." Her shoulders tensed. He could stand here all day and argue, but she wasn't in a place to see clearly. He sighed. "Right now, this camp is their best chance, Gwen."

She tugged her ear, her clouded gaze diverted for a moment before she looked at him. "Then you're going to forfeit whatever chance you and I might have had—if there even was one—because those kids are lost and there's no saving them.

You'll only lose yourself in the process." Her blue eyes filled with a sad resolve. "And that's a trip I won't help you navigate." Then she turned and walked away.

Chapter Nineteen

Fire burned in Gwen. Hot. Blinding. Alive.

Watching Nate with those boys? She didn't possess the words. The farther she walked from him, the more the scene replayed in her mind, the angrier she got. He was sticking his neck out there, and those kids would chop it off.

Her feet slammed against the asphalt. Before realizing where she headed, Granddad's door came into view. She shoved it open.

"Gwen?" His voice reached from his room.

"I'm done." She stomped to him. "I can't be here, Granddad. I was starting to think I could, but now I know I can't."

His attempt to sit up only left him ashen.

She hurried to him. "Stop. That's why we got you this bed." Pushing the button, she waited until it was at a forty-five degree angle and then propped a pillow behind him.

Color returning, he patted his mattress. "Seems you're the one who needs help."

Too wired to sit, she paced the worn oak floor. "I caught a few boys vaping, and Nate is letting them stay." She dragged her hands through her hair. "Why have rules if we don't keep them?"

And trying to compare this to Nyla only made her angrier. Nyla wouldn't hurt a fly. Keeping those boys around only endangered them all. Nate included. Watching Axel's cold eyes on Nate . . . She shuddered again.

"Did he give them a warning?"

Dry laughter scratched her throat. "The person who needs a warning is Nate." She looked at him. "Tell him he's playing with fire. Maybe he'll listen to you."

Granddad reached for his water and took a long sip. "Isn't it time for my medicine?"

She checked the clock. Great. So consumed with herself, she'd forgotten what he needed. "Let me grab it." She hustled to his nightstand. "I'm sorry."

"It's okay." He tossed back two pills and took another long swig of water. "With this broken hip, I need to stay up on my medicine or the pain will get out of control. Then even the slightest movement will hurt."

His eyes roamed over her. Yeah. An object lesson, only this time she wasn't sure of his exact point or even if she wanted to know.

Finally, she sighed. "Go ahead."

His grin contained part victory, part worry. He patted his bed again. This time she sat.

Granddad's hand took hers, so familiar. "When Danny died, you were hurt. Broken."

"Try shattered."

He nodded. "And you've been trying to manage that pain without God. But much like I can't manage my pain alone, neither can you."

"So you're saying God's like morphine?"

"You know what I'm saying." He squeezed her fingers. "You curled into yourself. Hiding here at the camp and disengaging from life rather than walking through the pain. And I allowed it, but I can't let you continue being the walking dead."

She tried to pull away. "Gee, thanks, Granddad."

"It's been four years." He held tight. "Do you realize this is the first real emotion I've seen on your face in all that time?" A pause. "You wouldn't be worried about Nate if you didn't care about him."

Wetness formed in her eyes, but she blinked it away. She tried to skirt his truth, but it chased her. Feeling one emotion meant she could feel the others. So she'd shoved them all down. Stayed in control. Because . . . She gulped, raw honesty whispering off her tongue. "I don't want the pain." It remained so close, the edges suffocated her. If its full weight descended, that would be the end of her.

"I know." He patted her hand. "I know." Silence descended for several long seconds. "But it's there anyway. Now all you can do is walk through it. And the only way you'll survive the journey is with God."

"He's the one who put me here to begin with!" She stood, fingers of anger squeezing her. "Now I'm supposed to take his hand and stroll back to a life I never asked for? Should I grab a lollipop and skip while I'm at it?"

"Sure. If it'll make the trip more enjoyable."

She stopped. "Excuse me?"

"We're not doing sarcasm then?" Granddad lifted his grey, bushy brows. "Just as well. It's not very helpful, is it?"

Her tongue nearly split, she bit it so hard. "I should go." She made it to the door before turning. "I thought you of all people would understand. You loved Grandma so much."

There was that warm smile. The one he had every single time he thought of Grandma. "I do understand." His gaze moved from past memories to rest on her. "Why do you think I said yes to Nate?"

"To torture me?"

His smile dipped. "To help you."

"Well, this isn't helping. It's hurting."

"Then it's time to decide. Face the pain or hide again?"

She turned and walked away.

Jude met Nate outside the mess hall. "Everything okay? You look like someone kicked your puppy, or you're about to do it yourself."

"It's been a tough morning." Not ready to stop moving, Nate continued walking, and Jude joined him.

"Axel?" Jude nailed the first half of the problem.

"How'd you guess?"

"He came into lunch late, and simmering with an attitude to match yours." He shook his head. "He's going to bust our butts all summer."

"Don't I know it." He'd seen trouble in Axel's eyes the moment he stepped off the bus. Made him want to reach him all the more. "Praying for a way to break through to him."

"You will. Just keep trying."

He wouldn't stop. "If Gwen had her say, he'd be on the bus back home."

They walked toward the lower clearing. "She's really got a chip on her shoulder, doesn't she?"

"Well earned." And if he could help knock it off this summer, the success would be as much a victory as making a difference in these kids' lives.

"She the other reason you're stalking around?"

"Don't really feel like talking about it." There wasn't much to say. They were over before they'd even gotten started.

Jude grabbed a branch as they walked under it, tugging a leaf free. "Okay." He shredded the leaf. "Calloway call recently?"

Apparently Jude preferred talking about things that personally bugged him, or he wouldn't bring up Nate's little sister. She and Jude had been engaged until Calloway abruptly called things off and disappeared a few months ago.

"No. But she calls at least once a week, so any day now." Beside him, Jude tossed the last piece of the leaf but remained quiet. There wasn't much to say that he hadn't already. Calloway, on the other hand, needed to fill Jude in on several things. But that needed to be on her terms, in her time. "Anything you want me to pass on?"

His lips tipped into a frown, and he shook his head. "What I need to say is better done in person."

Nate's heart hitched. Jude had been patiently waiting. Had his patience run out? "Jude, she's coming back."

No answer.

They approached the lower field. Kylie had a group of about ten kids attempting to fly kites. By summer's end, she'd have them making and flying their own. Nate and Jude stood by and watched.

"Elliot any closer to signing on the dotted line?" Jude swiped at a bee dive-bombing him.

"Bryce said he's happy with the weekly reports. I think those have really helped smooth things over. Right now he's scheduled to come out the last day of camp. Sign the papers and participate in our celebration. Hype up next year."

"He hasn't fully committed?"

"Only verbally."

That bee wasn't leaving Jude alone. "What are you going to do if he decides not to back you?"

Nate shrugged. "Guess I'll cross that bridge if it happens." He ducked as Jude's hand nearly clipped him. "What'd you do? Take a bath in honey this morning?"

Earned him a glare.

Across the field Nyla held a kite, her shoulders slumped. Kylie was busy with another group.

"Not that I want to leave you to face that bee alone,"— Nate nodded to Nyla—"but I'm going to check on her."

"I think I can handle it." Jude waved him off, then left to join a boy struggling to untangle his string.

Nyla didn't look up as Nate approached. "Need some help?"

"Nah." She shook her head. "I can't do this. I ain't no good at it." She dropped the string. "I ain't good for nothing."

She hadn't even tried. Twisted his heart. "Sure you are. Only takes practice."

"Why bother? I heard Ms. Doornbos earlier."

Nate stepped a foot closer, not impeding on her large bubble of personal space. "Heard her where?"

Her bottomless brown eyes peeked out from a chunk of frizzy blonde bangs. "Talking with you by the ropes." Oh no. "I wasn't spyin' on you. I followed Axel 'cause I saw what he was doin', and I didn't want him in no trouble."

Trying to keep up with her brother, in any form, would only wind up getting her hurt. "You're not responsible for your brother's choices, Nyla."

"He's all I got." An even bigger truth since she'd overheard Gwen. "She say you ain't got no chance of helping us 'cause we worthless."

His twisted heart flamed. "That's not what she said." Not that her sharp words hadn't launched an arrow straight into Nyla's heart. One he hoped to dislodge.

"It's what she meant." She stared at the dirt, no doubt thinking her value far less than it truly was. "She ain't the first to say it."

No. But she was the first to flicker hope in Nyla. Build a connection with her. Nyla had rushed to her aid, protected her. And in one sentence, Gwen shattered the young girl. Nate clenched his fists, then released them. Nyla would read any show of frustration wrong. This should be her safe place, and Gwen's words had decimated that. His anger wouldn't add to it.

That he'd reserve for Gwen alone.

He gentled his voice. "She might not be the first, or even the last, but it doesn't make their words the truth." He waited a beat. "You may not believe me, but Ms. Doornbos is hurting. Sometimes hurting people say mean things. Doesn't make it right, and it definitely doesn't make it the truth." That fact he couldn't overstate.

"What she got to hurt over?" Curiosity and annoyance coated her words. Not surprising. From where Nyla stood, Gwen's life was perfect.

"Maybe you should ask her." He held out the kite. "After you and I get this thing in the air."

Longing and insecurity swam in her eyes.

"You know what's so neat about kites?" he pressed.

A slight shrug. Trying so hard to be indifferent.

Nate held it up. "They fly the highest when they meet the most resistance. It's like the more something pushes against them, the better they do. The higher they go."

He let the words hang. And if he hadn't been watching, he'd have missed the tiny tip of her lips. Enough to keep him going. "So how about you hold that string again, and I run with the kite. I think together we can get it working."

Across the field, Jude raced behind another youth. Flying kites. Something most kids their age had outgrown, but for so many here, their innocence had been stolen in varying forms. They needed pieces of it back.

Nyla glanced at the other kids racing around, then back to Nate.

"So what do you say?" He offered her the string.

Her slow nod was all he needed. He jogged backwards. "Okay. You go the other way until the string is taut. Then start running. I'll follow and when I say pull, yank on the end of your string as hard as you can."

She followed his instructions and the moment no slack remained in the string, she started running. His long strides easily kept up.

Come on, Lord. A little breeze would be perfect right now.

A puff of wind slammed him, and he raised the red and blue kite into the air, tugging slightly backwards against the string. "Pull!"

Nyla gave a yank and the kite soared, but Nate didn't take his eyes off her face. That smile. Full of freedom and filled with laughter. She had no idea she could feel that always. But by the end of this summer, Lord willing, she would.

Nate looked over the clearing.

No matter what Gwen said.

All of them would.

Chapter Twenty

Gwen had managed to avoid Nate over the past two days. Not because she remained frustrated. She simply didn't know what to say to him. They were on such opposite ends—even if his end did tug at her. His words and actions echoed around her, creating slivers of truth that pricked at her heart. But moving forward didn't mean returning to the life that stole Danny from her. It couldn't.

Stretching into a Warrior Two pose, she let the smooth, warm rays cusping the tree heat her face. At her feet, her phone dinged a text message. She thought she'd turned it off. Meant to, seeing as she wasn't sure what she'd do today.

She changed positions and worked her way down to plank, enjoying how her muscles quivered. She held on, relishing the control. Today she needed to be in it.

Four years.

How could they pass so quickly and excruciatingly slow at the same time? The first year had swallowed her; she vaguely remembered pieces of it. The trial consumed the second year. And she spent the last two years helping Granddad reach his anniversary while working on the deal with the church. Setting the plans of her new life in order.

Then Nate slammed her back into chaos.

Her muscles screamed for release from plank.

But she forced them through another sixty seconds.

As her watch beeped, she folded her body into a sitting position with her legs crisscrossed. She stared over the lake as her phone trilled again. No doubt messages from all her friends, but they weren't who she was avoiding. That was Danny's parents. They'd want to spend the day focused on him, pouring over old photo albums, dining at his favorite restaurant, reliving old stories, and ending up at his grave.

Gwen dropped her chin to her chest. She didn't have it in her.

Crashing sounds erupted through the path connected to camp. She twisted. Nyla? She hadn't seen her since the weekend. The yoga class she'd added to the schedule remained empty. Worry started to set in, but yesterday Jude assured her Nyla remained around and doing well. Maybe she was coming to tell her she'd be at the class later today.

She stood to meet Nyla, but deep laughter froze her. Within seconds, a group of teenage boys rolled into view. Too busy tossing a football, they didn't see her. Most were the same ones caught smoking with Axel.

Oh, no. This was her time. Her space.

This stopped now.

Drawing herself up, Gwen stalked down the short beach. The boys' toes barely touched the water. "Hey!" she called. "You."

Two of them turned and nudged the others. The tallest held on to the football. "Yes, ma'am?"

His polite address nearly halted her pursuit. But she'd been fooled before. She dragged her gaze over their faces. Enough of them possessed hardened jaws and dark eyes. Tattoos snaked up several of their arms, and scars that could be from bullets or knives littered a few of their bodies.

"This isn't open swim time. You need to get off my beach. Now." Her hands rested on her hips.

Again, the tall boy spoke. "Renner said we could come down 'cause—"

"Renner?" Who the blazes was Renner?

His eyes widened. "Mr. Reynolds."

Since when did the kids give him a nickname? She didn't want to guess what they called her.

"Well, I'm saying you can't."

Axel broke through the group, towel around his neck. "This ain't your lake."

How had she missed him?

She pulled herself as tall as possible. "Actually, it is."

"Why you got a problem with us?" Another boy, shorter and with plenty of muscle, advanced.

Gwen refused to give any ground. "I have a problem with you not following the rules."

"Nah. That ain't it." Axel stepped closer and worked his jaw. Better than his fists. "My sister told me what you said. You think we ain't good enough—even for your water."

Who was his sister? Gwen didn't dignify him with the question or a response.

And his eyes lit with the same anger that laced her belly.

Bring it.

This time she'd fight.

And Axel saw it. With one long stride he stood in her face, but his tall friend held his arm back before he could lift it.

Tall boy tightened his grip. "Let Renner talk or you gonna be sent home."

Nostrils flared, his cold eyes pierced her.

Devon leaned close. "You gonna prove her right?"

Axel settled. He sucked in a breath and stepped away. "Don't have to. She already thinks she is. Ain't no changing someone like that." He stalked away. "But I ain't giving her no power to kick me out."

All six cast her glares . . . all but the tall one. He shook his head at her, his eyes digging into hers like he could see past her anger. Like he understood her.

She blinked, and he turned, following his friends back to camp.

A slight tremble ran through her, but it originated more from anger than fear. She dusted off her leggings and collected her things. Those boys only stacked another log of proof onto the case she'd built, and it didn't need to grow any bigger for her to do something. She should have after the vape incident. Now she would.

Her phone rang again, but she silenced it. She owed Danny more than standing by his grave today while history repeated itself right here around her. There had to be a way to stop Nate from purchasing this place, and she would figure it out. She wasn't going to share this land with him. It had been a mistake to allow Granddad to sway her, and she fully intended to rectify that error.

Towel wrapped over her shoulders, Gwen stalked toward camp. Any minute the bell would ring. She needed to be in her cabin by then, because she wasn't about to interact with any more of the kids who'd pour onto the paths.

She had work to do. Rather than spending the day in tears by Danny's grave, she'd do something. She slammed into her cabin. A quick shower and a bite of breakfast. She'd need her strength. She was going into battle.

Nate's phone buzzed on the counter. He wrapped his towel around his neck and answered. The boys would have to wait a few more minutes to start cooling off in the lake.

He pressed answer. "Morning, Ryker."

"I think this camp thing is good for you." His old friend chuckled. "You actually sound awake, and it's not quite eight."

"Been up for two hours."

"Hang on, I think a winged pig buzzed me."

Nate laughed. "Nice." He pulled out the small chair by his table and sat. "I'm guessing you finally got my voicemail."

"Yeah." Ryker bounced something in the background. No doubt that tiny rubber ball always in his hand. "You cooled down some?"

Nate cracked his neck. He didn't lie to Ryker. Not anymore.

"Your silence answers my question." The bouncing stopped. "So what are you going to do about it?"

"Not sure." Two days and he still didn't know. It's why he'd been happy Gwen was avoiding him. Kept him from the hard work of avoiding her. "Thought you'd have a suggestion."

"Talk to her."

"Not that suggestion."

Ryker barked a laugh. "Listen, we're about an hour away. How about you come visit for the day? Work out some of that anger. Toss some ideas around with us. Then you can talk to her."

He wished. "I can't leave this place."

"You think it'll fall apart without you for a couple of hours?"

With Gwen here and him not available to step in? "Yes."

A long intake of breath followed by a longer exhale. Ryker prepared to lay it on him. "Look. You and I both know God's got you there for a reason. How about keeping your pride out of the way?"

"Nice."

"Call it like I see it." Ryker started bouncing that ball again. "So when should I expect you?"

Visiting with Ryker would help clear his head.

"Couple of hours. I have to meet a few kids for a swim. They helped me tackle some yard work this morning." The crew he'd hired flaked again, and he wasn't offering a third try. He'd contacted someone new, but it'd be another week before they could fit them in. Last thing he wanted was for Gwen to try and take on the yard again. Why, he didn't know. He was mad as all get-out at her, and still trying to take care of her.

Ryker cleared his throat. "I'll let the guys know you're coming."

They said their good-byes, and Nate tossed his phone on the counter. By now the boys must be itching to attack The Iceberg. They might think they knew how to launch each other, but he'd show them how to achieve real height off that thing.

With a near jog, Nate made for the beach. He hit the "y" in the path and looked to his left. Stopped. And changed course.

"Guys!" He hustled to them.

Axel glared but kept moving. "She rat us out that fast?"

"Huh?"

Axel hacked. "You ain't talk to her?"

"Who?" Not that he needed to ask. His sinking gut provided a logical answer before Axel even said—

"Your lady."

"She's not—" Never mind. "What happened?"

"You actually asking?" Axel's eyes narrowed. "Not accusin'?"

"I prefer to get the facts before I accuse someone."

That gained most of their attention.

Anger still hardened Axel's face. "Tell that to your lady."

Nate sucked in a deep breath. "She's *not* my lady."

"Whatever." He blew him off. "I gotta get to breakfast."

Grabbing his shoulder, Nate stopped him but let go the minute Axel turned. "What happened?"

"She ain't lettin' us in *her* lake without *her* permission." His jaw worked. "And she ain't givin' it."

Red. He saw red. Yeah. So his anger from two days ago definitely hadn't disappeared. He swallowed. Axel saw his frustration, and it would give him approval to do something stupid. Gasoline did not need to be added to this fire. "You told her I'd given mine?"

Axel clipped a nod.

"I'll talk to her."

"Nah, man. No worries." He lifted his hands. "I'm just here to grab my hours. Nothin' she say wasn't straight."

Another camper that much farther from his reach. All because of Gwen Doornbos. Was she trying to make his job impossible?

"Axel."

He kept moving. "Better get our free meal before it's gone. Few more weeks and we be back to stealin' it. Ain't that right, Renner?"

They all trudged up the hill.

Nate spun and slammed down the path.

Gwen's cabin grew as he closed in, remembering every trick Ryker taught him to rein in his anger. It was working. Barely.

His foot hit her porch as the front door opened. Blonde hair in a tight bun, shoulders in an even tighter line, she closed the door and spun straight into his chest. She jumped back. "Nate!"

"Gwen." He didn't budge. "Tell me about the lake this morning."

Her lips flat-lined. She pulled to her full height as if it would intimidate him. "Boys came through for an early morning swim, and I sent them on their way. If you'll remember, your rules state that lake isn't open until after breakfast and not without a lifeguard."

"They've all passed their swim tests. I gave them special permission, and I was meeting them down there." He fisted his hands at his side. "I know they told you that."

"Most of it." Her eyes narrowed. "But you can't change the rules whenever you feel like it. You made them for a reason, and if the kids keep seeing you break them, you'll lose any authority and all order."

"You make no sense." And she needed a glimpse in the mirror. "It's the same rule you bent for Nyla. I thought we already had this conversation."

"So did I." Her hands clasped her hips.

Nate sucked in a long breath. "I'm trying to earn their trust and respect, Gwen. That's what gets them to follow my authority."

Her dry laugh scraped his nerves. "Those kids don't have respect to give, and that won't change no matter how much you wish it." Acid dripped from her words. "They won't change."

Each annunciated word only fanned his flames and fed his determination to show her how wrong she was.

He brought his face centimeters from hers. "Get your things."

She leaned back. "Excuse me?"

"Your things." He ignored the scent of roses rolling off her and focused on her prickly thorns. "We're going on a little trip."

Gwen attempted to sidestep him. "I'm not going anywhere with you."

He blocked her. "You are."

"What? Are you going to pick me up like a caveman and carry me to your car?"

He allowed a lazy smile lined with resolve. "If I have to."

"You wouldn't."

He bent, thrusting his shoulder into her middle.

She slapped at him. "Stop it!"

Nate straightened. "Then you better get a move on."

"I have plans."

"Yep." He nodded. "With me."

She held still.

"I wasn't kidding about carrying you if I have to, Gwen." He crossed his arms, and her gaze flicked from his biceps to his face. "Your choice."

"Why are you forcing this?" Delicate fingers rested on her slim hips.

"Because in your anger and hurt, you're hurting these kids."

"Because I didn't let them swim?"

Nate paused. The next words he used needed to stem from compassion, not anger. And he couldn't quite bring up Nyla without anger yet. "Like it or not, they're here for the summer and so are you." Shouts drifted through the camp, their sound punctuating the fact. "And I'm hoping to help you remember that once upon a time you believed you could make a difference in their lives."

Her phone rang. She looked at the screen, stiffened, then silenced it. Her face smoothed into cement, and she brushed past him. "Knock yourself out."

He chuckled at the truth in those words. Trying to help her mimicked constantly tossing himself into a boxing ring. Hopefully he'd win, but he doubted it would come without a few bruises—for them both.

Chapter Twenty-One

Gwen stared at the trees whipping past her window. After she'd agreed to tag along, Nate had detoured to his cabin to quickly change out of his bathing suit before meeting her at his truck. Now they were about an hour outside of Hidden Lake. With the exception of her two phone calls—one to Bay making sure Granddad would be cared for today, and one to Granddad himself—the ride remained conversation free.

Nate flicked on his blinker, following Siri's commands to stay on M25. He'd plugged in their destination as some address in Bay City.

"What's in Bay City?" Curiosity finally won out.

"Old friends." He didn't spare her a look.

"I thought you weren't from the area."

"I'm not."

He was a fountain of information, wasn't he?

She reclined and closed her eyes. He didn't want to talk? Fine. Bet he hoped their destination would help him make some point she'd finally agree to. Let him live in his fantasy world a little longer, because by the end of the day he'd learn how serious she was about shutting his camp down.

"You know"—Nate finally broke his silence—"those boys you didn't want swimming this morning spent two hours doing yard work in the upper and lower fields. Lawn, weed whacking, picking up waste and clippings." He pinned her with a look. "So you wouldn't have to."

She swallowed, allowing his words to hit their mark. Still, it didn't change anything. The boys who killed Danny once stood by their sides, regularly distributing meals and ministering to their classmates. Never in her wildest dreams had she believed Carson capable of murder. Now she lived in the nightmare reality that he had taken Danny's life.

Nate sighed and shook his head. He drove another silent fifteen minutes before pulling into the parking lot of a run-down . . . bar? A chipped blue sign blinked that Rupert's was open for business.

She tossed Nate a look. "A bar? It's only ten in the morning."

He hopped out and waited for her by the hood of his Bronco. When she reached him, he stalked to the building, opening the door for her.

"Okay. Hold up." She crossed her arms. "Why are we here?"

"To meet my friends."

"In a bar."

"In a bar." He looked bored. Or simply tired of her. "Or do your preconceived notions about such establishments prevent you from darkening their doors?"

She narrowed her eyes. "I don't drink."

"Not even water?" He waved at her to enter. "Because I find that hard to believe."

A stocky figure appeared in the doorway. "I'm not paying Rup to air condition the great outdoors. Either come in, Nathanial, or have your argument outside."

Nate's lip twitched, and his eyes lightened. Gwen peered into the dark interior. Whoever filled that silhouette resembled a wall. Like the Berlin Wall.

Nate tipped his head toward the entrance. "You heard the man."

"Yes." She hesitated. "But I don't know the man."

He closed his eyes, sucked in a deep breath, and then leaned into her space. "Would you trust me for a millisecond. Please?"

Trust or curiosity, she didn't know which, pushed her inside. Light hit the shadowed figure and Gwen blinked. Shaved head, dark stubble lining his cheeks and mouth, bulging arms and legs, the man only eclipsed her by a few inches but had to outweigh her by a hundred pounds of muscle. His eyes, rich and full of life, contained the clearest color of amber she'd ever seen, with a line of black rimming his pupils. They reminded her of tiger eyes, except nothing predatory lingered in them.

He stepped forward. "You must be Gwen."

Surprised he knew her name, she met his handshake, fully expecting his grip to crush hers. Instead, his smooth hands held hers like glass. She met his smile. "I am."

"Ryker Zane." He released her, then clapped Nate on the back. "Told the guys you were coming. They're in the back." He motioned for them to follow.

The rear opened to a larger room with a few high-top tables in the center. They stood about waist high, were padded with what looked like two rubber squares attached to the surface and two vertical handles to the side of those. Weight lifting equipment lined the far wall, while phone books, pans, and long metal tubes cluttered the corner. What was this place?

Four other men milled about, looking over as they entered. "Nate." Their faces lit, and they approached him, slapping his back and pulling him into hugs that better resembled chest bumps.

The shortest of the group greeted her. "You must be Gwen."

How did they know about her when she had no clue who they were?

"I am."

He grinned. "I'm Tanner." He motioned down the line. "Chuck, Owen, and Jett."

"Pleasure to meet you all."

They nodded.

Ryker stood beside Nate. "Spoke to Elliot. I'm meeting him and Bryce for lunch next week."

Her curiosity spiked another notch. "You know them too?"

"I introduced Nate to them. When he came to live with me, the rule was he attend church." She looked at Nate, but he simply shrugged as Ryker continued. "I made sure he bumped into Bryce. He needed a friend who wouldn't put up with his crap, and I knew Bryce'd fit that bill."

Nate grinned. "Most definitely did."

"Then you two brought in Jude." Ryker shook his head. "Good times. Loud. But good." He smacked his hands together. "All right. We have a youth group coming tonight. You want to warm up the guys?"

Warm them up for what?

Nate shrugged off his flannel shirt, his smooth skin tanned from long days outdoors. "Who wants first try?"

Jett stepped forward. "First and final. Been practicing since you last saw me."

Nate grinned. "I haven't been gone that long." He stepped to one of the tables and bent his arm. "Bring those scrawny arms over here."

Gwen cleared her throat. "Uh, you arm wrestle?"

Nate shot her a glance, but Tanner answered, "Man made a name for himself."

"As an arm wrestler." Each syllable dropped.

Red filled Nate's cheeks. Instead of addressing her response, he drilled a glance into Jett. "You coming?"

"Great." Jett stepped up. "Make him mad and send me to the table."

"Already making excuses for losing?" Nate wiggled his fingers.

Ryker joined them and clasped his hand around theirs. "Ready?"

Both men nodded, and Ryker let go.

For looking like he didn't have a strong bone in his body, Jett put up a good fight. But Nate dropped him in under thirty seconds. He looked up. "Next?"

He plowed through his next two friends, beads of sweat popping on his temples. Finding a table in the corner, Gwen settled in, her curiosity over why he'd brought her here momentarily tempered by the impressive show in front of her. Arm wrestling wasn't all that bad to watch. Not when Nate stood at the table. Definitely explained those arms.

After beating Owen, Nate straightened. "Tanner?"

Tanner shook his head. "I think I'm warm enough."

Nate laughed and then shifted his gaze through the room till it landed on Gwen. He crossed to her, using the cotton sleeve of his t-shirt to wipe his forehead. He pulled out a chair, flipped it around, and straddled it.

"Why are we here, Nate? Besides you wanting to play with your friends."

He raised a brow. "Does there need to be a bigger reason?"

"No. But I'm thinking there is."

"Anyone hungry?" An older man popped his head in the door, grey tuffs of hair shooting in all directions. Man could double for Einstein. He looked as out of place here as she felt.

She glanced at the clock. Her stomach rumbled from missing breakfast but a greasy burger and beer were the last things she wanted.

"Need a menu?" Nate stood.

She dug in her purse and hauled out a granola bar from Bay's. "Thanks. I'm good."

He tipped his head. "You sure? Rup's a great cook."

"Rup?"

"You did see the name on the door, right?" He lifted an eyebrow. "Rupert's?"

"Right." Reaching for a napkin, she scrubbed at the chipped, yellow laminate. Something sticky caught the thin paper. She placed a second napkin over the spot. "I'm good."

Shaking his head, he walked away. "Suit yourself."

Gwen untied the tiny string holding the parchment paper on her granola bar while Nate and his friends ordered with Rupert. Something the old man said had Nate tossing his head back, deep laughter bellowing from his lips. No denying he was handsome, and joy only deepened his appeal. Unfortunately, she didn't bring that feeling out in him.

She shrugged out of her wayward thought.

After chatting a few minutes with his friends, he rejoined her, two glasses of water in his hand.

"Thanks." She accepted the glass and the straw he held out. He turned his chair around and sat as she swiveled a look around the room. "So how do you know all these guys?"

Nate sipped his water. His gaze rested on Ryker. "Long story."

"You just ordered. We'll be here a long time." She leaned forward. "And it's a long ride home. So I think you have time."

"Rup's a fast cook. Man's always prepared."

"No one's that fast."

He grinned.

How had she missed his crooked bottom teeth? Only added to the charm of his smile. One which grew when Rupert pushed through the door with a tray full of food. He stopped by their booth and dropped a chipped white plate with a stack of pancakes bigger than her head in front of Nate. Huge oats dotted the cakes, and blueberries the size of quarters rolled on top. The lightest of maple syrup seeped into the stack. Next arrived bacon sliced thicker than the pig itself and a mug of steaming coffee.

Her stomach roared.

Rupert left to serve the others.

Nate peeked up from his prayer with eyes that matched the blueberries on his plate and a smile that sweetly taunted her.

Her heart skittered.

"Thought you were fine." He reached for his silverware.

She swiped at the drool surely draining from the corner of her mouth. "I am."

"Uh-huh." He sawed into the stack. "Right." His eyes closed with the first bite. "The old man can cook."

"Doesn't look like standard bar fare."

Nate shrugged and quartered off another bite. "'Cause Rupert's isn't a bar."

Gwen straightened. "You said it was."

"No." He pointed his fork at her. "You said it was, and I didn't correct you." After another swallow he reached for his coffee. "Looks can be deceiving, can't they?"

The bitter truth of his words only made her more hungry for the sweetness of those stinkin' pancakes. She slumped down, arms crossed. "I knew we came for a lesson."

"I came for the food and company." He grinned. "But if your take-home is a lesson, it'll make a great doggy bag."

Gwen wadded up a napkin and launched it at him. Without even a glance, he dodged it. She growled.

He chuckled.

A plate of pancakes slid in front of her.

"Goes against every grain in my body to serve the lady last, Nathanial." Rupert plopped bacon down next.

"Appreciate it, Rup." Nate paused his sip of coffee.

"You better." Rupert leaned down to Gwen. "You enjoy this, and if you need anything else, holler."

"Thank you." Her smile met Rupert's clipped nod.

Nate slid over a fork and knife wrapped in a napkin, then dug back into his food.

He'd ordered her breakfast?

And had Rupert deliver it last?

Sweet and obnoxious all in one. Which about summed up the man sitting across from her.

Cakey, buttery, syrupy—the assaulting smells watered her mouth. Unwrapping the utensils, she unfolded the napkin and placed it on her lap. Next she sliced the pancake stack in half, then turned her plate and cut another straight line down the middle. Another quarter turn and another cut.

Nate cleared his throat.

She looked up, knife and fork poised over another cut. "Yes?"

"You have a plan for how to eat pancakes?"

"It's called proper table manners."

"For OCD support meetings." He jabbed his knife at her pancakes.

Gwen yanked them back. "Hey."

"Sometimes you have to dig in." His smooth tone sent her stomach tumbling.

She swallowed, then reached for her water.

"Is he being nice, or do I need to come over there?" Ryker's voice boomed across the room.

Gwen set down her glass, heat in her cheeks. "I'm not sure he's capable of nice." The tease slipped out and met Ryker's laughter. She leaned across the table. "Is he your dad?"

Gratitude and longing collided in his eyes. "No." He cast a glance at Ryker, then met her stare, shoving the rest of his pancakes away. "I met Ryker when he arrested me."

Like Rupert flipping the sign from open to closed on his front door, Gwen's expression changed that quickly. "You've been to jail?"

Nate nodded. "I meant it when I said I could relate to these kids."

She sat back, her pancakes untouched except for the one bite he'd forced her to take. He should have waited to drop his bomb on her, but was there ever a good time to tell anyone—especially Gwen–his shady past?

He'd enjoyed, entirely too much, the few moments of friendship that sprang up around them. Her laughter. Her goofy, slanted smile. The way light changed her eyes from a dull blue to the color of Lake Hideaway when the sun bounced off it, the subtle shift inviting him to dive in all the same.

And now he sounded like the guys he made fun of.

But the thought of losing even the glimpses of something more chilled him.

"Nate. You plan on letting that slip and not filling in the details?" Her low voice lost any sweetness. "Because I can tell you that isn't happening."

Her stomach grumbled. She attempted to cover it with a cough, but that failed.

Nate nodded to her breakfast. "You eat. I'll share. Don't want your stomach interrupting me."

"See, and here I thought it was because you cared." She stabbed another slice.

"I do." The words escaped, and he cleared his throat trying to suck them back in. But the way her jaw stopped midchew said she heard them. He swiped his mouth. "So, me. Jail."

Here went nothing. But they'd been at an impasse since the whole vaping incident, and the only way he could see to build a possible bridge involved sharing his story. Least that was his hope. There remained the possibility his past would ruin their future.

"Waiting." Her fork full of bacon waved in his face.

"You eat bacon with a fork?"

"It's greasy."

He shook his head. The woman's quirks might be the end of him.

Her eyebrows arched.

Nate cleared his throat. "I never knew my dad, and my mom was an alcoholic who, uh . . . She entertained men." Thirty years old and he still couldn't call it straight about his mom.

"She was a prostitute?"

But Gwen could.

"Yeah."

Complete silence at their table created a stark contrast to the noise at Ryker's. He caught his friend's attention and Ryker stood. After a moment, the guys filed out of the room.

"She didn't bring men to your house, did she?" Her focus moved from their retreat to him.

"Sometimes. Though all I knew as a kid was she worked nights." He curled and uncurled his straw wrapper. "By the time I made it to junior high, I finally understood what that entailed. Did my best to keep Lo and me away from her."

"Lo?"

"Calloway. My little sister."

Gwen nodded.

"So I'd send her to her best friend's house most nights. The Thompsons loved having her." He closed his eyes, unable to rewind, but forever wishing he could. He would have kept her by his side. Protected her from all she endured.

"You were a good big brother."

He should have been better.

He swallowed against his suddenly dry mouth. "Right before I turned seventeen, my mom disappeared, and I dropped out of school to take care of Lo."

Her mouth tipped down. Sadness or judgment? "Didn't a truancy officer show up at your door?"

"Not in my neighborhood." It wasn't exactly white picket fences. "I signed my mom's name on the paperwork. The school office didn't look closely."

Everyone in their community turned blind eyes.

"Anyway, I kept my head down and tried to make some money. I did whatever I could. Ran drugs. Lifted cars. B&E." He swallowed. "Until I discovered I was good at fighting."

"Fighting?"

"Mixed martial arts." Nothing to be proud of, at least not how he'd gone about it. "It's also when I ramped up the gambling. At first it was a release. It quickly became an addiction right up there with the fights. Then the two worlds mixed together in a sick kind of lucrative way. "

"You were under eighteen."

He lifted his brow.

"Right." She shook her head. "Fake ID."

"Yeah." In truth, there were few places he'd needed to lie about his age. "Got by for nearly a year without anyone interfering. Honestly thought Lo and I were better off that way." Pride had come before his fall. "Arrived home one night to find a man in our house holding her on the couch. At least that's what it looked like through all the booze I'd put back."

"It wasn't?"

"He had his arm around her, and she was crying, but it wasn't what I thought." He shuddered under the memories. "I don't remember much until Ryker had me face down on the carpet." One long pause, then, "I nearly killed the man, Gwen. He'd been helping Lo, and I nearly killed him."

She pushed her pancakes away. "You thought you were protecting your sister." Her words sounded hollow. Felt hollow.

"I was too drunk and too angry to hear her tell me to stop. She had to call the police." Nate massaged his eyes, trying to erase the images. "The man I . . . He was Ryker's friend. A youth pastor she'd called. I didn't even know she went to church."

Gwen straightened. "What was he doing in your house alone with her?"

"He'd taken Lo from a . . . bad situation. She was a mess. He thought someone would be home at our house—she didn't tell him any differently. She worried he'd take her away from me. When they got there and the place was empty, he called his wife." He could still hear the woman's cries. "She showed up before the ambulance." Now he looked at Gwen. "That man . . . He was never the same."

Across from him, Gwen closed her eyes. When she opened them, she focused on her fingers, her breaths slow and measured.

"Ryker arrested me and took Lo home for the night. He and his wife were registered foster parents. Thanks to Ryker, I wasn't sentenced as an adult." The first of many times Ryker had protected him. "I was in juvie for six months, and when I came out Ryker took me in."

Now she looked at him. "You had to have been eighteen by then. Why'd you stay?"

He lifted a shoulder. "Lo. She loved it there, and I couldn't leave her."

"Can't imagine that went well. House full of rules when you were used to none."

"Nope, it didn't. But I'd do anything for my sister, and they had custody of her. If I wanted to see her, I had to play by their rules." He'd hated it. But slowly things massaged into the hard places of his life, softening them. "Ryk ran a strong-man group as a side job, and he brought me on board. Gave me a healthy physical outlet for my anger in place of the fights. If we weren't practicing, we were performing at youth groups across the country."

"So you can rip a phone book in half?"

He chuckled, taking the light moment in the middle of heavy. "I'll show you sometime." His gaze caught on the padded tables. "My specialty became arm wrestling. I started entering matches, but then Ryk caught me betting on them. Pulled me out so fast, it made my head spin. He was on me twenty-four seven after that. It was either a show, gym with the guys, or helping out his friend's family."

"The one you hurt?"

Nate nodded. "Every Saturday I was at their house doing anything the wife needed."

Gwen straightened. "And she was okay with that?"

A fact that had taken him the longest time to understand. "She forgave me." He swallowed. "But every time I saw her husband, I couldn't forgive myself. Because of me, he sustained a traumatic brain injury and needed full-time care. Never left a bed again. Couldn't recognize her or their baby." Tears pressed against the back of his eyes. "I might not have killed him, Gwen, but I took his life away all the same."

Her stare dropped to the table. "That's why you relate to them."

Them. He held in his flinch. She'd made the connection he'd strung. He'd been what she hated. And it was precisely the association he needed her to make. Now if he could walk her back across the bridge.

"Look at me, Gwen. Please."

One long moment before she complied.

"Is it my past you see or who I am today?"

She stared at him long and hard, tugging her ear. Finally, "I see you. Today." His breath released, but then she blinked, and the shadows of her past filled her eyes. "But it doesn't take away the fact that I've lived the other side. And I don't know how to bring those two things together." She shook. "I see your change, but I'm not sure I can be the one to bring it anymore."

She was stuck in the middle.

"I understand." He tried for a smile. "But every day of my life I was told I wouldn't amount to anything, and I lived those words until someone poured into me." He tapped his chest. "Even now I fight those voices in my head that call me a failure." He leaned in. "If I'm going to help these kids, I can't have your voice in the background screaming the same."

Her eyes widened. "I don't think you're a failure."

"Only that I'm going to fail."

Red ran through her cheeks. Her gaze looked anywhere but at him.

He took her hand. "Agree with me or not, able to help me or not, I need your support."

She clenched her fingers around his. "I don't know if I can give it."

He watched her. "Can you at least try?"
She waited a beat. Then a slight nod.
It was all he could ask for.

Chapter Twenty-Two

Bombshell. Dropped.

Gwen stared into the cloudy mirror and gripped the edges of the leaky white porcelain sink. Behind her, grey paint chipped off the cement walls. The bathroom in Rupert's might be run-down, but it sparkled. Not a speck of dirt or grime—corners included—and even the air smelled fresh thanks to the pretty glass flower plugged into the wall.

Unexpected. Just like Nate.

The word truly suited him. Suited life since he'd arrived, really.

Deep voices and rumbles of laughter penetrated through the closed door. A few moments ago, Nate's friends returned. Gwen used the distraction to excuse herself, hiding in the bathroom. She needed a moment to process Nate's story.

That required longer than she could hole up in here though, because what he'd shared stood in direct opposition to what she knew. Not about Nate. He remained the same man she'd grown to care for in the past several weeks. The same man who'd returned her laughter and cracked open her heart—and therein lay the problem. His past combined with his present challenged her current beliefs.

The mess brewing inside her would take more than a made-up bathroom break to work through, so she exited the room. Her focus immediately latched on to Nate's. Arms crossed, he leaned against the far wall and stared her way. He'd been waiting for her, concern and insecurity lining his normally confident gaze.

"By the look on Nathanial's face, I'd say he told you a little about his past." Ryker stood two feet from her left.

She turned. "He told me a lot, actually."

Pulling a red stir stick from the corner of his mouth, Ryker looked from Nate to Gwen. "He told you how we met?"

Gwen nodded.

"Hmm." His thick frame stepped toward the equipment wall. "Wasn't easy for him to tell."

"Wasn't easy for me to hear," she mumbled softly.

The man had to possess some sort of animal instinct to go with those tiger eyes because he caught her quiet words. "Then use that as common ground." He picked up a few of the scattered metal pipes and placed them in a barrel. "Nathanial." Ryker nodded, his focus behind her. "You two leaving?"

Gwen glanced across her shoulder. Nate stood there, keys in his hand. "It's a beautiful day outside. Thought we'd enjoy it."

"Always preferred the outdoors." Ryker tossed the last pipe into the container, then extended his hand to Gwen. "Pleasure meeting you." Next he hauled Nate into a hug, slapping his back. "If you need anything—"

"I'll call." The way Nate finished Ryker's sentence sounded like a family routine.

The look that passed between them showed a bond stronger than family. These two hadn't asked to be father and son, they'd chosen to be.

Nate made the rounds to each of his friends. Easy to see how much they all loved him.

Gwen followed along, saying a quick good-bye to Rupert, then walked out the front door Nate held open. She blinked against the bright sunshine as warmth wrapped around her. "They're a nice group."

"They are." Gravel crunched under his feet. "Are we okay, Gwen?"

Straight and to the point. A trait becoming synonymous with Nate.

And while there might be a lot to settle in her brain, this was an easy answer. "We are."

A relieved smile stretched over his face. "Then where to now?" He jingled his keys in his pocket as they neared his car.

"Well, I planned on spending a part of my day at Little Blue, but I was kidnapped."

"I did not kidnap you." A semi rumbled by, ripping at his words as he held open her door. "I stroncouraged."

She parsed the words, then laughed. "Strongly encouraged?"

"Exactly." After closing her in, he hustled to his side.

His dark hair curled at the edges, and he'd pushed it off his forehead enough today that it stayed there. She liked the look. Liked the stark edges that lined his face. The way his soft eyes contrasted with those hard lines. Suited him. Strong and soft, a walking oxymoron.

He slid in and pulled out his phone. "Know the address off the top of your head?"

"You really would be lost without that thing, wouldn't you?"

"I even get lost with it." He punched in the street name she offered, and they pulled out from the parking lot following Siri's voice.

After they'd been traveling for some time, Gwen leaned against the window, looking at him. "One thing your story didn't cover."

"Yeah?"

"How did you get the money to do what you're doing at the camp?"

His fingers tightened around the steering wheel.

She waited.

"Remember when I said my fighting and gambling worlds merged?"

"Yes."

His neck cracked as he stretched it side to side, tension lining his shoulders. "When I said it was lucrative, I wasn't kidding. Especially when it all occurred under the table. I was too young for the pro circuit, but there were people who didn't care. I fell in with some pretty bad guys who'd have me throw or win fights based on bets made. At its height I was taking home several thousand a night. No taxes. No waiting for checks from online gambling sites. Just cash. Making money off my anger and addiction seemed a perfect fit." Now he looked at her. "Until that night."

His focus returned to the road, and only the rush of passing cars filled the cab for one long moment. "After jail I didn't fight again, but I did sink farther into gambling. Wasted a huge chunk of change before Ryker stopped me." He slowly shook his head as if it still ate at him.

"You needed help."

"And he made sure I got it." At Siri's command, he slowed for their destination. "While I went through some serious rehab, I put him in charge of my money and he invested what was left for me. Man should have worked Wall Street. To say he grew my investments is a huge understatement. He's been holding them until I started this camp." He turned onto the old gravel drive nearly swallowed by trees. "With his help, I also set up a college account for the child of the man I'd hurt along with covering all of his medical bills . . . and eventually his funeral expenses. He died last year."

Even when he'd shared his past, pain hadn't coated his words. Not like this. She reached out and squeezed his arm. "You're a good man, Nate."

"Not good. Forgiven. Changed by God's grace. And still in need of it every day."

Weren't they all?

Those three words collided with her heart. Wasn't that exactly what he'd been trying to show her?

Only two cars were parked in the small lot as they pulled in. Nate ducked to peer up at the tall white structure through his windshield as it rose into view. "So why is this place called Little Blue, anyway?" He parked and shut off the engine. "Did it used to be blue?"

"Nope." Gwen climbed out. "It's always been white."

"Then why the name?"

"Because at sunrise the light hits the dark here and starts turning the shadows into this grey-blue color. Like it's not night, but it's not quite morning yet either. Somehow that low light makes the lighthouse appear to be a gorgeous blue tone. The fishermen leaving in the morning started calling it Little Blue." She shrugged. "It obviously stuck because that's been its name for over a hundred years."

"Does it happen at sunset too?" He shielded his eyes with his hand.

"Only when the sun is rising. Though sunsets are beautiful here too."

"Maybe sometime we could catch one together." Hands in his pockets, his eyes crinkled around the edges as his wide smile landed on her, and it was like someone ran a feather across the insides of her stomach. Not how she pictured today at all. Definitely not the feelings she thought she'd encounter. Her past and future collided. They'd been doing that a lot lately, but each collision became less jarring.

"Maybe."

"I'll take a maybe." Smiling, he bent to pick up a shiny blue stone. "Uniqiful!"

The man had mastered the move from serious to light. She couldn't stop her smile. She bent for her own rock. "Just can't stop making up words, can you?"

"Somebody made up all the ones we currently use." He stood and brushed his sandy hands on his jeans. "Who says I have to stop?"

"Merriam-Webster."

His chuckles rolled across the warm air. Where Danny's had been light and peppery, Nate's came from his toes, deep and bellowing. He was like the Barry White of laughter.

The mental picture yanked a tiny snort from her.

His brow lifted at the sound. "What?"

She stifled her giggles. "Nothing."

He stepped closer. "You're cute when you laugh." Amusement bounced in his eyes. In a blink, the amusement turned to something she hadn't seen in years. Something she still recognized. Something that had her fighting heat and cold all at once.

Her heart raced forward like a horse out of the chute, but tight reins yanked it back. "Danny used to say the same thing."

Nate's grin dimmed, and he bent to grab another stone. Better than the awkwardness she'd tossed out.

Short of a lobotomy, though, Danny would always be a part of her. How was she supposed to move forward when he would always occupy space in her heart? Every inch Nate worked into her life met territory already occupied. Flirting with him felt light and heavy all in one breath. His warm voice replacing Danny's was like recording over one of her most precious memories. And the mere thought of another man touching her? Kissing her?

She hooded her eyes, slowly sneaking a glance at Nate.

Yes. She'd thought about it. But couldn't wrap her brain around sharing those moments with anyone else. Her lips belonged to Danny. Any attraction was his and his alone. How could she let even a seed of another thought take root?

Her phone rang in her pocket. She snatched it out and checked the screen. Marlene. Again. She had to answer.

Turning from Nate, she connected the call. "Hello?"

"Gwen?" The strained voice only added to her confusion. To her guilt. Thinking of another man was bad enough, but today of all days?

She'd been wrong to think she could move forward.

Gwen stepped away. "It's me, Marlene."

"Where are you? You haven't answered your phone, and I sent David to check on you. Someone from the camp said you'd left with Nate?" *How could you?* She didn't say the three words, but they clanged through the air nonetheless.

"He had something to show me."

"Today?"

"Yes." She snuck a look behind her and found Nate watching.

Marlene inhaled as if resetting herself. "But you're still planning on Danny's grave with us later, right? Like we do every year."

"No. I . . . I should have said something sooner. I'm not sure if I'm going this year."

Nate stepped closer. "Need me to take you back?"

Gwen shook her head.

Marlene's voice could cut a diamond. "Is that him? Are you still with him?"

"Yes. But he isn't why I'm not coming. I hadn't planned on spending the day with anyone. Things kind of happened." And now she was rambling like a teenager caught with a boy past curfew.

"No. Not in this. In this you had a choice." Marlene's voice shook. "And you're choosing to be with that man."

Something shifted across the phone lines. Marlene's voice crept through in muffled tones. Gwen pressed the phone to her ear but couldn't tell what she said. Then David's voice came on. "Marlene needed to step away."

"Is she okay?"

"She will be." He cleared his throat. "We knew this day would come, Gwen. We knew you'd move on with another man. Doesn't help that it's today, though. Or that man."

"What?" Gwen straightened. "No. I'm not with—" Nate shifted, crinkling his brow. She faced the other way again. "Tell Marlene I'm sorry. I should have talked to her sooner about today, but I didn't want to hurt either of you. I just need . . ."

"To live again." David supplied for her. "It's time for you to do that. It's not easy for any of us, but I understand."

Was that what this was with Nate?

Gwen rubbed her temple. She didn't know. All she knew was she had to pull herself from the past, and maintaining this yearly ritual wouldn't allow for that. Thoughts of her future couldn't start until she faced forward again.

"Thank you, David."

"I need to check on Marlene."

"I'm not trying to hurt her."

He hesitated. "Everything about Danny's death hurts, Gwen. I'm not sure it will ever stop." The line went dead.

At first Nate planned to walk away and give Gwen privacy for her call. But then her eyes filled, her voice shook, her hand trembled. He'd sift through her words later. Right now all he wanted to do was hold her.

So he opened his arms. She hesitated, then stumbled into them. She wept, he stroked her hair. "Hey," he soothed. "It's okay, Gwen. You're okay."

Her head shook beneath his hand.

Framing her face, he pulled her shiny cheeks up until she looked him in the eye. "Yes. You are."

Her gaze locked on his, pulling the strength he offered. Then she stepped back. Wiped her eyes. "You're right. I am."

His empty arms rested at his sides. "How can I help?"

She massaged the base of her bare left ring finger. "It's the anniversary of Danny's death today. I normally spend it with his parents, remembering, and then we visit his gravesite."

Might as well have sucker punched him and expected him not to react. She didn't need any more emotion added to this day. "And you're here with me instead." Explained the phone call, but not why she'd come with him. "Why didn't you tell me back at camp?"

"You threatened to toss me over your shoulder."

"I wouldn't have." Did she really think he'd have kept pressing? "Not if you'd told me. You have to know that, Gwen."

A tiny smile. "I do. But I wanted to go with you."

That was news. "You didn't look like it."

"I might have been a little peeved at the moment, but if I didn't want to go, you couldn't have made me." Her focus drifted over the lake. "*You* have to know that."

"I do." She was more stubborn than he'd ever been. Might make for an interesting combination—not that they were anywhere near finding out. The breeze caught a strand of her hair, and he itched to brush it behind her ear. "So why come with me?"

"The last four years have been defined by one moment. Making it through today without it being a giant memorial was my crazy way of trying to take back control. To start marking my years by a normal calendar again. Not the one that begins and ends with Danny's death."

Her voice pinched on those last two words. He lowered his. "How's that working for you?"

She tugged on her earlobe. "How's it appear to be working?"

He offered a tiny shrug. "Not so well."

"And again today we agree on something." She rested on her heels. "Maybe friendship isn't too far out of the realm of possibilities."

"I thought we were already there."

Her head tipped. "Maybe we are." Then a long sigh as she stared into the crystal blue sky.

She had to be exhausted. "Want me to take you home?"

She shook her head.

"To see your friends?"

Again, her head shook.

"Then what?" He kept it gentle, even injected a teasing lilt. "I mean, I'm good, but even I can't read a woman's mind."

This won him a smirk. "Might help if this woman knew what she wanted to do right now."

For someone who always had a plan, admitting that she didn't know what she wanted couldn't be easy. He looked out over the rocky shoreline. Colorful stones ran in every direction. "Then let's hang here until you decide."

"You don't have to get back to camp?"

"Jude has things under control for the day."

Her hesitation lasted another minute before she nodded and headed to the right. Wanting to allow her space, he angled left. Every few minutes he'd cast a glance her way. Sunlight spilled across her blonde hair, pulling out the highlights and golden streaks woven through it. Her eyes crinkled along the edges as she concentrated on a stone she'd picked up. Pocketing it, she continued on her way.

Half an hour later, she strolled to his side and opened her palm. Inside lay two smooth stones that, when placed together, formed the ragged image of a heart. "Mind driving me somewhere?"

"Anywhere." He ran a finger along their edges. "Those are beautiful."

"Thanks." The lighthouse tossed a long patch of shade on the ground, covering Gwen.

"So where are we going?"

Light bathed her as she stepped from the shadow. "Danny's grave."

Chapter Twenty-Three

"You don't really have to come along. Not if you need to get back." Gwen peered across the cab at Nate, a grove of pine trees whipping past outside his window. Now that he knew the destination, she wanted to offer him an out in case he felt uncomfortable. "You could drop me at camp, and I'll drive myself."

A lock of his hair dropped over his forehead as he shook his head. Her fingers itched to brush it in place. He did so himself. "That's too much extra driving." He glanced her way, not a hint of discomfort on him. "I'll stay in the truck and give you privacy."

Gwen tugged her ear. "Not going today was my show of strength. And yet I'm still winding up there. What does that say about me?"

"That you loved your husband." Nate checked his blind spot and switched lanes. "Danny will always be a part of you, Gwen. It's okay to remember him. Doesn't mean you're living in the past."

"Feels like it." And that feeling grew older by the day, making her restless. "I'm not sure how to remember him and move on. Those two concepts seem counterintuitive."

"You'll figure it out." He squeezed her hand. "One step at a time."

"Think I've taken enough *one steps* to get me somewhere by now."

"You're just building endurance."

Interesting thought. She tipped her head. "Yeah. I suppose I am."

Except for the occasional direction, they stayed silent until Nate pulled into the cemetery. Gwen rolled down her window. A gentle breeze cupped her cheek. Birds called to each other and squirrels raced across the lush green lawn. Life where death wanted to reign. She directed him to Danny's grave.

He stopped a few feet away. "Take your time."

Her feet slipped to the black asphalt, and she slowly closed her door. She hesitated, then turned back to Nate. "Come with me?"

Three lines deepened across his forehead. "I don't mind waiting."

She didn't doubt that, not after how sweet he'd been to drive her here, but this year needed to be different. It was time to share today with someone new. Nate pushed her to remember and still move forward. Something she had no clue how to do in this realm but desperately wanted to discover— even if it scared her.

"I know, but I'd like you to come."

With a swift nod, he unbuckled and climbed out. He matched her pace, hands jammed into his worn jeans pockets, and his Camp Hideaway T-shirt stretched snuggly across his chest. His heart resembled Danny's in many ways, but that created their only commonality.

Grass crunched beneath their feet as they approached Danny's headstone. Daniel David Doornbos.

"I used to call him 3D." She ran her finger over the last name. The one tie she still held to him. "It sounds funny when people call me Mrs. Doornbos. It's me, but it's not." She didn't look at Nate, but she felt his presence. Sure and steady. Strong. Chaotic in so many ways, and yet still peaceful.

He stepped forward, squinting at the stone. "If we live, we live for the Lord; and if we die, we die for the Lord. So, whether we live or die, we belong to the Lord." His deep voice recited the words from Romans. Then he gently grasped her wrist and turned it. The rough pads of his fingers ran over her tattoo.

She watched as he traced each letter, their permanence a decision she'd never regret. "It was as much to make me drag myself out of bed everyday as it was to remember him. I needed the reminder to live when I didn't have the will to on my own."

"You know," he spoke gently, like his touch, "there's more ways to live than getting out of bed each day."

"What happened to one step at a time?"

"What happened to wanting that journey?"

Remember. And move forward.

"Gwen. Read that verse again."

She didn't need to. The thing was branded on her mind. Her wrist. Her heart.

But Nate didn't relent. "Is that how Danny lived his life?"

"He's dead, isn't he? Because he died for the Lord."

"Would he have changed a thing?"

His words stopped the churning inside. Stillness prevailed.

No. No, he wouldn't have. If Danny stood right here beside her, knowing his life would be taken, he'd still have run straight toward the same ending. Because he also lived for the Lord.

Nate spoke into her silence. "I looked the verse up after you told me about it. Explored the Greek word *záo*. Do you know its true meaning?"

He had to know she did. "To live."

"As in to experience God's gift of life." He brushed his thumb against the scrolled letters. "And from everything I've heard, that's what Danny did. He worked to show that gift to the kids around him." Nate paused. "It's time you start living again, Gwen. This shell isn't what God wants, and it isn't what Danny would have wanted."

She gently pulled from his grasp. "Easier said than done." Her shoulders nearly touched her ears, then she released them with one long, sorrowful sigh. "I look at those kids, and I see nothing but black holes." She tapped her chest. "I feel nothing except lingering resentment. I simply don't still have a fiery passion to reach them or the faith to believe they can change."

"What about Nyla?"

Her name pricked at the hard shell around Gwen's heart. No. The little girl had already cracked it, just like Nate. "She's different." He was different.

"She doesn't believe she is." He held her gaze. "Not since she heard you say otherwise."

Confusion stilled her. "What are you talking about?"

"Nyla overheard us at the ropes course."

Gwen squeezed her eyes closed. No wonder she had been absent over the past couple days. "No."

The boys' faces from this morning filled her mind, their hurt and defeated expressions morphing onto Nyla's face. What had she done? They'd offered help. She'd offered bitterness. "Nyla and then the boys this morning." Her harsh words ran on a loop, increasing in speed and intensity. She pressed her hand against her forehead. "I should stay away."

Nate didn't let her off so easily. "That right there shows me you see more than black holes." He stepped into her space and grasped her chin, lifting it until her eyes met his. "You care, Gwen. Fight it all you want, but you do. If you didn't, you wouldn't be upset about hurting them."

He was right. And it scared her to her core.

But who her bitterness and anger were turning her into scared her even more.

Softly tugging her chin from his grasp, she offered a tiny smile. "I think I do need a minute alone here."

He gave her a look full of understanding. "Take all the time you need." Turning, he strolled to his car.

Digging the stones she'd collected earlier from her pocket she knelt by Danny's grave. She took the right side of the heart—the side he stood on at their wedding, the side he slept on in their bed—and placed it in the grass beside his gravestone. "I'll always remember." She touched the sun-warmed granite. Her hand lingered for a long moment, then she stood.

And took one more step.

Darkness fully blanketed camp by the time they returned. Turning off his engine, Nate leaned his head back. "Long day."

"Long but good." Gwen smiled at him. "Thank you."

"Any time." Easy promise.

She hesitated before more words tumbled out. "Do you think I could speak with Nyla tonight?"

He glanced at his watch. The kids would be in their cabins, but it wasn't lights out yet. "We could probably do that. I'd like to be there, though."

"I assumed. And I think it's a good idea."

They both climbed from the Bronco and headed for Nyla's cabin. He loved the nighttime soundtrack of camp. Kids' voices floating through open windows. Crickets chirping. Even the slight rustling of the evening wind.

Gwen scuffed alongside him, scattering pebbles. "Nyla is Axel's sister, isn't she?"

"Where'd that come from?"

She shrugged. "Something he said at the lake today. It clicked into place when you told me she'd overheard our conversation." She shivered in the light breeze. "Do they live together?"

"No. Different dads. His wanted him. It wasn't a good thing."

Reaching the cabin, they jogged up the steps. Nate knocked, and Kylie stuck her head out. "Oh, hey, Renner. Did you need something?"

"We wanted to speak with Nyla."

Her brows rose, but she nodded and called for the girl. Nyla appeared at the door, smiling, until she caught sight of Gwen.

Beside him, Gwen dipped to look her in the eye. "Hey, Nyla. I wondered if we could talk?"

"Ain' got nothing to say."

"But I do."

Indecision marred the girl's features.

"I think you'll want to listen to her, Nyla. I'll stay too, if you'd like," Nate coaxed.

She met his eyes, nodded, then stepped onto the small porch. She stared at the rough wooden planks, her toes nudging sand into the spaces between slats.

Gwen didn't let the silence grow but spoke straight into it. "I've missed you for yoga these past few mornings."

Nothing.

Gwen peeked up at him, her eyes shiny, and he offered a tiny smile of encouragement.

"Nyla, I wanted to say I'm so sorry"—her voice broke, and she swallowed—"Those things I said, they weren't right. I . . . My husband was killed, and sometimes that hurt spills out of me in not so nice ways."

Nyla stopped fidgeting, but she remained silent.

Gwen didn't give up. "Will you please forgive me? I never meant to hurt you."

"You didn't hurt me." False bravado lined Nyla's limbs. "I jus' been too busy for your class."

"Even so, I said things I shouldn't have, and I wanted to apologize. I hope you'll find time to join me again, because I've missed you."

Now Nyla shifted a glance at Nate and then to Gwen, who offered a smile. She fidgeted with the edge of her t-shirt. "Won't matter none anyway. I'm gonna get kicked out."

Nate straightened. "Why would you say that?"

Her shoulders lifted in a defensive stance, as if bracing herself from the inevitable. Yet she twirled her hair like a lost little girl. "Ain't Mr. Jude told you yet?"

"Told me what?" Nate shared a questioning glance with Gwen, whose own face showed confusion.

She toed the ground again. "I lost my inhaler."

Lost it, or had it stolen?

"Nyla," Nate spoke her name gently.

When she refused to look at him, Gwen softly touched her arm. "You're not in trouble. Everybody loses things sometimes. Right, Nate?"

Gwen glanced from him to Nyla, offering her an empathetic expression that showed off how amazing she'd been at this work once. Her capacity to care. Did she realize she was tapping back into that ability?

"Right," he agreed. Though he needed to speak with Jude to obtain more details, he didn't think Nyla had done anything that would warrant them kicking her out.

When she cast her mocha eyes on him, he nearly broke with the worry there. Dipping to her height, he met her anxiety head on. "Mistakes happen. Owning up to them is the important part, and you did that. I'm proud of you."

"I am too," Gwen added.

She shifted uneasily at their praise. No doubt they were words she didn't hear often.

He straightened. "Any idea where you last saw your inhaler?"

"Campfire. Mr. Jude was going to search to see if I dropped it there."

Now that things had settled some, a little time alone between these two might be good. "I think I'll go help him and let you two ladies catch up, if that's okay?"

Gwen smiled at him and mouthed, "Thank you."

With a nod, he descended the steps and headed to where they held bonfires. Jude walked between the log benches, eyes on the ground. They lifted as he heard Nate approaching.

"Hey there," Jude greeted. "How'd your day go?"

"Good."

"You and Gwen bury the hatchet?"

"For now." And hopefully it remained buried. He much preferred the openness they'd shared today. Felt like progress in all the right spaces. "I hear Nyla lost her inhaler. Think Axel has it?"

Jude's mouth swished to the side, and he crossed his arms. "Maybe. But if he does, it's hidden well. Not in his cabin or on him."

"You already searched him?"

Jude nodded. "He didn't like it."

"The kid's definitely got an attitude."

"He does. Right now he's following the rules, but you can see in his eyes he's ready to bolt."

Nate dragged a hand through his hair. "Then why stay? We don't force him to."

"Free meals. Warm bed. Not having to live with his dad for the summer. Ability to keep an eye on Nyla. And access to the kids he's trying to recruit into whatever gang he thinks he can start."

"He wouldn't last two seconds."

"Maybe. Maybe not." Jude shrugged. "He's smart enough to realize he'd never make it under another gang. Prideful enough to think he can start his own."

"And that's what will get him killed." Nate paced. Frogs and cicadas called from the tree line. "It's like a timer in my head. Six more weeks to reach him."

Jude's eyes tracked him. "Not on you. You do your part, Axel's got to do his. No shouldering his responsibility, Nate. You'll burn out by summer's end if you don't get your head on straight." He paused, then, "You can't save them all."

A phrase he'd grown tired of. "Now you sound like Gwen."

"No. I don't. You two are on opposite extremes, and the truth is someplace in the middle."

A niggling in his gut had him listening.

"You think you can, which is what drives you, and that's good. It's essential. Each kid out there needs to know you believe in them, and you should because God can make a difference in every last one. But it won't happen before they leave here. For some you're planting seeds. Others will hear the Word and let it roll off.

"You don't give up because you can't reach them all, and you don't beat yourself up when you *don't* reach them all. You just"—he pointed a look at Nate—"do."

But if he couldn't use his messed up past to influence these kids, then what had it been for? "I'll try."

"That's all God's asking." Simply stated, as if Jude didn't question the fact. "You're looking at starting several of these camps, Nate. Don't limit God, but don't try to become Him either, or you'll crash and burn. Fast."

The words settled into his bones, feeding his soul. He clapped his friend on the back. "Thanks."

"Why I'm here."

Nate lifted a brow.

"Okay. So the advice is a fringe benefit." Jude's attention strayed to a nearby cabin where laughter poured out the window. After it quieted, he refocused on Nate, his face drawn and serious. "Maybe you could give me some back?"

No doubt the conversation turned toward Calloway. "Anytime. You know that."

Jude's hand cupped his mouth, as if he was trying to discern which words to release. As he looked at Nate, the way this situation wore on him shown in his eyes. "Why hasn't she called?"

"Give her time."

"I have." He stared at the trees. "I thought," his voice cracked and he swallowed. "I thought I was the one she'd run to." He hesitated, then dug in his pocket, pulling out the princess cut solitaire Calloway had left on his kitchen table. "Instead I'm the one she ran from, and I don't even know why." He twirled the ring between his fingers.

"She hasn't given up, Jude. She loves you."

"Has a funny way of showing it."

"Maybe." Nate might not be able to say much with certainty where Lo was concerned, but he was positive of this. "But she does."

Jude stood silently, no doubt twisting his thoughts like the ring in his hand. Finally, he pushed the diamond into his pocket and looked his way. "That inhaler isn't here. Nothing more we can do tonight. I'm headed for bed, and I'll talk to Paula in the morning. See if anyone handed one in."

Jude made it several steps before Nate spoke. "She's coming back, Jude."

"And I'll be here." He stopped but didn't turn around. "Though I'm not sure in what role." Then he disappeared into the night.

Nate's heart pinched. Lo needed to come clean with Jude. He should be her shoulder, not Nate. Convincing her of that was like digging to China. Sounded plausible but wasn't happening.

He tore a wrapper from another Laffy Taffy. If he survived this summer with his head and heart intact, it would be a miracle.

Chapter Twenty-Four

Five more days passed with ease. Though Nyla's inhaler remained missing, she no longer feared being kicked out. Paula issued her a new one, and Nyla hadn't let it out of her sight. She'd also returned for morning yoga and snagged two other girls to join her. Those three introduced Gwen to more kids throughout each day, slowly enlarging her circle of relationships. She still avoided the JCS crowd, which was easy since Jude had them working another project in town.

After two long afternoons and evenings filled mainly with rain, Nate had shown up on her front porch this morning begging to take advantage of today's sunshine and the new kayaks Huron Our Lake delivered yesterday. Kayaking wasn't on her list for the day, but truthfully, this entire summer hadn't been on her list.

Ever so slowly, she was moving forward. Tackling the fears that had been a part of life for the last few years. Maybe even the prejudices that had layered on without her noticing. When Nyla extended her a second chance, something pricked inside and made her take a long look. How could she ask for a fresh start but not extend one to others?

Maybe these kids could change. Hope slowly rebloomed, but even cacti produced flowers. Didn't mean they still couldn't inflict a world of hurt if not handled correctly. Which left her uncertainties alive and well. Was the known risk worth the uncertain outcome of transformation? The answer eluded her. Until one settled inside, she couldn't look farther ahead than this summer. But God had brought her this far, so she didn't have to know tomorrow.

Which, for this schedule girl, was nearly unheard of.

At least she could tackle the list in front of her. Picking up her clipboard, she set to work.

Half hour later she stood, hands on her hips, and surveyed the area. Kayaks washed. Paddles attached. Life jackets arranged by size. Two coolers packed with food, another with medical supplies, matches, and hot dog forks, and a last with beach towels. And one waterproof bag with walkie-talkies.

They were set.

She inhaled this serene moment. Chaos was about to descend.

Which meant she needed to grab her inhaler and change into a swimsuit.

Near the tree line she slipped into her discarded sandals. The hint of bacon wove its way through the trees, and her stomach growled. Okay. She'd need to eat too.

Hustling up the trail to her golf cart, she let the bacony aroma guide her. The low grumble in her middle turned to a roar. Eating came first.

Her cart practically drove itself to the mess hall. Voices swelled inside, each competing to be heard. Laughter topped it all. The longer these campers stayed, the more joy flowed over the campground. Each day these kids seemed more like kids and less like the worn-out adults they'd been forced to become. Even if they returned to their old life and nothing changed, at least they'd hold these memories. Maybe that alone made it worth this camp being here.

Gwen paused, her hand on the door. Life transformed around her. Not only in these kids, but her too. She hadn't expected it. Hadn't wanted renovation in this way. And yet it was happening.

The door pushed open, and Nate's lazy smile greeted her. "Coming in?"

She'd sort through her revelation later. Right now she needed to deal with the enticing distraction in front of her. Nate's worn navy T-shirt pulled over his muscles, the waves of his hair framed his high forehead perfectly, and dark stubble coated his cheeks in a way she used to find messy until him.

"I don't have an actual paper invitation, if that's what you're waiting for." The rumble of his voice lightened into a teasing lilt.

She snapped her gaze from his cheeks to his impossibly blue eyes, smiled, and stepped past. "Sorry. I was distracted."

"Yeah." He dipped low to her ear. "I noticed."

A shiver ran up her spine, and she nudged him away. "Get over yourself."

"I'd probably have an easier time of that than you."

She whipped to a stop, open-mouthed. "You're full of it."

He shrugged. "And you're easy to goad."

Maybe she'd turn the tables. "You know, when I was little, Granddad told me boys only bugged you if they liked you."

Nate crossed his arms over his broad chest. "Your granddad is a wise man." Then he spun and walked off. "Meet you down by the beach," he tossed over his shoulder.

No words. None at all. Nothing but a dry throat she tried to swallow past and failed miserably. What was up with this morning? Her thoughts were darting off in their own direction so fast they needed a leash. If she had any hope of catching the wandering rebels, she required protein and coffee in mountain-size quantities. She stepped to the buffet.

Flipping open the first silver pan, she frowned. Pancakes didn't belong over here, not with waffles and syrup at the other end of the table. Picking up the pan, she positioned it on her right hip before the searing heat registered. With a hiss she let go, and the pan clattered across the floor. Every head whipped in her direction, Nate's easily topping them all. Fire spiked up her spine and into her cheeks.

Two boys stepped forward along with Nyla and scooped pancakes off the floor. Nate strolled over, taking her hand. "You okay?"

"Just embarrassed."

He tenderly rubbed his thumb over her palm. "No blisters."

His touch heated her skin far more dangerously than the pan had.

She tugged from his grasp, and he turned to the boys cleaning up her mess. "We'll get it, you guys. But thanks for being willing." He nodded toward the door. "Bell's about to ring for your activities. Why don't you clear your plates and head out."

The two boys left, but Nyla stood between Nate and Gwen. "I'll stay."

The bell rang, and the room began to empty as fast as if it were the fire alarm.

"Go get your suit on. You're kayaking with us today, aren't you?" Gwen bent to pick up pancakes.

"Yes, ma'am."

Gwen peered up. Nyla stood over her, arms straight and taut at her side, feet braced like a warrior prepared for battle. Judging by the fact it was Nate she faced, the battle she anticipated included him.

Gwen slowly rose and placed a hand on her shoulder. "Nate won't hurt me, Nyla. He's not upset. He's only staying to help."

Nate's brows rose and dipped so quickly Gwen nearly missed it. He knelt down. "In fact, how about I clean and you two get your swimsuits? Girls take twice as long as guys to get ready." He tossed pancakes at the pan on the floor. Two hit, one missed. "Besides, I need to work on my aim."

A laugh escaped Nyla, and her whole body relaxed. "Yeah?"

"Yeah."

She stepped toward the door. "You coming, Ms. Doornbos?"

"Right on your heels." Gwen bent to Nate. "Thank you. That was sweet."

"It's all that candy I eat seeping out."

"Take the compliment, will you?"

"Go get ready, will you?" Like mini frisbees he tossed two more pancakes at the bin. They both missed.

"You'll be here until dinner." She laughed and crossed to the door. Her palm rested on the cool glass as she pushed it open. Off-tune whistling yanked her back. She turned and a pancake smacked her in the face. Nate's lopsided grin deepened.

Apparently his aim was perfectly fine.

Nate sliced his paddle into the water, chatter trickling over the surface as several groups made their way across Hidden Lake. They were more than halfway to the back bay, and all the kids easily kept pace. Nate snuck a glance at Gwen, her hair swept up in a bun not quite as tight as usual. A few strands escaped and cascaded along the curve of her neck. Nyla said something, and Gwen tipped her head back, laughing.

Life had never gone in a linear path for him and sometimes he'd begrudged it. But meeting Gwen? Best surprise he'd ever had around a blind curve.

"See those two logs there?" She called, pointing her paddle straight out. "That's where we're aiming everyone."

The boys let out a yell and dug in. No way they'd come in last. If he weren't in the canoe laden down with coolers, he'd be right up there with them.

Water splashed across his back, the cool wetness sliding beneath the neck of his T-shirt and trickling between his shoulder blades. Goosebumps rippled across his skin.

"Oops." Gwen's kayak raced past.

"Paybacks," he called.

She tossed a grin full of crazy back at him. "Exactly."

He stopped paddling and watched her free movements. With every layer she shed, another string attached him to her. Pretty soon she'd have him completely twisted up, and she wouldn't even realize it.

Unless he gave in and kissed her.

He tipped his head. Looked at where that loose hair tickled her neck again. Not a bad idea.

Storing the thought, he paddled for shore. The trees grew larger as he neared the bank, and moss-covered logs extended into the water. One of the boys reached down to steady his canoe as he came to ground. "Gotcha."

"Thanks, Henry." Nate tossed his leg over the side and climbed out. "Can you grab one of the coolers?"

"Sure."

Nate snagged the other and headed for shore.

Gwen passed him, wading through the water and out to his canoe. "Finally made it."

"Didn't want to show off." He winked.

By the time he'd dumped his cooler on the sand, she neared shore with hers. "You know, the guys and I can get those."

"I do know that." Arms full, muscles straining, she didn't stop till she dropped hers an inch farther on shore than his. "I also know I can help."

She turned and faced him. The breeze lifted the strands at her neck, and she shivered. She dug a bobby pin from her pocket and reached for them. His hand stilled hers. "Leave it."

Under the roughness of his skin, hers felt like silk. The barest thread of her pulse sped beneath his fingertips, but it was her eyes that made his heart speed up. Wide. Surprised. Curious. Even a hint of uncertainty. Beneath all those layers another emotion rose, pressing the accelerator on his pulse.

Awareness.

Something dropped by his feet.

Henry stood beside another tub he'd delivered. "Need me to get the last one too, Renner?"

Gwen blinked and stepped back but didn't look away. Nate bared a slow smile and when she matched it, he nearly reached for her again. Her awareness was giving way to curiosity, and he'd more than happily oblige her inquisitiveness.

"Renner?"

Gwen's smile grew. "Mr. Reynolds is looking a little overheated. I'll grab it. He better jump in the lake." Her palm patted his chest as she stepped past.

He caught her wrist. Leaned down. "Take a walk with me tonight?"

The tiniest hesitation held his heart in his throat.

"Cool! Rock N' Rye," one boy called from beside an open cooler. "That's old."

Gwen puffed laughter through her nose as her head shook. She peeked up at him. "I'd love to." Slipping her hand from his, she took off for the last load of supplies.

"Renner! We need another guy on our team." A group of boys tossed a football in the air.

Nate jogged to join them. An hour whipped by in a flurry of water football, chicken, and tag-team races. By the time he dragged himself out from the water, his muscles hurt and his stomach begged for lunch. Snagging a towel from the bin on shore, Nate dried off. Gwen stood beside a baby bonfire.

"How come you didn't join us?" He added wood to the tower.

She knelt down with giant tongs and repositioned the log he'd added. Behind him an army of boys descended.

"Food ready?" they asked.

Gwen pointed the tongs toward them. "That's why." She nodded toward where the girls already congregated beside the two make-shift tables created from fallen logs. "Through the line in order, boys."

Nate followed her nod. A line starting with plates and ending with hot dogs and roasting forks ensured everyone would find what they needed and move efficiently. Only problem was starving boys didn't want to be efficient. They wanted to eat.

"That'll take forever."

"This is crazy."

"Can't we eat the dogs raw?"

Their comments pulled the girls' attention who now nodded. Gwen's jaw clenched. Anyone else jumped in with a complaint, and she'd roll over the edge.

"Hey, guys. We can handle a little patience." He picked up one of the roasting forks. "How about I get a few dogs going while you get your plates ready? Eat some chips, get your drinks. Hot dogs'll be up in five."

He shrugged at Gwen. Her tightened jaw gave a little. "I thought they'd want to roast them themselves, or I'd have already done it."

Nate pushed five hotdogs onto a fork, handed it to her, then started another. "You've obviously never been a starving teenage boy."

"Obviously." She rotated her fork over the flames, the hot dogs browning evenly.

After a few moments, black bubbles raised along his. "You know you're missing the best flavor on those things."

"Charcoal and ashes?"

"Ever tried it?"

She didn't answer.

Nate twisted his to blacken the other side. "Don't believe me?"

"Nope."

"Then how about a blind taste test?"

"I'm not eating a charred hot dog."

"Not you." He pulled his out and examined them. Nearly perfect. "We cut a few pieces up of each and let the kids decide."

"Because a teenager's palette is that discerning."

"We're talking hot dogs here, not caviar."

"True." She held hers up, perfectly browned. "So what's the winner get?"

Only one thing he wanted. Had wanted for some time now. Dare he ask?

Hesitation nearly stole his words but then he leapt. "A kiss. Tonight after our walk."

He watched for her reaction. Waited.

She cut her eyes to the teens. "Hot dogs are ready."

Way to go. He'd moved too fast, and she shut him down. Would probably cancel their walk now too.

"And save room for a taste test later," Gwen called to them.

He turned so quickly his neck popped. "We're on?"

With that look on her face, tonight couldn't come fast enough.

"How could I pass that up?" She added more hot dogs to her fork to keep cooking. "Sounds like I win either way."

Chapter Twenty-Five

What on earth had she been thinking? Gwen stared at her reflection in the mirror. Scratch that. What *was* she thinking? Flirting with Nate had been bad enough, but actually getting cleaned up, hair flowing loose against her shoulders and minty gloss on her lips like this was a first date? She dug her fingertips into her forehead and sucked in a breath.

If she kept up this freaking out, she'd need her inhaler.

Things seemed so innocent and natural this afternoon. Flirty words and shared smiles as they played at the beach. But somewhere between packing up the picnic and paddling home, things changed. Memories of Danny. Their first date. His lips the only ones that had ever touched hers.

She peeked at the reflection of the woman behind her splayed fingers. "You can do this." Shaky words. As shaky as her legs. Tears welled in her eyes, and she closed them again. "I can't do this."

Knuckles lightly wrapped against her door.

Gwen swallowed. She'd set herself up. Even the idea of a date proved too much, but add on the kiss she'd promised? Idiot.

Another knock. "Gwen?" Nate's voice pushed its way through her door.

Stiffening her back, she crossed the room and with one big breath, opened her door. At the sight of his smile, competing bands of apprehension and excitement twisted her stomach. When his gaze flickered to her lips, the apprehension won out.

Gwen turned. "Let me grab a sweater."

His eyes scrunched up for a second, then he nodded. "Sure. It'll get cooler as the sun sets."

The buttery yellow cardigan coordinated better with this shirt, but she grabbed her ratty gray one and a hair tie to pull her hair back. She'd committed to going, but the night didn't have to end in a kiss.

She stepped onto her small porch where Nate waited, pulled her door closed, and flicked the lock. Twisting her hair into a ponytail, she clomped down the steps.

"Might be a bit hard to lead since you don't know where we're going." Nate's voice stopped her.

She half-turned. "True."

Her back warmed from his intense stare, but she couldn't fully face him. Danny was the only man she'd ever dated. The only man who'd ever kissed her, touched her. Would the memories remain as strong if she shared those experiences with someone else? Either answer hurt her heart.

Impossible waters to navigate.

Nate's footsteps shuffled closer, and his hand rested on her shoulder. She stiffened, but he didn't remove his touch, simply continued down the steps until they stood face to face. His thumb traced a circle against the beating pulse near her collarbone, not pushing but also not retreating. "No expectations. Okay?"

He didn't blink; instead, he let her search the depths of his blue eyes. Behind him, twilight stretched across the sky, the dusky light softening the rigid lines of his jaw. She'd offered him irrational and silly, and he offered her an out. He was such a good man.

Someone she never expected to meet in this place.

She could do this. One step at a time.

"Okay."

Susan L. Tuttle

He nodded, stuck his hands in his pockets, and waited for her to follow. They slid into the golf cart, and he turned the key. "I'd have gotten your door if there was one."

She laughed. "Thanks." They started up the small hill. "Where are we going?"

His eyes remained on the path. "It's a surprise."

"The camp isn't that big." And this way led to the lake, ropes course, archery field, and prayer trail.

He shrugged and remained quiet.

At the top of the hill, he stopped in front of the small walkway to the beach. Gwen hopped off and once again, Nate stuck his hands into his pockets. No pressure. No wondering. Her breath released. Her muscles relaxed.

Pine needles and dried leaves from seasons past crunched under their feet. Above, the last of daylight trickled through the trees. When they returned, they'd need a flashlight. Even now it was difficult to see distinct shapes in the woods. Gwen concentrated on the ground in front of her, trying to make out any obstacles in her way. She peered ahead, and bursts of white light twinkled through the leaves. What was that?

She stumbled, and Nate steadied her. "You okay?"

"I'm fine." She pointed ahead. "I was distracted by that."

"What?" His attempt at innocence failed.

"Something's lighting up the beach."

He squeezed her arm. "Guess we'll have to check it out." He stepped in front of her. "How about you hold the back of my T-shirt and follow me?"

She held on. "Lead the way."

A few more feet and the beach opened before them. Gwen gasped. A border of iron stakes with jars of candles marked a twinkling path to the dock where tiny white lights edged both sides of the wooden slates and reflected off the water. As if that wasn't enough, the trail continued past the dock to where the beach, woods, and lake all collided. Strands of old white bulbs created a canopy between several trees under which a small wooden table with burning lanterns sat only feet from the water.

"Surprised?"

More like speechless. Still as glass, the lake rolled out as if belonging only to them for the night, and even more lights blinked alive in the ever-darkening sky. Breathtaking.

Wait.

"Where's the blob?"

She could learn to love that laughter.

"Didn't think it went too well with the décor, so I towed it away for the night." He pointed down the lake. "It didn't go far, though." Then he motioned her in front of him. "Shall we?"

Sweetness in his eyes, he maintained his promise of no expectations. Simply waited for her motion. "We shall."

Her hand felt empty as she started down the path. Problem was, she still wasn't sure whose touch she missed. Tears welled again, but she pushed through. Focused on the beauty in this moment. When they arrived at the table, Nate held out her chair.

"Thanks." She scooted in, and he bent down behind his chair. The lake created a perfect backdrop, the twinkling lights of the dock and walkway jutting out into its navy waters. "You gave me the best view."

From a basket, he picked up a platter of food and set it between them before sitting across from her. "Thanks. I thought I cleaned up well myself, but it's nice you noticed."

"I meant all the lights."

"Sure you did." He held up a Rock N' Rye. "For you."

Her fingers brushed his. Warmth. She twisted the pop top and poured it into the clear blue plastic goblet he'd set by her plate. "Thanks."

He continued to unpack their dinner. Gwen smiled. All her favorites from NovelTeas. "Bay packed that, didn't she?"

Beneath the scruff on his face, his cheeks pinked. Or maybe it was the candlelight. Either way, something tickled her stomach. This wasn't simple attraction. This was a man who studied her. Who focused on her. Who cared for her in his patience. His words. His restrained pursuit.

"I'm no cook." He handed her a sweet potato and rice patty sandwich. "And definitely not of this food." The barest of shrugs lifted his shoulder. "I wanted you to enjoy your dinner."

She waited a moment. Let her eyes rest on him. And took a leap. "With this view, I'd have even enjoyed another hot dog."

"You better enjoy it. Took me all afternoon and lots of ribbing from several teenage boys."

"I wasn't talking about the lights." Bold words wrapped in a whisper, but sometimes bravery arrived in quiet ways.

Nate's response involved only a look, but his intense stare sent shivers up her spine. Simultaneously made her regret and relieved a table sat between them.

Small steps. Baby steps.

Then he cocked that half grin, and the shivers pulsed her heart to a thrilling race. "Wondered if you'd come around."

"I'm starting to."

"My boyish good looks are hard to resist." He produced a tub of Bay's pasta salad.

"No, but this food is." She stole the pasta, leaving him open-mouthed and laughing.

Dinner passed as evening firmly took over the sky. Every bit perfect. Every word linking them closer together. As she took the last bite of her meal, Nate pulled out a small white box.

"What's that?"

"A little bird told me this is your favorite dessert."

She flipped open the top, and a small hummingbird cake, coconut coating the white frosting, lay inside. She giggled. "Nice play on words."

Nate pulled out two forks, and they dug in. When only the last two bites remained, he set his fork down and leaned back. "All yours."

"You sure?"

"Positive."

The air shifted across them, tousling his soft waves of hair. He fingered them back, his stare never leaving her. She swallowed the final delectable bites and reached for her drink. After she downed all her pop, she dabbed her mouth with her napkin. Nate followed her movements, not bothering this time to hide his study of her lips.

She'd been cool enough moments ago to contemplate donning her cardigan. His look heated her enough, she no longer needed it.

He reached across the table. "Care to watch the stars with me, or would you rather call it a night?"

The twinkling lights on the dock provided testimony as to how he'd planned the evening, yet he again offered her an out. Putting her before his own desire.

She worked her bottom lip for a moment before placing her fingertips in his. "I can't promise anything."

He gently tugged her to her feet. "No promises needed." This time he didn't let go, but kept her hand loosely in his. Not staking a claim, not taking anything more than she willingly gave. Just being present.

She still felt protected and wanted.

The dock shifted under their feet and when she stumbled, he steadied her for the second time that night. "You okay?" His deep voice. So strong. So tender.

She tightened her grip. "I am."

Soft music drifted from the end of the dock. "Is that country?"

Again with the shrug, as if thinking of her first was the most natural thing in the world. It had been so long since she'd been this cared for. Memories of Danny floated toward her, but she held them at bay. Sweet companions that couldn't accompany her out here.

One blanket covered the worn and rough wood, the colorful fabric making soft the sharp edges. She slipped off her shoes and rolled up her jeans, then sat and dangled her feet over the edge. The cool evening water elicited a shiver. Nate reached for another blanket and draped it over her shoulders.

"Good?"

She nodded. Looked up. He lowered himself beside her, and they sat quietly for a few moments. Splashes punctuated the soft lap of water against the dock. Above, the best of connect-the-dots lit the sky. "Do any of them make sense?"

Nate nodded. "If you know what you're looking for."

"And you do?"

"I spent a lot of nights as a kid in my backyard staring at the sky." He swirled his legs in the water as if he wasn't opening a piece of himself to her.

"Avoiding your mother?"

"Helping Lo avoid the men Mom brought home."

The man was a protector. But who'd protected him?

"You had a tough childhood, didn't you?"

"I survived it."

She squeezed his leg. "You did more than survive." He inspired her. She'd gone through fire and remained gripped by its ashes. But Nate? He'd found strength in the searing flames and walked out shining. His light stirred up a desire inside to fully shed the grief still encasing her.

His leg tensed beneath her hand.

At some point she'd started rubbing her thumb against the soft cotton of his shorts.

She removed her touch. "So you know a lot about stars?"

He cleared his throat. "Yep."

"Then show me something, because I'm clueless."

After a long swallow, he pointed up. "See those four?" He drew across the sky with his index finger. Long fingers. Strong hands.

She leaned close to capture his viewpoint. The four stars leapt out at her. "I see them!"

His cheek pulled up in a smile. "That's Hercules' head."

"Where's his body?"

He took her hand and moved it across the sky. "This is his body." Still holding her, he motioned lower. "And those are his legs."

The scent of pine and something fresh rolled off his skin. She turned to inhale, and her nose pressed against his cheek. His intake of breath sucked in hers, but he kept his face toward the sky. "Do you see it?" Gravel rolled through his low words.

This time she couldn't pull away.

So unsure of what she was doing. Not wanting to retreat. Not wanting to travel forward. Her past and her future eclipsing each other in this one moment, she gave in and placed her lips against the stubbled skin where his jaw and neck met.

Keeping her fingers captured in his, Nate lowered their joined hands to his lap and turned his head slightly, nestling her cheek with his. With his free hand, he reached for her ponytail holder and released her hair. The soft strands tickled as they drifted to her shoulders. He brushed a few from her neck. Taking his time. Still allowing her to back away. When she didn't, he pressed a kiss to her forehead.

She leaned into the intimate touch.

He released her hand and both of his framed her face. He brought his lips inches from hers, his sweet stare asking but not taking. His thumbs brushed across her cheeks. So gentle. She stepped in.

Her mouth brushed feather light against his, and he hovered there for a moment. Her last chance to turn away. When she didn't, he tugged her to him. Sweet and slow, he kissed her. He slid one hand into her hair and cupped the back of her head, tilting her to fit him. His lips left hers for a breath, as if asking permission to continue. She pressed into him, and he smiled against her as he reached for more, exploring deeper.

His free hand skimmed her skin down to her shoulder where his thumb rubbed soft circles. Courage taking route, she lifted her own fingertips to his skin. His jaw new to explore, she placed kisses along it. His soft release of her name encouraged her discovery to continue as she worked toward his ear. She planted her other hand against his chest and felt his sharp inhale as he twisted to reclaim her lips.

When he'd planned the night, he'd hoped for this kiss. When he'd picked her up, he'd released that hope. Content to simply be with her tonight, to move at her pace, this sweet reward tested his control.

He slowed the kiss, nipping at her bottom lip, then freeing it to place kisses against her closed eyes. Salty dampness touched his mouth. He pulled away. Twin tears tracked from beneath her lashes. He swiped at them with his thumbs and pulled her close. "Too fast?"

She shuddered in his arms but shook her head, pressing a kiss against his throat.

The heat already inside notched up a few degrees. He set her away from him. "Why the tears, sweetheart?" He wiped another one. "Did it not feel right? Do you need more time?"

It nearly crushed him to ask, but if they were going to do this, honesty was the only way it would work.

She smiled a tiny, bittersweet smile. "I'm not crying because it didn't feel right." She took his hand and squeezed. "I'm crying because it did."

Emotions on every level thrummed through her voice. He pressed another kiss to her forehead. "That's a good thing, right?"

She looked to the lake and swallowed but didn't let go of his hand. "Danny's the only man I ever dated. The only man I ever kissed." She looked back at him. "You're the second."

Obvious words coated in such deeper meaning. The weight of what she'd offered stole his breath. She became a hundred times more beautiful and precious to him in that moment. Worth so much more than what he could ever offer her.

All things new, my child.

Those words settled in before his own could run away from him, reminding him he was God's now, not a sum of his past mistakes. And in so many ways, he and Gwen were doing these new firsts together.

He brought her close, his mouth inches from hers. "Thank you." Then he kissed her again, showing her how precious she was. Controlling his desire for more, he enjoyed the simple sweetness of her lips, the slight spice still lingering on them from her favorite dessert.

The dock swayed gently in the water. Crickets sung on the night air. An owl called. The perfect accompaniment to her crazy country music crooning in the background.

She had a mouth made for kissing and skin smoother than silk beneath his rough fingertips. He traced the line of her jaw. Pulled her in closer. Felt the enticement of what they built between them. He could stay here all night, but he wasn't strong enough. They'd both carried kisses farther than this, and he refused to ruin what she'd cared for.

Slowing them to a stop, he tucked her into his embrace. Her fingers found his, and she burrowed her hand into his grip.

"I wasn't looking for this." Her words muffled against his flannel shirt.

"I wasn't either."

"I've got a lot of baggage."

He chuckled. "So do I."

She started to speak. Stopped. Then plowed ahead. "I'm not ready to let him go yet."

Her honestly demanded his. He bent to look her in those icy blue eyes that glowed more like a warm summer day right now. "I will never ask you to." He tipped her chin up. "He will always be a part of you. But what he can't be is the man you compare me to." He pressed a light kiss onto her lips. "In any area. Fair enough?"

She nodded. "Fair enough."

It was all he could ask.

Chapter Twenty-Six

Sleep wasn't happening anytime soon. The kisses on the beach left his brain spinning, but the last one at Gwen's door keyed him up worse than the energy drinks he used to pound back. His attraction wasn't a surprise. That had been building for weeks.

The strength of his feelings, however, astounded him.

This wasn't a casual summer fling. What he felt tonight? Nate tugged his hair. Were either of them ready for this?

He stood at the bottom of her cabin stairs, the lights inside casting their glow. She'd taken another step from the shadows tonight, straight into his arms, and he hadn't taken advantage of the moment.

It still stunned him, how much he'd changed. Once, he'd have pushed for more, but with Gwen he held himself back. Enjoyed the sweetness of what she offered. Under Ryker's mentoring, he'd made the decision years ago not to sleep around any longer. He'd never fully believed Ryk that waiting would give him something better than his immediate gratification. Tonight he understood. Yeah, physical was incredible. He was a man, not going to lie. But what Gwen offered tonight? Her trust and honesty . . . her vulnerability . . . They were the building blocks of something that could last far beyond one moment.

It was a treasure.

And cue the sappy music. Might as well be in a chick flick.

See? Spinning brain.

He headed straight for the camp store and a huge dose of sugar. He'd demolished the Laffy Taffy supply in his cabin. As he crested the hill, shadowy movement beside the medical center and staff quarters drew his attention. Were some counselors out for a night stroll? The tension rolling up his shoulders said no. Nothing other than his own crazy instinct had him changing paths.

Pale moonlight broke through the trees to illuminate a flash of red darting behind the buildings. Nate took off, his long legs eating up the space between them as the figure raced toward the woods.

A familiar figure.

His heart lurched. "Axel!"

Axel skidded around a tree, not giving up an inch. Nate put on a burst of speed maintaining his line of sight. "Keep running, and it'll only make things worse."

Nothing.

Nate stopped. "I won't chase you."

Axel disappeared. No noise. He had to be hiding.

"Come out now, and we'll clear this up. Make me wait at your cabin, and it'll be too late." Quiet. "Either trust me, Axel, or you're on the next bus home." If he even came back to camp. He might choose to keep running. It was a chance Nate had to take.

Seconds ticked by. After about ninety, Nate turned.

"Wait." Axel stepped from behind a tree twenty feet away.

Nate stopped.

Slowly Axel walked over, shoulders back, head high. Still on alert. Still full of attitude. Except his tongue licked across his lips. Nerves played through the kid. And he was just that, a kid.

"What are you doing, Axel?" Nate tried to inject concern, not the worn-out frustration bubbling inside.

He held out a red drawstring bag and dumped its contents on the ground. Enough candy to restock Nate's cabin cupboards plunked out. Then he emptied his pocket, producing a can of Coke.

Candy he had access to every day?

"Had the midnight munchies?" Nate lifted a brow. "Or were you bored?"

Axel stood tall. "Don't matter, does it?" He held out the bag. "We square?"

Nate took it. "No. We're not *square*."

"You said I come out and we good." Distrust narrowed his eyes in the dim light.

"I said you come out, and we'd clear this up." Nate took the bag and filled it with the candy spilled on the trail. "We've only begun that process." He nodded. "Start walking."

Nonrepeatable words murmured under Axel's breath as he trudged forward.

"Excuse me?" Nate prodded.

"Nothing."

"Oh, that was most definitely something." Nate followed him. "Otherwise you'd have said it louder."

"Already in enough trouble, man."

Nate swallowed a grin. Finally some wisdom taking root. It was a start. A tiny one, but hope sprung from the smallest of wells. "You want to make it here all summer, Axel?"

"Woulda kept runnin' if I didn't."

"Wouldn't have broken into the camp store if you did."

Axel turned. "You lie to me?" He snorted. "Ain't no surprise. Go on. Send me home."

Nate shook his head. "I didn't lie to you, and I'm not sending you home." He prodded him to turn and keep walking. "I'm trying to figure you out."

"Ain't no figuring me out," he muttered. "What you see is what you get."

"And what do you think I see?" Whatever it was, the answer would be what Axel had been programed to believe and not the truth of what Nate saw.

"Some kid that won't make it to his next birthday, and that's a'right in your world." He shook his head. "Stealing that stuff, ain't hardly nothin'. It's what you expect."

Nate remained silent. He'd rather not talk than say the wrong words. As they neared the edge of the woods, he grasped Axel by the shoulder. "Is this what you really want?"

The boy pulled away. "Was tonight."

"Turn around." It took a moment, but he finally did. But his eyes stayed on the ground. "I see a kid with his whole life in front of him. With choices. But it's up to you to make the right ones." He got in Axel's face. "You don't." He paused. "*That's* the only thing that'll make those predictions come true. Others' words don't have power unless you choose to fulfill them. So choose the right ones to listen to."

"Easy enough for you."

"Not saying it'll be easy." The boy had a mountain to scale with a toothpick and string for equipment. "But I am saying you can do it."

A beam of light hit them. "Nate?" Jude's voice reached from beside the staff building.

Nate shielded his eyes. "Want to shine that thing at the ground? You're blinding me."

He complied, and Nate blinked, inky blackness all he momentarily saw.

"We done?" A sharp edge cut Axel's voice.

Nate held in his sigh. "Yeah. For now." He nodded to Jude. "Jude and I will walk you to your cabin."

He took off, stomping past Jude without a glance. Once he made it to his cabin, Nate stopped him with his words. "You need to check in with Jude first thing in the morning. He'll be adding a few things to your list for the next week."

"Thought we was good." Axel glared.

"We are. Doesn't mean there's not consequences."

"Shoulda kept runnin'." He stomped up the steps.

His counselor opened the door. Once Axel trudged inside, he looked out. "Everything okay?"

"Yeah," Nate answered. "Maybe move your bed in front of the door."

Eyes wide, brows lowered, the twenty-something started to close the door. "Um, okay."

"I was kidding," Nate added before the door clicked shut. Okay. So mostly kidding.

He turned and found Jude watching him. "Hectic night?"

Nate nodded. "Axel broke into the camp store."

Jude sucked in a breath, eyes closed. Then he opened them. "Nate, you can't keep giving the kid free passes."

Worried their hushed voices would carry, Nate motioned him toward his cabin. "What's he got to go back to? We're his best chance."

"Not if he won't take it." Jude shook his head. "It's not fair to the kids who are following the rules. Who want to change."

"He does want to change."

"He said that?"

"I see that." Nate looked up. "Each time I look in his eyes."

Jude slowed. "He's not you, Nate. And you're not Ryker. This isn't a repeat of your past."

Felt like it. Their pasts might not read identical, but the look in Axel's eyes echoed the same one Nate had seen in his own mirror for years. And if someone had reached him sooner, his life, Lo's life, could have been so different.

If even one person had told him it was possible.

His past had to be worth something. Saving Axel added value. Each child added another layer of appreciation on a past that otherwise depreciated to nothing.

"I'm not looking for a do-over, Jude. I want to help the kid."

"And if you can't?"

"Not an option."

"You can't force help on him."

"I know that."

"Do you?" Jude clasped Nate's shoulder, stopping him. "You're walking a thin line, friend. Putting this entire place at risk, bending rules to reach Axel. I don't want that cost to come at too high a price."

It couldn't. "No price is too high for any of these kids." He shook off Jude's hold. "Not one."

What would raise more questions? Missing her standard Sunday meal with the girls or showing up with the blush that wouldn't leave?

Gwen sat in her car parked directly between two white lines outside NovelTeas and checked her rearview mirror again. Yep. Definitely the blush. The brightness of her eyes and smile that erupted at every memory of last night didn't help either. She felt like a kid trying to keep a surprise party secret, and her friends would know something was up. Her fingers rested on the ignition as Bay waved from the front window. Great. She'd been spotted. Ditching now would only result in them tracking her down.

Exiting her car, Gwen turned and jogged up the front steps. NovelTeas closed on Sundays after brunch, but Bay remained for their weekly private lunch. It was their time to catch up. They'd taken guesses on how quickly the tradition would halt after Bay married Colin, but he only encouraged them to continue.

Good man.

Smiling, Gwen opened the door, and the scent of oranges hit her from Bay's homemade cleaner.

Bay looked up from where she scrubbed her floor. "Hey. Go ahead and lock it. Elise and Lucy are in the kitchen, and I'm finishing up."

Voices floated from the open door behind the counter, one low and one high. Gwen twisted the deadbolt, then avoided the still wet spots on the floor as she made her way to their small table in the corner.

Bay rolled the bucket away. "Let me take care of this."

Gwen slid into her seat as Elise and Lucy rounded the counter, hands full. Lucy deposited a small plate holding a roast beef sandwich and a green salad with beets, goat cheese, and some dark vinaigrette.

"This smells wonderful," Gwen said as she spread her napkin over her lap.

Lucy shrugged. "Just used up some of Bay's leftovers."

"Your parents taught you well." Bay joined the table. "I never would have put the ingredients of my fridge together into this."

"None of this is my parents." Lucy picked up her sandwich. "And I only did it because you wouldn't let me mop, and I was too hungry to wait."

"Down, Luce." Elise stabbed a lettuce leaf. "You might've picked up how to make a great sandwich from them, but that doesn't mean you share their character traits."

"They have none worth sharing."

Uncomfortable silence littered the room behind her mumblings. Gwen could break it wide open with one confession.

She shifted in her seat. The moment she told her friends about the kiss, it would become real. Not that it wasn't, but if no one else knew, she still had a drawbridge behind her. Telling people took her one more step away from Danny.

But as much as her heart at times still longed for what had been, it could never be. And she no longer only wanted to reminisce about beautiful memories. She wanted to make more. Possibly with Nate. They'd definitely created one last night.

She set down her fork. "Nate kissed me."

Their faces snapped toward her faster than fire on hay. "He what?"

"Did you kiss him?"

"I knew you liked him."

Anticipating their questions should have prepared her with answers. It hadn't.

"If you don't want to tell us, you don't have to." Bay took a bite of her salad. Kind words, but curiosity lined her eyes. So did compassion.

"No." Gwen pushed her plate away. "I want to talk about it. I just don't know where to start."

Lucy leaned forward. "How about with where. Followed by how you felt. And did you kiss him back?"

"It's not an interview, Luce." Elise broke in. "Give her a sec."

Gwen licked her suddenly dry lips. Three pairs of eyes watched her. Wasn't there a song that said to start at the very beginning?

After clearing her throat, that's what she did. "We went on what you could call a date, I guess."

"You guess?" Lucy's thick brows drew together. "Either it was or it wasn't."

"I don't know." She shrugged. "It's been a long time since I had a first date, and Danny was my only one."

"A kiss was involved." Bay smiled. "It better have been a date."

Gwen tucked a loose strand of hair away. "Nate came and got me from my cabin, and we walked to the lake." Her cheeks lifted at the memory of how hard he'd worked to make the night special. "It was decorated with lights in the trees, along the path, on the dock—"

"Date," Lucy said.

"Definitely a date." Bay nodded.

Elise shrugged. "Men don't date me. Go with what they say."

Bay squeezed Elise's hand but kept her focus on Gwen. "So a beautiful night that ended in a kiss."

Gwen's heated cheeks reignited.

Lucy studied her. "That look says more than one kiss."

"I don't kiss and tell."

"You kind of already did." Elise chuckled. "But I'm happy for you, Gwen. I know it can't be easy."

Gwen picked at her napkin. "It's . . . strange." She looked at them all. "But it's really, really good at the same time." She'd lived in some weird, oxymoronic state since last night. "I don't have words to describe how I feel."

"Happy and sad. Scared and bold. Excited but cautious." Lucy always had words. "It's the final steps away from Danny. You'll always love him, and you have to find a way to do that while you're falling *in* love again. It's going to take time to navigate those feelings." Her fingers ran along the smooth sides of her mug. "Now you decide if Nate's worth navigating them for."

Was he?

"It was one kiss." Gwen shrugged. Okay, one night with several kisses, but they didn't need to know that.

Bay speared a beet with her fork. "Question is, do you want another?"

"I don't know." Kissing Nate came easily, once they'd crossed that bridge anyway. But one date didn't make a relationship. Accepting another . . . Well, that placed them on the road to one. Not that Nate had asked, but she knew enough to understand they'd both enjoyed the night.

Elise swallowed a bite of roast beef, her sandwich half finished. "You don't need to know this very second."

But she didn't want to lead Nate on.

Stuffing salad into her mouth, Elise squinted as she watched Gwen. Then she turned. "So how was the township meeting last night, Bay? Did they okay your idea for the ice sculptures by the shops this winter?"

Gwen smiled her thanks to Elise. She'd happily vacate the hot seat. Except the look Bay flicked past Elise said she'd better grab a bucket of ice water, because she remained on the seat while it grew hotter.

"What?" Gwen prodded. "Did they not approve your idea?" What would that have to do with her, though?

The bracelets on Bay's arm clinked as she rubbed her hands together. "No. They loved it."

"So why the look?"

A moment's hesitation, then, "Marlene made an appearance at the meeting."

Gwen's throat tightened. Nothing good would come from that.

Rather than speaking she simply nodded for her to continue.

"She presented info on Nate's camp combined with juvenile criminal statistics." Bay cleared her throat. "Specifically citing—"

"Danny's death." She'd rather say it than hear it.

Bay nodded. "And using that information, she collected signatures from people who don't want a camp like this in our township. She plans to keep collecting until there's enough signatures to bring it up for a vote in November."

Gwen tossed her napkin on the table. "Vote on what? The land's already sanctioned for a camp, the grounds are maintained in good condition, and there's been no abuse. They don't have a legitimate reason to shut us down."

Us? When had her mind made that switch?

Or was it her heart?

She set the word aside to examine later because the *when* and the *how* didn't matter. The switch had occurred, and she couldn't see herself going back.

"They don't," Elise joined in. "But Marlene can cause enough backlash to create trouble. Right now the camp relies on the town's hospitality for a majority of their community service hours. If no one wants them around, that could affect the JCS program."

Even worse, the conflict could stop Elliot from investing, preventing Nate from running the camp after this season and effectively shutting his idea down. An outcome she'd not only wanted and planned on, but inadvertently shared with Marlene. "It won't come to that."

"Marlene won't back down, Gwen." Bay fiddled with the ribbon on her blouse. "She's scheduled to speak at the next township meeting."

"When is that?"

"Two weeks."

Fourteen days to fix this. "I'll call her."

For the first time in a long while, her worry didn't stem from plans changing. Rather fear rose over the idea of them remaining exactly the same and damaging the people she'd unexpectedly come to care for.

Chapter Twenty-Seven

G wen rolled up her yoga mat. Nyla, Haven, and Brittany were tucking theirs away as well. They grew more limber—and talkative—every day.

"You here tomorrow?" Nyla asked.

"Yep. Though we'll have to meet after your hike to Little Blue." Nate had scheduled a visit to the lighthouse in the morning.

Her lips pursed. "I don't wanna see no lighthouse."

Haven and Brittany nodded their agreement.

Routine had become a comfort for them, but they also needed to learn change could be good. She could teach her own course on that fact.

"Little Blue is one of my most treasured places to visit." Gwen ran her toes through the sand. "Seeing how tall and strong it is, knowing all the storms it's weathered"—she shrugged—"makes me feel safe."

After a long sigh, Nyla looked at her new friends. "Guess it might not be so bad."

Nodding their agreement, the girls raced off toward the mess hall.

Gwen stowed her mat in the bin on the beach. Three days had passed without any return phone call from Marlene. Until Gwen had a chance to speak with her, she didn't want to tell Nate a thing. Not when she held the blame for what Marlene was doing. She might not have encouraged it, but she'd definitely planted the seed. And she wanted to find a way to sidetrack her mother-in-law—even better, derail her completely—before sharing the news with him. If she could offer some good mixed in with the bad, maybe he'd believe she hadn't intentionally impaired his plans.

Especially since that had been her initial desire, and he knew it.

But he must sense the change in her. They'd spent the past few nights on her front porch, talking, laughing, and gorging on his stock of candy. She'd ingested more sugar in the past week than the past several years. But no more kisses. Nate gave her time and space. Slowly the shadows were shifting out of her life.

That movement provided enough light for her to see the outline of his camp and these kids. The picture coming into focus wasn't one she'd anticipated, but it was there nonetheless. It twisted into clarity on mornings like this with Nyla and the other girls, or when she worked alongside Nate. Then it blurred again when she'd pass by a group where a boy's cold eyes would scan her from head-to-toe, or a cloud of obscenities hovered over the beach. It only took one small thing for old memories to flare and erase all the good moments she was creating with a few kids.

Nearby, her studio took shape. Lew had added a wall of windows that faced the lake, and Nate had repositioned the blob, keeping it off-center so the view from the windows remained unhindered.

He was literally finding middle ground.

Could she?

Could she have this dream while allowing Nate his?

No answer slipped into place. Only ideas that floated around each other.

Her stomach growled. She couldn't feed her questions, but her body was another story. Gwen hurried toward the mess hall. Cresting the hill, she spied Nate with Kylie and a group of about ten girls on the archery field. Laughter peppered the air as they took turns attempting shots. Gwen changed course, stopping a few feet behind them as one small girl let an arrow loose. It sank into the hay in the second circle of the target. Girls bounced around, congratulating her.

"Nice shot," Gwen added her voice to the celebration.

Nate turned and broke into a grin. "Hey."

"Hey." The sight of him sparked nerves in her middle. She massaged her fingers, fighting the sudden urge to press a kiss against his cheek, but they were surrounded by kids. And she hadn't shared a kiss with him since their date. Not that the thought hadn't been edging in a little farther each day.

Based on the way his eyes kept dropping to her lips, he worked to control the same thought. He quirked his head to the side. "We were just finishing up here."

"Mind if I stay and watch?" She'd find a snack later.

"Not at all." He addressed the girls. "Three more arrows each." He lined them up, two deep across the five targets. "Take turns and help each other out. I'll be watching and come through to give you each pointers."

Gwen pointed to Nate's bow. "Mind if I try too?"

"Sure. When the girls finish you can grab one of theirs."

While he coached, she picked his up. Heavy, but not so much she couldn't easily lift it out in front of her.

Nate peered up from correcting one of the girl's aims. "You won't be able to shoot mine."

Really.

She lowered it. "Sounds an awful lot like a challenge."

There went his cocky grin, but instead of responding, he addressed the group. "Once you've finished, put away your equipment, then enjoy your free hour."

Within minutes, the girls scattered. Gwen held up Nate's bow again. She ran her hand along the camouflaged . . . Okay, she had no clue what the parts were called.

Nate did, and he filled her in on all of them before holding up an arrow. "You pull the string, and I'll let you shoot this. It's an arrow."

Kiss that smirk, or wipe it off his face? She wasn't quite sure.

So she lifted the bow like she'd seen the girls doing, gave him a look, and grabbed the string. "Funny man." She pulled.

It didn't budge. Not even a centimeter.

She readjusted her stance and pulled again.

Still nothing.

Unless Nate's laughter counted.

"Is this a trick bow?" She turned. "It only works for you?"

"Or someone with muscles." Nabbing it, he slid the string back like a rubberband. "It's a seventy pound bow, Gwen." He released it. "Made for someone my size, which you most definitely aren't." He smiled. "The girls were on ten pounders"—he strolled to the small shed—"but I bet you could handle a twenty."

"A whole twenty, huh?"

He returned with a bow and a few arrows. "Okay. Here's a thirty then."

"Your belief in me is staggering."

He lifted one brow and held out some contraption. "This is your release." Taking her hand, he helped her put it on and explained how it worked.

"It looks like a trigger."

"Because it is." He picked his bow up and quickly walked through all the same steps. He pulled back, muscles taut, hand perpendicular to his face, and the string barely touching his nose. His arrow twanged from the bow, thwacking into the middle of the bullseye. "Now your turn."

"Easy." She stepped up.

He set his down. "I'll help you."

She side-eyed him. "I've got this." She mimicked his earlier stance. "Pull back, look through that circle, and release. Right?"

He cupped his mouth, his forefinger tapping against his lips, those blue eyes dancing. "Mm-hmmm. Go ahead then."

"Oh, ye of little faith." Gwen tugged the string and sighted the target. Directing the tip of the arrow toward the big red circle, she squeezed the trigger. The arrow didn't even make it to the hay.

"Still going with *easy*?" Nate chuckled.

She picked up another arrow. "Fine, Mr. Expert. Show me."

"You are so teachable." His slowly shaking head softened his words as he stepped closer. His hands gripped her waist, and he swiveled her around so her shoulders connected with his chest. "Set your feet"—he gently nudged her legs with his left one—"here and here." Then his arms came around her, encasing her fully. His face pressed in, cheek against hers, his fresh pine scent filling her entire breathing space as much as his body filled her physical one. How was she supposed to concentrate?

His hands slid over hers. "Now pull the string while pushing forward on your grip."

Her arm trembled as she did, and this time it wasn't because the tension was too much for her muscles.

"Steady." He tightened his hold.

So not helping. She fought to stable herself against the shiver those softly breathed words evoked.

He gently shifted her aim. "Up a little."

Somehow she followed his directions.

"How does it look to you?"

Gwen turned slightly, his whiskers rough against her skin. "Perfect." Her movement brought his focus from the bow to her. The blue of his eyes darkened. Or maybe he blocked the sun when he leaned closer.

He grinned and pressed his lips close to her ear. "I agree. Ready to let go?"

Pulse jackhammering, she released. The arrow sunk into the outer circle of the target. No bullseye, but closing in. Dropping the bow, she turned in his arms. "With your help, I'm getting closer." Sometimes ambiguity made baring tentative feelings easier.

His hand engulfed both of hers and brought them to rest on his chest. There was nothing tentative about the look in his eyes. Goosebumps rose. She leaned in . . . and her phone rang.

Stepping away, she answered as Nate mumbled something about distractions. "This is Gwen."

"Hey. It's Jude. Any idea where Nate is? He's not answering his phone."

"About two feet from me." Still mumbling. She tossed him a grin.

"Could you tell him to come up to the office?" Something in Jude's voice seemed off.

She stiffened. "Sure. Everything okay?"

"I don't know. Bryce and Elliot just showed up."

"I don't remember that being on the schedule."

"Because it wasn't." Jude sighed. "Can you send him up here?"

Marlene.

Gwen's stomach bottomed out. "We'll be right there." She hung up.

Nate regarded her. "What's up?"

"That was Jude. He said he couldn't reach you on your phone."

"I forgot to plug it in last night, and it died on me." He moved to lock up the equipment shed. "What did he need?"

"Bryce and Elliot are here. They want to see you."

Nate tensed. "What?" He looked down at his T-shirt and athletic shorts, then back at Gwen. "They're not coming until the end of summer."

She hesitated.

"Gwen." He drew out her name. "What aren't you saying?"

One thing about Nate, he knew how to read people. Knew how to read her. It was something that deepened her attraction to him, but now she wished she had the ability to block that trait.

Wouldn't change the fact that she needed to own up. Hopefully, he'd understand. "There was a township meeting Saturday."

"Okay."

"Marlene presented information that didn't paint the camp in a very good light."

He slid his hand through his hair. "What else?"

She swallowed. "She's collecting signatures of people who don't want the camp here. She plans to address the council again at a special meeting in two weeks. Her goal is to have enough signatures to create a proposal for the November ballot that will prevent this camp." Her hand itched to smooth the deep creases above his brows. "But she doesn't have a leg to stand on. Even with the signatures, there's nothing legally she can do."

"No, not legally, but she can make enough noise to scare Elliot away. You and I both know that's all she has to accomplish." He looked across the field, blinked, then looked back at her. "Why didn't you tell me this earlier?"

"I don't know."

He shook his head and stepped close. "I don't know's not good enough." He took her hand. "Why?"

Here went nothing. She sucked in a breath. "Because I'm the one who told her if you didn't have an investor, your camp wouldn't succeed. I was trying to reassure her, reassure myself even." What was going on behind those blue eyes of his? "I'd honestly forgotten it until I heard about the township meeting. I've tried reaching her, but she's not returning my calls." A deep sigh. "I should have said something, but I was worried you'd think I'd done this on purpose."

His mouth remained in a straight line the entire time she spoke. Not a muscle on his face twitched. Until she finished. Those lips curved up. "I might have believed that weeks ago, Gwen, but not now."

Sweet relief rolled over her. "I'm sorry for the trouble I caused."

"Who says you have?" His thumb stroked her wrist. "Let's see why Elliot's here before we jump to conclusions."

With a nod she followed him to the golf cart, and they headed for the main building. Jude waited for them on the porch. "They're in your office."

"Thanks." Nate pushed inside, and Gwen followed.

"At least I'll finally get to meet Bryce. You two seem pretty close."

"We are." Distraction coated his words.

He opened his office door. Two people filled the chairs by his desk. An elderly gentleman and a beautiful—okay, beautiful was an understatement—woman.

The leggy brunette stood and hugged Nate. Hugged him. "It's so good to see you."

He returned the embrace. A little too eagerly. "You too, Bryce."

Wait. *This* was Bryce? Bryce was a girl?

No. Not a girl. A woman.

Everything Ryker mentioned about how important their relationship was now taunted her, right along with how completely at home Bryce looked in his arms.

Nate stepped from Bryce's embrace and shook Elliot's hand. "Good to see you, Elliot." Even if this visit arrived over a month early. He turned. Gwen flicked a glance between him and Bryce, eyes slightly narrowed under a wrinkled brow until she caught him watching. Then her face slid into a neutral territory he hadn't seen in days. One he'd hoped was completely gone.

"Gwen, I'd like you to meet Bryce Payton and her father, Elliot." Nate stood in the center of all three.

Bryce held out her hand. "Great to finally meet you, Gwen."

"Finally?" She looked back at Nate.

Bryce nodded. "Nate's told us a lot about you."

"Wish I could say it was mutual." Shoulders stiff, her mouth tightened into a thin line almost as if she didn't want any further words to slip out.

Nate tipped his head at her. What was up? He *had* told her about Bryce.

He raised his brow, but she ignored it. So he held out his hand. "How about we all sit? You can tell me what brings you out."

Elliot claimed a chair around the small coffee table. Bryce sat beside her father. Gwen remained standing, her eyes bouncing between Bryce and him. Wait. Did she think—?

"I need to finish my list for today." Gwen scooted toward the door. "So I'll let you two—I mean three—um, four, including you, Jude." Now she looked everywhere but at him as she retreated. "Anyway, you need to catch up. I'll see you at dinner. Actually after dinner. I'm having dinner with Granddad tonight. So maybe I'll see you tomorrow." She practically shut the door on her last word.

Gwen didn't ramble. Yet those words tumbled out faster than snow melting on the sun. Nate jumped up. "Give me a sec?"

Amusement glimmered across Bryce's face. "Take as many as you need."

He chased after Gwen, who'd already made it outside. "Gwen."

Nearly off the porch, she spun. "Sorry. I know that wasn't my smoothest exit, but it wasn't the time or place for questions. I'll find you later. Right now you need to get back in there."

"Elliot and Bryce can wait a second." In two strides he stood in front of her. She went as stiff as the wood post behind her. "What's going on?"

"Nothing that needs talking about right now."

"I disagree. You're obviously upset."

"I'm not upset, I'm—" she toyed with her lip. He did his level best to stay focused on her words. "Caught off guard."

Well, that arrested his attention. It wasn't at all what he expected. "How so?"

Her hands wiped against her shorts, and she looked everywhere but at him. A weighted silence stretched, then, "Bryce is a woman."

She uttered the fact so quietly, he thought for a second he'd made up her answer. But, nope. Those pink cheeks confirmed the words were hers.

He swallowed his chuckle. She was jealous. It warmed something in him. "Yes. She is."

Her eyes flittered over his. "You didn't tell me."

"I didn't hide it." He lifted one shoulder in a shrug. "Didn't realize you hadn't known."

"Well, I didn't."

"And that tossed you off kilter?" He inched closer until his toes nearly touched hers. "Why?" With the spindled railing behind her, she had nowhere to go. He placed a palm flat against the tall post, boxing her in as much with his presence as with his steady stare.

"Because." She swallowed and looked down at their feet. "I don't know."

"Chicken." Her eyes sparked to his, and he smiled. "Want me to tell you what I think?

"Not particularly."

"Too bad." He cupped her cheek with his other hand. "You're jealous." She sucked in that bottom lip again. Nervous? "Thing is, Gwen, you have no reason to be."

His eyes fixed on her lip still captured between her teeth, and he finally gave in to his weeks-long desire to help her curb that habit. In a gasp, her mouth released to his.

Their first kisses he'd restrained himself, taking things slow in case she wasn't ready. And he'd waited since then to see if she'd initiate, not wanting to push her. But after her reaction on the archery field and now, concerning Bryce, he wasn't about to hold back. He was staking his claim. Leaving her no room to negotiate herself out of her feelings.

Removing his hand from the post, he slid it between her shoulder blades and pulled her close, his other hand digging into her hair, cupping the back of her head as he gently slanted her to fit closer to him.

Her hands fisted in his T-shirt. He smiled against her lips, then let them loose before he gave in and pressed her farther into the railing. Holding her close with her hands creating a small barrier between them, he breathed in roses and gently kissed her forehead. "Feel better?"

She murmured something.

He tilted away. "Hmmm?"

"Feeling something."

He chuckled. "I'd like to stay out here and explore those feelings some more"—he added a few more inches between them—"but I have to get back into the meeting. You coming?"

She seemed to consider it before shaking her head. "I really do have a checklist to accomplish."

"Why am I not surprised?"

"Because I haven't hidden my amazing list-making talent."

"Yeah. That's it."

She made it two steps, then stopped. "Nate?"

"Yeah?"

Nibbling her lip. She was still nervous.

"Need me to help you with that again?" If she said yes, they might be out here all afternoon.

"Hmm?" She caught the direction of his stare and unclamped her teeth from her soft skin. Red filled her cheeks. "Yes. I mean no. I mean, did you date her?"

That's what had her worried?

He joined her and rested his hands on her shoulders. "No. Bryce has always been only a friend. I haven't dated anyone since I realized the next woman I do needs to be the one I can see marrying. That's not Bryce."

Did she understand what he *wasn't* saying? There remained a fine line between reassuring her and scaring her.

"Oh." So light, the word could be good or bad. It took a moment for her to meet his eyes. A tentative smile played on her face. "Better go inside." She pressed a kiss to his hand on her shoulder. "And I'll see you tonight." Then she jogged down the steps.

He watched her for a moment before returning to his office. His thoughts remained with her, but he needed them here. He took another thirty seconds before opening his door. All three looked up, smirks firmly in place on Bryce's and Jude's faces.

"That was longer than a minute," Bryce's voice lightly teased.

"Pretty sure you said to take all the time I needed."

Jude pushed off the wall. "Then I'm surprised you rejoined us."

Elliot cleared his throat. Might be almost like a second father, but this wasn't the conversation he'd come to have.

Nate settled into a seat. "Not that I'm unhappy you're here, but I wasn't expecting you until Labor Day."

"I've had a few phone calls that made me want to come and see for myself how things are going." Elliot leaned forward, his arms braced on his knees. "Sounds like this town might not be as open to us being here as you'd thought."

"Not so much the town as one woman."

"Who's collected several signatures."

Right. Nate shook his head. "I just found out myself. I'll talk to the town council. Not everyone feels the same way." At least the vibe he received in town hadn't changed.

Jude pushed off the wall. "I have to agree. The town was leery at first, but I've had the kids working service projects, and they're winning them over."

"Doesn't take but one to poison the pot." Elliot sighed. "And after multiple calls from Marlene, listening to her story, I wonder if what we're doing is the right thing."

Marlene had worn him down. Maybe it was good he'd come early. He could see the importance of this place. They were changing lives—for the better. "What we're doing is vital to these kids."

"Which is why I'm here. To weigh the benefits against the dangers."

"They're not dangerous." Nate stood. "They're teens." Felt like he kept dodging boulders on a steep hill while others rolled into place.

Bryce stood too and placed a hand on his arm. "We know that, Nate." She looked at her father. "But the Doornbos' story tugs at hearts and pulls out fears. It's shaken Dad up a little. Once he sees all the good you're doing, once he meets these kids, even talks to Gwen, we'll be back on track." She peered at her father. "Right, Dad?"

Elliot drew a hand across his chin. "That's what I'm here to find out. I'll be honest, Nate. I narrowed the field to you and one other nonprofit. This week will help me decide." He stood. "So how about you show me where I can unpack and then convince me why I should stay."

Chapter Twenty-Eight

"You're sure you want to do this?" Gwen asked for the—well, she'd lost count of how many times in the past twenty-four hours.

Nate's exasperated look said it had been more than ten. Probably more than twenty. "Yes." He yanked the strap tight over the final kayak. "You don't have to come."

Except she did.

With each passing day, their connection deepened, and it was important to her to be there for the people she cared about. If she were honest, she'd edged beyond the simplistic word *care*, but she wasn't ready to put another label on her emotions. They felt too familiar but not aimed at the right person. Not that Nate wasn't the right person, he just wasn't—

Nope. Wasn't comparing. She'd promised him she wouldn't—explaining why she wasn't naming the emotions yet. She needed time to wrap herself in these feelings again, which only seemed fair to them both.

"Gwen?" He stood at the end of the trailer. Stepping closer, he took her hand. "I promise I'll be okay."

Concerned for her even though she currently exasperated him.

"Which is why I'm coming. To make sure."

"There's plenty of adults going. You don't need to be one of them."

In the past four days, Bryce and Elliot had participated in every aspect of camp, getting to know the kids. Last night

Elliot asked if they could take the JCS crew on an overnight camping experience. Granddad had told him about the kayak trips to Turnip Rock and the Northern Lights they'd view. After hearing about all the work those kids had done in town the past few weeks, Elliot thought this would be a great reward.

Gwen had been invited.

And Nate offered her an out. He'd given it the moment the invite had been extended.

She so didn't deserve this man's unending patience or understanding.

She squeezed his hand. "I'm going."

Nate pulled on their joined hands, enfolding her in his arms. He clasped his hands at the small of her back. "You're pretty amazing, you know that?"

She breathed him in, all pine and something fresh and sweet she'd finally pinpointed as all the candy he ate. His strong arms around her—those arms she'd noticed from the first day—provided a haven she'd missed and thought she'd never find again.

Gwen tipped her head up and found him studying her. "Honestly, I was worried you'd get lost."

"Nah. Bryce can read a map."

Bryce. The woman he promised she didn't need to worry about, yet had mile-long legs and an effortless beauty—she even glistened instead of sweated. She also possessed a quirky humor that paralleled Nate's so much, Gwen nearly started calling them Abbot and Costello. Oh, and Bryce stood so firmly on board with his plans for this camp, she might as well be his co-captain.

Gwen shoved against him. "Of course she can read a map."

Nate tightened his hold. "Not nearly as well as you, though."

Poor attempt to pull out the foot he'd just eaten.

"Too little, too late, buddy."

"I could always kiss you again."

She tucked her face under his chin. "Not getting out of it that easily."

Chuckles vibrated against her cheek. "You're cute when you're jealous."

"Remind yourself of that when you're waiting for the search party to come rescue your sorry bum." Her lips rubbed against his soft cotton T-shirt. "Bryce might be able to navigate, but no one knows this area as well as I do."

He leaned away until he could see her face. "Then I'm doubly glad you're coming."

"You're just using me for my navigational skills."

"Well, that and you're cute to look at."

Their light banter rose to the top of her ever-growing list of things she liked about Nate. "It's going to take more than compliments to make up for your little slip."

He dropped a light kiss to her mouth. "Good thing I packed Rock N' Rye then."

The campfire had died down to red coals. Jude played his guitar. Most of the kids laid in sleeping bags on the soft green grass that met the beach. The families who owned the land had granted them use for the night. Already the teens talked about ways to show their thanks. Their quiet whispers filled the night while they waited for nature's light show.

Nate settled in beside Gwen, who chatted with Bryce. He handed her a burgundy can. It hissed as she opened it, then she made a small moan as she sipped. He shook his head and pulled out a Laffy Taffy.

Across from them, Elliot made the rounds with the teens, asking soft questions and listening to their answers. He'd been a walking questionnaire all day, trying his best to figure out what they needed, how the program helped, and what they'd do differently. It was classic Elliot and one of the reasons Nate wanted him for an investor. Much like Arthur, Elliot connected with the kids even if he was the age of their grandparents.

"Nice way to spend your last evening?" Nate peered around Gwen to Bryce.

"Won't need to hit the gym the rest of the week." She rubbed her upper arms. "Not that I could use my arms even if I did."

"Can't wait to see you try and eat a s'more." Jude grinned, softly plucking away a tune he'd made up.

"You making me one?" she asked.

"I might." He switched songs.

As Bryce and Jude continued their banter, Gwen set her can in the sand and looked at Nate. "Thanks for bringing my pop."

"Thanks for bringing the extra stash of Laffy Taffy." He tapped one against her soda in a toast. "We make a great team."

Too bad they had an audience, because he wanted nothing more than to kiss that full smile she leveled at him.

"Look." Jude nodded.

Greens, reds, and blues danced in ribbons above, while every color in between lined their edges against the evening's black canvas.

"Oh." Bryce's breath escaped on a puff, and her full attention fixed on the sky.

And it was beautiful. But not nearly as captivating as the woman beside him. Unable to stop himself, he captured Gwen's hair between his fingers and brushed it behind her shoulders as an excuse to trail his touch over her skin. She shivered.

He smiled.

Then leaned in beside her. "I'm glad you came."

She turned. Her eyes held his, and her lips moved temptingly close. "Me too."

He flicked his gaze past her shoulder. Jude and Bryce remained focused overhead and caught in their own quiet discussion. The soft strands of Jude's guitar played a soundtrack to the lights. Sneaking a quick kiss, Nate extended his arm in silent invitation for her to settle into his embrace. She snuggled in, her head tucked under his chin. Perfect night.

Something wasn't right.

Nate sat up, instantly alert though he'd been asleep only two hours. The Northern Lights had dimmed and the moon's pale glow slipped over the sand. Crickets chirped and the gentle lapping of water against the beach were the only noises, but something had awakened him.

He scanned the sleeping bags around him. The girls had moved to the other side of the campfire which left eight on this side, including himself. Jude and Elliot slept along the outside edges, and five sleeping bags separated Nate from them. One sat empty.

Axel's.

He'd bedded down in that spot. All afternoon he'd been quiet and polite. Kept his head down and did whatever they asked of him. Still hadn't opened up, but Nate continued to try. The sight of his empty bed pulled Nate out of his.

He stood and ran his gaze along the entire area. Moonlight glinted off the sand—and off a white T-shirt by the water. Nate jogged down the beach, hoping Axel battled a case of insomnia, not his destructive habits.

"Axel?" Nate called his name as he approached. The boy startled, then turned.

With glassy eyes.

"Hey, Renner." A sloppy smile. "What you doin' down here?"

His slurred speech confirmed Nate's suspicions. "Woke up, saw your empty sleeping bag, thought I'd check on you." He nodded toward Axel's hands locked behind his back. "What're you hiding?" He tried to keep the disappointment from his voice.

A sliver must have snuck in because Axel's face hardened. "Got a problem with me takin' a walk? You a warden now?"

"What's behind your back, Axel?" Nate pressed and took a step closer. "You can show me, or I can take it."

A dry laugh barked from the teen's lips. "You think you can take me?"

"I know I can." He deepened his voice and straightened his stance, suddenly reliving memories of standing up to Ryker. He'd come full circle. Nate held out his palm. "Last chance."

"Last chance?" Another laugh. "Naw, man, you don't do last chances. You keep givin' 'em." Now his eyes flickered, worry lining them.

Nate said nothing. Didn't move.

After a long sigh, a joint along with Nyla's inhaler landed in his palm.

Nate tensed. So she *hadn't* lost it.

"You're wrong." Couldn't stop the sadness in his voice. "You just forced my hand." He looked at the young boy. Things could be so different, but this time he couldn't look the other way.

"So you are like the rest of 'em." Axel shook his head. "I knew it."

"Like the rest of them?" Now anger laced up his spine. "I stood behind you. Gave you every chance to change, and I catch you sneaking off to get high?"

"That don't even count." Axel pointed. "Ain't like it's smack or speed. 'Sides marijuana's legal now, ain't it?"

"Not at your age." Never mind how he acquired it, which no doubt happened during one of his stints in town working off his community service hours. "And this inhaler isn't yours. Both are illegal, Axel, and I have to report you."

"You ain't got to do nothing." He straightened to his full height. At fifteen, he'd grown to the size of a man, but still smaller than Nate. "You didn't turn me in for smokin' or stealin', and those're illegal too. Why now?"

"Believe me, I don't want to." Ryker had said the same words when he hauled Nate to jail. Nate hadn't believed him then, but now he understood. "This isn't easy, but it's what I have to do." He'd put it off long enough. Axel wasn't responding to grace. Maybe he would to consequences.

"You foolin'."

"I'm not." Gwen's cold voice shook from behind him.

This situation shifted from bad to worse.

He turned. "Gwen, go back to camp."

Her hand gripped her waist so tightly, she ran the danger of breaking herself in half. She trembled. From anger or fear, he honestly didn't know. "So you can let him go again?"

"I just said I wouldn't, so please leave."

Instead, she took a closer step. "You caught him stealing too? And let him go?"

"Aw, made your ol' lady mad." Axel laughed. "B—"

Nate whirled. "Watch it."

Axel shrugged. "Just gonna say she don't like me." He glared around Nate. "Ain't that right?"

Nate fought an adrenaline-fueled tremble. His muscles coiled. Axel itched for a fight, and so did Gwen. Not a good combo. "Gwen, I want you to get Jude."

"I'm not leaving." It was as if he'd asked her to rob a bank.

"Please." He met her eyes with the plea.

Axel shoved him from behind. Not ready for it, Nate flew into Gwen. They both went down, her breath knocking away as he landed on top. "You okay?" In the same second he caught her nod, Nate launched to his feet, chasing Axel who headed for the kayaks. Did he really think he could make it away from here in one of those?

Feet digging into the sand, Nate called, "Axel, stop!"

He reached the boy and grabbed his arm. "You're only making this worse for yourself."

Pushing away, Axel tripped and landed chest to the ground. Nate reached for him, but he rolled and tossed a handful of sand into Nate's eyes. He recoiled, the grit digging in like tiny pinpricks. Nate fought the urge to rub them. He never saw the oar coming.

But he felt it.

Pain radiated across the side of his head. Wetness trickled along his temple.

"Nate!" Gwen's voice rattled him.

Nate righted himself, trying to put his body between hers and Axel's. Except he had no clue where Axel stood. "Get out of here, Gwen."

She reached his side. "He's already gone." She gingerly touched the uninjured side of his head.

His vision dimmed. His legs shook.

"Nate?"

"Go get Jude." He didn't want Gwen deciding to chase Axel.

She shook her head. At least he thought she did. He still couldn't see.

Something swished in the water. He tensed. Reached for Gwen, but she'd slipped out of his grasp. "Gwen?"

"I'm grabbing water to rinse out your eyes."

He needed to tell her to get Jude. Wait. Hadn't he already? His head throbbed. He needed to sit. The sand made a soft chair. Maybe if he laid down.

"Nate?" Fear coated her voice.

At least she didn't sound mad at him anymore.

He tried to tell her he was all right. He just needed a quick power nap. But everything went black before he could get the words out.

Chapter Twenty-Nine

——❧❧❧——

She hated hospitals. Loathed them. And in the past two months she'd been in them twice for someone she cared about.

Cared.

Her feelings for Nate had driven well beyond that line, which only made her angrier. Discovering he'd let Axel go not once, but twice, heated that anger to a near fury. What had he been thinking? She had no clue, but the revelation stuck on replay in her tired brain, and each cycle back only fortified her initial thoughts: this entire camp was a bad idea and someone would get hurt.

Along with another singular truth, none of this would have happened if she'd stood her ground and forced Granddad and Nate's hand.

Well, now she would.

She pushed past the curtain to where Nate waited to be released. A white bandage covered the twelve fresh stitches on his temple. He should count himself lucky he hadn't received worse.

His eyes collided with hers, uncertainty there. Worry created lines across his face. She had no desire to add more to his distress, but far better to experience a small pain now if it prevented a larger one later.

She'd start with the easy info first. "One of the counselors came with the van and trailers. Jude's helping him return the kids and kayaks to camp." She tipped her head toward the door. "And Elliot and Bryce are here."

He blinked. Looked like he wanted to say something, but she tightened her shoulders and her lips. He shook his head. "Go ahead, send them in."

She waved the two into the curtained area.

Bryce stood beside Nate. "How are you feeling?"

"Like I got whacked upside the head with an oar."

No one laughed.

Elliot pocketed his hands. "You gave us a scare."

"I've got a thick skull." He looked at all three. "Anyone find Axel yet?"

"No. The police are searching," Elliot answered. Then he cleared his throat. "Gwen told us about everything that's happened."

Red coated Nate's neck. "He needed help." He swallowed. "Needs help."

"At what cost, Nate?" Bryce asked. "Marlene Doornbos heard what happened tonight. She's spoken with us."

Gwen shifted, and he glanced her way. "I thought you'd decided not to listen to what she has to say."

"After tonight we feel there's credibility to her concerns." Elliot's voice issued low.

Nate's focus strayed from Gwen to Elliot. "Because of one altercation?"

"It wasn't just one," Gwen responded. How could he try to say that?

Elliot picked up where she'd left off. "We weren't aware of all the trouble Axel has caused, but that doesn't mean you can't count it."

"No one got hurt."

"Until tonight." Gwen pressed her fingertips into her thighs rather than reaching for him. "If you'd never brought those kids here, or if you'd tossed Axel out when he broke the rules the first time, you wouldn't be sitting here."

Nate sought out each pair of eyes. "Everyone makes mistakes. Everyone." He stopped on Gwen. "And they deserve a second chance when they do."

The intensity of his stare too much, she blinked away. This time he wouldn't sway her.

"How many second chances, Nate?" Bryce asked. "Because it sounds like you gave Axel quite a few."

"I caught him smoking once and stealing a few candy bars another time." He kept his focus on Gwen. "If anyone can understand him, you can. You make checklists and keep things in order. That's how you deal with your pain. Axel acts out too, only in a different way."

She laughed. "You are not even trying to compare the two."

He closed his eyes and sighed. "I wasn't giving him a pass tonight. I was going to turn him in."

"Too little, too late." Fatigue pushed at her muscles.

"Gwen."

She shook her head. "It isn't me." Now she nodded to Elliot.

Nate shifted toward his friend.

Elliot rubbed a palm against his chin. "I'm not investing at this time, Nate. There's some kinks to smooth out before this idea can work."

"Kinks?" He fisted the blanket beneath him. "And if I didn't include the JCS program?"

"We'd reconsider. Maybe." Elliot drew his shoulders up. "But you've got some personal work to do too. I know you can relate to these kids, and that's a good thing, as long as you don't see them as a second chance to fix your youth." He held up his hand at Nate's open mouth. "I think we both need time to think, and then we can revisit your proposal.

"Regardless of what we decide, Hidden Lake is off the table as a location. Marlene collected more signatures, and with the new support"—his eyes flicked to Gwen—"I believe they'll gain the full backing of the town. Leg to stand on or not, I simply don't want that fight or the publicity."

Nate's intense focus hadn't left hers since Elliot had outed her with a look. "You signed it?" She had, but his raw voice almost made her reach for an eraser.

Except they were in a hospital, and his blood still dotted the tan cotton of her shorts.

"I did." She lifted her chin. "And, if need be, I'll help her fight."

The lines around his eyes and mouth narrowed. "Gwen, please." He stood. "You know these kids need this place. Nyla—"

"Will be all right. I'll make sure of it."

"And the others?"

Now wetness coated her eyes. A battle inside she wouldn't allow herself to fight. "It's for the best, Nate." She backed away as he reached for her. One touch and she'd cave. "It's for *your* best."

Chapter Thirty

Thunder rumbled in the distance. Was the storm actually rolling off of her? Sure felt like it. Gwen slipped out of Warrior Pose and looked up. Thick clouds unfurled across the sky above, the perfect backdrop to frame her with, especially after what she'd done to Nate.

Second thoughts pummeled the door of her defenses, but she refused them entrance. Instead, she reinforced the wall with mental pictures of Nate knocked cold and bleeding on the sand while her every fear materialized.

Yep. Lending her support to Marlene was the right thing to do. Better a little pain for Nate now than a world of hurt later. How many times had she repeated that sentiment in the past hours? Too many.

Dawn still clung to the horizon when Elliot and Bryce had chauffeured Nate to camp. She only knew because, unable to sleep, she'd gone for a walk and caught their shadowy figures helping him into his cabin. After which she headed to the beach. Early sunlight bled into the darkness as she faced Hidden Lake and worked through the motions of her yoga. It didn't calm her. Not this morning.

Wrapping a towel around her neck, Gwen turned. Movement along the tree line caught her attention. Nyla perched under one of the oaks, her back pressed to its massive trunk. Same tree she and Nate had dinner under. Seemed forever ago.

She shook off the memories. Even if she wanted to keep moving forward with him, after last night he'd no longer feel the same. The pain in his eyes as she'd left tempted her to eradicate her signature from Marlene's petition. But she couldn't forget his blood on her hands.

As she approached Nyla, sobs poured from the little girl. The broken sound pried into Gwen's heart. She knelt beside her. "Hey. What's wrong?" Had she heard about her brother? They'd mentioned holding the information until he'd been located.

"I don't wanna go home."

Go home? Gwen tipped her head. "That's not for several weeks." And next year Gwen would ensure Nyla had a camp to attend. Wouldn't be Camp Hideaway, but it would still provide a safe place.

"No." She shook her head. "I heard about Renner. What Axel did to him." So she did know. Shudders wracked her body. "Is he . . . is he gonna be okay?"

"Yes. He's resting in his cabin."

Now her mocha eyes widened. "He is? Wh-when did he come back?"

"This morning." Knowing her brother had caused Nate's injury, seeing Nate for herself might be helpful. "How about you come check on him with me a little later? You'll see for yourself he's fine."

Nyla shook her head vehemently. Was she worried Nate would blame her because it was Axel who'd attacked him?

"Nate won't be angry at you."

"But they're kicking Axel out." She rubbed her arms.

How did she know all this? And how to explain? "They are." A slight nod. "But it's the safest thing for everyone."

"I don't wanna go home too." More tears leaked from her lids.

"That's not going to happen." She squeezed her hand. "Trust me, Nyla." Taking the edge of her towel, she dabbed Nyla's eyes. "Get yourself cleaned up, have some breakfast, and then we'll go see Nate." She stood and pulled Nyla to her feet. "You'll see. It'll all be okay. I promise."

Nyla slowly nodded. "Okay."

"Okay." Gwen smiled. "I'll walk you to breakfast."

Another nod. The walk remained completely silent. Nyla stood outside the doors as more thunder rumbled. They were in for a soaker. Dark clouds rolled toward them. Perfect day for rain.

"I'll come get you after I shower. Wait inside for me."

Without answering, Nyla stepped through the entrance. Gwen captured, then released her hair, letting it fall softly against her shoulders. Nate was the last person she wanted to see today, but Nyla needed the little trip. Maybe she could stand in the doorway while Nyla made sure Nate was not only okay, but also not angry with her simply because of her brother's actions.

Gwen hurried to her cabin and quickly showered, Nyla's concerns niggling at her. Not once had Gwen placed blame on the young girl for Axel's decisions. So why did she heap it onto the shoulders of other kids because their dress or actions resembled the one who'd killed Danny?

That question didn't erase the memories of standing by Danny's grave or kneeling beside Nate last night. But it did bring a new perspective to them. It felt as if Axel had proved her hypothesis correctly—only she no longer wanted it to be true.

Her emotions were too much to wade through right now. She shoved into her tennis shoes and grabbed a rain jacket. Thick clouds weighted down the sky, so close to breaking open. She hurried up the path and ducked into the dining hall as the first fat raindrops fell. The wind banged the door shut behind her. Inside, near silence filled the room. Most of the kids had finished breakfast and were on their free hour. Probably playing games in The Commons. Gwen surveyed the room for Nyla's face.

Lips turning down, she entered the kitchen. Maybe Nyla had been drafted to help with dishes. Nope. She spun and went to check the restroom. She pushed open the door. "Nyla?"

Silence.

Had she gone to her cabin?

Outside, rain thrashed against the windows. Gwen jerked the hood of her slicker over her head and raced into the rain, jogging all the way to Nyla's cabin. She thrust the door open and ran inside.

Kylie stood by Nyla's bed, eyes wide. "I was headed to find you."

"What?" Unease slithered up Gwen's spine. "Why?"

"Something's off."

Gwen stepped closer to Nyla's bed. "Like what?"

"Sid is missing."

"Huh?"

The counselor shook her head as if clearing it, then focused on Gwen. "It's Nyla's stuffed sloth. I gave it to her the day she came, and it hasn't moved from her headboard since."

"Is someone playing a trick on her?"

"No." Kylie shook her auburn hair. "I gave a unique animal to each girl. They don't want anyone touching theirs, so there's no way they'd mess with Nyla's."

"Okay. She was upset when I saw her earlier, so maybe she took it and found a quiet place." Which could be anywhere in camp. Though it was raining, so the spot would be inside.

"Except her backpack is gone too." Kylie pointed to the end of the bed as she paced. "Something was bothering her this morning, but she wouldn't tell me what. That's why I came to check on her."

"Somehow she heard about Axel and worried Nate would kick her out."

"That's crazy."

"Not to Nyla." She picked up the girl's pillow. "I brought her to breakfast and told her I'd be right back. That we'd go see

Nate together." She stood again. "But she wasn't in the dining hall when I returned."

Kylie's face blanched. "I never saw her there, and I came straight from breakfast."

The circling certainty landed like one of Nate's arrows into the bullseye. Nyla had run.

And Gwen would find her.

She zipped up her jacket, pulling her hood around her head.

"What are you doing?" Kylie blocked the door.

"Going after her."

"You have no idea where she is." Winds whipped outside. Their phones beeped. Gwen watched Kylie's face as she checked hers. "They've issued a tornado watch. We have to get all the kids to The Commons."

"Go." Gwen clipped a nod. "Find your girls. Help the other counselors."

Kylie placed a hand on Gwen's shoulder. "We have a camp full of kids who need our help, Gwen. You can't go out in this. You don't even know where to start looking. Just help me with the kids who are here. We'll pray Nyla is okay."

From the depths of her childhood, the story of one lost sheep slipped into Gwen's mind. She hadn't thought of it in years, but now its words hit her in a new way.

"I need to find her." Gwen shrugged away. "Go take care of the others. I'm bringing Nyla home." And she raced into the storm.

A crack of thunder sprang Nate awake. Sounded like it had landed in the middle of his bedroom. Was it the noise or his sudden shift in movement that had his head throbbing?

He pushed off his bed and shuffled through the dark room to the bathroom. Nighttime already? Rain pounded the roof overhead, and he flicked on the lone light. Grabbing a few aspirin from behind the mirror, he swallowed them dry, then headed for whatever cold liquid he had in his fridge.

The clock on his microwave glowed in the dim room. A little after ten. Still morning. He'd been asleep a few hours. It only looked like night. Changing course, he scuffed to the small window beside his table. Quite the storm.

Another boom of thunder rumbled and two more quickly followed. Wind thrashed rain against his cabin. He should check to make sure all the campers were inside The Commons, at least until this blew over.

Ignoring the searing pain in his temple, he slid his feet into shoes and headed for the door. It banged open. Jude rushed in, dripping wet. "Tornado watch. Warning to the southwest of us. We need to go."

Nate grabbed his jacket off the hook, every movement enforcing the sledgehammer whacking at his head. "Are the kids okay?"

"The counselors are rounding them up." But those words didn't match the worry in his eyes. Worry bigger than a tornado watch.

"What." Issued as a demand, not a question.

A split-second hesitation, then, "Nyla's missing."

Cold seeped in that had nothing to do with the storm outside. "What? How?"

"I'm not entirely sure. Kylie just found me. Seems Nyla thought you'd kick her out because of what Axel did, and she didn't want to go home." He wiped water from his face. "So she ran."

"Then we need to find her." Didn't matter that bright lights pulsed along the corners of his vision with every heartbeat.

"I agree." Then he sucked in a big breath. "So did Gwen, because she's already out there looking."

Thunder shook his cabin.

"In this?" His pulse picked up.

Jude nodded.

"Did she take the truck?"

Now he shook his head.

Nate slapped the doorframe. "What is she thinking?" He grabbed his phone and punched her on speed dial. It rolled to voicemail. Her phone never went to voicemail. It was never dead. Charging it every day lined the top of one of her stupid checklists. He was adding a new one: *Don't run off alone in the middle of a monsoon.*

He raked a hand through his hair, then winced at the excruciating pain from his bruises. "Did she at least take a golf cart?"

"Yep." Another pause. "Until she hit the woods."

His chest constricted. "What's that supposed to mean?"

"That she must be on foot now, because I found her cart parked outside the prayer trail."

More thunder, this time closer, pushed at him. "I need to get out there."

"I already walked it. She's not there."

He tried to tap down the freaking out. "Then where is she?"

Jude's full focus sank into him as if he was trying to anchor his friend. "I don't know."

Chapter Thirty-One

Never be in the woods during a thunderstorm. Granddad had drilled that into Gwen's head. And here she trudged, shoving branches out of the way, her voice stolen by the wind, as she tracked down a little girl she never meant to care for.

Like she hadn't meant to care for Nate. But he'd shown up out of the blue. Pulled her from the dark shadows life had become. Made her laugh again. Made her feel again.

Bright light blinded her and thunder shook the ground. Electricity crackled through the air, making the hair on her arms tingle and stand on end.

She should turn around.

But Nyla needed her.

The little girl had to be terrified—Gwen fought panic herself. But while walking the prayer trail, it hit her where Nyla would be. Little Blue. They'd spoken about it often since Nyla's visit there with the other campers. If she'd been caught out in this storm and didn't want to return to camp, the lighthouse truly would be the only other beacon of safety nearby.

Picking up her pace, Gwen pushed through soggy branches, keeping her head down and one foot in front of the other as mud seeped through her shoes. "Nyla!" She yelled for the umpteenth time, the wind snatching her voice before it made it an inch. But maybe, just maybe, Nyla would respond.

She couldn't have made it to the lighthouse yet. Could she?

Gwen spun in a circle seeking some sort of landmark. Anything familiar. Branches bent backwards, their leaves turned inside out. Rain drove into her. She wiped what felt like a river from her face, her tears mixing with the water as another lightning bolt struck. This storm raged overhead.

She had no control.

None.

She couldn't find Nyla.

Couldn't stop the wind and rain.

She was as lost here as the girl she was trying to find.

Thunder rumbled the ground beneath her, the force vibrating through her core, and she sank to the ground partway beneath the bent limbs of a bush, sobbing. So tired. So done. She curled down, her forehead in the mud as rain still lashed her back.

She breathed in the musty dirt, not caring that her lungs tightened. Even her own body defied her control. And she was done trying. Let God do what he wanted. He did anyway.

Water seeped through the dirt, trickling against her cheek where it touched the mud. She lifted her face.

Lightning slashed against the black sky, illuminating everything around like a camera flash. Then she saw it, as if looking down on herself from above. She was a living picture of her last four years. Stuck in a storm. Covered in mud. Knees bent in defeat.

Refusing to stand. Refusing to continue forward and find shelter. Unable to find peace because she remained so focused on being caught in a storm she never saw coming. It had nearly destroyed her. It would, if she stayed here.

But refuge stood so close. And it was so much stronger, safer, than this tiny bush she tried to make into a shelter. Like yoga or her checklists, these leaves would provide momentary relief but never what she needed to weather this tempest.

She had to stand and move forward, one step at a time, because remaining still locked her inside her pain.

And she so badly wanted out.

"Okay, God." She lifted her head. Rain pelted her skin. This storm refused to budge. But she could. Time to let God lead her to true shelter. "Okay."

She pushed to her feet, shaky, and scanned the tops of the trees. Still nothing familiar. So she took a step, and another, pushing aside limbs, wiping away rain, while the remnants of defeat continued to call for space. But she'd tried that path. For four years. It was time for a new one.

Five minutes? Ten? She didn't know anymore. Her throat sore from yelling Nyla's name, she kept pressing forward. Shoving another branch away, a clearing opened before her. Again she scanned the sky above the circle of trees, and a slow smile spread across her face. There! In the distance, the cap of Little Blue broke over the trees. Not taking her eyes from its gorgeous sight, Gwen raced across the small clearing and pressed back into the thick forest. Almost there.

With every step, more of the beach peeked through. Gwen reached the edge of the tree line and scanned the rocky area, not ready to step out from the forest. Nyla had to be near, and Gwen wasn't entering that lighthouse until she found her.

"Nyla!" she tried again.

Still nothing.

She scoured the area for any sign of white—the color of Nyla's T-shirt. Would the child answer her?

Please, Lord. The plea escaped her lips. The last time she'd said those two words was in a frantic drive to the hospital when Danny lay inside. They hadn't worked well then. But they were all she had to offer now.

Closing her eyes, she uttered them again. And again. Powerless to do any more. Finally realizing who truly held control and offering every drop to him.

And then she heard it.

"Ms. Doornbos." Quiet and unsure, but nonetheless there.

Gwen popped her eyes open and swung in a circle. "Nyla?"

Crawling out from under a bush, Nyla didn't come closer, so Gwen slid in the mud to her side. "Nyla." She gently grasped her arms. "Are you okay?"

She nodded.

Gwen smashed her into a hug. "Thank you, Lord." Sweet relief. And another flash of lightning. The storm refused to quiet, but they had shelter only feet away, and they were taking it.

"Okay." She ran her hands up and down Nyla's shuddering arms. "We need to get you dry." She cast a look over her shoulder at Little Blue. "Come on."

"It's locked." Nyla dug in her heels. "I already tried."

"This time, I'm trying." Gwen tightened her grip on Nyla. "Crouch down and run." She looked at her. "You ready?"

A fast nod, then they were off. Stones crunched under her tennis shoes, the uneven ground hard to keep steady on, but she never let up her fast pace as lightening splintered all around them and rain pelted like tiny bullets. Nyla kept up. Good girl.

Gwen reached for the old doorknob at the base of the lighthouse, but it resisted opening.

"I told you it was locked." Nyla cried.

"Had to try." Gwen bent and picked up the largest rock she could find and thrust it through the window.

Nyla released something between a yell and a scream. Gwen pulled her jacket down over her arm and reached inside, a shard of glass slicing her. She popped the lock and nearly tossed Nyla through the open door.

With her breath coming in gasps, Nyla wiped rain from her face. "You broke in here."

"I did." Gwen slammed the door behind her and looked for a light. She felt the cold wall, her fingertips finally touching a switch. She pushed it and a faint glow filled the space. Nyla stared at her, open-mouthed. "You broke in," she repeated.

"Sit." Gwen nodded to a chair in the corner, then grabbed a jacket off a hook. "Take off yours and put this one on."

Nyla was still shaking her head. "You—"

Gwen knelt in front of her. "Nyla. I broke in to keep you safe."

"You shouldn't have. Now you're going to be in trouble too." Tears slipped down her face. "I'm not worth it. All this is my fault."

"It's okay." Gwen tried to reach for her hand, but Nyla snatched it from her grip.

"No. It's not." She shook. "You never would have come for me if you knew."

Gwen rested on her haunches. "Knew what?" What could this little girl have done that would ever make Gwen not come for her?

"I didn't lose my inhaler." She sniffed. "I gave it to Axel."

Oh.

"Nyla." Gwen released the word on a breath.

"It's all my fault Renner got hurt. And I knew once Axel ratted on me, you'd kick me out too." More tears. "I'm no good."

"No. You made a mistake."

She pushed against the chair. "I am a mistake." Pain etched into her face. "Like you said that day. It's all true."

Gwen wrapped the resistant girl in a hug. "You are not a mistake, Nyla. You are not a mistake." Oh, how she wished she could take those words back. Erase them from existence. "I was wrong. You showed me that." Could she get through to her? "You taught me how to forgive. How people deserve a second chance, myself included." She cupped Nyla's face. "You did that. And even if I'd known you'd made a mistake, I'd have come for you."

"Why?" One word laced with pain, longing, and disbelief.

The story of Jesus leaving the ninety-nine for the one filled her mind again. "Because it's what Jesus would do." It's what he had done in the midst of this storm for her. She was a mixed-up mess. Spewing anger and hurt. So blinded by her own personal pain and unwilling to relinquish it all to him. She'd bowed to defeat instead of bowing to the one who could heal her.

Nyla's head tipped.

Gwen sighed and smiled. "Nyla, I may not have been the best picture of Jesus to you, but let me tell you about Him."

Tell her about the only true way to find peace.

While the rain beat against the concrete walls, Gwen told Nyla the story. Warmth filled the little girl's face right along with Gwen's heart. They'd found refuge from their storms in so many ways right there in this little lighthouse.

Chapter Thirty-Two

Nate was about to come unhinged. "Where are they?" Gwen might as well have disappeared into thin air and Nyla right along with her. He tried her phone again. Voicemail.

Jude stood near the door, unwilling to let Nate leave. What was supposed to be a quick trip to make a head count turned into Nate being caged like a wild animal. Arthur tried to convince him this is where Gwen would come. She could navigate these woods blindfolded, and they should wait for her, because the last thing they needed was Nate injured *and* lost in this storm.

His argument made sense ten minutes ago. Five more, and Nate would be tossing it out the window.

Arthur peeked an eye open from where he sat smack-dab in front of the door. "If you spent as much time praying as you did pacing, you'd actually be doing more than wearing a path in the floor."

Nate stopped. Looked outside at the bending limbs. Instead of passing over, the storm intensified. Counselors remained downstairs with the kids, keeping them occupied with games and loud music to drown out the howling wind.

Up here, Nate stood watch over the door. Where was she?

"I have been praying." He resumed pacing.

"In the midst of your muttering?" Arthur challenged.

On any given day he appreciated Arthur's wisdom, but right now? Not so much.

He kept moving. If he stopped, he'd have to think about how he'd failed. Axel sat in juvenile detention, angrier than ever and unwilling to seek forgiveness. Unwilling to change. At least that's what the last phone call from a random worker there conveyed. And if that wasn't bad enough, his own best-laid intentions had sunk this place before it even started.

His past truly remained unredeemable. His pain worth nothing. Why had God brought him through it if not to use it?

"Something not good's going on in that brain of yours." Arthur looked up. "Why don't you share it?"

Nate ignored him.

Jude leaned against the door frame. "My guess? He thinks he's failed."

"Because of one road block?" Arthur asked.

Nate ground to a stop. "One road block? Try *road ends*." He started to tug the tips of his hair, then remembered his tender head. "I just. . ." He looked at Arthur, then at Jude. "My past makes no sense if it can't be used for something." How could he reconcile what God had allowed if no good came from it? "Doesn't the Bible say God uses all things for good?" He'd clung to that verse. And if those words weren't true, then what about the rest of the verses between all those pages?

Only the rain thrashing against the roof filled the silence. Until, finally, Arthur spoke. "God did use it for good."

Dry laughter choked Nate. "Think we have a different definition of good."

"So your life isn't good?" Arthur pressed.

Nate flicked a glance to Jude, looking for shared clarification. Jude shook his head and nodded at Arthur. Nate changed his focus to the old man. "My life?"

"Yes." Arthur tapped his cane on the floor. "You might have never seen God if it weren't for the darkness around you." He pressed to a stand. "He tends to shine brightest where there's no light."

And he had.

Arthur wasn't finished. "Your past brought you to God, Nate. He turned what was meant to harm you into good. And if he'd used your past just to reach *you*, well then, good still occurred."

Thunder shook the walls as Arthur's words shook his core.

They cracked something in him. Pieces of truth pried into the fractured place.

"I never thought—"

The lights flickered, then went out. A few screams flew up the stairs, but the counselors quieted the kids—until, in the distance, a faint whine grew into a full alarm.

Arthur shuffled across the room. "Time for us to get downstairs too."

What? Wait. His brain rushed to switch gears. "They're still out there."

"They are." Arthur nodded.

Jude's voice of reason joined Arthur's. "We need to get away from these windows. That's the tornado siren."

"I know what that is." Nate's gut twisted. "And Gwen and Nyla are out there." He stepped toward the door.

Jude stood in his way, arms folded over his chest, legs braced, and his face near stone. "Don't make me."

"Don't make *me*." Nate stopped, toe-to-toe.

Jude's face softened. "I know you're worried, Nate. Believe me, I understand what it's like to not be able to help someone you care about. To not know where they are." He let those words sink in. "And you've been the one to tell me to be patient. To pray. To let God do what I can't." He relaxed his stance a fraction. "Now it's your turn."

The doors shuddered. Nate looked out the windows and back to Jude. "I'm not sure I can."

Jude's hand gripped his shoulder. "You don't have a choice."

What sounded like a freight train chugged through the distance.

"Come on, boys." Arthur stood half-way down the steps.

Jude propelled Nate toward the stairs. One last look out the windows showed trees bending to near breaking point.

He felt like one of those trees.

Following Jude, he raced down the stairs as something broke through glass. He didn't turn around to see. He just prayed.

In the last ten minutes the storm had ramped up beyond anything she ever remembered. Nyla clutched the sloth they'd pulled from her backpack. Rain pelted through the broken window pane in the door, but otherwise they remained dry.

"How's your arm?" Nyla asked.

Gwen had wrapped a T-shirt from Nyla's backpack around it, but blood still soaked through. It was a thin shirt, so she wasn't worried. Yet. "It's okay."

Another minute of silence. Then Nyla spoke again. "Can you tell me more stories?"

Gwen smiled and settled onto the floor beside Nyla's chair. She took her hand. "Sure." Reaching into her memories, she flipped through other parables. "So how many people do you think you could feed with a loaf of bread and a couple of fish?"

"I don't know." Her face screwed up in concentration. "Maybe five?"

"Try five thousand."

Her eyes widened.

And in the same instant, so did Gwen's. Off in the distance, were those tornado sirens?

She pushed off the floor. "Stay there." She held her hand out toward Nyla and walked to the door, pressing her ear to the window panes still intact.

Oh, no.

"Nyla." Gwen spun, looked around the room. There weren't any other windows, but the remaining panes on the door could still break. Could allow access to anything a tornado tossed. "Help me with this desk."

They tipped it on end and pushed it against the door. Something larger than any thunder she'd ever heard rumbled toward them.

"What now?" Fear lined Nyla's face.

"Now," Gwen began as she took her hand. If she was going to bend her knee again, this time it would be in prayer. "Now we pray."

Chapter Thirty-Three

———————————•♦♦♦•———————————

Destruction.

The entire camp lay broken into twigs. Cabins destroyed. The ropes course twisted. Trees demolished.

But everyone was safe.

At least he prayed everyone was safe.

Nate looked over at Jude and shook his head. He simply didn't have the words.

"They're okay." Jude offered his own comfort.

He wanted to believe him.

Sirens wailed in the distance, but this time they belonged to fire trucks and ambulances. Nate waved them over. The counselors stayed in the basement of The Commons with all the kids. Nate didn't want them out here. Not only due to danger, but he could hardly handle viewing the destruction. What was he going to say to them?

They'd have to go home.

Who knew when or if he could rebuild? He'd sunk everything into this and had no prospects for investors. Insurance would help, but putting in the claim and waiting for the reimbursement would take more time than he had. And when the money came through, it would be weeks before the damage was repaired.

A boxed red truck pulled into what remained of their parking lot, Hidden Lake Volunteer Fire Department in white letters on the side. A black Chevy followed on its tail.

One of the firefighters jumped from the red cab. "Everyone okay here?"

Nate nodded. "Yep."

Lew jumped from the Chevy. He wore a HLFD ball cap. Must be one of the first responders. "You took a direct hit."

He had bigger concerns. "Gwen and one of our campers are missing."

"Any clue where they might be?"

"None."

"We'll get a search team started." Lew motioned Nate to follow him. "Oughta think about pinning a GPS tag to each of your campers."

Nate jarred to a stop.

GPS.

He was such an idiot! Why hadn't he remem—

He tore out his phone and called to Lew. "I think I can find her."

Lew changed directions and raced to his truck. "Tell me where."

Nate met him there and jumped in, opening the *Find My Friends* app Gwen had installed on his phone to make sure he didn't get lost. Saw her face in a tiny circle beside her name. Beneath it, the word *locating* sprang up with a spinning wheel. He shook his phone. "Come on." And then her picture blinked open on the map. Relief flooded him. "Little Blue." He looked at Lew. "She's at the lighthouse."

Lew turned around.

Broken trees littered the road like an obstacle course. What should've been a two-minute ride turned into nearly ten. He had no clue what he'd find. Had the lighthouse been unlocked? Was she able to get inside before the worst of the storm hit?

The last stretch opened before them, pockmarked but free of trees. Lew barreled down it, and Nate braced himself—one hand on the door, one on the roof—as the truck bounced over the nearly washed-out road. "How's your head?" Lew nodded his way.

"I'm not worried about my head."

Lew pressed the accelerator down another notch.

Little Blue came into view, growing as they approached. No movement anywhere. Good or bad, Nate didn't want to think about it. He unbuckled before they slammed to a stop, then he leapt from the cab and raced to the lighthouse. "Gwen! Nyla!" The lower left panel of the window was broken. Something large—a desk?—rested against the other side of the door.

"Gwen!"

The desk screeched to the left.

Then her beautiful face appeared. "We're here."

Sweetest words he'd ever heard.

He yanked the door open, and she tumbled into his arms. He kissed her forehead. "You're okay." Mud caked her face, her hair lie plastered to her head, and she'd never been more beautiful. He crushed her into his embrace.

Her face nestled in his chest, her breath warming him, she nodded. "We're okay."

We're.

The word slowly penetrated his ping-ponging emotions. Behind Gwen, Nyla quivered, her wide brown eyes on him until he met them. She blinked her gaze to the ground. Pressing one more kiss against Gwen's hair, Nate gently set her aside. He stepped into the room. "Nyla. I'm so glad you're okay."

Her head slowly shook. "I gave Axel my inhaler. He didn't steal it."

His heart twisted with her confession. The guilt she carried. No wonder she'd run.

But she didn't need to be carrying it.

Nate knelt in front of her. "Nyla. I'm not angry with you."

She slowly met his gaze. "You ain't?" The quake in her voice showed she didn't believe him.

"No. I'm not." He didn't blink. "What Axel did was not your fault."

Her hand gently touched the bandage on his head. "If I didn't give him my inhaler, he wouldn't've gotten in trouble. And you wouldn't be hurt."

"Not true." Nate shook his head. "Axel made his own choices. He needs to own them, not you."

A small swallow bobbed in her throat. "I'm real sorry for what I done."

"I know you are." Nate smiled. "And I forgive you."

"What's gonna happen to Axel?"

"That's up to him." The truth of those words sunk in deep. "I've given him the chance to make it right. To change. But I can't force him to." No matter how much he wanted it. But even if Axel never changed, that didn't have a bearing on Nate or his past. His past had been redeemed the moment he'd stepped into God's grace.

It had been used to show him his need for that grace.

God brought good out of so much destruction.

Nate looked up. From Nyla to the brokenness behind him. The past twenty-four hours had delivered it in the physical and emotional.

And God could bring good out of this too.

Nate held out his hand. "Let's get you back to camp."

"You ain't kicking me out?"

"No, I'm not kicking you out." He helped her stand. "Though, after the storm, there's not much camp left. But I promise you, we'll make sure you have a safe place to go home to."

With her brown eyes full of trust, she let him lead her out of the lighthouse. Outside, sunlight attempted to chase away the remaining clouds. Gwen stood beside Lew, who stepped forward to wrap an arm around Nyla. "Let's go sit in my truck."

After one more hug from Nate, Nyla followed. Lew tucked her in the back seat, then jumped in the driver's.

Nate focused on Gwen, her eyes on the truck. Clearing his throat, he waited for her to turn around. She did, slowly. Then he saw the towel wrapped around her arm. Two steps and he stood beside her, gently grasping her soft skin. "What happened?"

"I broke into the lighthouse." Her lip tipped up. "But it's more of a scratch. It stopped bleeding."

He disagreed with her assessment, but it had stopped bleeding. "How very felonoic of you."

"Are you calling me a felon?"

"A heroic one." His eyes captured hers. "I was worried." Out of his mind. His heart wouldn't take a scare like that again.

"I was too."

He drew in a breath. "What were you thinking, going after her on your own?"

She shrugged. "That someone needed to." Her fingers wound in his. "That *I* needed to." And she nibbled her lip. "I've been so wrong about so many things."

A new softness sprang from her. Like she'd moved free from the pain of the past, or at least to the edges of it.

Nate tucked a loose strand of hair behind her ear and smiled at her nervous gesture. Did she remember the last time she'd toyed with her lip around him?

She released her lip into a smile that said, yes, she did.

He slid his hand along her neck. "We're all wrong sometimes." His fingers trailed over her skin. "I know I was."

She blinked up at him. "Yeah?"

He nodded "Yep. When I first met you, I told myself being friends with you would be enough."

"And you were wrong?" Her face tipped up to his.

"Very." Then he leaned down and kissed her, his hands gently framing both sides of her face. He sank his fingertips in her hair, his palms smooth against the softness of her skin, while his mouth gradually explored hers. She sighed into him, and he pulled her closer.

She hadn't expected to find this again. Tears sprang to her eyes as she allowed Nate to pull her closer. Her arms moved from between them to wrap around his waist. Releasing his lips, she ran soft kisses to his ear where she whispered, "You weren't a part of my plans."

He stilled. Looked down.

And she couldn't stop her smile. "You're faretter."

"Far better?" Chuckles rumbled from his chest. "Maybe leave the new words to me."

"Hey. I thought it was a good—"

Then his lips were on hers again, this time in a smile. She could stand here all day. Something new began to beat in her heart, the ties of the past no longer holding her. Sweet memories would always be that; memories. She'd cherish them.

But she couldn't live in them.

Nate's hand pressed the small of her back, arching her into him. His arms strong and confident in their hold on her. This. This she could live in.

A horn blared, and she jumped.

Oh! Lew. Nyla.

Heat crept up her neck.

Nate gently brushed his fingertip down her nose. "Maybe add me to your list for later?"

"Top spot." She grinned.

She glanced behind him, then tipped her head and looked up. Looked around. Sunlight broke through the clouds, the shadows casting their hue over Little Blue, transforming it from white to a shade typically saved for painting the sky or rippling through the water. "So beautiful."

"It is." Emotions she could spend a lifetime exploring swam in his eyes.

Behind them, Lew started his truck.

Nate held out his hand. "Ready?"

She cast one last look at Little Blue, then trailed her eyes to the sun crashing through the last of the clouds, and finally to her feet still grounded in the shadows. She took Nate's hand, this man she'd never planned for or expected, and squeezed.

And like he'd come into her life, she stepped out of the blue.

Epilogue

"I don't know how you convinced me to have an outdoor spring wedding in Michigan." Gwen smoothed out the wrinkles from her fitted gown and peeked through the flaps of the white tent housing her bridal room. A hundred feet away, Little Blue stalwartly stood. People huddled in the chairs lining the grass that rolled from its base to the stone-filled beach. The sun shone, but temps barely reached sixty degrees.

"Well, I wasn't about to wait till summer." Elise fixed a small jewel band in Gwen's hair. "I was done playing chaperone after your first date. You two should have gotten married months ago."

"Hey. We didn't ask you to be a chaperone. We were fine on our own."

Now Lucy and Elise laughed.

Bay snuck through the opening with Colin and Rhett in tow. Actually, her belly appeared first. "I think I'm the only one not cold out there." She rubbed her stomach, a tender smile on her face.

"Blame Lucy. She cast such a perfect vision of my wedding here, what was I supposed to do?"

Beside her, Lucy smiled. "After the story you told us, you had to get married in this spot."

"Always about the story, Luce." Rhett wrapped his arm around her shoulders. With his dark pants and gray jacket trimmed at the collar in black, he matched Lucy's outfit. Had he planned to?

"I'm a journalist. It comes with the territory." She peered across her shoulder at him. "And you shouldn't be back here. No men allowed."

"I'm a friend of the bride." He pressed a kiss to Gwen's temple. "You look beautiful." Then he turned to Lucy. "You too. Thought you weren't going to be here."

"As if I'd miss Gwen's wedding. Please." She nudged him. "You know me better than that. I told my editor he could book the flight, but if it was before nine, I wouldn't be on it."

"Of course you did." He brushed a long, loose curl from her shoulder. "Need a ride to the airport?"

"Already planned on you taking me."

"Of course you did," he repeated, then stepped through the flap and beckoned with his hand to Colin and Bay. "Going off the look on the groom's face, I say we should take our seats. Come on, you two."

Colin wrapped Gwen in a hug. "So happy for you."

Bay stepped up next with a side hug. "I'm glad I didn't miss this."

"It would have been worth it." Gwen placed a hand on her friend's little basketball. She made the cutest pregnant woman.

"It is so good to see you smile again." Tears slipped from Bay's eyes. "Every happiness, Gwen."

"Thank you." Now wetness tinged the edges of her eyes. She couldn't start crying already.

Bay slipped into Colin's arms, and they walked to their seats. Front row. Bay might not be able to stand through the entire ceremony, but she would be close.

Violin strings drifted from the beach. Jude ducked into the enclosed area, Shane McCoy on his heels.

Still hadn't sunk in that Nate not only knew the author they teased about, but had asked him to stand up in his wedding. Even more surprising? Shane broke every stereotype she'd set up in her mind about this man best known for his steamy romance novels. Or maybe she'd learned to get to know a person before forming an opinion.

"Nate's tapping his foot up there. We make him wait any longer for his bride, and he'll move the ceremony back here." Jude produced a slip of paper. "From your groom." Then held out his arm. "You ladies ready?"

Jude had been more reserved since learning Calloway wouldn't attend the wedding, but he took his role as best man seriously. His pasted-on smile hadn't dimmed all morning, though Gwen suspected it would the second the day wound to a close. Nate had shared a little of Calloway's story with her over the winter, but if she'd learned one thing this past year, it was that hope was never lost. And she held endless amounts of it for those two.

Lucy wrapped her arm around Jude's. "Let's do this." And she followed him outside.

Elise hesitated a moment before taking Shane's. He grinned down at her. "You look beautiful."

Pink crept up her neck, fully exposed since her red hair had been swept into a loose bun with tendrils escaping. Her friend did look gorgeous. The fact that she put on a dress today wasn't lost on Gwen. No heels though, and that was okay. It constituted the compromise for making her walk with Shane McCoy—though Gwen wasn't sure Elise had fully forgiven her yet. She had, however, made it perfectly clear to Shane that while she knew who he was, she wasn't one of his fans. Ever since she'd made that comment at the rehearsal dinner, he seemed as intent on making her one as she was at resisting his efforts.

Elise stared straight ahead. "Thank you."

Parting the tent's flap, Shane ushered her through.

Gwen stood alone as the flaps fluttered back in place. Granddad would meet her at the end of the aisle, but this part she had to do on her own. Each step cemented the end of her past and the beginning of her future.

God was so good. A tiny part of her heart would always ache with the loss of Danny, but it no longer consumed her. She was in love with Nate. Wholly in love. In a way only God could do, he allowed her heart to carry them both, and she was forever thankful.

She flipped open the paper Jude had given her and scanned the neat handwriting penned in red ink. Laughter poured from her.

OUR LIST

Get Married ☐

A few more things that made her blush.

Then *Live Happily Ever After* ☐

Spend a lifetime completing it with me?

Oh, yes. A million times over, yes.

The music changed. Gwen tucked the paper around her bouquet and stepped from the tent, her eyes immediately latching on to Nate's. The depth of love there pulled her forward. Bryce and Elliot sat in the middle of those who'd come to pledge their support today. And it went farther than simply supporting their new union. After the tornado, all the kids from camp—JCS kids included—helped clean up the town. They spent tireless hours doing backbreaking work while sleeping at the church, which hadn't been damaged. They'd given up the rest of their summer to put the town that wanted them gone back together.

And in the process they'd forged new relationships.

Once again God crafted good from the pieces of destruction.

Hidden Lake opened its doors, taking these kids as their own. Well, most of them did. Marlene and David led the charge of those still opposed to the camp, but that number was dwindling. So much so that her in-laws hadn't returned from Florida yet. Gwen had a feeling the move would be permanent.

That was the thing. Some people didn't change, like Axel. He remained in a juvenile detention center. No matter how often Gwen and Nate reached out to him, he chose to continue down a path that would only bring him hurt. Still, they wouldn't stop trying. He was too important to them and to Nyla.

Gwen wiggled her fingers at Nyla who'd turned around in her front-row seat beside Bay. She wore the flowy pink dress Gwen had picked out for her, accessorized by her bright eyes and huge grin. Jude had driven her and a group of campers here yesterday. Last night they'd shared their rehearsal dinner with them at the restored grounds of Camp Hideaway. The kids couldn't wait to return. A reality made possible when Elliot, seeing the impact in both the town and the kids, reversed his decision and invested in Camp Hideaway after all. Which was, in ways, proof that people could change.

They'd be reopening in a month.

Just enough time for Gwen and Nate's extended honeymoon. Something, with the look in her almost-husband's eyes and the list in her hand, she was looking forward to.

She reached the end of the aisle, and Granddad extended his hand. His weathered grasp took hold of hers. "Still mad at me for letting that boy have this place?" he whispered in her ear.

She chuckled. "Only mad you didn't find him sooner."

He kissed her cheek and walked her the three steps to Nate, who outstretched his palm, his eyes never leaving hers, more love there than she could live through in a lifetime. "Thought you'd never make it."

His words slipped the last fetters from her heart. She held tight to his hand and took her first step fully with him. "So did I, my love. So did I."

If you enjoyed this book, will you consider sharing the message with others?

Let us know your thoughts. You can let the author know by visiting or sharing a photo of the cover on our social media pages or leaving a review at a retailer's site. All of it helps us get the message out!

Email: info@ironstreammedia.com

 @ironstreammedia

Brookstone Publishing Group, Iron Stream, Iron Stream Fiction, Iron Stream Harambee, Iron Stream Kids, and Life Bible Study are imprints of Iron Stream Media, which derives its name from Proverbs 27:17, "As iron sharpens iron, so one person sharpens another." This sharpening describes the process of discipleship, one to another. With this in mind, Iron Stream Media provide a variety of solutions for churches, ministry leaders, and nonprofits ranging from in-depth Bible study curriculum and Christian book publishing to custom publishing and consultative services.

For more information on ISM and its imprints, please visit
IronStreamMedia.com